PENGUIN BOOKS

PLAYING TO WIN

Monica Murphy is a *New York Times, USA Today* and international bestselling romance author. Her books have been translated in almost a dozen languages and have sold over two million copies worldwide.

A native Californian, she lives on fourteen acres in the middle of nowhere with her husband, two kids, one dog and four cats. When she's not writing, she's an assistant coach for her daughter's high school cheer team. Maybe someday, she'll even write about this experience.

ALSO BY MONICA MURPHY

The Players

Playing Hard To Get

Playing By The Rules

Playing To Win

Lancaster Prep

Things I Wanted To Say (but never did)

A Million Kisses in Your Lifetime

Birthday Kisses

Promises We Meant to Keep

I'll Always Be With You

You Said I Was Your Favorite

Wedded Bliss (Lancaster)

The Reluctant Bride

The Ruthless Groom

The Reckless Union

The Arranged Marriage boxset

The Fowler Sisters Series

Owning Violet

Stealing Rose

Taming Lily

Reverie Series

His Reverie

Her Destiny

Billionaire Bachelors Club Series

Crave

Torn

Savor

Intoxicated

One Week Girlfriend Series

One Week Girlfriend

Second Chance Boyfriend

Three Broken Promises

Drew + Fable Forever

Four Years Later

Five Days Until You

A Drew + Fable Christmas

Standalone YA Titles

Daring The Bad Boy

Saving It

Pretty Dead Girls

PLAYING TO WIN

MONICA MURPHY

PENGUIN BOOKS

PENGUIN BOOKS

UK | USA | Canada | Ireland | Australia
India | New Zealand | South Africa

Penguin Books is part of the Penguin Random House group of companies
whose addresses can be found at global.penguinrandomhouse.com

First published in the United States of America by Monica Murphy 2023
First published in Great Britain by Penguin Books 2024
001

Edited by Rebecca, Fairest Reviews Editing Services
Proofread by Sarah Plocher
Printed and bound in Great Britain by Clays Ltd, Elcograf S.p.A.

The authorized representative in the EEA is Penguin Random House Ireland,
Morrison Chambers, 32 Nassau Street, Dublin D02 YH68

A CIP catalogue record for this book is available from the British Library

ISBN: 978-1-405-96975-8

www.greenpenguin.co.uk

PLAYLIST

"Ruby" - Geskle
"Shee" - quickly, quickly
"Thicc" - Remi Wolf
"Erotic City" - Prince
"Lavender Haze" - Taylor Swift
"Think it Over" - New Constellations
"On You" - The Hics
"No Role Modelz" - J. Cole
"Send Nudes" - Warpaint

Find the rest of the **PLAYING TO WIN** playlist here: https://
bit.ly/3Dst9ND
Or click the QR code below:

1

RUBY

New Year's Eve

"OOH, WHO'S THAT?" My gaze lands on the tall, built guy standing dead center in the living room, surrounded by girls, all of them watching him with adoring eyes and wide smiles. He grabs hold of two of them, inserting one under each of his thick with muscle arms, that grin on his face telling me he's enjoying every minute of their attention.

His confidence practically resonates throughout the room and it doesn't hurt that he's gorgeous. His best feature is his beautiful smile—it's broad and friendly and slightly mischievous. From where I'm standing, he appears to have a beautiful everything.

I'm in Colorado for the holidays to both visit my family and spend time with my brother and sister along with their friends and significant others. They all came back to campus early, specifically to attend this party, and I tagged along. I've had the time of my life in the span of only a few days, which is more than enough confirmation that I need to come back here to finish my degree. I went to the East Coast to college my freshman year thinking I needed something different. An escape from my supposed mundane life. I was craving a new adventure, and when I got into a university on the East Coast, I believed I would party my life away and have a great time. I firmly believed a different environment meant my life would change for the best.

None of that happened. Classes are boring. The campus life—boring. I haven't made any solid connections with fellow students. Definitely not with my roommate freshman year, who bailed out and wasn't in our room for the entire second semester. This year, I'm sharing an on-campus apartment with another girl, and while we're friendly and I think she's okay, I definitely don't feel...connected to her. And that's all I'm looking for.

A connection.

Someone who *gets* me.

Right now, that feels like an impossible feat.

"That, my friend, is Ace Townsend. Second-string quarterback on the football team and hopefully our starting quarterback next season," my new friend Natalie informs me. She's my brother's new girlfriend's best friend—whew, that was complicated—and guess what?

The moment we met, we instantly *connected*. We've been having fun hanging out together ever since. Natalie is down for anything. She likes to party and she's blessedly single. Everyone else that currently surrounds me while I'm here is attached to someone else, with the exception of Natalie.

Which makes her the perfect friend to crash holiday parties with.

Not that we're crashing this particular one. We were both invited, thank you very much.

"Ace? That's his actual name?" I blatantly stare at him, not that he notices. He's too busy putting on the charm and chatting up his fan club. "Not a nickname?"

I've never heard of him. Knox has never mentioned him to me before, and neither has Blair, but that doesn't mean anything.

"Maybe it's a nickname? I'm not sure." When I glance over at Natalie, she's already shrugging. "I don't know him that well."

"He's hot." I can't help but smile when he laughs, the pleasant rumbling sound drifting over to where we stand, and I'm suddenly compelled to walk over to him and introduce myself.

But would he care? Maybe not. He seems preoccupied enough. What's one more girl in the mix?

"He is, huh?" Natalie grabs my arm and hooks it around hers, dragging me over to where my sister Blair is with her boyfriend, Camden. He's the current quarterback for their college football team, though can I call him current? He's basically finished with his college football career and hopefully about to embark on an NFL career next. "Come on."

"Where are we going?"

"We need to talk to Cam. He can give us the scoop on Ace," Natalie says as we head toward them.

We stop in front of the newly, publicly launched couple, a pang in my heart when I see the way Cam looks at my sister. As if the sun rises and sets on her head. Like she's the only person he sees.

That's another thing I want...eventually. Maybe sooner than later, though I guess it depends on who I meet. But yeah.

I want a man who's totally into me. All the guys I manage to try to get to know either lose interest fast, or they're not serious. That's the biggest issue. They are never serious. Though am I ever serious? Not really. But also, when it comes to men...

I always pick the wrong one.

I like the good-time guy. The fun guy. The one *all* the ladies love, which always ends up being a giant problem. From what I see happening around Ace, I'd guess he's the same type, so it makes sense that I'm drawn to him.

Which means he's probably all wrong for me. I need to be a little choosier in my man crushes and not fall for the hot guy with the lazy smile and buzzing sexual energy.

Blair finally glances over at me, a faint smile on her face. "What's going on?"

"I want to talk to that one." I incline my head in Ace's direction, who isn't paying us the least bit of attention.

All thoughts in regards to being pickier fly right out the window.

What can I say? Attractive, confident men must be a weakness.

Cam groans. My sister grins. I can't help but frown.

"I think you two might be cute together," my sister singsongs.

My brows shoot up, curiosity coursing through my blood. Oh really? Hmm. Maybe I like the way my sister is thinking.

"No fucking way. Look at him. He's currently sitting with two girls," Cam grumbles, waving his hand toward Ace. I quickly glance over my shoulder to see most of the women have left, leaving him with...yep. Two girls.

Rolling my eyes, I bump my hip into Natalie's. "Duh, Cam. He'll take one look at me and forget all about them."

"Yeah, girl!" Natalie holds up her hand and I give her a high five, Cam muttering curse words under his breath.

"I wish I had an ounce of your confidence," Blair tells me, her voice sincere.

I've never understood why Blair isn't more confident. She's beautiful and smart and always so composed. While I'm over here acting like a hot mess most of the time. If I could learn anything from my older sister, it's how to better control myself.

"You were pretty confident in your pursuit of me," Cam tells my sister.

Blair glances over at Cam, her eyes wide with surprise. "You think so?"

"Oh yeah. You wore me down." He leans down to kiss her and she reaches out, pinching his lips together. "Ow."

"Wore you down," Blair mumbles, shaking her head. "More like you couldn't resist me."

"Same difference." He grins, reaching for her, and I realize I need to break this up fast or I'm going to get nowhere with these two.

"Hey." They both turn their heads to find me staring at them. "Introduce me, future brother-in-law. I want to meet that guy."

"Ruby." Blair's eyes are wide, like she hates that I just said that, but I couldn't resist.

Cam doesn't appear to mind though. The smile on his face is soft, like he might even enjoy the idea of being part of the Maguire family, and that's when it hits me.

This is serious. They're madly in love and he didn't even bat an eyelash at being called my future brother-in-law. He might even envision marrying Blair himself, and if that's the case?

Wow.

An unfamiliar feeling flows through my blood, leaving me uneasy. I'm not...jealous. Am I?

No way. I don't want to get married yet. I'm too young. I don't even think I'm ready for a serious relationship. Or am I? I just want to have fun. With a guy. Who isn't afraid to give me what I want when I ask for it. Or when he just...takes it.

Takes *me*.

Whoa. My feelings are taking a turn for the slightly dirty tonight and I don't get why.

"Come on," Cam tells me, releasing his hold on Blair.

I follow him, Natalie and Blair trailing behind us as we walk over to where Ace is currently sprawled out on the couch. One of the girls has disappeared, so he only has a cute redhead under his left arm, a red Solo cup clutched in his right hand. When he spots Cam, he grins, lifting the cup up in a toast.

"Number one QB! Who's the hottie?" Ace's attention shifts to me, his gaze slowly running up and down my body, checking me out. Making me tingle with just a look. I stand a little taller, thrusting my chest out and his gaze falls to my breasts, lingering there for a moment too long.

Well, well, well. Looks like I might be catching his attention after all.

"This is Ruby Maguire. Ruby, I'd like you to meet Ace Townsend." Cam pauses, his lips curling in the faintest smile. "The number two QB."

"And about to become number one." Ace rises to his feet, forgetting all about the redhead, his focus one hundred percent on me, those beautiful blue eyes leaving me frozen. Even a little breathless. "Nice to meet you, beautiful."

He thrusts his hand out and I automatically shake it, a jolt passing between our palms the moment they touch. I can't let go of his hand, and he can't seem to either. An uncomfortable giggle escapes me, which is just—weird. I don't giggle like that. Not really.

His gaze seems to darken, his fingers curling tighter around mine and when I glance over at the couch, I see the redhead scowling at me, crossing her arms in front of her chest.

"You did hear me say her last name, right?" Cam asks Ace.

"I caught it. Maguire. You a cousin?" he asks me. His gaze is hopeful and my heart starts to sink.

Ugh. This has everything to do with Knox. He's so over-protective of me and my sister, though I've rarely had to deal with it. We're a little farther apart in age, so Blair is the one who's had Knox standing guard over her with his friends.

"She's my sister," Blair pipes up from behind us.

Ace lets go of my hand immediately. "I forgot Knox had two sisters."

"Is that a deterrent?" I ask, my heart racing a little faster than normal. "That Knox is my brother?"

Is Knox really that much of a threat? What does he say to these guys to keep them away from us?

"It makes you off limits," Ace says, sending a smile in the redhead's direction, whose entire demeanor relaxes when he looks at her.

Okay, that's freaking annoying. Forget the redhead. Forget my brother.

Forget everyone.

My gaze goes to Natalie, her eyebrows shooting up in question, and I sort of love how she's always encouraging me. If we were to hang out much longer, I'm sure the two of us could get into some serious trouble, and have fun while doing it too.

"Ooh, I love a challenge," I proclaim, making Natalie laugh.

Ace returns his attention to me, his interest obviously piqued. "You do, huh?"

I nod, not letting the redhead's moody stare bring me down. "And my brother is not my keeper."

"Tell that to Knox," Ace says with a chuckle that he immediately smothers with his hand.

My gaze zeroes in on that hand. It's large, with a wide palm and long fingers I wonder if he knows how to use.

I have a thing about hands. A man's hands. I don't know what it is. I love a smile and a handsome face and a hard body but what really gets me?

Ace's hands are...perfect. I bet he knows just how to touch a woman. Hands cupped around my cheeks, holding me in place, or even better? A hand around my throat. Gentle yet firm. With just enough pressure to show his strength, though I know deep down he would never harm a single hair on my head.

Heat coats my skin and I part my lips, my tongue touching the corner of my mouth just thinking of Ace's hands on me.

"Damn, girl, don't look at me like that," he murmurs.

I jerk my gaze to his, surprised at the rough sound of his voice. "What do you mean?"

Okay, I let my imagination get out of control and unfortunately, he caught me.

"You're looking at me like I'm a tasty snack and you're dying to eat me." His blunt statement makes my skin burn.

Or maybe that's the image that's now floating in my head thanks to what he said.

"I just looked at you like that?" I blink at him, knowing exactly how I looked at him.

Busted.

His laughter is deep. A pleasant sound that makes me smile. "Yeah, you sure did. And don't play like you don't know."

"This is some bullshit," the redhead mutters as she leaps to her feet and stalks off with a huff.

We both turn to watch her go, eventually facing each other once more, and he scrubs a hand along his jaw, contemplating me. "Guess it's just you and me now."

I look over my shoulder to see that he's right. Everyone has abandoned us. Cam and Blair are leaning against the wall once again, completely wrapped up in each other, Cam's hand on her waist and their gazes locked. Natalie is nowhere to be found.

"I guess so," I say when I meet his gaze once more.

Ace settles his big body on the couch, his arms stretched out across the back of it, his legs spread wide. The man sprawl is strong with this one. "You should join me." He taps his fingers against the back of the couch.

"It's probably safer if I stand," I say. I get the feeling if I snuggled up close to him on the couch, I might end up doing something I'll regret.

Oh, who am I kidding? I wouldn't regret spending a little time with this man.

"For who? Me or you?" He seems amused, but not at my expense. I think he's just happy to be talking to me and not afraid to show it? Hmm.

How refreshing.

2

ACE

Ruby Maguire is a hot piece of ass.

That sounds shitty as hell, even in my thoughts, but it's true. She's got on a pale blue, tight in all the right places dress and it shows off her assets to the best of its ability. Meaning, she looks sexy as fuck tonight. Might be the sexiest girl at this party.

And that's saying something. There are a lot of beautiful girls here—both in this house and on campus in general. I should know since I've talked to a bunch of them and the night is still young. But most of them...I'm not really into. They're either too shallow or too grabby or scarily possessive and/or obsessive.

Some of them are flat out dumb, which is mean of me to think, but damn, it's true. And then there are others who are way too smart and onto my game so I leave them alone. They know what I'm about.

Which is absolutely nothing. When it comes to women, I'm not serious. Not even fucking close. Coming here to Colorado University after growing up in a super small town with conservative parents who tried their best to shelter me, while attending a tiny high school, I turned into a kid at a candy store. Only my candy of choice is women.

Lots and lots of women.

I know how to have fun and I know when to be serious. School and football? I'm serious as hell. Women and partying? Fun. I work hard and play hard, and so far, it's working out for me.

But shit is about to get even more serious come next year. I'm a contender for being the starting quarterback, taking Cam's place. And while I'm positive I can handle it and even more positive I'll get the coveted position, nothing in life—or football—is guaranteed.

Which means when spring hits—hell, when we return next semester—I'm going into full-blown serious mode. Right now, though?

It's fun all the damn time. I have a small window and I'm taking advantage of it.

Maybe I can have some fun with Knox's little sister. I might be an idiot to even consider it, but as I sit here listening to her explain her situation and how she doesn't even go to this school, she's sounding more and more...

Perfect.

The ultimate one-night stand. Have a little fun with Ruby, fuck her on the bathroom counter, maybe while we ring in the new year together, and then I'll never have to see her again. Knox is graduating. Blair should still be around next year, but Ruby won't be.

Sounds like the ideal way to spend the last night of the year.

"I'm feeling lonely," I say when Ruby pauses to take a breath. She's a talkative little thing, which makes me think she's nervous. I pat the empty spot next to me on the couch. "You should join me."

A delicate brow lifts and she crosses her arms, plumping up her tits. My gaze drops, lingering. "Does that work on other women?"

"All the time," I drawl, smoothing my hand over the couch. "Come on, pretty girl. Join me."

"Pretty girl? What, am I a parrot?" Both brows are practically to her hairline now.

I keep the smile on my face, not deterred by her sassy mouth. Her body leans forward, like she's subconsciously drawn to me, so I know I've got her. I just need to be a bit more persistent. "If you say so. And might I add, you're the prettiest parrot I've ever seen."

"What's with the parrot talk anyway? Are you a pirate?"

Now I'm the one with raised eyebrows. "Of course not."

She remains quiet. Just sends me a look that says, *okay?* Like she doubts me.

What the hell?

"I'm definitely not a pirate," I continue.

"If you say so." She tilts her head to the side, her long blonde hair sliding over her shoulder. It looks soft. I bet it's silky to the touch.

I have the sudden image of wrapping those wavy strands around my fist and giving them a hard tug. All while I fuck her from behind.

Damn.

"You sound disappointed," I say when she remains quiet.

"I can't figure you out."

What's she trying to figure out? We only just met.

I flex my wrists, lifting my hands, though I keep my arms planted on the back of the couch. "What you see is what you get, babe."

I sound like an absolute cheese monkey. I'm trying to impress this girl, yet I'm saying stupid shit. I really need to know when to stop.

But she does the most surprising thing. The very last thing I expected. Without warning, she settles in right next to me, so close our thighs are pressed together on the couch. The moment her warmth seeps into me, I'm on high alert. My arm falls from the back of the couch to settle around her shoulders and she doesn't seem bothered by it at all.

See? I knew she'd come around.

"You're a giant flirt," she tells me, and I open my mouth to argue with her, but she keeps talking. "Which is fine. I like it. You're actually just my type."

"You're just my type too," I tell her, leaning into her so I can murmur those words close to her ear.

"What's your type? A willing female?" She leans back some, as if she needs the distance, our gazes locking. "By the way, I can feel Cam's death glare penetrating my brain."

We both turn our heads to find Cam staring at us, Blair hanging all over him. She's another hot piece of ass, but I would never ever utter those words out loud. First of all, I'm never going to disrespect my number one QB's girl and I like her as a person. Second, Cam would hand me my ass and make me eat it for lunch if he ever heard me say that. He's a grumpy son of a bitch.

And if Cam didn't beat my ass, Knox would and he's another grump, though he's not as bad as Cam.

Honestly? I can't wait for the seniors to graduate so I can slowly but surely take over the team. I'll be a junior this upcoming season. Ready to lead our team and make it a well-oiled machine that takes us all the way to a bowl championship. It's going to happen.

I can practically taste it.

"Ignore him," I tell her, my attention zeroed in on her face. She's cute, not one of those sisters who looks like her brother wearing a wig.

Thank fucking God.

Her lips are coated with a faint pink, glittery shine and her eyelids are covered with a pale blue shadow that matches the dress. I just impressed myself that I even noticed. She looks good with the makeup, but I'm guessing she looks just as good without it.

I'm not anti-makeup, but some women wear it so thick it's like a mask, when that shit is absolutely not necessary. They take the cosmetics off and it's like I'm looking at a whole different woman. Sometimes I even feel tricked.

That won't happen with Ruby though. She's hot. Pretty. The dress she's wearing has a low-cut neckline that shows off the tops of her tits and I can tell...she's not wearing a bra.

Nice. Easy access. I'm all about that.

The dress hits about mid-thigh and when she sits, the hem rides up, showing off her slender legs. Wonder if she's got panties on.

Wonder if she's going to let me check.

I must stare at her thighs a little too long because she begins to laugh, murmuring, "Are you Superman?"

My gaze jerks to hers, guilt flooding me. "What do you mean?"

"Do you have X-ray vision?" She tilts her head again, all of that blonde hair spilling down her back and this time, I give in to my urges and touch it, slipping my fingers into the silky strands, making her breath hitch in her throat. "It's like you're trying to see what's under my dress."

"Ah. No." Well. Yeah. But I'm not going to admit that.

"Oh." She sounds almost disappointed.

"Wouldn't mind sneaking a look though." I lick my lips for emphasis because yeah, sometimes I can be a prick.

An over-sexualized, looking to get in a girl's panties, prick. I can't help it. I'm young and horny and women are throwing themselves at me constantly, thanks to being on the football team. How can I resist? I never tell them lies. They know what they're getting when they're with me. A good time. A quick fuck.

Then it's adios, baby. See ya around campus.

Ruby's gaze flickers in Cam and Blair's direction for the briefest second before she rises to her feet and bends over me, the front of her dress dipping, giving me an excellent view of her chest. Her tits. She's definitely not wearing a bra, and I think I can see her nipples. "Come on."

She grabs my hand and I let her pull me to my feet, which is impressive because I'm not small. I'm tall and I weigh a lot and it's all solid muscle. But she comes from a legacy football family, so maybe she's used to big dudes like me.

Ruby keeps my hand in hers and drags me through the house, her steps determined. All sorts of people yell out my name in greeting as we pass. Male or female, it doesn't matter. They all want to talk to me. They all act like they want a piece of me.

But Ruby won't let me linger. She's stronger than she looks, pulling me through the room. I have no idea where she's taking me. Pretty sure she doesn't know either, but within seconds, we're in a cramped box of a bathroom and she practically shoves me against the door, her body pressing into mine as she murmurs, "Show me what you've got, big boy."

Big boy?

Without hesitation, I wrap my arms around her waist and maneuver us so she's the one with her back against the door, her eyes wide when she tilts her head back, our gazes clashing.

We stare at each other, as if we can't look away, and I reach out, tracing the neckline of her dress with my index finger, goosebumps rising on her flesh where I touch her. Her skin is so damn soft and I swear I'm witnessing her nipples tighten into hard points beneath the fabric the longer I touch her.

Her gaze still locked on mine, she sinks her teeth into her lower lip, her breaths starting to come faster. Damn, she smells good. Sweet and heady, reminding me of candy, and I inhale deeply, breathing in her scent. The pulse at the base of her neck is fluttering wildly and I'm tempted to kiss it.

I'm tempted to kiss her everywhere.

She tips her head back, a soft exhale leaving her when I lean in closer, my mouth hovering above hers, sharing the same breath with her for a beat. Two beats.

Anticipation curls through my veins and I dip my head, about to kiss her when—

The door swings open, shoving Ruby into me, me stumbling backward with her practically on top of me, my ass hitting the edge of the bathroom sink. The redhead I was talking to earlier is standing there in the slightly open doorway, a sly smile stretching her lips just before they form an O, her eyes comically wide.

"Oh my gosh, I'm so sorry! I didn't mean to interrupt." She hides the laughter that spills from her lips with her fingers.

Ruby disentangles herself from me, straightening her dress before she brushes her hair away from her face. Her cheeks are flushed and she looks frazzled and I sort of want to tell the redhead to get the fuck out of here, but that's mean as hell, so instead, I just shrug at her.

"It's all good," I say, my voice easy, my manner much the same because what's the big deal? I can sneak Ruby into another room in the house and we can continue what we started later.

"I need something to drink," Ruby mutters, pushing past the redhead and exiting the bathroom without another word for me.

Huh.

The redhead watches her go—damn it, I wish I remembered her name—before she turns her attention to me. "Looks like you got ditched."

"Yeah." I scratch the back of my head, my butt still propped against the edge of the counter.

She shuts the door behind her, leaning against it with a sultry smile on her face. "I can pick up where you two left off."

Say what? This type of girl is always surprising to me. She has no clue if I was kissing on Ruby just moments ago. For all she knows, I had my tongue shoved down Ruby's throat and my fingers inside her pussy. She literally has no idea. Yet she'll happily offer herself up to me and that's kind of wild.

Okay fine, it's *really* wild.

"Thanks, but no." I rise to my full height, ready to get the hell out of there, but the redhead slaps her palms against the door, like she's not going to let me get by her.

"It's almost midnight." Her smile is now overly bright. "We can ring in the new year together."

"Maybe." I pull my phone out of my pocket to check that yep, it is close to midnight. "I need something to drink too."

"Let's go then." She shifts away from the door and opens

it for me and I have no choice but to walk out, the redhead right by my side.

I need to lose her. Fast. I need to find Ruby.

Where the hell did she go?

3

RUBY

Once I make it to the kitchen I lean against the counter for a moment, running a shaky hand through my hair as I focus on my overactive heart rate, mentally telling myself to calm down. But wow.

Wow.

That moment with Ace shouldn't have felt so intense, yet it did. I've been kissed before. By plenty of guys. I've even been felt up in a bathroom a time or two. But there was something about the way Ace touched me. The way he looked at me.

A shiver moves through me and I close my eyes for the briefest moment, willing myself to stop. I'm reading too much into it. Our encounter was a potential hookup in a bathroom, only to be rudely interrupted. I need to compose myself.

But it's like I got close to him and he put his hands— wait, only his *finger*—on me and my senses went haywire. Completely out of control.

It's weird. I don't like feeling out of control. I sort of hate it.

I also sort of want it—that moment between Ace and me —to happen again.

"There you are!" I turn to find Natalie approaching me, two fresh Truly cans clutched in her hands. She gives one to me and I take it gladly, cracking it open and practically draining it with a couple of gulps. "Where were you? Getting felt up by the cutie QB?"

"Sort of," I answer, lifting my can toward her in a cheers gesture.

She nailed that a little too closely for my liking.

Natalie laughs, clinking her can against mine before we both drink. "I need all the details."

"There's not much to share." I glance around the room, hoping to catch a glimpse of Ace again. Hoping against hope that he followed me out here, though he better not be with the redhead.

I mean, it's possible he could be looking for me. The tension between us was strong. Palpable. Did he feel it? When he touched me, I wanted to melt. I sort of did.

Remembering the moment now, I want to melt all over again.

"Don't be shy." Natalie's smile is sly. "Please tell me you at least kissed him."

"Hey, everyone! It's almost midnight!" A tall, beefy football player is standing in the middle of the kitchen, his hands cupped around his mouth as he makes his announcement. "Get ready to celebrate the new year!"

Natalie sends me a panicked look. "I need to find someone to smooch on at midnight. It's bad luck if you don't kiss someone!"

"Are you serious?" She doesn't even hear my question. Just hurries away from me, her head swiveling left and right as she moves through the house, as if she's on the hunt for a man.

Which she totally is.

I watch her go before leaping into action myself, on the search for a specific someone to 'smooch on,' as Natalie put it. And that someone is Ace Townsend.

This is probably a terrible idea, but what does it matter? I'm leaving in a matter of days. I might be coming back to this campus as a student next fall, though what are my chances of running into Ace again. Knox will be graduated and gone, so I'll have no reason to spend any time with the football team. No access to them whatsoever, which is fine by me. I get enough of that in my homelife. My entire family is made up of football players. I don't date them.

I swore I never would.

Exiting the kitchen, I move through the crowded house, but I don't spot him anywhere.

Where did he go?

"Hey! Did you just sneak off with Ace?"

My sister appears in front of me, her expression one of pure concern.

"Nothing happened," I immediately say, not wanting Blair to overreact. I know she's just watching out for me, but whatever happened between Ace and me a few minutes ago was no big deal.

That's what I keep telling myself.

"Between you and Ace?" Blair makes a tsking noise, shaking her head. "Well, that's a shame."

I'm frowning. My sister is sending me mixed messages. "You actually want me to hook up with Ace?"

"I don't know. Maybe?" She shrugs. "I mean, it wouldn't be a hardship, spending a little one on one time with Ace. Look at him. He's adorable."

Adorably sexy. Adorably magnetic.

"I've always had a soft spot for him." Blair leans in close, her voice barely above a whisper. "Don't tell Cam, though. I think he'd be jealous."

"Please." I dismiss her worries immediately. "Like you look at anyone else."

"I don't," she agrees. "But he'd still be jealous. Sometimes he acts like Ace is coming for his entire life."

It's kind of weird to hear that Cam has any insecurities, though he's only human, so I guess it makes sense. He definitely acts like he's got his shit together. Both personally and out on the football field. But if anyone knows the real Cam, it's my sister. They've become super close in a short amount of time, and I love it for her. For them.

They make a great couple.

"Get a drink everyone! The countdown is about to start!" the same football player screams, his voice booming through the house.

"I need to go find Cam." Blair gives my arm a squeeze before she leaves me alone.

Geez. I'm the guest here tonight and everyone keeps ditching me, I swear.

Determined, I go on the hunt once more for Ace, peeking around every corner. Looking behind every closed door, except the locked ones. He's nowhere to be found and the beefy football player—I think his name is Derek—has officially started counting down from thirty, which is obnoxious as hell.

I guess he's trying to give everyone enough time to find a drink and someone to yell Happy New Year with, but all he's doing is filling me with panic. Leaving me with the urgent need to find anyone—okay fine, a particular someone —now.

"Ten, nine, eight…"

I race up the stairs, my heart pounding, my hands shaking when I reach for yet another closed door. An ominous feeling washes over me, my breath stalling in my lungs, and when the door swings open, I swear my heart lodges in my throat.

"Three, two, one…HAPPY NEW YEAR!"

The sounds of cheers and party horns blaring fill my already ringing ears as I take in what's happening directly in front of me. It's another cramped bathroom and Ace is in it, and this time the redhead who busted up our earlier encounter is the one in his arms, her lips fused with his. His broad back is to me and her hands are buried in his hair, long pointy red nails stroking through the short strands. When she breaks the kiss, our gazes meet, the triumphant smile on her face telling me she's absolutely thrilled I caught them together.

That she's the one who got to kiss him at midnight and not me.

Frustration ripples through my veins and I clutch my hands into fists. I hate losing control of a situation, and I hate even more looking like a fool.

Right now, I feel like the biggest fool out there.

Ace quickly extracts himself from the redhead's arms, shaking his head. Rubbing his hand across his mouth like… what? He didn't enjoy the kiss?

Please. I must make some sort of noise because he jerks his head in my direction, his eyes going wide when he spots me, the panic in his expression obvious.

Panic that he just got caught, I'm sure.

"Oh shit. Ruby." He starts toward me and I hold up my hand, stopping him.

"Fuck off, Ace." Before I can hear him say anything, defend himself, whatever...

I'm gone.

4

RUBY

L*ate August*

"WE'RE EXCITED to have you as a part of this program, Ruby." My advisor smiles at me, his teeth blindingly white. Jim Williamson was in the NFL for about a minute, before my dad and uncle's time, and he's been using that 'connection' with me since the moment I met with him via Zoom over the summer to discuss my goals and aspirations as part of the sports management and marketing program.

I didn't call my plans 'goals and aspirations,' he did. But anyway...

I decide to give Jim what he wants.

"I'm excited to be here." I sit up a little straighter, my gaze wandering over all of the stuff in his office, taking it in. He has an entire shelf devoted to his college and NFL career, with photos and plaques and ribbons and a signed football encased in plexiglass. I'm sure he's proud of his accomplishments but that was a long time ago and I can't help but wonder if he's the type who revels in the glory days.

My father isn't. He was in the NFL for years—part of that time when I wasn't even born yet—and Dad doesn't brag about it. He doesn't even really talk about it much. With Knox he does, of course, because my brother is just like him. Whenever Knox needs advice, Dad is always willing to give it to him. And now Knox is on a professional team like our father, about to play his first season opener in like what... two weeks?

Yikes. I bet Knox is nervous. Excited. I can't wait to watch him.

"An opportunity has come up," Jim says, his voice serious and I return my gaze to his. "We have paid internships with the teams here on campus and one of the students had to pull out of the program, due to her withdrawing from the university. You were the first person I thought of for the job."

"Oh, wow. Thank you." I'm flattered. I took classes at the other college I went to, but nothing specifically for this major. The sports marketing major that Colorado University offers is right up my alley. And while I'm not a diehard football fan—I'm not a huge fan of any type of sports—I do know my way around athletes. Plus, I enjoy marketing and promotion, specifically in social media, and I've put together some great projects in the past. It seemed like a natural fit. "But I've barely been in the program."

It's only the second week of school. How am I the first person Jim thought of for the job?

"I know, but I truly believe you're the perfect candidate." He smiles at me, looking pleased, but doesn't say another word.

"What's the position?"

"Social media for the football team." Jim leans back in his chair, resting his linked hands on his chest. "Running their Instagram and Facebook pages, I guess. Oh, and that clock app. Twitter? Is anyone there anymore? Reels and videos and whatnot."

Spoken from a man who sounds like he doesn't have a firm grasp on social media. "Are you saying I would be the social media manager for the football team?" I'm shocked they don't have one currently.

"Not the manager. They already have one of those. You'd be an integral part of the team though."

"How big is the team?"

"Not sure. It varies. Would you care to interview? They need someone right away, so they're willing to talk to you ASAP." He smiles. "I already put in a good word for you and told them you're Knox's little sister."

Frustration ripples through me at his using my family name as a selling point. Though I suppose I can't blame him because the Maguire name is well-known on campus, thanks to Knox. "I appreciate the mention, but I can get by on my own merits, Mr. Williamson."

"Call me Jim," he insists. "And trust me, it doesn't hurt to say who you're connected to, young lady."

Ugh. I want to roll my eyes, but I just nod and smile instead.

"They like the fact that you're so steeped in football history. Your family is a legacy. That you want to carry it on in a sports-related field is a smart move. You'll get far with the Maguire name on you."

That's not necessarily why I chose this major and potential profession, but it's definitely influenced me. I've been immersed in football pretty much my entire life. I understand athletes and they don't faze me. They're just people. I don't get dazzled by their massive fame or strong confidence or outrageous good looks. Many of them are sweethearts. Some of them are egotistical assholes. I can handle any of them.

All of them.

"The interview is later this afternoon if you're interested," Jim continues, grabbing a piece of paper from a notepad and thrusting it toward me along with a pen. I take both from him, the pen poised on the paper, ready to take down...what exactly, I'm not sure. "Three o'clock in the athletic department. You know where the building is?"

It's attached to the stadium. "I do."

"The meeting is with Marilee. She's in charge of the entire athletic department's social media section." He smiles, nodding toward the paper and I jot that little fact down. "You'll like her."

"Are there any other positions available?" I ask, offering a weak laugh at the sharp look Jim sends my way. I don't mean to act ungrateful and I do want to work with the football team. Sort of. Though there is someone on the team I'd rather avoid...

I'd rather not think about him at all. That's been my plan since I walked onto this campus.

"Not that I know of," Jim answers. "You can ask Marilee that particular question, but I figured you'd jump at the opportunity to work with the football team."

"Oh, I want to. Of course, I do." I smile and nod, hoping I look more enthusiastic than I feel.

Minutes later, I'm walking around campus, the notepaper crammed into the pocket of my denim shorts with the meeting details written on it. I should probably change into something more professional. Or maybe I should go to the student store and buy a Golden Eagles T-shirt. Would that be too obvious?

Whipping my phone out of my pocket, I FaceTime Natalie. My new roommate and bestie. She answers on the second ring.

"Why can't you call like a normal person?" She's still at home. From the looks of it, she's still in bed.

"I like to see your face, especially when you're so cheerful," I tease.

I lucked out getting Natalie as a roommate. My brother's girlfriend, Joanna—and Natalie's best friend and now former roommate—left campus to be with Knox. She's still a full-time student, taking her classes online and she'll come back to graduate here in May, but she wanted to be with Knox during his first NFL season after he begged her to go with him. The man is obsessed with her and she seems to feel the same way about him. I guess I can't blame her.

They're madly in love. They want to be together as much as possible.

With Joanna gone, Natalie needed a roommate and so did I, since Blair did the same thing as Joanna and she's now living with Cam. Considering Natalie and I got along so effortlessly when we hung out over the holidays, it made sense.

Natalie rolls her eyes. "Why are you calling so early?"

"It's eleven," I point out. I'm not a total early bird, but come on.

The day is almost half over.

"That's still early for me. My first class doesn't start until one."

"Must be nice," I mutter, plopping down on a nearby park bench. "I need advice."

"About a guy?"

It's my turn to roll my eyes. "You wish. No, not about a *guy*. About a job."

Natalie makes a face. "Why do you need a job?"

"It's for my major. I spoke to my advisor and he said there's a social media manager position open for one of the teams."

"That sounds perfect." Natalie sits up a little straighter, pushing the hair out of her eyes. "Why do you need advice?"

"I still have to interview for it, though he made it seem like I already have the job." I can't count on that though. I can't really count on anything unless I achieve it myself.

"Would it be for the athletic department or for a specific team?"

"A specific team." I hesitate. "The football team."

Natalie is a shit friend because she immediately starts laughing.

Like...hysterically.

"It's not funny," I try to interject, but she's not listening to me. And she knows how I feel about the football team, but it's obvious she doesn't care. "Seriously, Nat. What am I supposed to do?"

"Take the job if they offer it to you. Make his life a living hell," Natalie says, sobering up quickly.

"Wouldn't it be better if I just ignored him?"

"How can you? He's the freaking quarterback. He struts around campus like he's the top dog and damn it, he *is* the top dog." She sounds irritated. I appreciate her undying loyalty to me, I really do. Even if she was laughing at me only a moment ago. "I hate him."

"You do not."

"I do. If you hate him, I hate him."

I don't hate Ace Townsend. Though I am still pissed over

what happened on New Year's Eve. I thought we had a connection. We definitely had chemistry. That almost kiss in the bathroom still ranks as one of the hottest moments I've ever experienced, but then he had to go off and ruin everything.

Kissing another girl on New Year's Eve isn't necessarily a crime, but I don't want to deal with a guy like that. He can't commit. Not even to a kiss at midnight. And that sucks.

At the time, my thoughts were all about someone temporary. The good-time guy who knows how to have fun. But he couldn't even manage that and over the last eight months, I've had some...thoughts.

No more settling for the guy who obviously doesn't want to commit. I deserve a man who's totally into me. It should be painfully obvious.

Which means Ace definitely isn't the guy for me.

After the NYE Incident as I call it, I also swore off men. There was no point in trying to get with any at my other college. I was leaving anyway so I threw myself into my school work and ended up getting all A's last semester. I impressed my parents and myself.

See what happens when you forget about guys and don't party as much? You actually get things accomplished.

But now I'm here at CU and Natalie is a gigantic flirt, who is always on the prowl for hot guys and while that makes her sound awful, she's not. She just knows how to have fun, like I used to. She also knows when to get serious. And this is where we differ.

I'm the type who goes all in. I either wanted to party all the time like I did my first year in college, or like last semester, when I threw myself completely into my studies and focused on nothing else. I need to learn how to balance myself out a little more, where I can have fun, but I can also be serious. It's like I don't know how to be one with the other.

"I have to get over myself," I finally say with a sigh. "And get over what he did."

"You're allowed to hold a grudge," Natalie says, giving me the permission I didn't know I still sought. "He was a jerk to you."

"Not really. He didn't even know me." I didn't know him either.

"He knows your brother. He knows Blair. He led you on." Natalie's voice is firm, telling me I can't convince her otherwise.

"I can do this, right?" My voice drops and I glance around before I continue. "If I get this job, I can ignore him and go about my business? And still work for the football team? I'll be able to keep things professional...right?"

The doubt that lives within me lately is nearly crippling, and I hate it. Why am I second-guessing my every decision? Maybe because the first university I went to, I didn't like. I think that happens a lot more often than we think. And it's okay to make a mistake and change my mind. That's what my mom said.

Plans change and that's okay. Yet here I am questioning every move and choice I make, scared shitless to actually do anything.

Like, who am I right now?

I stuck it out for two years at that stupid college I hated and now I'm back in my home state, wondering if I'm doing the right thing, even though deep down, I know I am.

I know it.

"Of course, you can. You're Ruby Fucking Maguire. You

can do anything you set your sights on," Natalie says, as if she's reading my mind and knows how full of doubt I am.

I smile, thankful for her encouragement. "Should I go to this interview wearing an Eagles T-shirt?"

"Ew, no. You need to play it cool. Can you come home right now?"

"I have an hour break." Meaning going home will be cutting it close to make it back to class on time.

"Then get your ass here and I'll help you pick out an outfit. I'll start going through my closet right now." She climbs out of bed.

"I'm sure I have something."

"Oh, I'll be going through your closet too. I just want to check and see what I have first. A cute dress always works."

"Okay. But nothing too cute, you know?"

"Always professional," Natalie says with a firm nod. "You've got this in the bag."

"If you say so." Yep, there's that doubt creeping in. I don't know why it happens. My parents have believed in me ever since I can remember. My entire family is supportive. I've never let my insecurities get me down. Throughout high school, I was a total overachiever, both in class and in my extracurriculars. I love a schedule, staying busy, creating things, doing things.

But the moment I graduated high school and went away to college, I've felt...wayward. A little lost. Unsure of myself. I can't explain why. I'm not sure what I'm supposed to be doing here, if that makes any sense. What's my purpose in life? Why are we expected to have our life plan in place at eighteen and know what we want for our future career?

Over two years have passed since I graduated high school and I'm still unsure as to what I want to be. What I want to *do*. I've changed my major twice already. I'm hoping I've zeroed in on something that will make me happy and give me purpose, but we'll see.

We will see.

5

ACE

"Can't wait to see you play this weekend." The attractive brunette with extraordinarily long, thick eyelashes clings to my arm as I try to walk.

Would it be rude to shake her off? Probably but damn, she's making progress difficult.

"Thanks, babe." I tug my arm away from her grip and she digs her nails into my skin, making me mutter, "ow." Only when she hears me complain does she let me go. "Appreciate the support."

I flee from her, my steps hurried as I hustle toward the student center, my stomach growling the closer I get to the quad. It's like my body knows I'm about to feed it, and it doesn't hurt that the scent of cooking food lingers in the air.

Lately I'm always hungry, but I blame our workout and practice schedule. It's intense. Unrelenting. We're out on the field when the sun is barely rising and we're still out there when it sets. I don't even want to think about how many hours I'm currently devoting to the gym, honing my body into the well-oiled machine it's become, one of our trainers barking at us to do another rep. Just. One. More.

We work hard, we play hard and we're ready for our first game this Saturday. And for the first time ever, our team is playing during week zero, which means an extra game has been added to our schedule.

Too bad it's not at home, but we're gonna make the best of it.

I can handle it. I'm the starting QB on the team and scouts have been frothing at the mouth discussing my potential lately, so I better be able to handle it. Though my number two is always nipping at my heels like an annoying little dog, constantly showing off for the coaches. Aaron Maloney is a giant pain in my ass and I finally understand why Camden Fields gave me constant shit.

God, I must've been so obnoxious and I didn't even realize it. But I'm not gonna let anything get me down. I'm in the number one slot for a reason. Aaron is a freshman. He may have excellent passing skills and look damn good on the field, but he still lacks maturity. And while I would never describe myself as mature in the past, I act like a middle-aged man compared to that fool on the field. Aaron's always goofing off, always here for a good time.

I love a good time. I *am* a good time, but I'm not an eighteen-year-old jackass with nothing to lose either. That's how he acts every God damn day.

Again, I feel for Cam. I should text him an apology because this shit is hard.

"Yo, Townsend." Derek calls from his usual spot at our usual table. He's already got a tray in front of him piled high with food. "Come here."

Derek is a defensive lineman and as solid as a brick wall. I've been tackled by him more than a few times in practice and it's always rough, getting taken down by him. I swore he was a senior last year and would graduate with Knox and

Cam, but turns out the joke's on me and Derek is still here, tormenting me every chance he gets, but always good-naturedly with it.

Can't complain. He's a decent dude. An asset to the team.

I head for the table where he's sitting and dump my backpack in an empty chair. "I'll be back. Gotta get something before my stomach starts eating itself."

Derek laughs. "I know the feeling, bro."

I grab a cheeseburger and a giant basket of fries, plus a salad and a banana because I'm trying for a balanced meal, damn it. If any one of my coaches saw me right now, they'd be disappointed—the fries and packets of ketchup I grabbed would send them over the edge. They've been pushing us to eat a healthier diet and I try, man. I try hard.

But it's difficult when all you crave is pizza at eleven o'clock at night. Plus, I work out like a crazed motherfucker. How much more balanced do I need to be?

Once I've made my purchase, I settle back in at our table, diving into my food with gusto. Derek keeps pace, both of us eating quietly, our focus on the plates in front of us versus the girls we can sense swarming on the periphery.

I can sense them at least. Not sure about Derek. He seems too focused on his lunch to worry about anything else, but I know those girls are there. Lingering. Waiting for a signal from me that will have them sitting at our table and begging for an ounce of our attention.

"Your groupies are growing," Derek mutters out the side of his mouth after he polishes off his second cheeseburger.

Yep, he's paying attention. "Don't remind me."

"You love it."

Okay fine, I do love it, but sometimes I want a moment of peace and while I'm on campus? I never get it. These girls don't understand that sometimes I just want to...be. Instead of dealing with the constant fangirling I can't shake.

Here's where I can admit I'm a bit of a celebrity on campus—I sound like an asshole, but it's true. I'm kind of a big deal. Even though I haven't really proven myself yet. This could all go to shit after Saturday's game.

My palms start to sweat at the realization.

"They're probably staring at you too, bud," I remind Derek because he has quite a way with the ladies and this is his last year. Their last shot at nabbing the unattainable lineman with the goofy laugh and crass pickup lines.

Somehow it all works for him.

"They probably are." Derek grins and lifts his head, casting his gaze around the cavernous room. I swear I hear a few of the girls giggle. Even a couple of squeals. Jesus. "Yep, some of them are definitely here for me."

I let him revel in the attention, thankful they're not all here for me.

Who am I kidding? I glance around, flashing a quick smile at anyone who's looking, and I hear more giggling. One of them waves. Another one winks. One girl even tugs down on the neckline of her shirt, offering me a glimpse of the tops of her breasts.

A text notification hits both my and Derek's phones, indicating that it's our team group chat and I check mine first, frowning when I read what it says.

The social media team will be at practice tomorrow afternoon filming content. Be on your best behavior and give them what they want. We need to build buzz for this Saturday's game!

Shaking my head, I deposit my phone on the table and continue eating.

"Content? Buzz?" Derek snort laughs. "You telling me one of our coaches wrote this text?"

"Hell no. Someone from the social media team did." They're ramping up our social media presence this year. They've always been there, but the program has grown and now they're supposedly going to have a social media crew assigned to every team on campus. We haven't met ours yet, but I can count on a few people being on the team.

That one chick, Gwyneth, who's intimidating as shit. She's always barking commands, her phone aimed at us, trying to get us to cooperate, but most of the time we ignored her.

We were shits last year and it was kind of fun, not gonna lie. I just rolled with the older guys and did what they wanted. Until the assistant coach came to me a few weeks ago and asked to speak to me privately. He requested that I convince everyone else on the team to be a little more cooperative with the social media people.

"I know you all just followed the seniors' lead, but they're gone. And it'll go a long way, acting agreeable and working with the social media kids," he'd said with an encouraging smile. "You'll get more attention on the team's accounts."

At the time I loved the idea of more attention, but as it grows in its intensity, I'm starting to realize I don't enjoy it.

Not nearly as much as I used to.

"Hopefully they're hot," Derek says, a slow smile spreading across his face as he stares across the room. I don't even bother to see who he's looking at.

I think of Gwyneth. She's pretty, but she's also a fucking bossy bulldog so no thanks. "Remember Gwen?"

"Oh yeah. She's mean as a snake." Derek drags a fry in

ketchup before popping it into his mouth. "Tell me she's not still around."

"Pretty sure she's still around."

"Great. I'm guessing she'll have us doing trending TikTok dances or some shit," Derek mutters, looking disgusted.

I can't help but laugh. "You really think she wants us to dance?"

"You can probably get away with it. You're a graceful motherfucker compared to me."

Anyone is a graceful motherfucker compared to Derek. He's as big as a tank and bulldozes his way across the field, doesn't matter who's in front of him. He also bulldozes his way across campus. Into a classroom. A bar. A frat party. Just about anywhere.

"I'm not dancing," I say firmly.

"You'll just smile and look pretty like you do." Derek laughs when I scowl at him. "What? You don't like me calling you pretty? Or do you hate it because, deep down, you know it's true."

I ignore him, knowing he just wants to get under my skin. I'm trying not to react as easily or as much as I used to because guys like Derek? That's all they're looking for. A reaction. Back in the day, I gave him one all the time because I couldn't control myself. Now, I'm considered a leader. I can't keep fucking around and acting like a fool.

That's been my plan since the summer—working on myself this semester. It started at the beginning of the year, after I got back to school and realized I needed to get serious about my future. What I want more than anything is to continue to play ball. It's my love, my passion and I'm really fucking good at it.

But I could be better.

"Cam hated that pretty boy talk too." Derek smirks.

"I don't blame him." I shove the rest of my cheeseburger in my mouth, regretting I didn't get two.

My gaze snags on a woman in the distance, her back to me, long blonde hair spilling down her back. She moves in a way that feels familiar and I sit up straighter, hoping it might be—

The woman turns, her profile visible and I slunk back in my seat, disappointment filling me.

She's not Ruby Maguire. Not even close.

Maybe that's a good thing, that I haven't run into her yet. I know she's on campus. I remember Blair mentioning her sister was going to start here this fall and...this is where I admit something that feels almost shameful but...

I stalk her social media.

Yeah, I know. I'm cringe, but I was curious.

She's already shared photos of her being here at school. Moving in with Natalie of all people. Joanna Sutton's best friend and now former roommate. It makes sense that they know each other, that they're all friends. I vaguely remember them hanging out at that New Year's party. I've stalked Joanna's social media too, and Blair's. Natalie's.

Shitty, right? Like who the hell am I? I don't stalk *any* woman's social media because, quite frankly, I don't have to. Women make themselves readily available to me at all times. I don't need to go in search of anyone.

Except for her.

Ruby feels like the one who got away. The one I blew it with. That tantalizing moment with her in the bathroom on New Year's Eve still lives rent free in my head and I can't shake it. I didn't even kiss her.

It's one of my biggest regrets—that I don't know the taste of Ruby Maguire's lips. I should've tried to explain myself better after she caught me at midnight with someone else. I should've never let that girl drag me into the bathroom in the first place.

Talk about a colossal mistake.

I've been with other women since then. Not a lot of women—my number is always exaggerated, I was warned of this a long time ago by my fellow football players, specifically Cam—but enough that normally, I should've forgotten all about her by now.

But it's like I can't.

"That blonde is hot," Derek says, and I realize he's looking in the same direction I am.

"She's all right." I shrug, hating that I got caught staring, too caught up in memories of another woman. Fleeting memories that were really nothing but a quick moment in time.

Yet somehow, I'm still hung up on her.

It makes no damn sense.

6

RUBY

It was way too easy getting the social media manager position. I guess Jim did put in a good word for me, because the next thing I know, after I chat for a few minutes with Marilee, the head of the Athletic Department's social media, I'm being introduced to the rest of the football social media team. There's a very intimidating looking woman with sharp features and dark, wildly curly hair named Gwyneth and a totally dorky looking guy named Eric. He wears thick glasses and is long and lanky and knows more about the Colorado Golden Eagles football team than any person should.

He's currently rattling off stats and facts as he escorts me around the office where our headquarters is—his words, not mine—and I just nod and smile, ignoring the way Gwyneth stares as I wander around the tiny room.

Because our headquarters is exactly that: a single, cramped office with two desks, each topped with a massive computer that has seen way better days.

"We don't use these." Eric slaps the top of one of the monitors, dust rising and making my nose itch. "We bring our own laptops into the office sometimes, but mostly, I do my best work on my camera or my phone."

"That makes sense," I say.

"You have a laptop?" Gwyneth asks me from where she sits at the other desk.

I nod. "Yeah."

"And a phone?" She raises her brows.

What the hell? "Um, yeah." I pull my phone out of my pocket, holding it up for her as proof.

"Come on, Gwen. Knock it off. Don't forget she's a Maguire." The look on Eric's face tells me he might drop to his knees in front of me at any moment, like I'm royalty. I suppose to him I am part of football royalty, thanks to my family. The respect in his gaze is clear. "Knox's little sister."

"Ugh, that guy." Gwen blows out a harsh breath, her expression turning guilty when she notices I'm glaring at her. I mean, I know she's my superior, but she's bashing my brother. Right in front of me.

That's not cool.

"We'll be out with the team tomorrow afternoon when they're at practice, creating content," Gwen says briskly, all business. "We'll meet here first before we head out. Four o'clock sharp. Does your schedule allow for that?"

She asks the question like it's a challenge and she knows for sure I'm going to fail.

"Definitely," I say with a nod, keeping it strictly business too. I don't care if Gwen doesn't like Knox. She might not like me either because I'm related to him, but I'm not about to let that get in the way of my job.

If she's trying to scare me away, it's not working.

"Good." Her smile is faint and it doesn't quite reach her eyes, but I return the smile anyway because if I'm anything it's a people pleaser. "I was worried you might be spoiled because you're a Maguire."

"Gwyneth," Eric softly chastises. "Ease up."

"No, it's okay." I send him a blinding smile before I aim it at Miss Doubter aka Gwyneth. "I get it. You probably think I've been handed everything I could ever want my entire life."

"You do get it." Gwen inclines her head toward me. "You're going to have to prove yourself before I accept you as a bona fide member of our team."

Eric makes an irritated noise, but I talk right over it.

"That's fine. I wouldn't want you to be fake with me."

"The very last thing I can be is fake." Gwen scowls.

"Isn't that the truth," Eric mutters under his breath, pushing his glasses up the bridge of his nose, his gaze filled with longing as he stares at her.

I blink, surprised. Does Eric have the hots for Gwyneth?

The longing look is gone in a second and I tell myself I was seeing things.

I fill out paperwork and Eric discusses the pay structure. Minimum wage to start, with the pay increasing after ninety days. Perfect. Sounds like every other job I've had. Considering I've only had two jobs prior to this one, both of them part-time, that's not saying much.

"Is there a dress code or anything?" I ask Eric when I finish with the last of my paperwork.

"Not really," Gwen answers for him. "Casual clothing is best. Team colors on game days—we have a staff shirt we can give you too. What size are you? Small?"

"Medium," I tell her. "And thank you."

She doesn't even crack a smile. "One word of warning. Don't flirt with the team. It's not allowed. You can't date them."

Ugh. Like I'd want to.

"Don't dress to get their attention either, if you know what I mean," Gwen tacks on.

"Jesus, Gwyneth. You need to chill," Eric says, clearly irritated.

"Look, I don't think so. Remember that girl last season? She wore a low-cut tank top during every game she was at, even in October, and her boobs practically fell out of it. One of the coaches even came to me after a game and said we needed to get rid of her because she was a complete distraction."

"Maybe she couldn't help it," I say, trying to defend this poor girl who just might be cursed with huge breasts she can barely contain. I don't know. And why should we be responsible for how a man looks at us?

"Please." Gwen makes a dismissive noise. "She was hot for one of the tight ends. When we canned her, she was so pissed. Despite her admitting to me the only reason she wanted the job in the first place was to date a football player. She never took the position seriously."

"She was mad, and she admitted that to me too," Eric adds, his voice soft, his gaze shifting to me. "Look, we don't discriminate. Or judge. But I have to agree with Gwen. Flirting with any member of the team is...dangerous. We have to keep it strictly professional."

I did notice there was a professional behavior clause in the contract I signed, but I must've skipped over the no dating athletes clause. "I know a few of those guys. And I have zero desire to flirt with them."

"Good to know. I'm guessing the majority of them would want to get with you because of your connections," Gwyneth mutters, jumping to her feet. She points at me, her tone fierce. "Be careful, Ruby Maguire. All those guys on the football team? They can be—a lot sometimes."

I nod, not bothering to say another word. There is no reason for me to be intimidated by any member of the football team. I can handle them. I was always able to handle Knox's friends. Most of the time, they paid zero attention to me anyway. I was just the annoying little sister.

But now with Knox and Blair gone, I'm the lone Maguire left. Do they even care?

I know there's one who might, but from the vibe I got from him that night at the New Year's party, I'm sure he's already moved on. I don't matter to him.

And he doesn't matter to me either.

Considering I'm going to avoid Ace Townsend at all costs, I'm not too worried about this.

At all.

I'M JUST WALKING into my apartment when I get a FaceTime call from my mom's phone number. I answer immediately, not surprised at all to see both of my parents' faces fill the screen.

"Hey, honey." My dad's deep, warm voice immediately calms me and I settle onto the couch in the living room, eager to talk to both of them. "Your mom tells me you've found a job."

We've been texting about it. I like to keep her up to date with what's going on in my life, and I think they've been extra anxious about me since I've made the move back to Colorado.

Funny how I come back to my home state, only for my parents to move to California to be closer to my aunt Fable and uncle Drew. I get why they left—Blair was pissed and I think she might still be, even though she's moved too—but once they became empty nesters, they wanted to do some-thing for themselves. They've given us so much, it's only fair they have a little fun now and live where they want.

Since I've always loved going to my aunt and uncle's house throughout the years, I don't mind them all living close to each other. It's like a one-stop visit now.

"I did." I explain to them both what I'm doing and how it's all for the football team. I can tell this pleases my foot-ball-loving father immensely.

"That's great," he says once I finish describing my duties. "Sounds like you'll enjoy it. You're always on your phone so you've got the skills."

"Ha ha, Dad," I say, making him grin. "I think anyone my age could qualify, according to your standards."

"True." His expression turns serious. "I'm excited for you, honey. You seem happy there and I'm sure finding a paid internship related to your major is a relief."

"It is," I agree. "It'll look good on my resume and it'll be fun. We're going to create videos featuring the football team. As long as they're good-natured about it, it should be easy."

"I'm sure they'll love it. Most of those guys are a bunch of show-offs anyway," Mom says, Dad sending her a wounded look.

"What, was I a show-off back in the day?"

"Definitely," Mom says without hesitation, laughing when Dad utters a soft *hey* in defense.

Dad can still be a show-off, but in the best way. He's always been full of joy. The good-time Dad, the one who used to toss us high into the air, into the pool, wherever. Blair and I would scream and carry on and he'd just laugh. As we got older, he was there for us. A steady influence, someone we could count on. Mom is the nurturing one. The one we come to for hugs and comfort, our dumping ground when shit goes wrong.

"Do you know many of the guys on the team?" Dad asks, pulling me from my thoughts.

"A few," I hedge, not wanting to mention anyone in particular. "Not many though. I only met the guys from Knox's close circle over the holidays and the majority of them are gone now. They all graduated."

"Makes sense," Mom murmurs, her smile gentle. "Any good-looking ones?"

"Mom." I drag the word out, a little embarrassed. I don't want to talk about hot football players in front of Dad. Talk about awkward.

"Just asking. Look at your sister."

"I'm not going to be like Blair," I say, my voice firm.

"You never know," Mom says with hope in her voice and I try my best to ignore her.

"That new quarterback is looking pretty good out on the field," Dad observes.

Ugh. We just went into the direction I didn't want to go.

"He's also very handsome," Mom says, sounding one hundred percent like a mother with that particular assessment.

I roll my eyes. "Ace Townsend is kind of an asshole."

My parents share a look, laughing.

"So you have met him," Mom says, her tone knowing.

"At the New Year's party when I was here for the holidays. It was no biggie." The lies that come out of my mouth are astounding, but maybe if I say it often enough, I'll start to believe it. "How's Knox? Have you talked to him lately?"

I change the subject quickly and Dad rattles on about how great Knox is doing with his new team, which is exactly what I wanted to hear. I don't talk to Knox as often as I do with Blair so I appreciate the update, though I'm only halfway listening.

The other half of my brain is wondering how I'm going to deal with seeing Ace tomorrow.

Am I making a bigger deal about this than I need to be? Probably, but that's always been my mode of operation. I sort of make a big deal over...everything.

I guess Ace is no exception.

He definitely blew it that night. I would've done pretty much anything with him to experience that heady, all-consuming chemistry I felt with him during that moment in the bathroom. I haven't experienced something like that with a guy before or since. And it really better not be a one-shot moment only with that guy. If that's the case?

I'm freaking doomed.

7

ACE

Practice is halfway over when Coach Mattson calls a water break, his gaze zeroing in on something across the field. I glance over my shoulder, trying to figure out what he's staring at when I spot it.

More like when I spot *them*. Three people are heading toward the field. A tall, skinny guy and two females. One with dark, curly hair that I immediately recognize.

That social media chick from last year. Gwyneth. The mean one, according to Derek. When I look over at him, I see he's already watching them approach, a disgusted expression on his face that shifts and morphs into something else the longer I watch him.

"Wait a minute. I recognize that blonde," Derek mutters.

I check out the blonde he's speaking of, my heart tumbling over itself when I realize I recognize that blonde too.

Oh shit. I'm pretty sure that's Ruby Maguire.

What is she doing out here?

"The social media team has arrived," Mattson

announces, his booming voice carrying across the field. "Get prepared to put on a little performance, boys."

I grimace, dropping my head for a moment to stare at the blindingly green grass. I really hate it when he calls us *boys*, but I live for putting on a show and I'm ready to perform.

Especially for Ruby Maguire.

Is she on our social media team? Looks like it. How fucking lucky can I get? From what I remember last year, we had a lot of interaction with them. After a while, we didn't even notice they were there, because they were always around.

Don't know how that'll be possible with Ruby. I mean, look at her. How can I *not* notice her?

The social media team approaches Mattson and he talks to them, while I sit there and blatantly watch them. Everyone else on my team is sitting around chatting, hyping each other up about getting filmed or whatever, but all I can focus on is Ruby. She looks better than ever, her long blonde hair falling down her back in silky waves, the tight red T-shirt she's wearing stretched across her tits, emphasizing their size. Not too big, not too small.

They're just right. Because of course they are.

She's paying zero attention to me so I blatantly take her in, my gaze lingering on the denim shorts she's wearing, and how they show off her long, tanned legs. The tall guy and Gwen are both talking to Mattson, I'm guessing explaining what they want to do while Ruby remains mute. She's gotta be the newest member on the team. Wonder if she requested to work with the football team.

Maybe she's trying to find a way to stay connected to me.

I sit up a little straighter, puffing out my chest, willing her to look my way. My gaze is still stuck on her, lingering on that T-shirt that has no right to be so damn sexy but some-how, it is. Maybe because I'm imagining what she looks like without it on?

There's tiny writing on the front of the shirt and I squint in the sun, trying to make it out. It's only when my brain computes exactly what it says that I start to chuckle.

Three small white letters stitched into the dead center of her shirt.

IDC.

I don't care.

"What are you laughing at?" Derek asks me.

"Her shirt." I wave a hand at Ruby. "The IDC."

"I-D-C?" Derek frowns. "What's that mean?"

"I don't care."

"You should care. What if it's some sort of secret code...ahhhh." Derek nods when he gets it. "I don't care. IDC. Makes sense."

"Who's it directed at though? Us? She doesn't care about us?" I'm probably reading too much into this.

"I don't know. Why don't you go ask her." Derek grins. "Weren't you two flirting at the New Year's party? Whatever came of that anyway?"

"Nothing," I say way too quickly. From the knowing look on Derek's face, he caught it too. "She's not my type."

"Are you fucking serious?" Derek sounds incredulous.

"Well, yeah. I mean, I have a type."

"No, you really don't. You go after pretty much anyone."

Fuck, he's not wrong so I may as well own it.

"I don't need to 'go after' anyone," I remind him. "They all come to me."

"True. They all come to *us*," he clarifies. "But when it comes to a type? You definitely don't have one, Townsend.

You're down for any of them. As long as she's cute and flirty, you're into her."

Mattson blows his whistle, silencing all of us.

"Townsend!" His gaze is right on me and he waves his hand. "Come here."

Reluctantly, I walk over to where he's standing with the social media team, my gaze never wavering from him, though I can feel Ruby watching me.

I send her a quick look, noting how she turns away quickly, her cheeks the faintest pink at getting caught staring. Being this close to her, I can smell her perfume. See the faint pink glittery gloss on her lips, the same color she wore on New Year's Eve. I stare so long at her sexy mouth I see the quick flick of her tongue as she licks her lips and I finally tear my gaze away from her.

Hot. That's the only word in my brain, flashing like a bright red neon sign. Hot. Hot.

Ruby Maguire is sexy as fuck and she's not doing a damn thing. Just standing there, while my body reacts like I've just been completely overstimulated.

Damn it, I need to focus.

"What's up, Coach?" I ask, flicking my chin at him.

"You remember Gwyneth and Eric from the social media team." Mattson tilts his head in their direction.

I glance over at them, offering a quick smile. Eric's reaction is instant, his friendly smile making mine grow while grouchy Gwen just scowls. "I definitely remember them. How's it going, E-Dog?"

I offer my fist to Eric and he eagerly bumps his against it.

"Glad you're the starting QB, Townsend. Can't wait to watch you on the field this season," Eric gushes.

Gwen just rolls her eyes.

"Thanks, bro." I appreciate his support. There have been

some—okay a lot of—grumblings about me and how difficult it'll be to fill Camden Fields' position. I can't lie that seeing those articles, hearing them talk on podcasts or whatever, it shakes me a little. And leaves me feeling like I've got more to prove than ever.

"We have a new member of the social media team," Gwen says, waving a hand in Ruby's direction. "Ruby Maguire."

Coach Mattson frowns. "Wait a minute. Knox's little sister?"

"Yeah, that's me." Ruby nods, smiling at Mattson. "Hi." She waves.

More eye-rolling from Gwen while Eric just nods enthusiastically.

"Happy to see you here. I miss your brother." Mattson turns his attention to me. "Do you know Ruby, Ace?"

"We've met once." I keep my voice purposely casual, my gaze finding hers. Sparks fly from her eyes and I realize that yep, she's still not over how I dissed her on New Year's Eve. Not that I meant to. Not like she'll let me explain myself.

If she was open to hearing what I have to say, I'd tell her I didn't kiss that girl. She kissed me first, and her lips barely touched mine when the door flew open and Ruby was standing there, disappointment written all over her pretty face.

I still feel like shit over it. Hell, I can't even remember that other girl's name.

"Look, Ace, we won't take up too much of your time," Eric says, getting right down to business. I've always liked that about him. "But we're hoping we could get you to align yourself with us and convince the team to be a little more, uh, willing to allow us to film them for content."

"Weren't we mostly willing last year?" I always was. Sort of.

Okay I gave them endless shit and I remember the text one of our coaches recently sent the team, asking for our cooperation.

"Uh..." Eric and Gwen share a look before he replies, "Not really."

"Why not?"

"Because you're all just a bunch of egotistical assholes?" Gwen blurts, her gaze jerking to Mattson. "Sorry, Coach."

"Not a problem, little lady. You're actually right on the money with that assessment." Coach chuckles, scrubbing his hand along his jaw. "We have a new crew this season, meaning we have lots of new guys on the team who might not be so hung up on the old ways, if you get what I'm saying."

"What sort of old ways are you referring to?" Ruby asks, sounding defensive.

"I think he means that we're a little more open to allowing ourselves to be filmed," I answer for Coach. Ruby's attention swings to me, her fiery blue gaze seeming to burn me where I stand. "We try not to take ourselves too seriously around here."

"Oh." She crosses her arms, plumping up her tits. I know because my gaze lingers there. She's got a nice set. "So last year's team took themselves too seriously then."

I paste a smile on, trying to ease her ruffled feathers. "I appreciate how supportive you are of your brother. I get it."

"Do you?" She arches a brow.

I roll right over her comment. "But have you seen some of the team accounts out there on social media? They're hilarious."

"You've seen them too?" Gwen appears surprised. "And you think they're hilarious?"

"Yeah." I shrug. "They are. And I know where you guys are coming from. We need to lighten up and play along. I can talk to the guys and get them to agree. Don't worry."

"You have that much influence over your team already?" This comes from Ruby, who sounds downright hostile.

I take a step closer to her, regretting my decision the moment I do it. Her scent is even stronger now. And I can see the delicate spray of freckles across the bridge of her nose. Actual freckles.

She's adorable.

"I do," I tell her, my voice low, my gaze locked on hers for a beat too long. She doesn't look away. Doesn't so much as flinch and I finally flip my attention back to Eric and Gwen. "I'll help you guys out. You can count on me."

Ruby snorts, but I ignore her.

"Be sure y'all give them good footage," Coach Mattson says, his voice firm.

I send Ruby a look. "Trust me. I give good footage."

"I'm sure you can," she murmurs. "Hopefully you're up to the challenge."

"What challenge?" My eyebrows shoot up at her tone of voice.

"You'll need to be the stuff of every girl's fantasy."

Something unfamiliar inside me rises up and I swallow hard. Maybe it was hearing Ruby's sweet yet vaguely sarcastic voice say fantasy? The hint of doubt I heard in her words, like I can't manage it? "I can handle that."

"Really?"

"Definitely." I grin. "I'm sure I've starred in a few of your fantasies."

8

RUBY

"You and Ace have a past thing we need to know about?" Gwen asks me as we march over to the sidelines, our phones clutched in our hands, ready for action.

Filming action, that is. Of the team on the field. Eric has his Nikon, already taking photos. He likes to use them in his video creations he makes in iMovie. I watched the videos he posted on the team's Instagram account last night and they were great. His editing skills are top notch, everything syncing to the music perfectly. He's talented.

"There's no past thing between me and Ace," I lie, keeping my gaze aimed on the field, purposely not looking at Ace. They're not wearing their gear today so he's got a T-shirt and shorts on, and when my eyes mistakenly landed on him only a minute ago, I caught a glimpse of his thick thigh muscles flexing.

Ugh. I can't think about muscular thighs and six-pack abs and rock-hard biceps. I know Ace has all of that and more, but I can't like any of it. Because I don't like him.

He's an asshole. So arrogant. Like I've actually *fantasized* about him.

No way.

"He openly flirted with you," Gwen points out.

I turn to her. "Doesn't he flirt with everyone?"

"Not me," she's quick to answer.

"No one flirts with you, G." This comes from Eric, who has his back to us but must still be listening to our conversation. "You scare the shit out of every guy on campus."

"I do not."

"You kind of do," I say quietly. She turns to glare at me and I shrug. "I barely know you and you terrify me."

She looks away, her lips forming a straight line. "You need to be careful."

"Why?"

"The agreement you signed, there's a 'no dating athletes' clause." Gwyneth's gaze finds mine once more. "You did read the agreement, right?"

Barely. More like I skimmed it. Nothing alarming stood out so I signed on the dotted line, so to speak. "You don't have to worry about me dating an athlete. I'm not interested in any of them."

"Good, because if you do, you'll get fired," Gwen says, her voice firm.

Oh shit. That's serious.

"Hey!" We all turn to see Ace standing in the middle of the field, his hands cupped around his mouth. "We're ready for you if you want to start filming."

"Go ahead." Gwen waves her hand toward the field. "I'll let you film first."

Great. This feels like a trial by fire. And she's mad at me because I admitted she's terrifying. Probably didn't like the flirting part either, that's why she brought it up. I signed the contract, meaning I have to abide by the rules.

No flirting with Ace Townsend allowed.

I go to Eric, fighting the panic growing inside me. "Gwen wants me to film."

"You've got this." The sincere glow in his eyes isn't reassuring.

"What do you want me to do?"

"You and Gwen discussed it earlier. Just—go with what she said." Eric shrugs.

The earlier discussion was Gwen telling me what she wanted to do for the season. There are a lot of accounts out there right now that really interact with the players. Introducing them, letting the casual viewer know who they are and what position they play. These accounts manage to show them at their best—and their silliest. Sometimes even their worst, which is always good for a laugh, but never at their expense.

Gwen wants to do something like that for the football team. She even wants them to mouth along with trending songs, maybe even do a dance here and there. *Something lighthearted and fun*, were her exact words earlier.

Meaning the complete opposite of Gwen's behavior. Got it.

An irritated sound leaves me as I march out onto the field toward Ace, hating the butterflies that flap in my stomach at seeing that shit-eating grin on his face while he watches me approach. Am I wrong that it feels like he loves seeing my discomfort? It's annoying. He's annoying.

Though I can't deny just how gorgeous he is. Because he so is.

Gorgeous.

Ugh. No. Football players are a no-go.

"Ready to film us, Maguire?" His teasing tone on anyone else I would think is cute, but on him, I sort of want to sock him in the gut. This has me thinking about his stomach and how ripped I'm sure it is and how my hand would probably ache after trying to punch him and now I can't stop thinking about it.

"Not quite yet," I say, keeping my voice cool. Downright blasé. He doesn't affect me. I can't let him get to me. "I need to look up a few things first."

He rests his hands on his hips, glancing around. Feels like every member of the football team is out on the field and they're all circling us like a pack of wolves, curious to what's going to happen next. "Well, hurry up. We can only give you a few minutes before we need to get back to it."

"I thought you were going to be supportive."

"And I thought you had your shit together." He grins, and while I'm stewing in anger over his remark, clearly, he's just teasing me. "Take a couple minutes, babe. However long you need. We'll be here making plays and securing wins."

"Did you really just call me babe?" I roll my eyes, opening my camera on my phone and switching it to video. "I'm ready."

He'd already started walking away from me and he comes to a stop, slowly turning to face me once more. "Really?"

"Yes." I nod. "Are you?"

"You want to film *me*?" He glances around as if he's shocked.

"I want you to make a pass, yep." I hold my phone in front of me as if I'm ready to start recording him. "Let's do this."

"Hold on, hold on." He jogs over to a couple of his team-mates, their heads bent close as he discusses something with them. They all clap once at the same time and get into position just as I do the same, glancing around to make sure no one is going to run into me. "Ready, Maguire?"

I hate how he calls me by my last name, but it's better than hearing him say my actual name with that sexy rumble of his, so I'll deal. "Give it to me." I give him a thumbs-up.

Ace gets into position with the offensive line and when the ball is hiked to him, he stands there like the quin-tessential quarterback god, his arm cocked back, squinting into the sun, his eyes shifting as he figures out who's the best one to throw to. And when he does finally throw that ball, it goes long, a perfect spiral arcing through the air.

I capture it all with my phone, every single second and when the ball lands into a receiver's open hands, the player tucks the ball to his chest and runs it into the end zone. Ace throws his arms above his head. "Nice one!"

"Perfect throw," his teammate yells back at him.

I'd really hoped for a blooper, but damn it, he's just that good.

"What do you think?" Ace asks, his focus all on me.

I don't stop filming. "Pretty great."

"Don't you know it."

"Are you always so confident?"

"Only for the camera."

"I bet you'd say the same thing if I wasn't filming."

"Probably." He rests his hands on his hips again. One of the coaches is blowing his whistle in short, quick jabs, screaming for the defensive line to join him and I glance over my shoulder to watch as Gwen follows them. "You going to shut that off?"

I hit the button and stop filming, my fingers literally

itching to watch back what I just captured, but I restrain myself. "I'll have to come up with a dance for you and your offensive line to do for me tomorrow."

"You'll be back out here tomorrow?" He actually sounds excited by it.

"We'll be out here a lot this season. We need to film a lot of content." Gwen's goal is to grow the account by constantly posting, which means we probably need hours of film to work with. "We want to do a variety of things."

"Like what?" He sounds genuinely curious and I realize my mistake.

I hate that we're making casual conversation, and how it's so easy to talk to him. Look at him. I should still be mad at what he did. How he ditched me for another girl.

But it's hard to hold on to resentment when he's being so friendly and he's so freaking attractive. Makes me forget that he did me dirty in the first place.

"Interviews. Funny bits. Bloopers."

He frowns. "I don't like bloopers."

"It keeps you guys real." I roll my eyes. I feel like I do that a lot with him. "You can't be perfect all the time."

"I can if I try hard enough." He chuckles.

I make this obnoxious snorting sound that's not attractive whatsoever, but it's like I can't help myself. "Seriously, Ace. Making a mistake here and there, being able to laugh at yourself, keeps you human."

"You said my name." He rests his hand on his chest, full of drama. "Does this mean you forgive me?"

"What do I need to forgive you for?" My tone is overly-exaggerated and I'm blinking at him like I'm some sort of dumb doll.

He drops his hand at his side. "You know what I did. At that party."

"Oh, how you kissed some other skank at midnight? After trying to feel me up in the bathroom?" I hate that I just called that woman a skank, but I do think she finagled getting Ace alone at midnight on purpose to get back at me for turning his attention away from her.

"Yeah. That." His expression turns serious. "I feel bad about it."

"It was nothing." I wave my hand dismissively.

"Just to let you know, she kissed me first. I didn't kiss her." He levels his gaze on me, his expression dead serious.

I stare at him, hating the fact that hearing him admit she kissed him instead of the other way around makes me feel...relieved.

It shouldn't matter, who kissed who first. I don't own him. I don't *want* him.

Seriously, I don't.

"Oh." I shrug, trying to play off what he just said.

"Does that make a difference about how you feel towards me?"

"Not really." *Yes, really.*

"You sure about that?" He sounds like he doesn't believe me.

"I'm sure." I nod. "I don't care."

"About that. I like your shirt." He waves a hand at my chest and I glance down, seeing the three letters stitched on the center of my T-shirt. "I don't care?"

"Exactly." I wore this shirt as a silent message for Gwyneth and her crappy attitude toward me. I was trying to show that she doesn't affect me but looks like it came in handy for Ace too. "You like my shirt?"

"I love it. Fits you nice across the chest, if you know what I mean." He's grinning again, just before he turns away and rejoins his teammates on the field.

His words sink in only after he's left me alone and I blow out a frustrated breath, heading for the sidelines. I should be disgusted that he'd so blatantly refer to my chest—aka my breasts—like he just did. I should think he's a sexist asshole and want to steer clear from him as much as possible.

Instead, I can't help but enjoy our conversation. Even if he was staring at my boobs while giving me compliments about my shirt. He's flirtatious and there's no way I can take anything he says seriously.

Nope. Can't do that at all. I need to leave him alone.

But as I play back what I just filmed, I can't help but let my gaze linger on his tall, strong form. The way his muscles rippled when he threw the ball. That look of pure satisfaction on his face as he watched it fly through the air. He knew it was a good one. He knew it would land in the receiver's hands, and I wish I could've got his face on film when the ball was caught.

The camera loves him, that much is clear. The main reason Gwen wants to get so much footage of the team is because of Ace. She admitted as much to me earlier, when we were back in the office having our discussion while Eric was setting up his camera.

"He may be a cocky asshole, but Ace Townsend is gorgeous but like...in this unintimidating way? There's something about him that makes women feel like he's attainable, and Cam Fields never had that. Women loved him but he was really intense. But Ace? He seems—sweet." Gwen's nose scrunched up like she was disgusted by her assessment. "The women go nuts over him. Now don't get me wrong, we'll definitely focus on the games and all the normal football-type stuff, but we need to turn this into a fan account so girls can lose their minds over him. Over all of them, really."

Her words linger in my head. My job is that I'm going to be filming Ace all season, so we can play him up as a sex symbol for the masses.

Gee, can't wait.

9

ACE

We enter Logan's Bar downtown and the crowd parts for us as soon as we walk into the building. Guys greet us by holding their hands up for a high five, lots of, *looking good so far* type comments coming at us from all angles.

Plenty of women greet us too. All of them with hopeful expressions on their faces, their soft voices sounding almost frantic as they try to speak over each other, all of them vying for our attention.

It's like this every time we come to Logan's as a team, and tonight is no exception. It's a Wednesday night. Our first game is Saturday and it's an away game, though not too far and we plan on leaving first thing Saturday morning.

Practice today was rough. I know they're going to put us through it again tomorrow. And the next day after that. Tonight, I just want to relax. Shoot the shit with my teammates. Flirt with some pretty women. Maybe even take one home—or wherever—and have a quick hookup. Nothing too complicated. A hand job in the bathroom? A blow job in the back seat of my car?

I'm definitely looking to release some tension.

The odds are in our favor this evening. I notice quick that the ratio of women to men is three to one and I nudge Derek in the ribs, who sends me an irritated look.

"What's up with all the chicks?" I ask.

"Pretty sure they're all members of your fan club, bro." He laughs when I scowl. "It's ladies' night. They're trying something new at Logan's. Women get drinks for a cheaper price every Wednesday."

"Fucking unfair," I mutter as we head for the back of the bar, where we usually like to sit. Last year all I wanted to do was drink with my fake ID, and the bartenders and servers let me get away with it. Some of them had to know I was underage, but they always looked the other way. Plus, I had a really stellar fake driver's license that cost me a pretty penny. I wanted to make sure and use that bitch every chance I got.

Now I'm legal, thanks to turning twenty-one back in June, and I can drink whenever I want, but this season, I'm trying to remain mostly sober. It's not like I lose control when I drink or anything like that, but I'm trying to keep up a semi-healthy regimen here. There's no need for me to get shit-faced all the time and besides, I don't need the extra calories.

God, the team nutritionist would so be giving me a high five right now.

"Ladies' night brings more women into the bar," Derek points out as we settle into a booth. "Don't think you'll complain about that."

Logan's is already full of women any night of the week, but the estrogen is damn near overpowering tonight. "You drinking?" I ask Derek.

"Hell yeah." He smiles. "You?"

"One beer." Maybe I shouldn't even have one. Might be smart to just sip on some water and call it good.

"Boring." Derek shakes his head. "But I get it. You'll probably make the nutritionist jizz his pants when he finds out what a good little boy you are."

"Fucking gross." Grimacing, I shove at Derek's shoulder but he barely budges. The guy is so damn solid. He needs all the extra calories he can get to mow down anyone on the field. A few beers won't make a difference with his weight.

"What, it's true. We've got a whole new regimen going on here." Derek shakes his head, and I wonder what he thinks about all of the changes.

Our support staff has grown thanks to Mattson making his requests and the athletic department finally granting them. We have personal trainers, nutritionists and even therapists now on staff to assist us with any of our needs, both mental and physical. It's kind of nice, knowing we have access to so much help.

"Hey, Ace." I glance up to find a group of girls standing in front of our table with hopeful expressions on their faces. It's weird how they all look the same with their matching dark, wavy hair and extremely short denim skirts. It's like they planned their look on purpose.

"Hey." I offer them a quick wave, unsure of which one greeted me first.

One of them steps forward, her dark eyes latched onto my face. "Ready for this weekend's game?"

I nod, leaning back against the booth seat. "Sure am, sweetheart. What about you? You going?"

She slowly shakes her head, her other look-alike friends stepping forward, giving me eerie vibes. "I'm so sad it's an away game."

"There's a bus that takes students to the games," I remind her.

Her expression turns sheepish. "I can't take it."

I'm frowning. "Why not?"

"She got into a fight on the bus last season," one of her friends pipes up. "Got kicked off."

"I was drunk," the girl adds with a brilliant smile.

Derek and I share a look before I return my attention to her. "You're feisty."

She leans over the table, pressing her palm on the scarred wood, giving us a perfect view down her shirt. "You don't even know the half of it."

I squirm. Derek covers up a laugh with a fake cough, bringing his fist to his mouth and muttering some sort of insult under his breath.

"Can I buy you a drink?" she asks me.

Her friends start to wander off and I'm grateful there's less of them but still.

I'd rather just chat with my friends. This chick's intensity is kind of freaking me out.

"I've already got a beer coming," I tell her.

"I'll order you another one."

"I'm on a one-drink limit tonight, sweetheart."

"I can get a deal since it's ladies' night." Damn, she's not going to give up.

Derek is laughing and I send him a panicked look, wishing he'd come to my rescue.

"It's all good," I tell her with an easy smile.

"Oh, come on. My treat."

"Hey, Townsend." Derek nudges me extra hard in the side, making me grunt. "Isn't that your girlfriend over there?"

I whip my head around, ready to claim whoever the next female I set eyes on as my girlfriend. "Where do you see her?" I ask, playing along.

"Right there, idiot," Derek mumbles, and when my gaze lands on the familiar face, I nearly pass out with relief.

It's Ruby.

"Hey, sexy girlfriend!" I shout at Ruby, startling the girl who is currently trying to flirt with me.

Of course, Ruby looks in my direction, and of course she rolls her eyes the moment she sees it's me. She's got Natalie trailing after her and the only reason I even know who Natalie is, is because she lived with Joanna last year.

Natalie is kind of intimidating. Not like the girl who's currently staring me down like I'm a piece of meat she wants to gnaw on, but still. Natalie can be intense. She's never afraid to ask for what she wants.

"Come here," I mouth at Ruby, whose body is literally leaning backward, like she doesn't want to have anything to do with me. Natalie is the one who takes Ruby's hand and starts dragging her over to our table.

"You have a girlfriend?" the girl asks me.

"Definitely," I say with a firm nod. "And she's hot as fuck and super jealous so I'd suggest you steer clear of her, if you know what I'm saying."

"God, why do you even have a fan club if you're already taken?" The girl rolls her eyes and huffs out a breath, stalking away without another word.

"Nice one," Derek tells me once she's gone. "She was scary."

"They've all been coming on a little stronger than normal this season," I admit. I don't mind a bold, know-what-she-wants kind of woman, but the girls who've been swarming around me lately have been a different kind of confident. A lot more demanding than usual.

I blame it on the position I'm playing. Being the backup gets you just enough attention to make you feel like you can snag any pussy you want. But being the starting quarterback?

That's a whole new kind of intensity that's going to take some getting used to.

"Hey, guys," Natalie greets us brightly when she stops in front of our table, Ruby beside her. "Derek."

"Nat. Looking smokin' hot as usual." Derek's voice dips low, his gaze for Natalie and no one else. The way they're staring at each other reminds me that they had a thing before. About a year ago.

Before Derek moved on, which he does pretty quickly.

I'm the same way.

But then there's Ruby Maguire. For whatever reason, she's always lingering in the back of my mind. Seeing her now standing in front of me in a pair of long black flowy pants and a cropped black top that shows off her tanned stomach, I'm stunned silent.

Pretty sure she's not wearing a bra either. As in I can see the outline of her nipples.

Jesus.

"Hey, Red," I tell her, my voice rusty. I clear my throat, feeling like an idiot.

Ruby frowns. "Red?"

"Well, yeah."

"My hair is blonde." She picks up a chunk of it, showing me like I've never noticed before.

"I know."

"Why are you calling me Red?"

"Your name is Ruby. And a ruby is red, you know?" I

smile, glancing at the empty spot beside me in the booth. "You should join us."

She hesitates, glancing toward the front of the bar, and I can tell she wants to bolt. Man, I really fucked everything up on New Year's for her to act this way.

"Swear you won't try any funny stuff." She points a finger at me.

I hold up my hands, wanting to laugh at her saying 'funny stuff'. "I swear."

We watch each other, the silence between us stretching, and I swear to God, I'm starting to sweat.

"Okay," she finally says, shocking me. My gaze tracks her as she makes her way to my side of the rounded booth.

"Are we staying?" Natalie asks her.

"I am," Ruby says.

"Sit by me, Nat." Derek pats the empty spot next to him.

This is how we end up with two girls we already know sitting at our table on Wednesday night. And while this isn't normally how Derek and I operate, I can't help but feel a little relieved at having Ruby sitting with me, giving me serious side-eye while she watches Derek and Natalie launch into an immediate flirtatious conversation. Natalie even twirls a lock of dark auburn hair around her finger as she bats her eyelashes at Derek, and he's eating this shit up.

Ruby watches them, her eyes wide with shock and her lush lips formed into the slightest frown.

Damn, she's pretty.

The waitress finally shows up with our beers and I'm taking a giant gulp the moment the server hands it over. She glances over at Ruby.

"You want anything, honey?"

"I'll take a watermelon margarita."

"Ooh me too," Natalie adds.

"Coming right up." The waitress watches me as I steadily gulp from my beer. "You want me to bring you another one of those?"

I'm about to say no when Derek speaks for me.

"You better. I think he needs it."

I glare at him, ready to tell the server to cancel that request, but she's already gone.

"You watching what you drink tonight?" Natalie asks me.

"I'd planned on only one beer," I tell her, hoisting my beer mug into the air like I'm raising a glass and eager to say cheers. "But I guess Derek ruined that."

"He ruins a lot of things," Natalie says, her expression pointed when she studies Derek.

He doesn't seem affected by it at all. Either he's oblivious or he flat out doesn't give a damn.

"Red, huh?" Ruby asks once the waitress is long gone and Natalie and Derek have resumed their flirtatious conversation.

Glancing over at her, I find she's already watching me, her full lips curved into a faint smile. I probably amuse her, but not in the way I want. "It makes sense."

She neither confirms nor denies my statement. "No one has ever called me Red before."

"Kinda funny, considering your name is Ruby and a ruby is red."

"I've never really had a nickname," she admits. "I'm just always...Ruby."

"Nothing wrong with that. I don't have a nickname either. I'm just Ace."

"Ace sounds like a nickname," she admits. "Though I'm sure you've heard that before."

"I have." I bring my beer to my lips and tip my head

back, taking a long pull. The alcohol courses through my veins, warming me up. Relaxing my tense muscles.

"How did you get the name Ace anyway?"

I smile at her, pleased she wants to know. "It was my dad's favorite name growing up. He played some video game where the main character was Ace and he always loved it. So when my mom finally got pregnant and they found out they were having a boy, he immediately wanted to name me Ace. My mom could see how much it meant to him and that's how I became baby Ace."

I don't bother telling her how my parents struggled for years with infertility. My mom had a lot of miscarriages and went through IVF treatments until finally I was born. They considered me their lucky baby, their only child and completely overindulged me when I was growing up.

But my dad also taught me how to work hard and I channeled all of my energy into football. If I can pay the two of them back in any sort of way for the love and devotion they've shown me my entire life, it'll be by taking care of them financially, if I ever get the chance to play professionally.

It's the least I could do.

"Baby Ace," she says, her voice soft. "Were you cute?"

I make a scoffing noise. "Fucking adorable."

"So modest."

"That's me," I say. "Always playing down my best qualities."

Ruby laughs and fuck, it's a pretty sound. "Most of you guys are downright insufferable."

"When you refer to 'you guys', are you meaning us football players?" She nods. "Yet here you are, always hanging out with us."

"Guess I'm drawn to what I know?" She shrugs. "And I wouldn't say I'm always hanging out with you."

"You're right, and you should. Always hang out with us." I keep the smile on my face while hers fades a little, her expression turning unsure. I hate seeing that look.

"Yo, Maguire." We both turn in Derek's direction. "Your boy here called you his girlfriend."

10

RUBY

What? Is Derek serious right now?

"You did, huh?" I watch Ace's cheeks turn a little red, as if he's embarrassed by what Derek just said. How cute is that? Though he's not the type to ever be embarrassed. Not from what I've seen.

Meaning, I can't think it's cute, or that he's charming. Orrrrr that he's easy to talk to.

This man is off limits. I can't think about doing anything with him because it puts my job at risk.

And I like my new job. I don't want to lose it for some dumb jock who'll eventually disappoint me anyway.

"There was a girl at our table earlier," he explains to me, his voice low. "She was giving off a really weird vibe. I needed to get rid of her."

"By claiming me as your girlfriend?" I arch a brow.

He smirks, scratching his jaw with those long fingers of his. "Claiming. I like your word choice."

"Please." Nope. No way. I'm not going to let him leave me feeling all sorts of flustered. "You can't claim anything when it comes to me."

"Look I'm not even the one who mentioned I had a girl-friend in the first place. Derek did." He jerks a thumb in his friend's direction.

"Only because I was trying to save your ass from that weird chick," Derek says, confirming Ace's earlier explanation.

Not that I think Ace is a liar, but come on. These guys will say anything to get our sympathy. Or to get us to fall under their spell.

Look at Derek and Natalie. She told me on the drive over to Logan's that she's sworn off athletes forever. That they're all the same and just looking for a good time that lasts exactly one night.

Nat speaks from experience. She's already hooked up with Derek before and here she is, staring at him with stars in her eyes, her hand resting on his meaty forearm while he says God knows what to her.

Men. They're kind of the worst. And I'm not what I would consider a manhater either...

Maybe I shouldn't lump all men together. More like athletes.

Though my dad isn't awful. Neither is my uncle or my cousins or the guys my cousins married...

"Trust me, she was pretty weird," Ace tells me, reaching for his beer mug and draining the last of it. As if I would ever trust him. I'm not a complete idiot. "Tell me how you got on the social media team."

"Oh." I sit up straighter, surprised he'd ask something about me. From my experience with football players—even my brother sometimes—all they want to do is talk about themselves. "Well, my major is sports management and marketing and a paid intern spot opened up. My advisor let me know, I interviewed and now I'm on the team."

"Nice." Ace nods, drumming his fingers on the table. I stare at those fingers. They're long and almost elegant and they can throw a ball like no other.

I wonder what else they can do?

My body goes warm, thinking nothing but dirty thoughts. His fingers undressing me. Sliding around my neck. Pinning me in place...

"You like it so far?" he asks, pulling me from my wayward thoughts.

"I do. Eric is nice." I wrinkle my nose, not sure what to say about Gwyneth.

"Gwen is kind of a bitch," Ace adds.

"She's not that bad," I say in her defense.

"She's mean."

"She's a little mean," I agree and we both laugh and damn it, he has a nice laugh. "I think I just need to get on her good side."

"Does she have a good side?"

"I'm going to find out." I glance around the bar, wondering where our server is with our drink order. I need alcohol, stat, if I'm going to continue this conversation with Ace. "I think it's going to be fun. We have a lot of ideas we want to implement for you guys."

Ace groans, tipping his head back against the booth to stare at the ceiling for a moment before he glances over at me. "Were you serious about the dancing thing?"

"Maybe," I hedge, pausing for only a moment. "Definitely."

Another groan escapes him and I can't help but think the sound is kind of sexy. "Are we going to have to like, mouth along to songs and shit?"

"Um...yeah?" My voice is hesitant because his reaction isn't the best. "Dancing, singing, making fun of yourselves in general. We want you guys to have a sense of humor. Girls love that stuff."

"They do?"

I nod.

"What does Eric think of all this?"

I'm impressed he remembers Eric's name. "He claims he's cool with it, but I don't think he likes Gwen's ideas much. He'd rather showcase the team at their best, rattle off stats, share highlights from games and get the fans hyped every weekend."

"That sounds perfect." Ace nods his approval.

"Of course, you agree with him. If we did it that way, we'd only shine you guys in a perfect light. But Gwen thinks we need to show off how hot you guys are and get all the girls swooning. She's hoping you'll all eventually go viral and the team in general will become a social media sensation."

"This is all Gwen's idea?" He looks surprised and I can't blame him.

"Yep." I nod, smiling. "She says this kind of thing happens a lot, especially with college hockey teams. Get ready. She's going to put you all through it by creating a bunch of beefcake content."

"Beefcake?" Ace sounds amused as he runs a hand through his hair, the muscles in his arms rippling with the movement. My gaze lingers on his arms, my mouth going dry, my thoughts kicking into creative mode. He's in a black T-shirt, but I'm thinking we should make content with some of the team in tank tops, flexing their muscles, but not showing their faces.

Arm porn, if you will.

The server shows up with a tray filled with drinks, doling them out to everyone at the table before she moves onto the booth next to us. I pull my watermelon margarita closer to me and take a sip, glancing over at Ace to find him watching me, his lips parted.

His gaze fixed on my lips wrapped around the straw.

Releasing the straw, I lean back against the booth, knocking my knee into his, slightly taken aback by how warm he is. The man is a furnace. "You're staring."

"You're hot."

I'm taken aback by his blatant statement. "Seriously?"

"Are you fishing for compliments?" His brows shoot up. "Come on, Red. You have to know you're sexy as fuck."

Ummm...I wasn't expecting that. "I'm definitely not fishing for compliments."

"Right. You just want to hear me call you hot again." He leans in a little closer, his gaze lingering on my lips once more. "You're pretty fucking hot, Red."

"That is a dumb nickname," I murmur, refusing to let his words make me feel a certain way. "People won't get it."

"We don't need anyone else to get it." His smile is small and a little sneaky and a lot sexy. Ugh. "It'll be our little secret."

Oh. He has no right being this attractive. And he's so flirty. How many other girls does he flirt with like this?

I bet the number is shockingly large.

"I don't date football players." I sniff, tilting my chin up.

"I'm not looking for a date."

I roll my eyes. "And I'm definitely not looking to hook up with a football player either."

"That's too bad." He shifts away from me, reaching for his beer, his fingers curling around the glass. "I have a feeling we'd be really good together."

I hate how rattled his words leave me. How intrigued I am by him. Maybe we would be good together. In fact, we might even be freaking *fantastic* together. I get the sense Ace knows exactly what he's doing sexually. He's in peak athletic form. I saw the way he moved out on that field earlier.

If I let him, I'd bet he could fuck me into oblivion and I'd die happily satisfied.

But it's never going to happen. That's not what I'm looking for. He's the type of guy who pulls you into his orbit, makes you feel like no one else matters but you, and then promptly dumps you without warning when someone else catches his attention.

I've dealt with this sort of thing—this sort of guy—before. I'm not interested in putting myself through that again.

"Well, you're never going to find out," I chirp, taking another fortifying sip of my margarita. "We're probably better off as...friends."

"Friends, huh?" He rubs his chin, which of course is a complete distraction and I become fixated on his hand and his fingers and I wonder what it would feel like, having that wide palm smacking my bare ass? Would he be into that sort of thing? I'm not talking full-blown kink here, but I do think the occasional butt slap is kind of hot.

"Friends," I say firmly, shoving all thoughts of ass slapping out of my mind.

"How's the drink?" he asks, changing the subject.

Frowning, I stir the slushy concoction with my straw before I take another sip. "Delicious."

"You get drunk off tequila?"

"Well, duh." I sit up straighter. "Not like I'm looking to get drunk tonight though."

"You're not?" He leans in, nudging my shoulder with his. "That's too bad. I bet you're a lot of fun when you loosen up."

Okay that was the wrong thing to say. "Are you implying I'm uptight?"

"Around me? Ever since New Year's Eve?" His gaze locks with mine and he nods. "Definitely."

"Ace! Ace!"

At the sound of a bunch of high-pitched feminine voices chanting his name, we both turn to watch a group of women approach the table. Every single one of them is wearing a team jersey that can be purchased at the student bookstore. And every jersey has Ace's number on them.

"Hey look. It's my fan club." He grins, spreading his arms out along the back of the rounded booth, his fingers danger-ously close to my shoulder. "Aren't you girls cute."

They all giggle and flip their hair over their shoulders. There is a lot of skin on display since they're either wearing short skirts or shorts, with heeled sandals on their feet. They're also wearing a lot of makeup and their hair is perfectly done. Like they all got together and got ready before they headed over to the bar in the hopes they'd run into Ace.

This is truly...wild.

"You have an actual fan club?" I ask him, my voice incredulous.

"I mean..." His voice drifts and he shrugs those wide shoulders. "Not officially."

"But you know these girls exist." I incline my head toward them, noting the way a few of them glare at me. As if they're pissed that I'm sitting with him when I haven't even earned the right.

That's what it feels like.

"Oh, I definitely know they exist. We've met up before, right ladies?" He aims his million-watt smile in their direction and they all giggle and flutter their fingers at him, their bodies shifting and moving as one entity.

It's kind of weird.

"Okay, I'm leaving." I move out from under his arm, snagging my glass as I go, and rise to my feet. I offer a quick wave to the unofficial Ace Townsend fan club and they all wave at me in return, their gazes full of matching curiosity.

Wandering around the bar, I absently sip at my drink, my mind preoccupied by the giggling fan club and a very proud Ace watching them with lust in his eyes.

I get this image of Ace in a hot tub with all of these girls and they're all naked. Rubbing on him. Having a big ol' orgy and Ace is the star of their every fantasy. And while I can't deny that he is superhot with an amazing body as well as funny and charming—I just...

Can't get on board with this.

I don't know how my mother put up with this sort of thing back in the day when my dad played for the NFL, but they were together for so long by then and he was so madly in love with her, I guess she never had to worry about it.

Not that I can imagine Ace madly in love with *me*. Or that we'd end up in a relationship. I mean, come on. He just told me point blank he's not interested in that.

And I believe him.

11

RUBY

W e're out on the field, standing on the sidelines and watching the football team practice. Eric is as quick on his feet as the team is, running along beside them, following their every movement with his camera. He's busy snapping photos and taking videos, while Gwen and I just sit on the grass and watch everything, hot and bored.

Well, I'm hot and bored. Not too sure about Gwyneth.

"This isn't what I planned," Gwen says with an exasperated sigh halfway through practice.

Okay, that sounds like confirmation that we're feeling the same kind of way.

The team has gathered on the sidelines on the away team's side of the field, taking a water break. My gaze snags on Ace, as if I have no control over myself, lingering on the way he tilts his head back and drinks from the bright red Golden Eagles water bottle clutched in his hand. He's wearing a cropped white jersey shirt that shows off his washboard abs to perfection and white football pants that cut off just below the knee.

Any other guy I think would look ridiculous, but not Ace. More like he looks ridiculously *hot*.

I fan myself, turning to Gwen. "What do you mean?"

"This feels just like last year, when Eric filmed all this footage, while I sat around doing nothing and that other girl —Jamie—jumped around hooting and hollering and showing off her boobs for the guys in her endless collection of tank tops."

Right. Tank top girl who got fired for being a distraction. "That sounds…"

"Awful? I know." Gwyneth sighs, her gaze stuck on the football team. "I spent a lot of hours in that office trying to create the kind of content I wanted to see with Eric's footage, but it was impossible. Eric ended up editing a lot of it, though I helped him. It was nothing but the team running out on the field and trying to look like a bunch of macho bad asses."

I burst out laughing, ignoring the way Gwen scowls at me. "Why don't we continue creating some content of our own? Don't forget, I have the footage of Ace throwing that ball."

"Again, that's kind of boring." She makes a face. "I'm not trying to be rude. I just—I want to do something different."

"Then let's do it."

"It's not that easy."

I frown at her. Is she being purposely difficult or what? "Why not?"

"Because Eric is a control freak and he'll only want to use what he's made," Gwen points out, making her words sound logical but…

"He can go ahead and use his stuff and make a bunch of boring bro videos set to AC/DC songs. The dads and alumni will love it." I send her a look, noting the curiosity in her gaze. "I'm down to put together whatever you want to do, Gwen. We can do this."

"You want to help me? Really?" She sounds skeptical.

"Yes," I emphasize. "Let's go talk to them."

We both jump to our feet and I start walking, but she grabs my arm, stopping me.

"We probably shouldn't interrupt their practice." Gwen nibbles on her lower lip, her gaze going to the team.

I do the same, watching them for a second, how they're all clustered together, their deep, boisterous voices drifting across the grass as they give each other shit. Eric is standing among them with the camera hanging from his neck by a thick black strap, nodding and smiling and looking so happy, he could practically cry.

I bet he was the sort of kid who loved football growing up but either never gave it a try, or never made the team. Or maybe he played when he was a little kid but then all the guys grew taller and bulked up, while he never really did. Perhaps his parents wouldn't let him play, too worried he would get hurt, which is a valid concern.

It's obvious though, that this is all he wanted. To be out on the football field, accepted by his teammates. And now he's living that glory moment in a different way. This is why his content is like this. He wants to be a part of the team, and I get it.

That appeals to the guys.

But Gwen and I are trying to get the ladies on board. That's what will take these boys further, social media-wise. Having a bunch of women drool over them. And what hot-blooded football player wouldn't want a bunch of girls going on and on about how sexy they are? From what I've seen with this bunch, they'd freaking love it.

I know Ace would especially enjoy it. He has an actual

fan club, for the love of God. He would eat that sort of thing up.

"Coach Mattson said we could approach them when they're having a break. We need to before they start practicing again." I shake her hold off my arm and march across the field, pasting a pleasant smile on my face.

They all turn toward me as I draw closer, Eric forgotten, and I know the only reason is because I'm a woman, and there aren't many women out here during practice. I offer up a friendly wave, coming to a stop directly in front of them, shielding my eyes with my hand.

Damn it, I really should've worn sunglasses. The sun is so bright out here.

"Hey, guys!" My voice is overly cheerful and when my gaze drifts, I see Derek standing at the back of the crowd, an amused look on his face. "Um, I was hoping I could get a couple of volunteers to make a quick video for social media?"

Gwen approaches, stopping to stand right next to me, but remains silent, glaring at them all.

God, she's intimidating. She seriously needs to relax.

"What are you looking for?" one of them asks, his voice wary. He's got his arms crossed in front of him, in pure defensive mode, and I realize he's a perfect candidate for my planned video.

"I'm looking for someone who looks exactly like you," I tell him and he appears surprised. Even a little pleased.

"Guess I'll help you out." He comes forward, but no one else does, all of them remaining quiet.

I'm struck by how reluctant they all seem. Like they're terrified to step forward.

Mattson watches all of this go down, his gaze sliding to Ace, giving him a pointed look. Something unspoken passes between them and then Ace is shouldering his way through his teammates, approaching me with that ever-present affable expression on his face.

"I'll volunteer, Red," he drawls.

"Red?" Gwen mumbles, sounding confused.

"Don't ask," I say out of the side of my mouth, standing up straighter. "Anyone else want to participate?"

A few more players step forward, all of them with bulky, muscular arms, and I nearly want to jump up and down in glee at our choices.

"Okay, guys," I say, clapping my hands when I've got all of them surrounding me and Gwen. She's got her phone out, ready to record. "I need you take your shirts off."

All of them glance at each other before they look at me, their wary expressions telling me they're not too sure about this.

"This feels vaguely inappropriate," Ace says, and while I can hear the teasing in his voice, I also don't want these guys to feel like we're objectifying them.

Even if we sort of—okay, fine, we are totally objectifying them, but it's all in good fun. We would never make them do something they don't want to.

"Look, I promise this won't be sleazy. We don't want to make gawking videos of your naked torsos," I tell Ace, my gaze sweeping over all of them. "Our plan is to make an ode to arm candy."

"Oh my God, I love it," Gwen murmurs, and I stand a little taller, thrilled to earn her approval.

"Arm candy?" the first guy who volunteered—Evan—says. "What exactly do you mean?"

"We need you to flex and show off your muscles," Gwen says loudly. "You can manage that for a few minutes, right guys?"

They all grumble, but within seconds, we've got six guys with their shirts off and um...

Wow.

We're surrounded by men who are in top physical condition. Smooth skin, rippling muscles, thick forearms, bulging biceps. Firm pecs, flat stomachs, that naughty little trail leading from their navels and disappearing behind the waistband of their shorts, pants, whatever.

Okay, specifically I'm eyeing Ace's happy trail and it's making me feel very, um...

Happy.

Reminding myself I need to keep this professional and stop ogling them, my sensibilities take over and I line them up. Gwen films each guy, zooming in tightly as they hold up their arms and flex. She never films their faces, which causes them all to start protesting. They want to be known, want to show off their grinning faces so the girls know who to scream for, but Gwen shakes her head.

"We need an air of mystery at first. Eventually you'll be revealed," she reassures them.

"Maybe you should have them guess who we are in the comments," Ace suggests and Gwen's face lights up, glancing over at me.

"That's a good idea," she says, and I reluctantly nod.

Ace's gaze slides to mine and I can tell he's pleased. It's his turn to flex and I do my best not to watch while Gwen films him, but I quickly give up and just blatantly stare.

His arms are like works of art. He's bulky but not too much. Sleek, smooth skin that's tanned from the sun. Bulging biceps and thick forearms corded with muscle, lightly dusted in golden hair and those damn hands.

My gaze lingers on his hands, and I'm immediately lost in thought. I imagine them touching me. Pushing my hair away from my face, drifting across my cheek. Along my jaw and sliding farther down, curving gently around my throat, tilting my face up for a kiss...

"Okay, next!" Gwen shouts, snapping me out of my reverie and when my gaze finds Ace's once more, he's grinning, looking mighty pleased with himself.

Ugh. I turn away, ready to call the next guy to get filmed, but I realize Ace was the last guy.

Mattson blows his whistle. "Back to practice! Now!"

They all jog away, Ace the only one lingering, that smirk still on his face as he watches me. "Can't wait to see the final result."

"We'll be posting tonight," Gwen tells him, her gaze locked on her phone as she runs through all the videos she just took.

"Thank you," I tell him, wishing he'd walk away. Wishing he'd continue to linger.

My conflicting feelings are so...conflicting.

"Anytime," he says, his voice lowering, his gaze never straying from my face and I part my lips, ready to say...

What? Want to hang out? Want to meet at my apartment and make a mess of my bed for a few hours? No.

No.

"Townsend!" Mattson screams and Ace turns away from me without another word, heading back to the center of the field, his T-shirt still clutched in his hand. He stops, slipping it back on, his torso disappearing from view and a sad sigh leaves me.

"I think he likes you."

I turn to study Gwen, who's attention is still on her phone.

"No way."

"Yes way. He has a nickname for you that doesn't make

sense and everything," she says, like that's the logical conclusion for why he must like me.

"My name is Ruby. A ruby is red," I tell her, and she glances up, her brows furrowed.

"Oh yeah. Duh."

I turn my back to the field, not wanting to look at them anymore.

Or Ace. Instead, Gwen shows me what she got and I go in search of a trending sound, the two of us eventually plopping down onto the grass.

"I want to prove this kind of content will work," Gwen says at one point, lifting her head to glare at Eric, who is still capturing more of his usual content of the football team. "They've been filmed by the male gaze for way too long. We need to change it up."

"I agree."

She turns toward me, the surprise on her face obvious. "Really?"

"Yeah, of course. Why do you think I came up with the arm candy idea?"

Gwen drops her gaze back to her phone, chewing on her lower lip as she edits the video, shaving off a few seconds here and there, trying to get it just right. "It's a good one."

"Thanks."

"We need something different. I keep telling Eric that. Our follower count has grown stagnant, but he's in denial." Gwen shakes her head, her gaze returning to Eric.

I see it then. She's trying to prove something to him because she likes him. And I think it's in more than a friendly way, but maybe I'm wrong.

I don't know though. She's got something to prove when it comes to Eric, and I'm here for it. He's a nice guy, but I'm starting to realize Gwen's not so bad either. She just seems to get rubbed wrong by...everyone.

Well, maybe not me.

Fine. I'm sure I rub her wrong. I know I did the first day I showed up to work. She was ready to send me packing and she didn't even know me.

"I know this sounds silly, but I want to make a difference and leave my stamp on the social media team." Gwen offers me a weak smile when I glance over at her. "I know we're not changing the world by showing off shirtless football players but if we can grow our follower count, I'll feel like I at least contributed something here. Instead of just putting together yet another slow-mo video of the quarterback throwing a football into the air."

I remember seeing a lot of those videos last season. Blair showed me most of them, ridiculously proud of Cam, and while I can't deny those videos definitely made them all look great, I'm on Gwen's side.

"We're going to shake this up," I say, my voice firm, my gaze going back out to the field. Ace is doing a little dance, the ball gripped in his hand, his eyes shifting as he tries to find someone to throw the ball to. I can see the moment he spots whoever his target is, his arm rearing back, the cropped T-shirt lifting, my gaze dropping.

Lingering on his abs that shine with the faintest sheen of sweat.

Oh lord help me.

I'm in serious trouble.

12

ACE

I'm walking across campus, hurrying to my next class, noting how many women pass me by with big smiles on their faces, all of them saying hi and sounding extra flirtatious.

I guess this isn't too unusual, but I swear there's something different in the way they look at me. A gleam in their eyes that's extra sharp. Like they know something I don't.

Huh.

Minutes later, I'm striding into class and settling into my usual desk, whipping out my phone when I hear the text notification sound. It's from one of the guys on my team.

Evan: **Did you see this?**

There's a link to a video and I hit it, wincing when I hear the song about hot guys making girls feel a certain way, and it's one short video shot after another of us flexing our muscles for the camera. I check the caption: *Football team who dis? Recognize anyone? Name the player in the comments!*

The caption is accompanied by the giant eyes looking to the side emoji.

I smile, glad they took my suggestion.

Me: **We look good.**

Evan: **Not the usual content the team shares, that's for sure.**

Me: **Maybe that's a good thing?**

Evan: **Maybe. It already has over a thousand likes.**

I check the stats. Well, damn. Evan's right.

Me: **Damn.**

Evan: **I know. Impressive.**

I scroll through the football team's account, checking the stats of past posts. They have okay likes but very few comments, and not a single post or video has over a thousand likes. Just the latest one.

Looks like the ladies knew what they were doing when they posted this.

"Hey, Ace." I turn to find the girl who sits to the right of my desk is smiling at me. "Are you in that video?"

"Guess you'll have to find out." I flash her a grin.

"Oh, is there going to be a reveal?" The girl's eyes go wide.

"Pretty sure that's the plan." I have no idea if that's what they wanted to do, but I'm suggesting it the next time they join us for practice.

Hopefully that's soon. I get a little thrill out of knowing Ruby is watching me out on the field. It's like I can feel her hot gaze on me, tracking my every movement, and I end up putting my all into my game play. Some might call that showing off and they're probably right but ultimately, it's got me playing better and that's kind of cool.

No, it's actually *really* cool. When she's watching me, I want to impress her. But does she notice?

That remains to be seen.

Ruby Maguire is not one to gush on and on about me, and I wonder if that's because she grew up with a father who played professional football? Or does her attitude have to do with her still feeling wronged by me over the New Year's Eve party?

Not sure. But I'm thinking even if I hadn't wronged her that night, she'd still treat me like I'm not that big of a deal. She's been surrounded by football players her entire life. Her whole family is made up of professionals. Like, legit.

Her *entire* family.

What's that like? I can't imagine. To be raised amongst such greatness. I bet it can be intimidating, but Knox always seemed to handle it with ease, though I'm guessing that's because he doesn't know any other way. Cam's an uptight motherfucker most of the time, but I'm thinking if him and Blair go the distance, he'll end up being a part of that family football legacy by marriage.

It's kind of wild to think about. To be linked, related to the Maguire and Callahan dynasty. And I'm not even touching on all the players included in that dynasty. Can't forget Asher Davis or Eli Bennett either.

Damn. That's a lot of football greatness.

I shake my head, impressed. Wonder if I could ever get on Ruby Red's good side and someday meet her family? Not sure what I would do if I was confronted with all of that football talent in one room, but I do know one thing.

I would talk their ears off in search of advice. Stories. I love a good story. I'm sure they all have a bunch they'd love to share.

And it's not like I'd be using her to get close to her family either. I don't use people. That's not my style. Here's the thing when it comes to Ruby.

I like her.

A lot.

I can't stop thinking about her. I'm dying to spend more time with her.

How do I convince Ruby I'm not such a bad guy?

Once classes are over, I head to the student center and grab something to eat, shoveling it down while I sit with a few of the guys from my team. My gaze scans the quad continuously, in search of a familiar blonde head but Ruby is nowhere to be found.

A few girls join our table, two of them flanking my sides, their whispery soft voices and constant giggling grating on my nerves almost immediately.

"Tell us, Ace, are you in that video?" one of them asks at one point, both of them staring at me like I'm going to strip naked at any given moment.

I smile at each of them, not minding the way they cling to my arms at all. I even flex a little, hoping they notice how hard my biceps are. "I can't make the reveal yet, ladies. Gotta listen to the social media team."

"You can tell me," the other one says, her free hand landing on my thigh, creeping up higher.

Everything's happening under the table so no one can really see what's going on but when I glance up, I find Ruby standing in the distance, her gaze stuck on us. A look of disgust on her face.

Shit.

Now Ruby is going to believe I'm an even bigger asshole than she first thought.

"Sorry, sweetheart." I grab the girl's wandering hand, removing it from my thigh and dropping it into her lap. "That's top secret."

She mock pouts, but I ignore her. I don't even know this chick's name. Don't know who the other chick is either.

Ruby leaves the student center and I fight the

disappointment that wants to crash over me. She's not stupid. I bet she figured that I was getting felt up, and she would be right.

I feel kind of cheap, can't lie.

We chat for a few minutes, but it's nothing but them trying to flirt with me and outdo each other. It feels weirdly competitive and the longer it keeps up, the more I want out of here.

It's time for me to go.

"Ladies, sorry but I have class soon." I raise one arm, then the other, their still grasping hands trying to keep hold of me. I jump to my feet, ready to bolt. "See you later."

Their high-pitched goodbyes trail after me all the way to the doors and I push through one, pissed at myself for running away like a giant pussy.

When have I ever wanted to run from a bunch of girls trying to lavish me with attention? I normally live for this shit. But for whatever reason, their attention today felt like too much. Too fucking obvious because that shit felt fake.

I'm sort of over it. Where's the real connection? Where's simple conversation and getting to know someone? Not around here. I have a legit fan club for God's sake, and while I love that those girls love me, they're not anyone I can take seriously.

Sometimes, I wonder if *anyone* can take me seriously.

That's when I spot her sitting at a picnic table under the cool shade of a massive pine tree just ahead of me. She's alone, a textbook spread open in front of her, her hair up in a sloppy bun on top of her head. She's tapping a pencil against her lips, and she's got...wait a minute.

Glasses on her face?

I slow my steps, just taking her in for a moment, entranced by the brainiac look she's got going on. Ruby Red is pretty damn cute in those glasses, though I bet if I told her that, she'd roll her eyes and blow me off.

She's good at that. Blowing me off.

Too bad she won't give me a shot and just blow me...

"Ace fucking Townsend! What's up man!" A short, stocky guy approaches on the pathway I'm standing in the middle of, holding his hand out for me to slap.

"Hey." I give him a high five, and I can already feel Ruby's gaze on me. I'm sure she heard this dude call out my name, and I hope like hell she didn't catch me staring at her like some sort of stalker.

The guy passes and I chance a look at her to find she's already watching me, the glasses gone, discarded on top of her textbook. I can't read her expression. Meaning I can't tell if she's annoyed by me or not and I stand there for one excruciatingly indecisive moment, trying to decide if I should approach her or not.

Fuck it.

I make my way toward her, walking up the gentle grassy slope and stopping right next to her table.

"Hey, Red." I grin, knowing my nickname irritates her.

She rolls her eyes, stretching her arms above her head, which makes her tits pop forward in that cropped white T-shirt she's wearing. Fuck me running, I can't get over what a great rack she has. "Ace."

"Homework?" I gesture toward the open book, dying to say something about the glasses, but I keep my mouth shut.

"Always." She drops her arms at her sides, glancing up so our gazes meet. "What's up?"

"Nothing much." I incline my head toward the empty bench across from her. "Can I join you?"

"Where's your fan club?" The pointed look is a reminder

that she saw me with those two girls and she's calling me out on it.

"Left them back in the student center." I jerk my thumb over my shoulder.

"Uh huh."

I gesture toward the park bench again. "Mind if I sit?"

"Sure." She sounds a little reluctant but I ignore her tone and settle in across from her, dropping my backpack on the bench beside me.

"Nice glasses." I nod toward them. "Yours?"

"Oh. Yeah." Her cheeks turn the faintest pink and she grabs them, slipping them on her face. "I always feel a little silly wearing them."

Silly? They make her green eyes pop and she's got a sexy smart girl thing going on that's making my dick hard. Not even that girl earlier actually touching my dick managed that.

I decide though, that my response needs to be restrained. Telling Ruby her glasses give me a boner isn't the right move.

"You look—good in them." I smile and so does she and damn it's like a zinger straight to my dick, making it twitch, and just like that, my mouth gets away from me. "Hot nerd vibes."

Her smile transforms into a scowl. "Did you just call me a nerd?"

"A *hot* nerd," I clarify and she snorts.

"Like that makes it so much better." She shakes her head, but she's still smiling so I take that as a good sign.

"Saw the video you posted." I keep my tone casual. "That you and Gwen made yesterday."

She squirms a little, a laugh escaping her. "It's done really well so far."

"I noticed." I pause. "Must be the subject matter."

"Oh, I'm sure." She smirks.

"Guess it's cool, though you objectified us."

"With your blessing," she reminds me. "And trust me. We have a feeling all of that objectifying is going to bring the team a lot more followers on social media, which is always the goal."

"Right. Gotta get those followers." I'm teasing her but she doesn't seem to mind.

"Well, we're also trying to prove a point to Eric."

I frown. "What do you mean?"

"Our content was looking too similar. You couldn't tell one post from another and we needed some variety. Not the same old videos of the team running down the field with heavy metal playing in the background."

"Hey, I take offense to that." I rest my hand against my chest as if I'm actually offended. "My dad likes those videos. He's always talking about them."

"Exactly!" she practically screams, pointing at me. "That's the problem."

"What?" This girl is confusing. "That my dad likes them?"

"Yes." She's nodding enthusiastically. "We're trying to appeal to people that are our age, not dads. And not necessarily guys either."

"Women?" I tilt my head, giving her my slowest, panty-melting smile. Will it work on her? "We already got a lot of those type of fans, Red."

"Not enough online though." She points at me again, not fazed by my smile whatsoever, so I let it fade. "And don't try to woo me with your sultry voice and flirtatious words, Townsend."

Ha. Okay, she did notice.

"Sultry? Flirtatious?" I rest my hand over my heart, solemn as a priest. "I would never."

"You are. You're doing it right now. You know how—cute you are." She spits out the word cute like it's a curse.

"Only cute, huh?" I'm only mildly offended. "I was hoping for manly. Sexy at the very least."

She grabs her textbook and slams it shut. "You're too sexy for your own good."

Heat rushes over my skin at her confession and my dick twitches yet again, pleased with this woman and her choice of words. Did she even hear herself? She thinks I'm sexy. And I fucking love that. "You really think so?"

"I know so." She picks up her book and shoves it in her backpack, then zips it shut. "I have class soon."

"You coming out to practice today?"

"Probably not."

Disappointment hits me, deflating my dick and I try to fight it. "Too bad. I was hoping to flex more for you."

"I wasn't impressed." There is no feeling in her voice whatsoever, but her eyes flash. I think I annoy her.

Actually, I know I annoy her and while it's fun, digging at Ruby, I'm realizing that every single thing I say is an annoyance to this woman and that...

Sucks.

Should I call her out? I don't believe she's completely immune to my charm. This might be the wrong approach but...

"Please. I caught you looking at me when I was out on the field." I rest my forearms on the table and lean across it, trying to get closer to her. A breeze hits, her scent drifting toward me, and I inhale as discreetly as possible, taking a hit like it's a drug and I need to get high. "You were staring, Red."

It's like I can't help myself. I enjoy teasing her.

"You threw a great pass."

"You weren't looking at the ball."

"I was sitting on the sidelines creating content with Gwen."

"While staring at my abs."

Her cheeks turn the faintest pink and she pushes her glasses up the bridge of her nose with her index finger. "Your abs are no big deal."

"My abs are pretty fucking stellar, considering how hard I work out." I lean back, barely lifting up my shirt and showing her what I'm talking about. Her gaze immediately drops, lingers almost lovingly.

"You're ridiculous," she mutters, her gaze still locked on my abdomen.

Uh huh. My abs are no big deal.

Sure.

13

RUBY

W e don't go back onto the football field for the rest of the week, much to my secret disappointment. Part of the reason is because the coaches asked us to stay away because they didn't want the team distracted. Their first game was away, and it was important, so totally understandable.

We were supposed to attend that game but were unable to go because Eric forgot to get permission from administration and it turned into this big mess, Gwen and Eric arguing over it for a solid thirty minutes. They were so snippy with each other, I've never been more grateful for the weekend to come because I needed to get out of there. Couldn't take the tension.

Those two? I think they got a little thrill over being mad at one another. Like their arguing was foreplay.

Hmm.

Over the weekend when I was sick of homework, I'd scroll through the hours of content Eric shared with us via Google Drive, trying to put something together that felt fresher.

It was a struggle, but I managed something and ran it by Gwen. I posted the video Saturday right before the scheduled kickoff, and while it was decent, and we got about two hundred likes, it was nothing like our arm candy post.

That one now has over ten thousand likes, which means it's gone semi-viral. And it has almost five hundred comments, pretty much all of them from women trying to guess the players by the guys' arms. Or they're demanding to know who they are. Some of the guesses are right, which is kind of impressive.

When Monday rolls around, Gwen sweeps into the office, the last one to arrive, a smug expression on her face as she deposits her book bag on her desk.

"Eleven-point-five-k likes, Eric." She shoves her phone in his face for emphasis and he averts his gaze, annoyed. "I told you that type of content would work."

"You had one lucky post, okay?" He shakes his head, crossing his arms in front of him. "Let's see if you can do it again."

"We can," Gwyneth says smugly, and I wince.

"Saturday's post didn't do so well."

"It wasn't new content we filmed," Gwen says. "It was Eric's."

"Hey," he protests. "You're making it seem like I don't know what I'm doing."

"You don't," Gwen says, not mincing words. Her gaze shifts to mine. "Ready to go film?"

"Oh, thank God." I leap to my feet. "I can't take it hanging out in here with you two fighting all day."

"We don't fight," they say at the same time, which is weird and proof that they're secretly in sync with each other.

"Afraid to break it to you, but you guys do. And I'm over

it." I grab my backpack and sling it over my shoulder, heading for the door. "Let's go."

When I realize no one is following me, I turn and lean against the door, contemplating them both. Their matching sour expressions. Their narrowed eyes. Ugh, these two. I can't with them anymore.

"Are we really going to waste away in this office today because you're mad at each other?" I snap, feeling as if I'm going to actually snap.

Eric and Gwen share a look, Gwen speaking first.

"Maybe we should still go over the video content first—"

"Give me a break," I interrupt. "You don't want to go over Eric's content, and Eric doesn't want you touching it either." Eric opens his mouth to speak but I shoot him a look that has his lips pressing closed. "I don't know what's going on, but I feel like you're in some sort of weird standoff that feels more like foreplay than actual anger, and I can't take it anymore. The tension between you guys is thick enough to slice through, and I'm sorry, but you're both being stupid."

Gwen's eyebrows shoot up and Eric grimaces.

"Foreplay?" he croaks, sounding uncomfortable.

I nod, not backing down from my assessment. "Definitely."

Gwen snorts. "Not even."

Fine, we won't go there, but my frustration is bubbling close to the surface and I don't care if I've been on this team for like, a week. They're both being so stubborn it's like they want to sabotage the team on purpose.

"Seriously, you two. Just...Eric, it's okay to admit our post has done better than all of the football team posts you've made combined."

Eric's mouth drops open. "That's not quite true—"

"And Gwen, stop gloating and trying to tell Eric what to

do. I think we can all co-exist and post a variety of content to appeal to all of our fans. The dudes and the dads and the women. Wouldn't you agree?" I cross my arms, feeling like I've somehow become their mom.

I don't even know them, yet here I am, bossing them around.

They both reluctantly nod, keeping their gazes averted.

"They're getting restless online, by the way. They all want to know whose arms we featured, which means we need to go film more content with the guys and reveal who they are."

Ugh, meaning I'll have to interact with Ace. Maybe I should leave that up to Gwen and I can go do...something else.

Anything else.

"It's a home game this weekend," Eric murmurs, staring off into the distance. "We should start pushing it."

"Of course, we should, and it's Monday, so we have plenty of time to push."

"We should post multiple times a day," Gwen suggests, keeping her focus on me, not once looking in Eric's direction.

"You know I think that's a bad idea—" Eric starts, but I hold my hand out, stopping him from talking.

"Have we ever done that before?" I ask them.

Gwen and Eric shake their heads.

"Then maybe we should try it." I take a deep breath, hating how I'm taking over this situation and turning it into some sort of meeting-lecture, but nothing was going to get accomplished until I said something. "Think we can get out there and film?"

"I should ask Mattson," Eric says. "Sometimes they don't like the distraction. He kept us away Friday, remember?"

Gwen snort-laughs, like she doesn't believe him, and I send her a look, silently asking her to explain.

"They usually love it when we're out there filming them. I think they actually play better when we're there because they're all a bunch of show-offs." Gwen rolls her eyes.

I smile. "I think you're onto something." I glance over at Eric. "Do you want to reach out to Mattson or should we live on the edge and just show up?"

"I can text him." Eric pulls out his phone and sends a quick message, his expression uncertain. "He might not answer me though. They're already out on the field."

Love how Eric keeps tabs on their schedule. He knows it by heart.

We wait for a few more minutes, Eric gathering his camera equipment, while Gwen remains at the desk, stewing in her feelings. I approach her carefully, sending a quick look in Eric's direction before I settle into the chair next to hers, knocking my shoulder into hers gently.

"You okay?"

"I'm annoyed," she tells the table, where her gaze is currently fixed.

"At Eric?"

She nods.

"Why?"

Gwen turns to me, her voice lowering, her gaze shifting from me to Eric and back to me as she talks. "He's being stubborn. And rude. I think he's mad that our post did so well and he doesn't want to admit his content is stale."

"Yeah, well you're both being really stubborn," I say, keeping my voice purposefully gentle. "I agree he's struggling to admit that our post did great, but you two sitting in this office constantly arguing or not speaking to each other at all isn't working. We need to get out there and get more content. We have a game to push. An entire team to feature."

This office is tiny. I'm over being locked away in here. And besides...

I hate to admit this, but I want to get outside and watch Ace in action. I haven't seen him since he stopped to talk to me when I was sitting at the picnic table struggling to take notes on the most boring chapter I've ever read for my ancient history class, and I...

Miss him.

No. I don't miss him. That's just weird. How can I miss someone who irritates me every time I talk to him? Hell, I *look* at him and I'm irritated.

I definitely don't miss him, but I do miss his...smart mouth and charming smile.

God, if he ever knew I thought that, he would be so smug.

"Have you heard from Mattson yet?" Gwen asks Eric, her tone even. Not hostile like it has been.

He shakes his head, remaining silent.

"We should go out there anyway." She pushes back her chair and stands. "You ready, Ruby?"

I nod, leaping to my feet with a smile. "Let's get out there."

WE HEAR them before we can actually see them, their angry shouts filling the air. A whistle constantly being blown. Lots of curse words, including a blasted "Fuck!" that seems to vibrate in the air.

Sounds like the football team is in crisis, much like their social media team.

"Throw the fucking ball, Townsend! Get rid of the *damn* ball!"

They finally come into focus, just in time for us to witness Ace scrambling, launching the ball at the same time he's sacked from the side, the lineman taking him down hard.

A gasp escapes me when Ace hits the ground and I clamp my lips together, hoping no one noticed. Gwen and Eric are too wrapped up in their own bullshit to notice me anyway and I try to play it cool, though my heart is thumping twice as hard as I watch Ace lie prone on the field.

He pops up seconds later, as if a current of electricity ran through him, bringing him back to life, and I breathe a sigh of relief, my gaze tracking his every movement as he claps hands with the lineman who just took him down, performing some sort of complicated hand shaking ritual that eventually has me shaking my head.

Boys. They're kind of ridiculous.

We launch right into capturing content, Eric protesting at first that we should ask Mattson if it's okay, but Gwen ignores him, holding up her phone and filming Ace as he gets back into position.

I stand behind her, my gaze stuck on Ace. He's wearing a practice uniform with pads and everything and he looks positively delicious. He's also got a sweatband around his head, though he's wearing it more like a head band so it keeps his hair out of his eyes.

Most any other guy wearing that, I'd think he looks dumb, but not Ace.

Nope, he's hot as hell in just about anything.

When he finally notices us, he does a double take, a slow smile sweeping across his face when our gazes lock, his dropping to my black T-shirt, lingering there. For a minute I think he's just checking me out but then when his smile shifts into a shit-eating grin, I remember what my shirt says.

Future MILF.

I can't help that I love a good silly T-shirt, but I'm particular too. I won't just wear some dumb shirt for the sake of amusing myself or others. I have to really like it—I might even need to believe in it. I also need to feel a little cool when I wear it.

Natalie bought me this shirt when we first moved in together and I immediately loved it, because of course I did. Future MILF—definitely goals.

Gwen catches some footage while they continue to practice until Mattson blows his whistle, calling a water break.

"We'll let them rest for a bit and then maybe you could go over there and grab all the guys we used in the video from last week?" Gwen's brows shoot up, her expression hopeful.

"I can gather them up," I tell her.

Gwen acts like a boss most of the time, so it's funny how she gets nervous around the football players. Though I guess they're pretty intimidating. Tall and broad and boisterous and confident. It's a lot.

After giving them a few minutes, I walk across the field, stopping just in front of them and pasting on my brightest smile. "Hey, guys! How are you?"

They all offer me a halfhearted greeting and I realize these guys are still in a funk, which sucks. I don't get it either. They should feel pretty good after pulling out a win Saturday. The game was close but they ended up on top.

Right now, though? I need them in a better mood to make this video.

"Can we get the guys who appeared in the video last week to film with us for a few minutes?" I glance over at

Mattson, who's observing all of us, his gaze narrowed. "If that's okay with you, Coach?"

"Go ahead. Don't take too long though. These boys need some serious work." His voice is tinged with irritation.

Okay then.

There are a few groans from the group, but all six of the guys who filmed with us last week approach me with friendly smiles, including Ace.

"What's up, future MILF?" His light blue eyes are twinkling as he stands directly in front of me but I choose to ignore him.

"Follow me, boys." I wave a hand and they all fall into step behind me as I lead them to where Gwen is waiting. She has them stand in front of her and smile, even flex their arm muscles if they want and most of them do. With the exception of Ace.

"Trying to stay modest," he tells Gwen with the utmost sincerity before she starts recording and I roll my eyes.

This man. He's full of it.

Once Gwen is done, Mattson looks ready to get them back on the field, his fingers curled around his whistle like he's gonna blow at any second. Ace stops right next to me before he rejoins the team, his head tilting toward mine.

"You should go to Logan's tonight." His voice is deep and sincere and I'm baffled.

Where did this come from?

"Why?" I fight the giddiness that rises at his request. I could assume he was asking me on a date, but requesting I meet him at a bar doesn't qualify as a date.

"It's Monday night. Half-price night."

"So?" I mean, I love a deal like anyone else but come on.

"I don't know. I thought it could be—fun." I chance a

look at him, steeling myself from the power of his smile. "We should catch up."

"Catch up about what?" I ask warily.

"Anything. Everything. I like talking to you, Red." He reaches out, his fingers curling around my chin, tilting my face up. "I like looking at you too. Whatcha think? Tonight, say around nine?"

What in the world is going on? Am I dreaming?

No. No, I'm not. I stare at Ace's smiling face, my brain scrambling to come up with a reply. I should say no. I don't know what he's about or why he's asking me to meet him at Logan's. Is he trying to charm my panties off? It wouldn't be too difficult for him to do. I try to look tough. Remain resilient.

But the way he's looking at me right now, the confident smile and easygoing attitude, his warm fingers still curled around my chin, it's enough to make me say yes and forget all about my earlier concerns in regards to this way too sexy man.

"Did you knock something loose earlier?" I ask, and he frowns. "When you took that hit?"

He chuckles, the warm sound winding its way through my blood, leaving me a quaking mess. I lock my knees together so my legs won't give way. "Nah. I'm stronger than I look."

I say nothing. The man definitely looks plenty strong.

"Why are you asking me to meet you at Logan's?"

"Why wouldn't I?"

"Oh, I don't know. Maybe there's the fact that you have an entire fan club at your whim whenever you want them?"

He presses his thumb to the corner of my mouth, his gaze hot as it lingers on my lips. I wish he wouldn't stare at them.

Fine, I like it when he looks at me. But this is nothing! It means nothing.

"Can I confess something?" he murmurs.

"Okay," I say, suddenly breathless.

"Can't stop thinking about you since our last encounter, Red. I missed having you on the sidelines." He pauses for a second. "You didn't come to the game."

"We were supposed to be there. There were—paperwork issues."

"Uh huh."

"I'm serious."

"Okay, well, you need to come to Saturday's game." His voice is firm and he releases his hold on my chin.

"We'll be there," I reassure him, wondering if he's for real.

How much does it really matter that I'm not on the sidelines? I think he's just saying this.

"And you need to come to Logan's. It's half-off night. Everyone comes to Logan's on half-off night."

"Really?"

Ace nods, his gaze locked on my mouth. As if he's thinking of the many things he can stuff in it. Or maybe that's me having those filthy thoughts. "Definitely."

"Do you go out and drink every night or what?"

"No." He frowns. "I'm not a total party animal—not anymore. In fact, I've been drinking less this season. Treating my body like a temple."

Ace waves a hand at his body for emphasis.

I roll my eyes. "My brother used to say the same exact thing."

"Really?" He actually seems pleased by this. "Love that."

"You would," I mutter, glancing around, noting how Gwen is watching us.

I look away from her, not wanting to see the suspicion in her gaze. She's already mentioned that she thinks Ace likes me, which I firmly believe is a stretch. He might want to *fuck* me, but *like* me?

I'm not buying it.

"Say yes that you'll come to Logan's tonight." Mattson blows his whistle and Ace starts backing away from me. "Come on, Red. You know you want to hang out, at least for a little bit. Nine o'clock? I'll save you a seat."

"I have homework." I always have homework, but I can work on it when I get home. There are still hours to go until nine o'clock...

Seriously though? I shouldn't do it. I absolutely can't meet up with this guy. I'm not interested in him like that. A casual thing. He's the type who chews up a woman and immediately spits her out. And besides...

I get caught with him? I'm out of a job.

"Just say yes, Ruby Red. You'll make my day. Oh, and stick around, will you? Pretty sure I'll have a better practice today thanks to you."

I don't answer him, but we do stick around for the remainder of practice and he was right.

He played like a champ. They all did. I even overheard the pep talk Mattson gave them as practice was winding down.

"Don't know what got into you boys today, but let's keep it up."

The pointed look Ace sent in my direction left me feeling helpless. I had nothing to do with their improved practice.

Did I?

14

ACE

I am an anxious motherfucker. A bundle of nerves. A finger-tapping, knee-bouncing asshole who's earning dirty looks from everyone who's sitting with me every time my knee hits the underside of the table.

"Calm your tits, bro." This comes from Derek, who's sitting right next to me in our usual booth. It's like it's become a habit, us hanging out together at Logan's. "You're so fucking edgy you're making me nervous."

And Derek is never nervous. About anything.

It's nine-thirty and there's no sign of Ruby yet at Logan's. I check my phone—wait, scratch that. It's actually *nine-forty-three* and she's still not here.

Fuck. She's ditching me.

If she doesn't show up tonight, this is it. I'm leaving her alone. I don't need some girl stringing me along. Even if she's hot. Even if her skin is kitten soft and her greenish-hazel eyes were eating me up earlier. Even if she's the reason I play that much better whenever she's close by.

Not sure if that's the real reason I started to play better, but it sure felt like it. Our practice Friday was terrible. The game Saturday was a scrambling shitshow and we only pulled out a win by sheer brute force and a little bit of luck. The speech Mattson gave us after the game left me feeling like a failure. His pep talk this morning when he spotted me in the gym did nothing to make me feel better either.

I was out on that field, throwing balls away left and right and getting fucking sacked but then Ruby appeared...

And I started playing better.

Way better.

It's like a miracle occurred. Or maybe it's Gwen and Eric bringing the luck, but I doubt that. I could give two shits about them. I mean Eric is nice and he's a loyal fan. Gwen is scary and I would never want to cross her. I don't want to show off for the two of them.

For Ruby? All I want to do is impress her.

Guess I didn't impress her enough though because her pretty ass still isn't here. And if that isn't low-key depressing...

"Sorry." I reach for my beer bottle and try to drain it, only to discover it's already empty. "I need another one. Where's the server?"

It's extra busy tonight, thanks to the half-off promotion. The bar is wall to wall filled with people, including lots of women.

Like a lot.

The majority of them are attractive. A lot of them are making eyes at me from where I sit at our usual booth in the back of the bar, fully expecting me to make eyes at them in return because that's what I do. I flirt. I put on the good ol' boy act like Derek calls it and next thing I know, they're cuddling up close to me and asking if we can get out of there, and of course I oblige them.

Tonight though? I'm not interested in a single one of them.

What the hell is wrong with me? Why *wouldn't* they interest me? I've never felt like this before. Women throw themselves at me and I catch them. Take them somewhere dark and quiet and shower them with all the attention they're searching for. I leave them satisfied and I'm always satisfied too. Until the next one. And the next one.

And the next one after that.

Some might call me a manwhore, and maybe I am, but who am I to turn all those beautiful women away? They're willing and so am I. We're consenting adults so where's the harm in it?

My gaze scans the room, touching on every pretty woman I see. Fuck Ruby Maguire. She's missing out on a good fuck and she'll regret not showing up tonight. This was her last shot.

Looks like she blew it.

"That one's staring at you, bro," Derek murmurs, blatantly pointing at an attractive brunette with a giant rack. "Look at those titties."

"Titties, D? Seriously?" I send him a withering stare before I refocus on Miss Titties because damn, that rack is huge. I should wave her over. Hell, I should be waving a couple of cuties over to join us because then I'll have options.

She waves at me, her boobs bouncing with the movement, and holy hell.

I'm. Not.

Interested.

I'm not interested in a single one of them. The blonde that's shifted into my line of vision isn't blonde enough. The girl with the long, tanned legs and decent tits—her legs aren't right. Neither are her tits. And neither of them is wearing a T-shirt with a funny message.

I like that about Ruby. Her funny T-shirts.

Hell, I like a lot of things about Ruby.

Yet I don't think she likes *me* much.

Our server eventually makes her rounds and I order two beers, which has Derek looking at me funny.

"You okay there, QB?"

I sit up a little straighter, honored he'd call me that. I only ever heard him call Cam that and it feels good. I finally feel accepted. "I wanna get drunk."

"Not a smart move during the season, bro. Isn't that your plan?" Derek studies me, rubbing a hand along his jaw. "Forget the beer. Go find a cute girl and lose yourself in her for a while. Burn some calories."

He knows that's what I've done in the past, which makes sense why he's pushing me to do it right now. But I shake my head, my voice firm when I say, "Nope."

The p makes a popping sound that is oddly satisfying. And I try the word out, saying it over and over again with the hard p.

"Are you already drunk?" Derek asks when I finally stop.

I think about how many beers I've already had. I count them on my fingers. One, two...

"I've had three."

"And you just ordered two more?" Derek's brows shoot up. "I'm cutting you off."

"No, you're fucking not."

"I am." Derek nods, reaching out to grab my beer bottle, seeming almost disappointed to find it's empty. "No more for you. You can't get trashed before the next big game."

"It's Monday, Derek. We don't play until Saturday." I

shoot him a look like he's fucking crazy. "Didn't you see how I played today?"

"You played pretty damn good." He hesitates, tipping his bottle toward his lips. "Eventually."

All I can do is snort in response because damn it, he's not wrong.

And I hate that. I need to get focused and not let the little shit distract me.

Then I think of Ruby showing up at practice. Watching me. How I felt a jolt vibrate through my body the moment our eyes made contact. Something came over me and next thing I knew, I was playing better.

Much better.

Feels like lately I'm always thinking of Ruby, which is fucking annoying, especially when she doesn't think of me.

The server reappears with our orders and I take both of my beers, placing them as far away from Derek's grabby hands as I can get them. I notice the empty spot beside me, wishing a cute ass was filling it, and when I glance up, I shake my head, positive that I'm hallucinating.

I blink. Close my eyes for a second. Two seconds. Crack them open.

Oh shit. Now she's even *closer*.

Ruby. Fucking. Maguire.

She's got on black shorts that are too damn short and show way too much skin and there are white Nike Air Force sneakers on her feet. She's wearing another one of her T-shirts. This one is pale pink with black lettering in all caps that says:

DUMP HIM.

Straight across her perfect tits.

I scrub a hand over my face, waiting for her to evaporate,

but she's still there. Approaching our table with a friendly look on her too pretty face.

God, she drives me crazy. I don't like it.

"Hey, guys." She stops right in front of our table, offering us a little wave. As casual as she pleases, not singling me out but acting like she's come to speak to all of us. "How are you?"

"Ruby, what's up?" Derek nudges me in the side with his elbow, making me grunt. That fucking hurt. "You should join us. Loverboy here has been pining away for you."

I send him a sharp glance and he shrugs.

How the hell did he know? Not like I told anyone I asked Ruby to meet me here.

"Sorry I'm late." These words, the smile, it's all aimed directly at me. "I was talking to my sister and lost track of time."

Uh huh. I bet she was second-guessing herself the entire time tonight. Should she come here? Should she stay home? Surprised that she was able to convince herself to show up.

Alone.

This feels major.

"How is Blair?" I nod, remembering her older sister. Only pleasant thoughts filter through when it comes to that particular Maguire sister.

"She's doing great. We haven't talked in a while so we needed to catch up. She's just so busy with everything going on with Cam."

"How's Cam doing? He's playing his first game this week-end, huh?"

"He's actually playing his first game in a few days. His team is playing the first Thursday night football game of the season."

"Oh damn, seriously? We gotta get together and watch

our fucking homie tear it up on the professional field!" Derek practically screams, making Ruby laugh.

I sit there and savor the sound, taking a big swig from my beer, realizing my mistake a second later.

My head is spinning. I swear I can see two Ruby's standing in front of me.

Shit. I need to stop drinking before I do something stupid.

"You should totally put something together," Ruby encourages. "I'm sure Cam would appreciate the support."

"He wouldn't even notice the support."

She glances over at me, frowning. "What?"

"Cam. He won't know we're supporting him. How can he appreciate it?"

Ruby squints at me, tilting her head. Did I mention she's got her hair in a high ponytail and my fingers itch to tug it?

Yeah. It's true. And it sucks.

"Are you drunk?"

"Yes," I say firmly. "Well, not drunk. More like pleasantly buzzed."

"Ah." She's smiling. "Okay."

"Sit down." I pat the empty spot next to me on the booth seat. "Join us."

"You sure about that?" Her brows rise.

"Hell yeah," I tell her, slapping the seat again, my palm cracking against the vinyl. "Come on, Ruby Red. Just sit down and let me stare at you for a minute."

She pauses, her eyes wide and I realize what I just said. Feels like I gave something away.

Like my feelings.

Fuck.

Eventually she does as I request, sliding onto the booth seat, her knee knocking into mine when she settles in close.

I can smell her perfume, the bare skin of her thigh pressing against mine and I remind myself that I can't touch her.

All I wanna do is touch her. It feels like a switch flipped on inside me and it pounds out her name with an incessant drum.

Ru-by. Ru-by. Ru-by.

Too much beer. That's my problem. I've got it bad. I've got it so bad and I'm living for it because now that she's here, I've forgotten all about my earlier anxiety. How twisted up I was over her not showing up.

She's finally here and all of that disappears.

"I thought you were going to be a no-show," I tell her, my head bent so I can speak directly into her ear.

"Better late than never?" She gazes up at me, her eyes wide and I dip my head closer, my lips practically brushing her ear.

"Worth the wait," I whisper, wishing I could bite her lobe. Trace the length of her neck with my fingers.

Ruby leans back a little as if she might prefer the distance, though her expression is amused. "You're definitely drunk."

"Not quite. Getting there," I say agreeably. "It's your fault."

"Oh yeah? How?"

"I had nothing else to do but drink while I waited for you."

"Aw, poor Ace. Waiting for a woman for once? You weren't flirting with your fan club to distract you?" She's teasing, her lips curved into this sexy little smile I want to kiss off.

No. What the hell am I thinking? There's no kissing this girl. That will only lead to trouble. I need to just—fuck her hard once. From behind? Yeah, that sounds perfect.

Tugging on her silky hair and making her moan with every thrust...

That should get her out of my system once and for all.

"Haven't seen the fan club around tonight. Don't really care either." I stare at her lips, wondering what she'd do if I just leaned in and kissed her.

Jesus, I need to get it together. Why am I so fixated on her mouth?

"What?" She sounds and appears genuinely shocked. "But you're all about your fan club."

"Not lately," Derek says from somewhere over my shoulder. The asshole has been creeping in on our conversation. "From what I see, they bore him. You might have the power to turn Ace here into a one-woman man, Maguire."

I close my eyes for the briefest moment, basking in my humility as I hear Derek laugh like he just told the funniest joke ever. But when I pop my eyes open—and I had them closed for like a second, tops—I find Ruby sitting a little closer, her hand resting on my thigh. I want to take that hand and settle it right over my junk.

Would she let me? Or slap my face if I tried?

Probably the second scenario.

"Oh, Derek, leave him alone. He's drunk and a little too in his feelings." Is she making fun of me?

When our eyes meet though, I see the sympathy there and I realize she's not making fun. Her tone is soft and her gaze is only for me and her fingers are burning through the fabric of my shorts. Seeping right through until it feels like she's touching my bare flesh.

Shit.

Derek just laughs some more and turns away from us.

Thank Christ.

"He's an asshole," I mutter.

"I know he's just joking." She pats my leg like she's my grandma and when she starts to remove her hand, I drop mine on top of hers, keeping her hand pinned there.

"Maybe he's not joking." My tone comes out way more serious than I intended and I swallow hard, hating myself.

No more beer for me.

"Ace." She tilts her head to the side, her ponytail swinging and I reach out with my other hand, slipping my fingers into the silky strands. "You know you don't do serious."

"You're right." I nod. "I don't."

"Meaning this is nothing." She waves her hand between us.

"I don't know about that. I did ask you on a date."

Ruby blinks at me, her lips parted, though she's not talking. Like I stunned her silent. "You did not."

I nod. "Did so."

Skepticism flares in her gaze. "This isn't a date. It's a meeting at a bar."

"Sounds like a date to me." I shrug.

"Definitely not." Ruby shakes her head.

"Tell me what constitutes a date then," I challenge, sounding like a dickhead.

Because I am a dickhead.

"Well, first, if you were asking me on a date, you'd offer to come pick me up."

Uh huh.

"And when you'd pick me up, you'd take me to dinner or a movie, or some sort of form of entertainment that'll keep us occupied for a few hours," she continues.

Sounds fucking boring as shit. "Keep going."

"And then you'd take me back home and—"

"Kiss you at the front door, convince you to go inside and

end up in your bedroom and fuck you until you were screaming my name?" I suggest helpfully.

Her cheeks go bright red. "Absolutely not."

"What? Why not?"

"I don't fuck on the first date." She manages to make the sentence sound prim but come on.

Ruby just said the word fuck.

That's hot.

"How many dates does it take until you're fucking the poor guy?" I ask, truly curious.

"At least three. Maybe more." She's nodding. "Yeah, definitely more. Like five dates. Six?"

I'm starting to sweat. That's a lot of work for what sounds like little reward. "I've never really dated anyone before."

Her brows shoot up. "Seriously? Not even in high school?"

"I never really had to." I shrug. "Girls just...wanted to hang out with me, but we never actually dated."

"No surprise," she murmurs.

"What's that supposed to mean?" I'm vaguely insulted.

"It means nothing." She shrugs. "I guess when you're —you, you don't have to work hard to find a random girl and hang out with her for the night."

"That's not what I'm looking for." I'm not? "And I don't give a damn about random girls," I say vehemently. "They don't know me."

Shit, where is this coming from? I blame it on Ruby. She makes me feel...I can't even explain it. I just know one thing.

I want her. I want to spend more time with her. I want to kiss her and talk to her and get to know her better. I want to strip off her clothes and fuck her nice and slow. Then fuck her hard and fast. Make her come. Make her shout my name. Stuff her mouth full of my dick. Go down on her until she's coming all over my face.

Yeah. That's what I want. With her.

Ruby.

"I don't really know you either," Ruby points out.

"You know me better than any other woman does." I curl a few strands of her silky blonde hair around my finger and gently tug. "You actually have conversations with me."

She sucks in a sharp breath but otherwise, there's no other reaction to me touching her. "Are you just starved for conversation, Ace?"

"I'm starved for a lot of things." I let go of her hair and give in to a sudden urge, tracing the side of her neck with my fingertips, curling them around the front of her throat so I can lightly hold her there, pressing beneath her chin and tipping her head up so our gazes meet. Her breath catches, her lips parting and a shuddery exhale leaves her. "Love the shirt. Trying to send a secret message to anyone?"

Ruby tries to glance down at herself, but she can't thanks to the way my hand is currently wrapped around her neck. Not in a threatening way. But damn, I like the way my fingers look, curled around her throat. It's fucking sexy.

She's sexy.

I have a feeling we'd be so damn good together.

Like we have the potential to burn down the world, if she'd just let me show her.

15

RUBY

Ace is...different tonight. His mood has shifted, and I can tell he's a little drunk. And like I said to Derek earlier, he's also somewhat in his feelings. Do those feelings have anything to do with me?

I'm thinking yes. Most definitely. And they're all conflicted.

Great. Feeling's mutual, bud.

He'd looked so down and out when I first spotted him sitting at the table. The moment he noticed me, though, his eyes lit up. His entire face brightened and I knew then.

He was sad because I hadn't shown up yet. He thought I was going to be a no-show. And while I shouldn't look too much into it, this guy was most definitely just feeling low because he thought I was going to reject him. I'd bet big money women don't reject him. I mean...

Look at him.

What rational woman would reject him?

Me. I almost did. I'm still kind of rejecting him at this very moment. Though I don't know if I'd qualify as rational...

Now he's got his fingers on my throat, skimming my skin, making me shiver as he stares at my mouth like he wants to eat it and I don't know want to say. Don't know what to do.

He's much easier to handle when he's Mr. Casual Flirtation, which is his normal mode of operation around me. And I'm cool with that. I'm fine with it. I can walk away from him with zero regrets, chalking up his behavior to casual flirtation.

Tonight, he's edgier. A lot more intense. And all of that intensity is currently focused on me.

I don't know how to handle it. Handle *him*.

I'm just wasting my time and his anyway. This is going nowhere.

Absolutely nowhere.

"I-I need a drink," I say, suddenly flustered.

He removes his hand from my neck and I immediately miss his possessive touch. He hands me a bottle of beer and I take it from him, offering a murmured thank you before I take a big swallow. It's cool and fizzy and while I'm not the biggest beer fan, it'll do in a moment of crisis.

And right now, that's what this feels like. But not like in a bad way, oh no. More in a, *oh my God, what are we doing* way?

"You never did answer my question."

I frown. "What question?"

"The shirt? Is it a secret message?" He reaches out, his index finger drawing over the giant D on my shirt and I feel that touch right down to my very core.

It helps that I'm not wearing a bra. And that his finger just basically flicked across my nipple by accident, making it hard.

And, of course, he notices immediately, his gaze lifting to mine, his blue eyes stormy.

"Sorry," he whispers, not sounding sorry at all.

Just before he does it again. Proving he is one hundred percent not sorry.

"Ace..."

"Is it a secret message to anyone?" He streaks his finger across the front of my shirt, from my right breast to my left and my mouth goes dry.

"No." I croak, shaking my head. "I just wear shirts like this for fun."

"Without a bra?" His brows lift.

"Sometimes. Like tonight." I hate bras. And my boobs aren't that big so I can get away with it, which I do often. Bras are such a hassle and sometimes even painful. Why can't we go braless all the time?

"I shouldn't have touched you like that." He drops his hand, and I'm sad at the loss. "I overstepped your boundaries."

Right now, I want to toss any boundaries I might have aside completely for him to touch me like that again. I've been fixated on those hands for a while now and I want to feel them on me.

"You didn't know I wasn't wearing a bra?" I sound like I don't believe it, because I don't.

I mean, come on, he had to have known.

"I don't think I did." His smile reminds me of the one you'd see on a boy who just got caught with his hand in the cookie jar. Or on a woman's boob.

I back away from him slightly, reaching for my beer. "I really hope you didn't drive yourself here."

"I did." He's frowning. "What does it matter?"

"Because you, Ace Townsend, are drunk. And you shouldn't drive."

He sags against the seat, his expression downright forlorn. "You're right. I can't drive."

I nod, sipping from my beer. It's already a little too warm and kind of gross. "Have Derek take you home."

"Have me do what?" Derek asks, butting his head in between us. Lord, he has a big face.

"You need to drive your friend home." I wave my beer bottle at Ace. "He's wasted."

"Can't," Derek says, withdrawing himself from our conversation.

And that's it. There's no explanation, no reason given. Just a simple, *can't.*

"He's a shit friend," I tell Ace.

"Yeah, he is." Ace nods in agreement. "Did you drive here?"

"I did."

"Then you can drive me home." He smiles.

Oh. That sounds...

Complicated.

He crowds me, blocking my view of the bar so all I can see is him. "You ready to get out of here?"

"Um, not really?" I'm not ready to leave just yet. "I'd like to finish my beer first."

"Oh yeah." He's smiling that smile again, the little boy one. It's a little crooked. A lot sweet. He's adorable. His earlier intensity has worn off him some and I'm a little relieved. Only because it—he—is a lot to handle. "Hurry up then."

So impatient.

"Sorry to break it to you, but I'm more of a sipper." I shrug, trying to play coy as I purposely take another small *sip* of my beer. I think about what he did to me only a moment ago. The way his fingers curved around my throat. My chin. God, I liked it way too much when he did that. That secret little kink of mine I usually keep buried deep inside is flaring to life and my body is hoping it'll happen again.

No guy has ever done that to me before unless I asked him to, and even then, not a single one of them was comfortable with it. Which made me uncomfortable making the request so I stopped.

It's not like I was begging them to choke me, but I guess I sort of was?

I might be a complete deviant, but I loved the way Ace grabbed my face without asking. My neck. Like he wants to claim me. As if he might already own me.

I wanted to melt, it felt so good.

"A sipper, huh?" he asks, his gaze shifting to my bottle of beer. He stares at it hard, as if he's mentally trying to empty it and I almost laugh.

"Can I ask you a question?" I smile at him, pressing my back against the booth seat when he leans forward, his face practically in mine.

"Go for it," he murmurs, his gaze now zeroed in on my mouth. He's staring so hard, my lips are tingling and it almost feels like he's actually kissing me.

"It's a personal question."

"My favorite kind." His voice is smooth, the look in his eyes...

Smoldering.

I swallow down my nervousness, hoping he won't judge me once he hears what I have to say.

"Do you ever do that hand thing when you're...having sex?"

He frowns, his brows drawing together in confusion. "What hand thing?"

"Like how you put your hand around my face and around my...neck." I can feel my cheeks grow warm and what little confidence I had to ask the question vanishes in a flash.

I wish I hadn't said that out loud. What's he going to think?

His gaze locks with mine, his expression serious. "You like that sort of thing?"

I nod, breathless. No longer able to speak.

"I don't really remember doing that to a woman before. Sexually." He's frowning, seemingly lost in thought. "Like I don't think ever."

"You did it earlier. To me." His frown deepens. "At practice. You touched my face. Curled your fingers around my chin and tipped my face up."

"Oh yeah?" He lifts his brows.

"Uh huh." My mind goes back to that moment. The way all the air stalled in my lungs when he did it. The pressure of his warm, rough fingers on my skin...

"Like this?" He reaches for me, holding my chin with his index finger and thumb, tilting my face up. His finger streaks slowly across my skin, like he's savoring touching me, and I want to die, it feels so good.

"Yes," I whisper, my eyes falling closed when he slips his fingers under my jaw, streaking them down my throat, his touch featherlight. He pauses at my collarbone, just above the neckline of my T-shirt and I can feel my nipples beading into hard, aching points beneath the fabric.

All from him barely touching me. As if he knows exactly what I want, and how I want it. His fingers are light, yet exert enough pressure that I know he's there. That he has the power to crush me.

But he never would. Ever.

His lips kick up on one side in a closed-mouth smile as we continue to stare at each other. "You're a dirty girl, Red."

"What do you mean?" I can't even take offense to him calling me dirty because I think he's right.

I think I might be.

"Getting off on me putting my hand around your throat." He then drifts his fingers upwards, all four of them pressed against my neck, his thumb coming up to trace along my jaw. "You like this?"

A sigh escapes me and I practically melt into the seat. When Ace's hand falls away from my neck, I miss his touch so bad, I physically ache from the loss. I'm reaching for my beer, drinking as much as possible, because I remember I told him I wanted to finish my beer first.

And now I'm desperate to finish it so we can get out of here.

Together.

"You two look cozy."

We both glance over at Derek, who's watching us with a suspicious gleam in his eyes.

"It's nothing," I say at the same time that Ace admits, "She's driving me home."

Derek's gaze jumps between us, his smile sly. "If Knox were here, he'd lose his shit."

"Well, he's not here, is he," I say, sounding vaguely bratty, but I don't care. "And what he doesn't know, won't hurt him."

"Truer words were never spoken," Ace says in agreement.

Derek watches us for a moment. Silently assessing. Then he shakes his head, chuckling. "You kids are on your own. I said my piece."

He turns his back to us, resuming his conversation with another team member who's sitting next to him and I breathe a sigh of relief, glancing over at Ace.

"Where's Nat?" Ace asks me, taking a sip from his beer.

"Nat? Oh, she had to work." She was beyond excited that Ace asked me to meet him here because all she wants is for me to get laid and have fun, which I appreciate.

It's what I want too, but with Ace?

I might be walking into a situation that'll be tough for me to get over.

"That's too bad," he murmurs, his focus on the sweating beer bottle sitting on the table in front of him. He shreds the damp label with his fingers, peeling it off, and the more I stare at his hand, the more I start to squirm, imagining those fingers touching me everywhere.

Specifically, between my legs.

Clearing my throat, I try to clear my brain of all dirty thoughts lingering. I need to change the subject, fast.

"Are you feeling all right?" When he frowns, I explain myself more. "After you took that hit at practice?"

He makes a dismissive noise, leaning against the seat once more. "Oh yeah. That was no big deal."

Athletes. They blow off any sort of injury all the time. Knox hurt himself a few years ago and told all of us he was fine. Yet in the end, he needed surgery. Because of course he did.

"Are you sure? How's your head?"

"You wanna play nurse for me, Red? Make sure I'm feeling okay?" He's teasing, his eyes sparkling and I can imagine tucking him into bed. Just before I slip in between the sheets and maul him. Take care of his...other needs.

And my own.

Okay, I am not one to just wallow in my dirty thoughts but being this close to him and all the innuendo in our conversation, has me fantasizing about him putting his hands on me again...

It's got me thinking all sorts of thoughts. None of them proper.

"Is that your kink?" He sits up straighter at my question and I carry on. "Seeing me in a nurse's uniform, my skirt so short you can see my panties every time I bend over?"

His eyes flare with heat. "I didn't know it was a kink of mine but I like the image you just put in my brain."

I start to giggle. I can't help it. "I bet you do."

"I figured you were the type to not wear panties." I go still when our gazes lock yet again. "Since you're not a big fan of bras."

"Oh." I swallow hard.

He grins. "That's all you can say? *Oh?*"

I nod, struggling to find words.

"Well, I much prefer the image of you bending over me wearing no panties at all." He grins, seeming very pleased with himself. "You have a great ass."

My cheeks go hot. "Um, thanks?"

"You're welcome." His gaze shifts to my neglected beer bottle on the table. "You done with that yet?"

I clear my throat again. "Why do you ask?"

"Because I'm dying to leave with you." He tips his head toward mine, his voice lowering. "Get you alone."

"Yeah?" I feel stupid, but it's like I can't come up with anything else to say.

"Unless you don't want to do that. And if that's the case, it's cool." He leans back, spreading his arms across the top of the booth, his fingers drifting back and forth across my shoulder, making me shiver. "It's completely up to you, Red."

16

ACE

I'm coiled tight, waiting for her answer. Anticipating a no because she's probably come to her senses by now and figured out a thousand reasons why we shouldn't do this.

But I'm dying to fuck her. Though it's more than that. I haven't even kissed her yet and I want to know what she tastes like. I want to see if her lips are as soft as they look and what might happen when I get my hands around her neck again. That's a turn-on, knowing she likes that. I've never been into that sort of thing. Never even really thought about it.

Now Ruby's got me thinking all sorts of things, all of them filthy, and feature me dominating her. Holding her down while I fuck her hard.

Or nice and slow.

I'll take it any way I can get it.

Swear to God I'm breaking out into a cold sweat just *thinking* about it.

"Should we leave? Together?" she asks, her voice so soft I almost didn't hear her.

"I thought that was the plan. I'm too drunk to drive," I remind her.

"Are you too drunk to do…anything else?" She bites her lower lip, her eyes wide.

Fuck me, she's sexy as hell.

"I'm up for whatever you want to do." I'm leaving this up to her.

"Okay." She takes a deep breath, glancing around the bar before her gaze returns to me, her expression dead serious as she murmurs, "Let's go."

I don't hesitate. I'm urging her out of the booth with one hand against her lower back and she moves just as fast, the two of us slipping out of the booth and walking away without a backward glance. No one says a word to us, not even Derek, as we move through the crowd toward the front door, my focus on nothing else but her.

Ruby.

Girls don't wave or say hi. Guys don't stop me to talk about football. Only when we're outside can I breathe easy, fucking thrilled that this girl is standing next to me in her DUMP HIM T-shirt, looking hot as fuck and a little frazzled. Like I might leave her on edge.

The feeling is mutual.

"Where are you parked?" I ask once we're outside and staring at the parking lot full of cars.

"Come on." I follow after her, my head swimming and I keep my gaze on her blonde head, which helps with the spins.

Clearly, I drank too much. It's been a while, but it's kind of wild that four beers would trash me so completely.

Or was it five?

Damn, I lost count.

"My car," she says as she hits the key fob and a sleek white BMW makes a chirping noise, its yellow lights flashing.

I whistle low, shaking my head. "Damn, Red. That's a nice ride."

"It was my mom's car. She gave it to me." Ruby grabs hold of my hand and leads me over to the vehicle, stopping at the passenger side and opening the door. "Get in."

I do as she demands, sliding into the passenger seat. She shuts the door and rounds the car, climbing behind the steering wheel and starting the engine with a push of a button before she grabs her phone. "Give me your address."

I rattle it off and she punches it into her maps app. Setting her phone in the cupholder of the center console, a map shows up on the built-in screen on the dashboard. She pulls out of the parking lot seconds later, tapping at the screen when we stop at a light and bringing up a playlist on her Spotify account.

Taylor Swift's voice booms from the speakers and I slide lower in my seat, closing my eyes. I don't mind that this girl is a Swiftie, but I don't really know much of her music. And women who are Taylor Swift fans always get offended when I admit I don't know whatever song is playing.

I brace myself for Ruby to do the same.

"Don't like it, huh?" She's smiling as she hits the gas when the light turns green, her fingers tapping against the steering wheel.

"I don't mind it. Taylor has a good voice." That's not a lie. "But it's not like I'm a secret Swiftie or whatever."

"That you even know the term 'Swiftie' earns you a point." She laughs, turning up the music louder as she starts to sing along.

She's no Taylor, but Ruby's voice is actually pretty good and she knows all of the lyrics. She's singing about a lavender haze and 1950s shit, and I have no idea what she's talking about but it's fun to watch her get into it.

"I like your voice," I tell her when the song is over.

Ruby laughs, shaking her head. "You really are drunk."

I frown. "Hey, I take offense to that."

"I'm just okay." She shrugs.

"You need to learn how to take a compliment, Red."

She's quiet for a moment, her fingers curled tightly around the steering wheel and when she finally murmurs, "Yeah, you're probably right," I realize something.

That took a lot for her to say.

Huh.

We're at my apartment complex in a matter of minutes because I don't live too far from downtown and I'm relatively close to campus. The majority of the football team lives in this complex, which makes it convenient for us to commute together to school, practice, or the bars.

"That's my building," I tell her, and Ruby pulls into an empty parking spot directly in front of it, putting the car in park and turning toward me with an expectant look on her pretty face.

"This was a fun night," she chirps and I frown at her.

"Yeah," I say slowly, reaching for the handle, my fingers curling around it but not opening the door.

"Is your car still downtown?"

"It is." I nod.

"If you need help getting it tomorrow, just give me a call." She smiles.

"But I don't have your number."

"Oh." With a frown, she reaches for her phone and pulls up a new contact. "Give me yours."

I tell her my number and she enters it into her phone, then sends me a quick text.

Hi.

"You've got this?" she asks hopefully.

"Got what?"

Ruby rolls her eyes. "You're drunker than I thought."

"And you're trying to get out of going to my apartment," I throw back at her, calling her on her shit.

Her face falls but only for a brief moment. She schools her expression and it shifts into neutral. No emotion showing. "Maybe this isn't such a good idea."

I ignore her cautious tone and open the door. "Fine. I'll just stumble to my apartment by myself, though who knows what might happen. I could trip and bump my head. Get a concussion."

She makes a scoffing noise. "You will not."

"You don't know that for sure." I climb out of the car and slam the door, fighting the disappointment that threatens to consume me as I make my way toward my front door.

I hear another car door slam and the sound of footsteps, then Ruby's voice.

"Wait up, oh my God."

I stop and turn, watching her approach as I wait. I shouldn't have pulled that kind of shit but she's the type who lets her doubts get in the way of a good time. I didn't realize she was that kind of girl, but apparently, she is.

At least when it comes to me.

"You're annoying," she mutters when she's close enough that I can hear her.

"It's part of my charm," I say drolly as we resume walking, Ruby following me to my apartment. I sort of want to shout in triumph that I got her to come with me but that might be a rash move.

She can still bail. And seriously, I'm not going to push a girl to do anything she doesn't want to do.

I'm not a total asshole.

It's just that every girl I end up with is always willing.

Always.

Is that part of Ruby's appeal? That she pushes me away instead of always being so accepting?

Maybe. I don't know. I might just be a sucker for a pretty face and bad treatment. A girl who gets off on me wrapping my hand around her throat. Never was my kind of thing but now I can't help but think...

New kink unlocked.

We're standing in front of my door and I'm digging in my pockets, looking for my keys. The worried expression on Ruby's face says she has zero faith in me and when I finally pull them out, I'm smiling in triumph.

"Got 'em."

"Thank God." She snatches them from my hand and unlocks the dead bolt, opening the door for me. "It would've taken you five minutes to manage that."

"No way," I say with confidence, grabbing her hand at the last second and dragging her into the apartment. She goes willingly, not saying a word when I gently shove her against the door once it's closed, reaching around her to turn the dead bolt back into place. My body brushes against hers, keeping her in place and I swear sparks light up between us.

"Ace—"

"Ssh." I rest my index finger on her plush mouth, silencing her. It's dark inside, but light still shines through the small half-moon window that's at the top of the door, enough to see Ruby's eyes are wide as she stares up at me. "I want to test something."

Her delicate brows draw together. "What do you want to test?"

My gaze drops to her lips. "To see if we're truly compatible."

She swallows hard, I note the movement in her throat, and when my gaze shifts to hers, I lean in closer, until I can feel her breath feather across my lips.

"And how are you going to test that?" she whispers.

"Like this." I press my lips to hers, keeping still for a beat. An electric current pulses through me the moment our mouths touch, settling in my dick, and when she pulls away slightly, I fight the disappointment.

But then she's back, her mouth somehow even softer when it reconnects with mine, her lips parting, catching around my upper lip and I put more feeling into it. Returning the kiss, brushing my mouth across hers again and again, my lips a little firmer with every pass.

When I sneak my tongue out to trace along her upper lip, her tongue teases mine. And when I cup the side of her face, my fingers drifting downward to curl around the side of her neck, it's on.

The kiss turns wild, our tongues sliding. Circling. A soft moan escapes her and I groan in return, my other hand landing on her waist, pressing her against the door, pinning her there and she doesn't seem to mind.

No, from the way she's reaching for me, her hands curling around my shoulders, clinging to me, I'd say she likes it.

Eventually she ends the kiss first, her breaths coming fast, her gaze fixed on my chest. She slides one hand down, her fingers slightly curling, gathering the fabric of my shirt and clutching it in her fist.

"You're so warm," she murmurs, her gaze fixed on my

chest, and I wish there was a light on in here so I could see her clearly and stare at her pretty face.

I don't answer her. Instead, I curve my hand around her cheek and tilt her head back, kissing her again. Devouring her mouth, plundering it with my tongue. She kisses me with the same enthusiasm, a low hum leaving my throat when her hand drops and slips beneath the hem of my shirt, her fingers brushing against my stomach.

My dick leaps to attention at her bold touch and I press more firmly against her, letting her feel what she does to me. Her hand shifts to my side, sliding up and around to my back, her mouth never leaving mine, and I skim my fingers down her throat, giving her what she wants.

When I wrap my fingers around the front of her throat, she gasps, her lips falling from mine. I pull away slightly so I can look at her, noting her wild eyes, her swollen lips. Her heavy breaths.

"You're fucking beautiful," I whisper.

Her face flushes and her eyelids flutter. "Such a flatterer."

"I'm serious, Red. You're the sexiest woman I've ever seen." I press her more firmly against the door, my fingers still around her neck, and fuck, I swear she goes limp. "You like this?"

She nods, her lips parting, her eyes fully closing.

Leaning in, I press my mouth to her ear, whispering, "Are you wet, Red?"

Her head barely moves in answer, a shuddery breath escaping her.

"Because of how I'm touching you?" I tighten my grip slightly, not wanting to hurt her but still testing her.

"Because of everything," she admits, her eyes still closed.

I go silent, studying her face. The way her chest rises and falls, her nipples hard beneath the T-shirt. Pretty sure this girl's got it bad for me.

Fairly certain I feel the same way about her.

He's got his hand around my throat and I should probably be terrified. He whispers in my ear and his voice is almost menacing, which is such a contradiction from how Ace is perceived by everyone else.

Including me.

He's the easygoing guy. The friendly, flirty, hot football player.

But in this moment, there's nothing easygoing about Ace.

I'm still surprised that I'm even here. I know how these guys operate. Football players. Athletes in general. Bringing a woman back to their apartment is usually a no-no because it could lead to bigger expectations. Like a woman thinking they could become something serious.

And none of them want serious. Especially Ace.

I don't want serious either—not with Ace. I can't be serious with this man, but the way he's currently touching me, how he kissed me?

I want more. More of *him*.

Every bit of him I can get.

"Everything, huh?" His hand slips from my throat and I want to cry out at the loss. But he makes up for it by slowly sliding his hand down the front of my chest, catching my nipple between his fingers. He gives it a quick pinch, and even through the fabric of my T-shirt, it sends a stinging sensation that lands right between my thighs, pulsating. A delicious reminder that leaves me all fluttery and breathless.

"Uh huh." My voice is shaky as his fingers toy with the hem of my T-shirt before he tunnels his hand beneath the fabric, his fingertips brushing the underside of my left breast.

"Like, this?" He cups my breast fully, his thumb drawing slow circles around my nipple, and I nod, letting a whimper escape.

The sound seems to encourage him because the next thing I know, the shirt is shoved up to my chin and he's staring at my naked chest, a rough sound leaving him that makes my knees weak.

"Jesus, Red. You're perfect."

I'm about to protest, about to deny his compliment, but when he wraps his lips around my nipple and gives it a tug, my brain shuts off and I can't form any words. A strangled sound leaves me instead, my hands coming around the back of his head, fingers sliding into his soft hair to hold him in place. He sucks and licks and pulls, his tongue working the hard bit of flesh, and I'm grateful I'm braced against the door or else I'd be on the floor. Too weak to stand.

Too overcome to think.

Oh wait. Pretty sure I'm already there.

He lavishes my other breast with the same focused attention and all I can do is take it, my fingers buried in his hair, clutching him to me. His hands are on my waist, his fingers splayed, like he wants to touch as much of my skin as he can possibly reach, and I realize I'm in big trouble.

This guy is going to ruin me.

I just know it.

His hands slide down farther and he lifts away from my chest, his palms sliding around my hips and over my ass, urging me up. I go with his silent command and he lifts me, my legs automatically winding around his hips, bringing my core to rest directly on his erection. And oh yes, he's gloriously hard.

My God, he's big.

He rubs me against him, his mouth finding mine once more, devouring me completely, and I let him. I bask in the way he kisses me, his hands on my butt, his cock nudging against me over and over, my entire body a mass of tingles. He pins me to the wall and ends the kiss, pulling away slightly.

I open my eyes to find him studying me, his expression intense. Downright thunderous. I'm on total display, vulnerable and open to him with my shirt shoved up and my chest exposed. I can tell from the heat emanating from his gaze that he likes what he sees but still.

It's a little unsettling.

"We need to get rid of this," he mutters, and a thrill runs through me when he tugs at the shirt. I help him take it off, a moan leaving me when he runs his mouth across the top of my breasts, worshiping my skin with his mouth.

A girl could get used to this kind of treatment, especially one who hasn't had sex with anyone else in a long time.

That would be me. It's been forever and maybe I'm just primed and ready for action because it's been so long, but I don't know.

I think it might be him. And the way he touches me.

"Come on." His hands shift beneath my ass, holding me tighter. "Let's go to my room."

I don't say a word, just let him carry me through the dark apartment, clinging to him. I sling my arms around his neck, my face pressed against it and I breathe in the spicy scent of his cologne, the clean smell of his skin. He carries me like I don't weigh a thing, and I wonder why I haven't hooked up with any athletes before.

It's true. I avoid them for the most part because they're such a part of my life that I think I subconsciously sought out someone different. But here I am, wrapped around a football player, impressed by his strength. He makes me feel small and dainty and completely protected and I can't lie.

It's hot.

Everything he does is hot.

Once we're in his bedroom, I barely have a chance to lift my head and check things out before he's depositing me on the bed and following right after me, his big body pressing me into the mattress. His mouth finds mine for a quick, tongue-sweeping kiss before he ends it, reaching across me to flick on the lamp that sits on the nightstand, the room illuminated with soft, warm light.

"I like to look," he explains before he rises above me and gets rid of his shirt.

I practically swallow my tongue at the sight of his chest and abs so close, suddenly grateful he turned on the light.

Seems I like to look too.

His mouth returns to mine and I lose myself in the sweep of his tongue. The sting of his teeth tugging on my lower lip. His hands are wandering all over my body, big and hot and with slightly rough fingertips that leave a trail of sparks wherever he touches me. I rest my hands on his broad shoulders, my fingers curling around the muscles there, marveling at how hard he is, clinging to him.

There's not an ounce of body fat on this man and that leaves me feeling more than a little intimidated. And while I'm usually pretty confident when it comes to this sort of thing—messing around with a guy—I can't help the self-doubt that slowly washes over me. I'm not what I would call at peak physical fitness, meaning my belly is a little soft from too many late-night pizza deliveries with Natalie because we're always hungry around midnight.

And when his fingers drift across my stomach, I'm suddenly batting his hand away, thinking of how bloated I felt last night, blaming it on how much salt I consumed.

He ends the kiss, lifting up so he can look into my eyes. "What's wrong?"

"Um…" I bite my lower lip, feeling stupid. "Nothing."

He's frowning. "What is it, Ruby?"

I sort of miss hearing him call me Red, which is silly. "You're just—really muscular."

He grins, and I'm sure he's pleased I noticed. How could I not? "I work out every single day for hours. I should be muscular."

"Well, I'm not. I eat pizza. And Subway, which I've heard they don't even use real bread. Not that bread is good for you. It's not. And I drink too much Diet Coke. Oh God, and I have a total sweet tooth. Did you know that? I can bake a mean chocolate chip cookie, though I'm guessing you don't eat them."

He's smiling, and the glow in his eyes is downright tender as he studies me. "I love chocolate chip cookies."

"Do you eat them right now? During football season?"

"Not if I can help it," he admits.

"See, that's the problem. I eat too many. I eat raw dough

too." The horror. Why haven't I died of food poisoning or whatever? "I'm gross."

He chuckles. "You are the furthest thing from gross, Red."

There it is. The nickname I thought I hated but really don't. I smile at him. And he smiles at me, just as he shifts downward to press his mouth upon my skin, making me suck in a breath, forgetting all my troubles. He kisses my breasts. Licks and sucks my nipples until I'm clutching him to me again, writhing beneath him, my body needy, my mind growing hazy and unfocused. Until all I can think about is the pulsating between my thighs and how much I want him to touch me there.

I'm desperate for him to touch me there, but are we moving too fast?

Yeah, we're definitely moving too fast. I gave him a big speech about dates and how many it takes before I'll get naked with someone, yet here I am...

Meeting him for our non-date and letting him have his way with me. If he ditches me after this, I'm going to be so pissed.

He shifts lower, his mouth on my stomach, and I'm tempted to talk about my junk food diet again, but I remain quiet. Reminding myself that I need to let go of my insecurities. I should focus on the way he makes me feel so incredibly sexy.

And he does. He kisses the skin just above the waistband of my shorts, his fingers reaching for the button at the front. He lifts his head, his gaze questioning, and I nod before I overthink what's about to happen.

He slides back up, his face in mine, his mouth returning to mine, and I get lost in his kiss, my mind vaguely comprehending that he is undoing the front of my shorts. Sliding the zipper down and spreading the fly open, his fingers barely brushing the front of my panties.

A jolt runs through me at first contact and I moan against his lips, immediately wishing he'd touch me more. As if he's a mind reader, he slips his hand into the front of my shorts, pressing against my throbbing center, cupping me completely.

I break away from his still seeking lips to catch my breath, focusing on the way his fingers mold to my pussy, his middle finger pressing harder, parting me.

"You're soaked," he whispers at the same time he slides his fingers up, like he's going to stop touching me, only for his hand to shift back downward, once again cupping me fully.

I don't know what to say, so I just reach for him instead, pulling him down so our lips touch once more.

He continues rubbing, pressing against me, making me shiver and moan. And when he slides those magical fingers beneath my panties and touches my bare flesh, his thumb brushing my clit, I almost shoot off the bed, it feels so good.

His mouth never leaving mine, we kiss and kiss, my hips moving with his hand, his thumb strumming my clit. He slips a finger inside me and oh my God, that feels good too. It all feels so good.

I'm already close.

It takes maybe another minute of his continuous attention to my throbbing clit and I'm coming, my body shaking as the delicious waves take over me. I break away from his kiss, lost in the sensations sweeping over me and when it's finally over, I lie there for a moment, trying to catch my breath.

Ace kisses my forehead. My temple. My cheek, while slowly removing his hand from between my thighs. I cuddle close to him, overwhelmed with exhaustion. He wraps his arms around me, tucking me into him, and press my face against his chest, thinking I could fall asleep so easily like this...

And I do.

18

ACE

I wake up to the mattress shifting, my eyes cracking open to find my bedroom is still shrouded in darkness. And the girl who fell asleep in my arms after I gave her an earthshattering orgasm is no longer in my bed.

There's rustling in the dark, a muttered curse, and I sit up, trying to see in the dark. "Ruby?"

"Oh." My eyes adjust and I spot her standing at the foot of my bed. I can just barely make out what I think is a sheepish expression on her face. "Hey."

"What are you doing?" I clear my throat, scratching the back of my neck. I don't remember turning off the light before I fell asleep, but maybe I did?

"I'm headed home." She sits on the edge of the mattress, her back to me and I can tell she's putting on her shoes.

I don't remember her taking off her shoes at any point when we were so—heavily focused on each other, but she must've. I don't remember a lot of details from our interaction, thanks to drinking a little too much, but I do remember all the kissing. How much she enjoyed me focusing on her perfect tits. And the way she coated my fingers when I stroked her hot, wet pussy.

I'd wanted to do more after I fingered her. I was willing to give her another orgasm—specifically with my mouth—and was hoping for some reciprocation, but ultimately, she fell asleep. Just...passed out within minutes, her breathing evening out, her body going soft.

Eventually I fell asleep too, too tired and drunk to keep my eyes open, I guess.

"You, uh, really leaving?" I ask when she still hasn't said anything else.

"Yeah. I have an early class tomorrow. Well—today." She glances over her shoulder, offering me a quick smile. "I had fun."

She had *fun?* That's how she's phrasing what we just shared?

I mean an orgasm is fun, don't get me wrong, but...

"Um, yeah. Same." My answer is lame and I fall back onto the mattress, closing my eyes.

What the fuck is happening right now?

Ruby stands and I can hear soft footsteps as she rounds the bed to my side, bending over and giving me a quick kiss on my fucking forehead. "I'll see you later?"

I crack my eyes open and nod, staring up at her, hating how the roles have somehow...reversed? I seriously don't know how to feel about this. "See ya, Red."

She smiles. "Bye, Ace."

The moment I hear the front door click shut, I'm bounding out of bed and running into the living room, peeking through the blinds. I feel like a shithead for not walking her out to her car, but it's directly in front of my apartment, giving me an excellent view. I watch as she climbs into the fancy BMW, shuts the door and starts the engine, backing out and speeding away.

I drop the blinds and stand there for a moment, my mind reeling. She just...left. What if I hadn't woken up? Would she have walked out without saying a word? I'm thinking yes.

Damn. Can't help but feel kind of...

Used.

What the actual fuck?

NEXT DAY at practice and I'm still sore over my encounter with Ruby. Not the sexual part of it because that was hot—she's a dirty girl with some secret kinks I'd love to explore further if she gave me the chance, but I'm starting to think she doesn't want to explore much else with me.

Which is a fucking strange feeling, I cannot lie.

I've hooked up with plenty of girls since I came here, doing a variety of things, including a quick little finger sesh. Most of the time, they're so damn grateful that I got them off, they're willing to do whatever I want afterward. Sometimes I take advantage of what they're offering and sometimes I don't. Depends on what I'm in the mood for.

Ruby didn't offer anything. She fell asleep, for the love of God. Like my orgasm-giving skills have the ability to take her out, which I can't help but feel proud of, but still.

I haven't seen her all day and like a jackass, I don't even have her number. Any other girl and I'd think I don't need it anyway. But with Ruby?

I want it.

I fucking need her phone number.

Memories come back to me, one after the other. Ruby

offering to help with my car—though I ended up having Derek help me. Me telling her I didn't have her number when she said just call me. How she took mine and sent me a quick text.

Shit. I *do* have her number.

I need to text her. After practice.

We're an hour in and I'm playing like a giant fuck-up. Constantly throwing the ball away when my receivers are too covered, which is like every time I try to pass. I even throw an actual interception that has me cursing up a storm, walking in circles with my hands on my hips as I mutter under my breath on the sidelines. Mattson eventually puts the second string in to play, supposedly to give me 'a break,' as he calls it.

Already cracking under pressure is how I'm describing what's currently happening to me. I'm a fucking hot mess and pissed about it, too. One game in and this is what happens? What the hell is my problem? I can't cut it?

"What's your deal?" Mattson asks me at one point, when it feels like everyone is out on that field but me.

"I don't fucking know." I throw my hands up in the air, frustrated.

"Well, knock this shit off. You're too in your head and it's messing with your ability. Stop overthinking." He stalks off, grumbling much like I was only a few minutes ago, and I exhale raggedly, pissed at myself.

Coach makes it sound so easy. Just get out of my head and play right.

I'm discovering it's not that simple.

I never want to disappoint my coaches, especially Mattson. He took a chance on me from the start. He's the one who came to my high school and watched me play. Talked to me and my dad after the game, encouraging me to apply to CU. While I didn't come from a big high school and we didn't win state championships, my team was still pretty good and I was a superstar in my hometown.

Mattson told me he saw great potential in my game play and felt that he could mold me into an even bigger star.

And here I am, learning under Mattson, letting him mold me and I'm failing.

To clear my head, I jog around the track, thankfully no one is calling out to me as they continue practicing. I run a mile, then another one, until Mattson is telling me to stop so I can conserve my energy.

Feels like I can't win no matter what I do.

It's near the end of practice when I spot our social media team of three approaching the field, my gaze snagging on Ruby's familiar blonde head. She's hot as usual, wearing a red Golden Eagles T-shirt today, the mascot on the front, and a pair of denim shorts, standing in between Gwen and Eric talking.

I try not to look over at her, but it's damn hard when I've got nothing else to do. I end up blatantly staring at her like some sort of jackass and she finally glances over at me, a faint smile curling her lips.

I smile back, about to lift my hand in a wave, but she's already looking away, talking to Eric.

My hand drops to my side, useless.

Mattson blows his whistle and calls for a break and my teammates head toward me, many of them offering me mini pep talks. I nod but don't say anything, keeping my feelings inside so I don't blow up on someone who doesn't deserve my wrath. There's no one to blame for my fuck-ups anyway.

Just myself.

"Hey." I turn to find Evan standing in front of me, his hair all sweaty from his helmet, clutching a reusable water bottle that's in the university's school colors in his hand. "You okay, bro?"

"Rough day," I admit, not sure how else to explain it. I shrug. "You know how it is."

"I do." Evan glances around like he's making sure no one is paying attention before he continues, "Not trying to make you feel bad or anything, but Mattson is freaking out."

"Yeah, no shit." He's definitely not making me feel much better.

"You seem to be really in your head." I start to protest, but he keeps talking over me. "It's something I've been guilty of too. I just wanted to make you aware of it."

"How'd you make it stop?" I ask, genuinely curious.

"Well, I'd take a walk or run or whatever, but I see you already tried that." Evan winces. "Maybe you should try and talk to someone that centers you? Mattson maybe?"

"That guy doesn't center me. He's too keyed up." Like I am.

"Okay...what about Derek? Or any of your other friends on the team? I know we're not that close, but if you ever need someone to just vent to, I'm here," Evan offers.

"I appreciate that." No one makes an offer like he just did. Everyone is too worried about looking like a wuss, I swear.

I remember hearing about Cam last season, how after the season was over, he went to counseling and it helped him a lot. All of that was thanks to Blair. He fell in love with her and wanted to be a better man for her.

And for himself.

Glancing across the field, I watch Ruby laugh at something Eric or Gwen says as she holds her phone out for them to all watch something. The pleasant sound drifts over to me, settling in my chest and easing some of that tension that's making it so tight, and I realize in that moment who I need to go talk to.

Someone who could possibly center me.

I stride across the field, ignoring the guys who call my name, thankful that Mattson doesn't blow his whistle or worse, try to get me to talk to him again. His idea of a pep talk isn't what I want right now.

Pretty sure I need something else.

I don't stop walking until I'm standing directly in front of the social media team, dying for Ruby to lift her head and acknowledge me before I have to say anything. And like she knows what I'm thinking, she lifts her head, her eyes lighting up and her lips curving into a faint smile when she spots me.

"Hey, Ace."

There's no point in mincing words. "Can you talk for a minute?"

Her smile fades, most likely thanks to my serious tone. "Sure."

I glance at Gwen and Eric. "Alone maybe?"

They share a look, Gwen saying, "Hey, let's go film some footage," to Eric as she practically drags him away.

Once they're gone, I step a little closer to Ruby, breathing in her scent, noting how it immediately seems to settle my rattled thoughts. Or maybe that's just because I'm standing close to her.

"Tell me what's going on," she says, her voice full of concern.

"I've had a shit day."

"Oh." She tilts her head to the side. "Why is that?"

"I don't know. I can't keep it together out on the field. I fumble. I keep throwing the ball away. I threw a fucking interception. More than once." I shake my head, grimacing. "I'm sucking shit out there and I don't know why."

She's quiet for a moment, absorbing my words, and I send her a worried look, fighting the panic growing inside me. I can't let one bad day get to me, but I am. I'm panicking and it's stupid and I don't know how to stop it.

"Why did you want to talk to me?" she finally asks. "How can I help?"

I stare at her, unsure how to explain it. What can she do to help me calm my wayward thoughts? I run a hand through my hair, cupping the back of my head, and she studies me, her gaze lingering on my biceps for a second too long, her gaze jerking to mine.

"Just...let me look at you for a minute." I really take her in, liking how the T-shirt fits snug across her chest. "Loving the show of support."

"Oh." She glances down at her shirt before returning her gaze to me. "Blair gave me this shirt. It's kind of small."

"I think it's perfect."

She rolls her eyes. "Because it's tight across my boobs?"

"That might have something to do with it." I grin, already feeling better.

Thanks to Ruby.

19

RUBY

Ace and I chatted a few more minutes along the sidelines about nothing in particular, never mentioning what happened between us last night. How he gave me an orgasm and I promptly fell asleep after it.

When I woke up hours later with the lamp still on and Ace passed out next to me, I felt guilty. I should've done the same thing for him. A hand job, some dry humping...something to pay him back, so to speak.

I tried to sneak out of there without waking him. He looked so cute while he was sleeping, and I turned off the lamp so not to disturb him.

Ugh, he was adorable. I can still envision his face.

He woke up anyway and seemed confused by my leaving early, but I had to. Snuggling close to his hard, warm body is a recipe for eventual disaster.

I'm not trying to get my heart broken here. Meaning I should steer clear. Besides the fact that I absolutely can't date him, hook up with him, whatever you want to call it.

But I can't resist him. It's like he's fire and I'm drawn to the flames. I need to remember...

Spending more time with Ace will only result in me getting burned.

Once we finished talking, he returned to the field and played his little heart out. Seriously, he was so good. I couldn't even wrap my head around him playing terribly because clearly, something clicked in his brain when he got the ball back in his hands. Everyone was cheering and clapping at one point, Mattson losing his mind to the point I couldn't tell if he was happy or upset.

Turns out he was happy. He just has a weird way of showing it.

Eric and I captured everything that unfolded on video and AirDrop'd it to Gwen's phone, so she could start editing right away. By the time practice was over, Gwen had already posted the arm candy reveal video and it was racking up the likes.

"Over two hundred comments already," Gwen reveals as we leave the field and head back to our office.

"You only posted like thirty minutes ago!" I chance a look in Eric's direction to find him scowling over this news, but the moment our gazes connect, the scowl is gone.

He's still not thrilled by this when he really should be. We're all in it together, after all.

"I know, it's like...I don't even know how to describe it." Gwen is actually grinning—something she never does—and she's shaking her head. "It's unbelievable!"

"Well, I think it's great." I send a pointed look in Eric's direction. "And it tells me this is the kind of content that will work and help us gain new followers."

"We've grown," Eric admits, sounding almost reluctant. "By almost two thousand followers. I've been keeping track."

"See?" Oh, I sound smug. I feel smug. "Gwen, you were so right."

"You're the one who came up with the arm candy idea," she says, giving me my props. "Looks like it worked."

"We keep this up, we're going to have so many followers!" I offer up my hand and Gwen gives me a high five.

We talk like this the rest of the way back to the office, with Eric interjecting here and there. He's not as grumpy as he has been, so maybe he's seeing that it actually works. Which it so does.

I'm gathering up my stuff and slipping my backpack strap over my shoulder when I receive a text.

Ace: **Thank you.**

Frowning, I read the text again, confused.

Me: **Thank you for what?**

I was the one who got an orgasm out of last night. Shouldn't I be thanking him?

I'm climbing into my car, tossing my backpack on the passenger seat when my phone buzzes with his response.

Ace: **For talking to me earlier at practice. I played better because of you.**

A snort leaves me at his answer. Come on. I had nothing to do with that.

Or did I?

Hmm.

I decide to play it off.

Me: **You're welcome for nothing.**

He immediately sends me a text.

Ace: **It wasn't nothing.**

Ace: **I want to see you again.**

Ace: **Tonight.**

Uh huh. Why? So he can collect what I supposedly owe him? Is he one of those types of dudes?

Me: **I can't tonight.**

Stowing my phone in the center console, I try to ignore it as I leave the parking lot and drive back home. It's not until I'm pulling into my parking spot at the apartment complex where I live that I finally check my phone to see I have more texts from Ace.

Ace: **Whatever time you can meet, I'm game.**

Ace: **I just really want to talk to you again, Red.**

Ace: **There's something I want to ask you.**

I stare at the three texts he sent, confused. What does he want to ask me that he can't via text?

He's not making any sense.

Shoving my phone into the front pocket of my backpack, I make the short walk to our apartment, grateful when I spot Natalie sitting on the couch when I open the front door, shoveling a mouthful of Lucky Charms cereal into her mouth via a giant spoon.

"Oh. Hey." The guilty look on her face stops me in my tracks and I start laughing.

"Hungry much?" The bowl she's eating the cereal out of is one we usually reserve for making a salad in.

She sets the silver bowl in her lap, crunching away until she swallows. "I was starving and nothing else sounded good."

I walk over to the kitchen table and drop my backpack on top of it, deciding to get right to the issue. "I have a dilemma."

She takes another big bite of cereal, her teeth loudly crunching. "Please explain."

Taking a deep breath, I tell her mostly everything that happened last night. About Ace being drunk and trying to hit on me. How I explained that my meeting him at Logan's didn't make it a date and how I don't have sex with anyone until at least the fifth one.

Nat's mouth hangs open in shock at that reveal.

Then I tell her how I ended up taking him back home and that he gave me an O—I don't go into too many details about that—and that I tried to slip out and he woke up. And lastly, how he needed to talk to me at practice today and how he's now claiming that I helped him so much.

"...he said he played better because of me." I throw my hands up in the air, flopping down in the recliner my parents gave me. "That he wants to see me tonight. He has something to ask me."

"What did you say to him in response?" Natalie asks.

"I haven't responded," I admit.

"Ruby!" she practically shrieks, leaning forward to set her disgustingly giant bowl of kids' cereal on the coffee table. "Girl. You need to answer him."

"I was waiting to talk to you." I climb out of the chair and grab my phone before I sit down again, staring at Ace's last texts. Wondering if he's waiting by his phone right at this very moment, anxious for my response. "I don't know what to say."

"Tell him you'll meet with him tomorrow. Like for coffee?"

"I mean...I could meet with him tonight. I don't have plans."

"Why did you tell him you couldn't meet tonight?"

"I don't want to look like I'm desperate and boring." I turn my phone face down and rest it on my thigh, closing my eyes. "This is a mess."

"What are you saying? It's a *great* mess. The best kind of mess. He's chasing after you. Claims he has something to ask you that must be important because he wants to say it to your face. Right now, you're a queen and he's put you on a pedestal, ready to worship you," Natalie explains, her eyes flashing.

"You're being really dramatic."

"I'm speaking truths! Ace doesn't chase after girls. He never has to. All the women flock to him wherever he goes. He has a fan club for God's sake."

"You know about the fan club?" I ask incredulously.

"Everyone knows about it. They try and recruit members like they're a fucking sorority! It's madness." Natalie starts laughing, shaking her head. "You have to meet with him."

"Not tonight," I say firmly, making her frown. "What? I can't run to him every time he asks me to. He'll think I'm easy."

He probably already thinks I'm easy. He had his fingers inside me last night.

I'm the epitome of easy.

"Oh yeah. That reminds me. Your date rules." She watches me carefully, like I'm a puzzle she's trying to figure out. "Were you for real about that?"

"About what? The five-date rule?"

"Yeah. Because if you ask me, that's some straight-up trash."

"Why do you say that?"

"First of all, if a girl gets with a guy immediately after meeting him, does that make her a slut?"

"No, of course not."

"Well then, why do you have that stupid rule with the stipulations and the minimum of five dates?"

"I was trying to prove a point to Ace that I'm not the type of girl who gives it up during the first date." I cover my face with my hands, irritated with myself. "Instead, I took him home after our non-date and let him finger me until I came all over his hand."

"Ooh, Ruby! That's a juicy detail you didn't originally share!" Natalie's so excited she leaps off the couch and starts pacing. "I think you might've hypnotized him."

"How?" I drop my hands to stare at her. She's talking nonsense.

"With your magical hoo-ha, of course." Natalie waves a hand in said hoo-ha's direction. "He's had a tiny taste and now he's hooked."

"He didn't taste it," I admit softly.

She rolls her eyes, stopping directly in front of me. "Well, he stroked it and now he's eager to get back to it. Proving your dating rules are nothing but bullshit."

"He only wants to talk to me so we can hook up again."

"And that's a big deal because these guys on the team, they don't really hook up with someone twice. Trust me, I've tried," she retorts.

"With Derek?" I wince.

"Um, yes. I've thrown myself at that asshole and he still won't touch me. Claims he just wants to be friends." She huffs out a breath, crossing her arms. "Who wants to be 'just friends' this day and age? You're either fucking or you're not."

"Natalie..."

"I'm serious." She settles on the edge of the coffee table, directly in front of me. "Go meet with Ace tonight and find out what he wants from you."

I slowly shake my head. "I'm not meeting him tonight. I'll do it tomorrow."

Natalie doesn't respond. Just stares into my eyes for at least five seconds, maybe longer. I start to squirm, but I don't look away until she finally breaks out into a smile, slowly nodding her head. "I'm so proud of you. Yes, that's perfect. Make him suffer."

My shoulders sag with exhaustion. "You are so confusing."

"I was seeing if you'd change your mind and you didn't. This is exactly the kind of treatment these assholes need. Every woman they encounter, they snap their fingers and the girls come running. It's annoying. We need to be stronger. We need to learn how to resist."

"Are you turning into a man-hater, Nat?" I ask with a sigh.

"No, I'm turning into a *woman supporter*. Fuck these guys who think they can get all the pussy they want, just because they know how to throw a ball or whatever. I say if Ace Townsend wants more of you, he should have to work for it." Natalie smiles and it's almost evil. "He's probably going to spiral, having to put some effort into seeing a woman for the first time in his life."

"He's not that bad—"

"He's awful, Ruby. Don't defend him. He's a *man*, he's on the *football team*, plus he's a *jerk* and women fall at his feet. Don't let him get away with it." She points at me. "Let's answer him."

She is seriously making my head spin, but hey. At least she saw the light and is now on my side.

We work on the response for far too long, to the point that Ace has probably given up on me replying at all, and when I finally send it, I immediately feel nervous. Like maybe I just made a mistake.

Oh well. Too late now.

20

ACE

It takes what feels like hours for Ruby to respond, and when she finally does, it's not the answer I was looking for.

Ruby: **I can't see you tonight. Maybe tomorrow?**

I blink at her text, imagining more words came along with it. Another text, a fucking meme maybe, but no.

That's it.

A frustrated growl leaves me and I stalk out of my bedroom and down the hall until I'm in the living room where my roommate Javier Sanchez—he's an excellent tight end, good eyes, great hands—and Derek are sitting on the couch, playing X-Box. Some violent game that I'm not into whatsoever, which means I rarely play with them.

I'm more of a Madden Football kind of guy. That's my game of choice. Oh yeah, and anything to do with Spider-Man because what guy my age doesn't love Spider-Man?

"What crawled up your butt hole and died?" Derek asks after taking one look at my face.

"I'm sick of women," I spit out, though really, I'm just sick of one woman in particular.

And I don't want to tell them about her because I will never hear the end of it, especially from Derek. A lot of *I told you so's* will be coming out of his mouth at first mention of her name.

"Best way to get over one is to fuck another," Derek claims.

Javi glances over at him. "What the hell are you talking about?"

"Get with a woman who's nothing like the ones who annoy you and fuck her. That'll get those other chicks—chick—whatever, out of your mind for good." Derek nods, looking pleased with his explanation.

"That's the dumbest thing I've ever heard." Javier has a girlfriend back in his hometown and she's already visited him twice since he started here. He's a junior like me, a transfer student. His girlfriend Piper is totally into him and I had the unfortunate luck to listen to them bang repeatedly when she was staying here with him last weekend.

It sucked. Their constant sex noises eventually drove me out of here to a bar downtown to try and find some random girl to hook up with. When not a single one of them interested me, I came back home only to discover they were *still* banging.

I'm surprised they could walk when they finally ventured out of Javier's room Sunday afternoon.

"Your opinion doesn't count," Derek says to Javier with a snort. "You're completely pussy-whipped."

"Your opinion is exactly what I'm looking for," I tell Javier, earning a confused look from Derek. "Tell me what I should do."

"First, what is your exact problem?" Javier sets his game controller onto the table in front of him.

Derek pauses the game and does the same thing, leaning

back against the couch and crossing his arms behind his head. "Yes, please enlighten us, Townsend."

How do I even begin to explain this without sounding like I've lost my mind?

"Let's just say there's a girl...and I'm into her. And I'm never into just one woman," I start. "But this one is different."

Derek groans. Javier jabs him in the ribs to shut him up. "Keep going."

"I don't even know her that well. But there's something about her..." I stare off into the distance for a moment, thinking about what I want to say about Ruby. Why I feel so connected to her when I barely know her. It makes no sense.

But I'm starting to realize that life in general doesn't make any sense. Just when we think we have something figured out, boom. Everything changes.

"What is it?" Javier asks, looking genuinely interested. Unlike Derek, who's shaking his head repeatedly.

"I can't even put my finger on it. But whenever we're together, it's like she calms me down and I feel at...ease. Yet I'm also amped up and unsure, if that makes any sense. It's like I can't wait to get my hands on her."

"Sounds like you really like her," Javier says.

"Yawn. Boring. Sounds like your typical crush," Derek says, punctuating his statement with an actual yawn that he doesn't bother to cover up.

His reaction has me shifting into pure hostility, which was probably his goal. "What the hell do you know about a typical crush?"

"Look, before I was a football god, I had my fair share of crushes over the years. And I've had *plenty* of women crush on me. Just because you're dying to fuck the youngest Maguire, doesn't mean you're in love with her, dumbass."

I fucking knew Derek would reveal her. The schmuck.

"You don't understand," I start, but Derek cuts me off, talking right over me.

"I definitely understand, bro. I've been in your shoes and it fucking sucks, but that was a long time ago and I don't let that happen anymore." He pauses, his gaze full of all sorts of sympathy. This dude. He's confusing. "What I'm going to say will hurt, but you need to hear it." He pauses. "Move on. She's not the one for you."

"And how the hell do you know?" I toss at him.

"Because I just *know*. Women like her, she's really just like you. Like all of us. Well, maybe not you, Javi. Anyway, she can have her choice of men. Anyone would want to be with Ruby because of her dad and her uncle and every other motherfucker in that family who plays football. I'm sure that's half the reason you're attracted to her."

"That isn't it—"

"Yeah, yeah, whatever." Derek waves a hand, dismissing my protests. "You need to act like you don't care about her."

"What?" Javier asks incredulously. He turns to me, his brown eyes downright pleading. "Don't listen to him."

"No, you should absolutely listen to me. You need to act like this girl doesn't matter to you. Play her off, brother. Don't beg her to see you. Don't chase after her. Make her come to you," Derek explains.

"That's what I've been doing since I started here. And there hasn't been a single woman that's interested me enough to want to pursue her. Until...Ruby," I admit, somewhat reluctantly.

More snorting from Derek. "Do whatever you think works then, since you believe you're so much smarter than me. I've said my piece. And when you come running to me crying that she's dumped you, I'll be the one who said I told you so."

He grabs his controller and resumes playing the game, Javier reluctantly going along with him, though he sends me a sympathetic look.

"Don't listen to him," Javier finally says. "Follow your heart."

Derek whacks the back of Javier's head like the douche that he is and I stare at my phone screen, wondering what I should say to her. There's a war in my head, and one of the voices sounds suspiciously like Derek.

Don't go chasing after her. Let her come to you.

My fingers hover over the keyboard so long they start to ache.

Fuck it.

I'm just typing and sending. I can't think about this any longer.

Me: **You sure you can't meet tonight? Doesn't matter how late.**

The moment I hear the whoosh sound of the text sending, I have major regret. I sound like a wimp. Like a fucking pussy.

Chasing after a woman who's not as interested in me as I am in her. I've never had this happen before.

It's fucking weird.

Almost depressing.

My phone dings and I grab it, reading her message immediately.

Ruby: **Well...if you don't mind waiting until around 11?**

Eleven? That's hook up time. And I don't want her thinking I want to see her just for a hook up. It's more than that.

I think she might mean more to me than that.

Oh God, I sound like such a sap, even in my thoughts.

Me: **I can do that.**

Ruby: **Okay. Want to come over then?**

Excitement bubbles up inside me and I remind myself to stay calm.

Me: **Sure.**

Ruby: **See you around 11.**

I'M PULLING into the parking lot of Ruby's apartment complex when I receive a text from her.

Ruby: **Don't go to the front door.**

Say the fuck what?

Me: **Why not?**

Ruby: **Natalie is...entertaining...a guest.**

Me: **So?**

Ruby: **I don't want you interrupting them.**

A growl escapes me and I glance down at myself.

Me: **How am I supposed to see you then? I'm already here BTW.**

Ruby: **Crawl through my window?**

Seriously? I feel like a teenager out after curfew about to sneak into my girlfriend's bedroom so I can have my way with her. Not that I've ever had an experience like that...

Me: **Please tell me you're on the ground floor.**

Ruby: **I am.**

Thank Christ. I took a shower and chose my outfit carefully and don't want to fuck it up by climbing through a damn window.

She texts me her apartment number and lets me know her bedroom is the second window on the right from their front door. I send her a thumbs-up emoji before I pocket my phone and climb out of the car, heading toward her building.

I feel just like I described to Javier earlier. Amped up and excited to see her. Wondering why the hell she's having me crawl through her window. Not sure if I believe the 'Natalie has a guest' excuse, but it's not like I can call Ruby a liar.

I don't think she is one. It's just—this entire situation is odd.

Or maybe I'm just overthinking everything, my new hobby now when it comes to Ruby. And I'm not an over-thinker. Not usually.

Damn, it sucks.

I find her apartment and go to her window, noting the light that glows from within the room. I lightly knock on the glass, trying to peek through the tightly closed blinds, but I can't see anything.

There's no response to my knock and I pull out my phone, sending her a quick text.

Me: **I'm here.**

I rap on the glass again, a little harder this time, but still nothing. It's kind of cold out here. Despite it being the beginning of September and late summer/early fall is notoriously still fairly warm in this part of the state, sometimes the nights can get cold.

Like tonight for instance.

I'm not really dressed for it either. I've got on black joggers and a light gray T-shirt with CU slides on my feet.

I send her another text.

Me: **Ruby. I'm outside your window. Let me in before someone calls the cops and reports that I'm a stalker lurking around the place.**

That gets her. Within seconds, the blinds shoot up,

revealing Ruby standing there in—oh fuck me—a fitted black tank top and a pair of Christmas print flannel shorts. She leans forward, the neckline of her tank dipping down and offering me a glimpse of her tits, which I just had in my hands and mouth only last night.

My skin grows tight and I start to sweat despite the cool air outside. She's got an amazing body and I swear to God, my fingers are literally itching to touch her again.

The window slides open and she's within touching distance, smiling at me. "Sorry."

She offers her hand and I take it, letting her guide me in while I hop over the sill and step into her room before I turn to the window and shut it for her and lock it.

"Is it safe for you to live on the first floor and not have a screen over your window?" I ask when I turn to face her, letting the concern show in my voice.

"When we moved in the screen wasn't there. We've put in a request multiple times with maintenance to get it replaced, but they haven't gotten around to it yet." She shrugs, seemingly not worried, while all I can think about is some legitimate creeper-stalker type sneaking into her room and doing something fucking awful to her.

I focus on the window again, glaring at it. "I'll talk to someone tomorrow and get this handled."

She laughs, reaching around me to pull the string so the blinds drop back into place, covering her window. "What, are you going to tell them you're my dad?"

"How would your dad feel if he knew this was an issue?" I glance down at her in time to see the guilt flicker in her eyes.

"He'd probably be pissed," she admits.

"Yeah, well so am I." I scrub my chin with my hand, fighting the urge to run to Walmart to purchase a screen. I think they sell them there and our local Walmart is open twenty-four hours.

"Hey." She steps closer, smiling up at me. "I appreciate your concern. Really."

I tell myself to shake it off and focus on the pretty woman standing in front of me, my gaze dropping to those Christmas print shorts. There are decorated trees, ginger-bread men and Santa Claus faces all over the red shorts, and they're pretty freaking cute. "I like your shorts."

"Oh." She drops her head, studying them for a second before she glances back up at me. "I've owned them forever. They're so soft."

"They're cute." Testing her, I reach out, brushing my fingers against the fabric right at her hip. "And they are soft."

"My favorite shorts to sleep in." Her smile is slow.

"Oh yeah? I usually sleep naked." Why the fuck did I just say that?

"Not that I asked, but thanks for the info." She laughs, shifting away from me and going to the bed, where she sits on the end of the mattress. Watching me with amusement still flickering in her gaze. "You mentioned that you had something to ask me?"

Oh right.

I did.

Glancing behind me, I lean against her desk, crossing my arms as I contemplate her. She looks ready for bed. Her face is scrubbed clean and a little dewy from what I assume must be her nightly skincare regimen or whatever it's called. I see stuff on TikTok like that on occasion that I find myself watching for no good reason.

"You're ready for bed," I finally say.

She smiles. "I am."

"Why'd you encourage me to come over then?"

"You mentioned earlier that you wanted to see me. I remember how important it was for you to see me earlier at practice so I figured I better say yes." She shrugs, her hair sliding over her bare shoulders and I'm tempted to go to her. Kiss her bare skin. Her neck, breathe in deep her fragrance just behind her ear.

No other woman smells as delicious as Ruby Maguire.

"You were a big help to me today at practice."

"I did nothing."

You exist, is what I want to tell her. *Just looking at you calms my chaotic thoughts. Like right now.*

Having her in front of me, looking at her is enough.

Well, I'd also like to touch her. Kiss her. Hear her sigh with pleasure when I slip my hand under her clothes...

"But I'm glad I could help," she adds, her voice soft.

I inhale deeply, keeping my gaze on her face, deciding to hell with it.

"I was hoping I could take you out on a date."

Ruby blinks, tilting her head to the side. "What do you mean?"

"I mean what I said. I want to ask you on a date."

"Oh." Her face falls a little and my heart drops into my fucking balls at that look.

"What's wrong?"

"I think I'm going to have to decline."

21

RUBY

I am blown away that this big, beautiful, sexy man crawled through my window late at night just to stare at me and ask me on a date with so much sincerity in his voice, it made my heart ache. For whatever reason, he's into me, and while I am definitely attracted to him and even might like him as a person—fine, I totally like him as a person—I am going to have to say no.

And it hurts. It hurts to turn him down and see the crushed expression currently on his face. I feel like a shithead.

"Why?" he asks, sounding like he's had the shock of his life, which he probably has.

"I signed an agreement," I admit.

"An agreement to not date me?" His brows draw together in total confusion.

"An agreement to not date anyone on any athletic team at CU," I clarify, wincing when he tips his head back to stare at the ceiling.

Wow, his neck is thick and not in a bad way. His chiseled

jawline is way too attractive as well. I want to go to him right now and kiss it. Kiss *him.*

But I remain where I'm seated on the edge of my bed, waiting for him to storm out pissed off.

I'd let him leave through the front door too. That whole Natalie is entertaining someone was a lie, and I don't know why I said it. To see if Ace would crawl through my window?

Yes. That's exactly why.

Natalie is most likely in her room and already in bed. Her nightly ritual includes scrolling through TikTok for approximately fifty hours before she finally falls asleep due to complete exhaustion.

That's an exaggeration but I'm not too far off.

"Is that because you're on the social media team?" he asks the ceiling.

"Yeah. I guess there was a girl on my team last year who was deemed a total distraction and she tried to date as many football players as possible. I'm not allowed to date anyone. I could get fired." I hesitate. "And I'd really like to keep my job."

Ace doesn't say anything, still staring at the ceiling, and I finally give in to my feelings and go to him. He spreads his legs when I draw closer, letting me step in between them and when I rest my hands on his shoulders, he closes his eyes.

Swallows hard.

I press my face into his neck, breathing in his intoxicating scent. He smells like the ocean. Clean with the vaguest hint of salt. I stay like this for way too long, inhaling him, my head beginning to swim when he wraps me up in his thick arms and holds me close. But not crushing me to him close. More like...

Perfectly close.

Ugh, I like it. I like *him*. I've had fun spending time with him, and I firmly believed he wasn't looking for anything serious so that's why I wasn't worried about the no-dating clause included in my employment paperwork. I know Gwyneth has some suspicions about us, but I fully planned on reassuring her tomorrow that nothing is going on between me and Ace.

Then he had to go and make all of my secret dreams come true by asking me on a date. He looked so cute when he did it too. Normally, I would've said yes. Thrown all my worry aside and just agreed because what good is life if you're not taking any chances?

I'm almost positive my dad said that to me once.

Can't risk my job though. Even though I'm only like a week in, I sort of love it. I enjoy working with Eric and Gwen —it's a fun challenge, trying to get on her good side. I like editing content and creating fun clips that showcase the team in silly ways. That's what I was doing tonight when Ace texted me. Editing content and scheduling posts on Instagram. I'm having a lot of fun with this and it's going to look great on my resume someday.

"We probably shouldn't do this," he finally murmurs. "I don't want to get you fired."

"Just...let me hold you for a few minutes," I tell him, nestling closer. I feel him swallow and I turn my head slightly, dragging my lips across his skin.

He shivers, his arms tightening around my waist and he dips his head, his mouth at my ear. "You should stop if you don't want me to do something you might regret later."

"What would I regret?" What could I possibly regret when it comes to this man? I know I just turned him down but...

He has to understand I did it with extreme reluctance.

Maybe we could date later. After the football season is over? Though he probably wouldn't wait for me that long. I might not either. He could have any woman he wants and I might meet someone too.

Or maybe I won't. I don't know.

And that's the tough part about life. All of the unknowns. Sometimes I wish I had a crystal ball so I could see into the future, but then I wonder if that would just freak me out?

Probably.

"I don't know. If we keep this up, you might find yourself naked on that bed with my head buried between your thighs," he says conversationally, as if he's talking about the weather.

Now I'm the one who shivers at the vision his words put in my head. I know how he kisses. He's, very um...

Thorough.

"That would probably be a colossal mistake," I murmur when he traces the curve of my ear with his tongue.

"Right? Just imagine it." He kisses my ear. Nibbles on the lobe, his hot breath coating my skin. "Probably shouldn't admit this, but I've been dying to taste that pretty little pussy of yours, Red."

Oh...

Oh God.

Dirty talk never did much for me in the past, not that I've ever tried it with anyone. I was always too embarrassed and I've never been with a guy that I'm comfortable enough with to just...let my freak flag fly.

I have a feeling Ace is the one I could do that with. I already told him I liked it when he put his hand around my throat. He didn't even bat an eyelash. He did it again for me, knowing I liked it.

This man...he just might be my sexual unicorn.

Though I'm most likely getting ahead of myself. And I shouldn't think of him that way because this can go nowhere. We can't date.

His hand shifts up my back, and then slowly down. Over my hip. Tracing the waistband of my old sleep shorts until he slips his fingers beneath the threadbare waistband and slides them over the curve of my bare ass since I'm not wearing panties.

Lucky him. Lucky *me*.

His touch is featherlight, yet it's like a brand. Making his mark on me.

"Are you wet?" he whispers. I hold my breath as he shifts lower to check, but at the last second, he pauses. "Ah."

That's it. That's all he says.

Ah.

A whimper escapes me and I lean into him more, my forehead pressed against his jaw. I can't speak either. I just wait for him to continue touching me.

"I should stop." His fingers slide lower. Just barely. Teasing the very edge of my pussy. One nudge forward and he'd be there. Right where I want him. "I shouldn't do this. We can't see each other. And besides, this breaks all of your date rules."

He's right. I know he is. So why am I widening my stance to give him better access? And oh God, why is he taking it?

"Fuck, Red." His fingers sink into me easily because I'm freaking drenched and a soft moan sounds low in my throat when he teases my entrance, slipping just a single fingertip inside. "We. Can't. Do. This."

Those last four words out of his mouth are punctuated with his finger thrusting into my welcoming body and it feels so freaking good.

"We shouldn't," I choke out.

His hand disappears and I cry out at the loss. But he's back in an instant, diving into the front of my shorts, his fingers searching me. Teasing me. Pinching my clit and making me see stars.

"Tell me to stop," he demands, his fingers busy, the sound of my wet pussy ringing loud in my ears. It's like the most erotic thing I've ever heard and I sink my teeth into my lower lip, unable to take it much longer.

"Red. Baby." His thumb strums my clit, his other hand circling around my chin, lifting my face to his. His expression is stormy, his eyes dark and turbulent as he watches me slowly fall apart. "Make me stop."

He stares into my eyes and I can't look away. And when his hand slides down from my chin to curl around my throat, he thrusts two fingers deep into me, his thumb pressing against my clit, rubbing it in tiny, quick circles. His fingers tightening around my neck, he rests his cheek next to mine, his lips at my ear as he whispers, "You're close, baby. Come for me."

My climax hits me hard, going on and on. Wave after wave of pleasure sweeps over me, leaving me breathless. Mindless.

I swear to God I might even black out for a second.

When I come to my senses, I'm panting, little whimpers falling from my lips, his fingers still thrusting into my pussy, his other hand still clamped around my neck. I don't even know how I'm still standing. My legs are shaking and my skin is hot. Itchy.

He lets go of me. The moment he removes his hand from my neck and the other hand from my shorts, I'm stripping, my movements jerky. Tearing off my tank and tossing it over my shoulder. Shimmying out of my shorts and kicking them aside. All while Ace watches me with lust-filled eyes, his broad chest rising and falling. Rising and falling. His fingers flexing like he's dying to touch me.

"What are you doing?" he asks incredulously.

"Getting naked." I basically tackle him, climb the man like a tree and he grabs hold of me, his hands lifting my ass as I wrap my legs around his hips. Our mouths connect and he turns me away from the desk, carrying me over to the bed, where he gently sets me on the mattress, leaving me alone on the bed as he stands by the side of it.

I prop myself up on my elbows to watch him, my eyes wandering over him greedily, drinking him in, lingering on the tent in his freaking track pants. Something pulses low in my belly and I wait for him to strip. To at least join me on the bed but...

He doesn't.

"What are you waiting for?" I don't recognize the sultry tone of my voice. The way I spread my legs so he can see everything I've got isn't familiar either.

His hot gaze lands on the spot between my thighs and he rubs at the corner of his mouth with his thumb, his tongue sneaking out for a quick lick. The same thumb he used to rub my clit only moments ago. He's tasting me. I know he is.

Oh my God I swear my pussy just got wetter if that's even possible.

"I should go," he murmurs, his gaze going to the closed door.

I sit up, slapping my palms against the comforter beneath me. "No, you shouldn't."

"You said so yourself that we can't date. And I—I really want to date you, Ruby." His gaze is still stuck on my pussy, so it's like he's talking to it instead of me.

"Maybe you could date me only for tonight?" I rest my

hand on my lower belly, propping myself up on the other hand and spreading my legs open once again. "Just for a little bit?"

His gaze tracks my every movement as my fingers go lower, until I'm touching myself between my thighs. Oh God, I am really wet. And my skin is so sensitive—as if it's electrified. I tentatively brush my fingers against my clit, tilting my head back and closing my eyes, getting lost in the sensations my own fingers are bringing me.

It helps, knowing he's watching my every move.

"I don't know." His voice is rough and he clears his throat. "It feels all sorts of wrong. You told me no, baby. And I will never make a woman do something she doesn't want to do."

The tone of his voice. His word choice. It's all a turn-on, making me hotter. Making me need him more.

I open my eyes and watch him, my fingers still stroking, my nipples so hard they freaking ache for him. His talented mouth. I swear the bulge in his pants is bigger than before and I stare at it, watching as it twitches.

Ace wants me. And I want him.

So why won't he do anything about it?

22

ACE

Fuck me, she's spread out for me like a present, her slender fingers stroking her pussy. Showing me exactly how she likes it. I already know a few things. The hand around the throat thing is hot. I clamped my fingers round her neck earlier and rubbed her sweet little clit for only a couple of minutes and had her going off like a fucking firecracker.

I want to make her do that again but...

She said no to my asking her on a date. She signed some damn agreement that said she can't see anyone on the football team and fuck me, isn't that just my luck?

The job means a lot to her. I can tell. And I won't ask her to choose me over her internship because not only is that bullshit, I can't even guarantee that whatever this is between us will work.

But man, we're hot together. I feel like I could come in my pants just from watching her. There's a light sheen of sweat coating her skin and her hair is a sexy mess. Her cheeks and chest are flushed pink and her nipples are stiff little points just begging for my mouth. And her pussy...

She's so fucking wet, it's all I can hear and see. And when she slides a finger inside of herself, that little gasp escaping her?

Damn it, I'm only a man. And I can only take so much.

I lunge across the bed, reaching for her, my hands clamping onto her hips, pinning her down. Her thighs fall open and I rest in between them, nudging her hand aside with my face just before I stick my tongue out and lick her cunt.

Her hands immediately land on top of my head, guiding me. Holding me to her like I'm going to leave, but she has nothing to worry about.

I'm going nowhere.

I eat at her pussy like I'm fucking starving. Licking and sucking every single part of her, teasing her clit with the tip of my tongue just before I draw it in between my lips and suck it. She bows off the bed, her breaths coming in short, hard pants and I can feel the bit of flesh pulsate against my tongue.

She's already close, and I like this about her. How responsive she is. A little bit sweet, a lot filthy.

Deciding I should help her get even closer, I release my hold on her left hip and slide my index finger along her folds before I push it inside her, steadily fucking her with it while I continue to focus on her clit with my mouth. She strains beneath me, her hips lifting, smashing her pussy against my face and I crack open my eyes to find her watching me, an almost frantic look on her face.

I pull away from her, still fucking her with my index finger. "You like this?"

She nods, not speaking.

"Use your words, pretty girl."

"I love it," she breathes and I smile, increasing my pace.

Adding another finger.

My cock is aching, pressed up against the mattress and dying to break free but this is all about her still. I might get my chance. And then again, I might not, but we'll see.

I'm enjoying this moment though.

Enjoying *her*.

"Want me to lick your clit again?"

"Please," she whispers.

"Such a polite girl." I dip my head and stick my tongue out, giving her swollen clit an exaggerated lick, putting on a show just for her. A keening cry slips past her lips and when I glance up at her again, she's got her head thrown back, her tits rising and falling, her nipples pointed at the ceiling.

Forgot to lick them, damn it. Will have to do that another time.

If I get the chance.

I circle her clit with my tongue at the same time I remove my fingers from her pussy, pausing long enough for her to start begging.

"*Pleaseohpleasedon'tstop.*"

"Lift your hips." She does as I ask and I slip my hands under her, gripping her ass, kneading her soft flesh. "Come on. Get 'em higher. Get yourself all over my mouth, Red."

She gives in to her baser needs and does as I ask, rubbing her pussy all over my mouth and chin, her upper body bent forward, her hand coming around the back of my head, holding me to her. I stare at her as I lick her everywhere I can reach, my fingers slipping toward her ass crack, sliding deeper, touching her in a forbidden place—

"Oh *fuck*." The curse falls from her lips just as she throws her head back, her body trembling with the force of her orgasm. Her pussy throbs against my mouth again and again and I continue licking her. Searching her. Teasing her clit.

Until she's pushing me away, her hands in my face, her legs swinging to the side, bent at the knee as I rise away from her. I rub the back of my hand across my mouth, breathing in her musky scent and fuck, the woman is sexy as hell, even all curled up in a ball and mumbling nonsense to herself.

She remains like that for a while and I reach inside my pants, trying to readjust my aching dick. Fuck, I'm dying to come but I don't—

"Ace." Her soft, seductive voice wraps all around me, making my skin tingle and I realize she's watching me. "Are you...are you jerking off?"

My hand stills in my pants, I feel caught. I *am* caught. "I, uh, was readjusting my—"

"Come here. I want to help you." She rises on her knees, crooking her finger and like a man possessed, I go to the side of the bed that's closest to her, not sure what she wants me to do.

When I'm close enough, she's reaching for my pants, shoving them down my legs along with my boxer briefs, my cock springing free. It bobs in her face and I kick my clothes off, nearly toppling over I'm so fucking excited.

"God, you're big." Her wide eyes shift upward to stare into mine and I wrap my fingers around my shaft, giving it a firm stroke.

"You can handle it," I tell her.

Fuck, I'm hopeful.

She watches me as I continue to stroke my cock in front her, her lips parted, her tongue darting out to touch her upper lip. I'm sweating, my pace increasing, getting myself there way too soon, so I slow down. Squeeze just the tip, a drop of precum pearling in the slit.

Without warning, she leans forward, her tongue sneaking out to lick at the precum and I groan so loud, I worry I might've woken up the neighbors.

"Shh," she warns, and I nod once, taking a deep breath between my teeth, my stomach muscles tightening.

Fuck, her mouth feels good on my dick.

Ruby bats my hand away and curls her fingers around the base, licking at the tip of my cock like it's her favorite ice cream treat. I watch her, sliding both of my hands into her hair and pulling it back from her beautiful face so I can watch the show. The head of my cock disappears into her mouth and I thrust my hips a little, sending it deeper.

Making her moan.

I thrust again, testing her and she gags a little, the sound such a fucking turn-on.

Jesus, what's wrong with me? I actually want to make her choke on my dick?

Seriously?

Seriously.

She pulls me out of her mouth and licks at my shaft, her tongue tracing the veins, circling around the head before she draws me back into her mouth. Her tits sway with the movement, her hot little body on total display only for me, and I reach behind my head for the neck of my shirt, yanking it off with one swift jerk because I want to be as naked as she is.

Her eyes widen as she stares at my chest, her mouth full of my dick and damn it, if I had my phone on me, I would take a picture of this.

It's a moment I want documented forever.

I forget all about taking photos when she starts to suck

my cock in earnest. She sucks me deep, her fingers squeezing the base of my shaft, her cheeks hollowing out. I pump my hips, pulling almost all the way out before I thrust back in and she takes it like a champ. The muscles in her neck relax and the head of my cock bumps against the back of her throat once. Twice.

Swearing, I pull out, her hand falling away, her expression disappointed. "What are you doing?"

"I wanna come on your tits." She has perfect ones and fuck, I'm so goddamn close, I'm done with the teasing. The pressure is building.

I just need to come.

"Okay," she agrees without any hesitation, and I realize that I like that about her. She's into whatever I suggest, no questions asked. No doubt or any funny looks.

Always agreeable. Even eager. Like we're on the same track.

"Come here." I pull her back onto the bed and she's lying on the mattress, her legs spread and me kneeling in between them. I eat up her body with my gaze, tracking her smooth, flushed skin, those pretty hard nipples and slender arms and legs.

She gathers her hair up in her hands and arches her back, her chest thrusting forward as she bends her knees and plants her feet on the mattress. Reminding me of a living, breathing sex goddess, on total display and ready for me.

I close my eyes for only a moment and swallow hard, my self-control slipping away. All it takes is a couple of squeezes, my gaze locked on her pretty naked body, and that familiar sensation builds at the base of my spine. The depths of my balls.

194   MONICA MURPHY

Ruby cups her tits in her hands, pushing them together, giving me the best visual and I'm done for.

"Oh God," I choke out, that first spurt of cum shooting from my cock and landing dead center, dripping in her cleavage. "Fuck, Red."

She scoots closer, another splatter of cum landing on her left breast, sliding down her skin to her nipple. I groan, trying to squeeze out every last drop and when I'm finally done, I fall onto the bed on my side, pleased when she turns and lies on her side too, directly across from me.

I'm breathing hard, and I close my eyes, focusing on calming my racing heart. Goddamn, that was good. I'm still shivering, the remnants of my orgasm lingering, and when I open my eyes, I find Ruby watching me, a look of fascination on her beautiful face.

My cum dripping all over her chest.

Reaching out, I dip my fingers in it, smearing it all over her body. Her breasts. Coating her nipples with it. An unfamiliar feeling sweeps over me, leaving me breathing deep, my head swimming. One single word beating like a drum in my brain.

Mine. Mine. Mine.

But she can't be mine. We're not supposed to do this.

Maybe that's why this experience was so fuckin' hot.

23

RUBY

I walk across campus the next morning, feeling like a new woman. A completely transformed human. All of my senses are heightened, like I'm ultra-aware of everything going on around me. The scents, the sounds, the color of the sky, the tinkling of someone's laughter, the annoying blare of a car alarm in the parking lot—it's all intensified.

I want to throw my arms out and do slow circles in the middle of the quad, while staring at the bright blue sky. I want to shout to the world that I just had the most transformative sexual experience of my entire life last night...

And we haven't even had actual sex yet.

A secret smile plays upon my lips when I remember how he came all over my chest. One of my secret fantasies come to life. I've seen this sort of thing on porn, but never really thought I could ask a guy, *hey would you mind coming on me instead of inside me?*

Yeah, that doesn't feel like a normal conversation for me. And it's not like I have lots of guys *literally* coming inside me. The men I've been with—all three of them—they always wore a condom. I'm a big supporter of safe sex because I'm not stupid. One, I don't want a sexually transmitted disease, and two, I don't want to get pregnant.

God no.

When Ace said he wanted to come on my tits, I agreed immediately because oh my God, that's like the hottest thing alive. The look on his face when that first spurt hit me. The way he smeared it all over my skin afterward. It felt like he was branding me for real. Claiming me... Rubbing his scent all over me so no one else will make a move.

A shiver steals through me at the memory.

My day is normal. I go to class. I eat lunch with Natalie, who digs me for details about what happened with Ace last night. I told her as little about it as I possibly could, still holding on to the moment myself, wanting to savor it. The things he said, how he looked at me, how he let me rub my pussy all over his face. Hot. All of it.

Every single moment.

Reality crashes down upon me when I walk into the social media office, remembering that one part of our conversation from last night that I purposely pushed from my memory.

How I signed the contract that states I can't date anyone from the football team.

Figures that I'd get my dream job on campus and meet my dream guy at the same time, and he's on the football team. Always told myself I should avoid football players and I should've listened to my own warning.

Even crazier? It hasn't been that long since I've reconnected with him. How do I really know he's my dream guy anyway? Because he doesn't hesitate to wrap his big hand around my throat and come all over my chest? That's just surface stuff.

Hot, sexual surface stuff, but there's not much depth in my reasons for liking him.

Is there?

Oh God, I don't even know what to think anymore.

Within minutes of my arriving at the office, we're out on the football field, Eric filming from the sidelines, while Gwyneth and I have a quick brainstorming sesh. My gaze strays to Ace every few seconds, like I can't help myself, my entire body going warm when our gazes meet, which is often.

Too often.

"What is going on with you two?" Gwen asks after about the twentieth time Ace and me look at each other.

"What?" I turn to her, flustered.

"You and Ace." She shifts closer and her voice lowers. "You two aren't...seeing each other, are you?"

If seeing each other means we got naked with each other less than twenty-four hours ago, then yes. We are definitely seeing each other. Allllll of each other.

God, his body is unreal.

"No way," I lie, my voice scratchy. I clear my throat. Shake my head and shrug at the same time, hoping I'm playing it off. "I mean, he's gorgeous but—"

"But you can't see him," she finishes for me, her expression serious. Her expression is always serious, though it's a little extra right now. "I warned you about this."

"Chill. I have no interest in Ace Townsend," I say with as much sincerity as I can muster.

Since when did I become such a skilled liar?

"Good. Because it always ends up getting weird," Gwyneth says with the authority of a woman who's never been interested in an athlete in her life. I've sounded just like that over the years, firmly convinced I didn't want another football player in my life.

Don't I have enough? God, all of that competitive alpha male testosterone in my family tree is positively overwhelming sometimes.

"Did something happen beyond the girl you had on the team last season who would always chase after the players?" I ask, curious. I can't imagine she's the only reason they instilled that clause in the agreement.

"Oh yeah," Gwyneth says, her eyes going wide. "You don't know the story?"

Unease creeps over me. "What story?"

Gwen glances around like she's making sure no one is paying attention to us before she leans in closer, her voice going low. "A few years ago, there was a woman on the baseball social media team—this was before TikTok and Reels really took off—anyway, she got involved with a star player. They were in this super serious relationship and she followed the team to all of their games. For her job and because he was her boyfriend, but no big deal, right? They were in love. Well, she caught him cheating on her, like literally caught him and took photos and everything."

My stomach cramps. "Oh God."

"Yeah, it was awful. But it's what she did with those photos that sent the athletic department over the edge."

"What happened?"

"She posted everything on the baseball team's social media channels. Like, photos of him in bed with the girl. Videos. Then she posted naked selfies he sent her. His gargantuan penis was all over the baseball team's Facebook page for almost twenty-four hours. No one had the log in but her because she changed it. It was awful."

"Whoa." The humiliation that guy must've felt. I can't even imagine.

"Yeah, whoa." Gwen nods, her gaze shifting to the team. "I know they're all attractive and confident. I get the allure, I really do. I find them intimidating so that's why I avoid them, but you? You fit right in with those guys."

"Is that a compliment?" I'm half joking, but sometimes it's hard to tell with Gwen.

"It is. You're used to those types of guys, thanks to your family. I can see why you're drawn to Ace. He's also incredibly charming."

My skin warms as I study him. Charming in the best way. The twinkling eyes and the easy smiles and the growly words in my ear...

"But untouchable to us. If anyone in the athletic department found out you were dating a football player? You'd lose your job, no question," Gwen says.

I don't want to lose my job. I love it. I like Ace a lot, but in this very moment, I think I like my job more. It will help my future, guaranteed.

Messing around with Ace? There are no guarantees in that. He might forget all about me next week. Hell, it could happen tomorrow. He already knows I can't see him, thanks to the work agreement I have with the athletic department.

I can't risk it.

"But you have to avoid him like the plague," Gwen finishes, making me laugh.

My laughter dies quick when I see the way he's watching me. His blue eyes are heated and I can tell he's looking at me like he can see right through my clothing, remembering the way I look naked with vivid detail.

I return his stare, thinking the same exact thing and I realize...

This is going to be really difficult, avoiding Ace Townsend. Worse?

I don't want to avoid him.

Not even a little bit.

"I've made a decision," I announce when I walk into the apartment and see Natalie lounging on the couch, a pillow in her lap and her laptop sitting on top of it.

She glances up from her screen for a moment, her fingers still moving across the keyboard. "What's your decision?"

"I'm going on a man ban."

Her fingers stop typing and she's staring hard at me, her head tilted to the side. "Excuse me?"

I shut the door behind me and lock it, leaning against it with a sigh. "A man ban."

"An Ace Townsend ban?" she corrects.

"That too," I agree, pushing away from the door, dropping my backpack on the floor before I flop onto the couch next to her. "I can't see him anymore."

"Says who?"

"The entire athletic department at Colorado University." I go on to explain the story Gwen told me earlier, Natalie nodding again and again the deeper I get into it.

"I remember hearing about this," she finally says, interrupting me. "My sister went here when it happened. She knew that girl. Her name is Annette and she's positively unhinged."

I'm frowning. "What do you mean?"

"She was already one of those crazy types, you know what I mean? Oh, I hate saying that. I don't want to slot her in the 'she was the typical psycho girlfriend' category, but she kind of was." Nat winces. "He'd been trying to break it off with her for a while and he realized quickly she wasn't getting it. So he...hooked up with another girl on purpose to send the message loud and clear that he was done with her."

"That's horrible." I can't fathom the idea of a guy doing that to me. I imagine walking in on Ace hooking up with another girl. Naked with another girl.

I'd probably want to rip his balls off.

"Uh huh. Well, it worked too much in his favor. She went completely overboard in her revenge toward him. The naked posts on Facebook, oh my God. What a nightmare. Not just for the guy being exposed, but the entire university took a hit. It was a bad take for a lot of people, and administration has worked hard ever since to make everyone forget it happened. Plus, they put all sorts of new rules into place, which makes sense."

"What happened to her?" I ask, curious.

"Oh, she was expelled, and that *never* happens," Natalie answers. "She tried to sue the school, but it didn't work. They threatened her with a countersuit and she backed off."

"What about the guy?"

Natalie sighs. "He's still playing in the MLB."

"WHAT?" I pull my phone out of my pocket and thrust it toward her. "He's a professional now? So his life continued on unscathed?"

Nat nods. "Of course, it did."

That's always the way, I swear. "Find his profile for me."

She does within seconds and we check out his photos. He's hot. Not lose your mind and post naked photos on the internet so you can ruin your life forever hot, but hot enough. And he's married. With a baby.

"They're a cute family." I glance up at Natalie. "What about her?"

"What about her? You mean Annette?"

I nod.

"Oh. Well, last I heard from my sister, she's working at the Walmart on the other side of town."

"No freaking way."

"It's true! She kind of went through a rough patch, obviously. She had a hard time coming back from this."

"I can only assume."

"Right? Anyway. It was tough. I'm guessing it's still tough. All because she dated a baseball player."

"That would never happen to me," I say firmly.

"Of course, it won't," Natalie says. "You're not allowed to date athletes. You'll never get the chance to let it happen to you."

Ugh. She has a point.

"Why are you on a man ban anyway?"

Another sigh leaves me and I lean back against the couch, staring up at the ceiling. "If I can't have Ace Townsend, I don't want anyone else. At least through the football season, you know?"

"That could go on until the end of the year," Nat points out.

A groan escapes. "Don't remind me."

"Is he that good?"

I turn my head in her direction, staring her down for a moment. "He is that good, Nat."

"I want deets."

"No way."

"Come on. You're holding out on me."

"And I will continue to hold out on you because I want to keep it to myself for just a little while longer."

Natalie studies me, slowly shaking her head. "He must have a magical dick."

I burst out laughing. "He does."

He's my every freaking dream come true.

Too bad he's off limits.

24

ACE

For the next two longest weeks of my goddamned life, I do my best to avoid Ruby Maguire as much as possible. I'm not a rude asshole toward her or anything like that, but I keep my distance. Try to remain respectful. We play our first home game Saturday afternoon and crush our opponents. It was fucking awesome. I went out later that night and we celebrated at Logan's like we usually do and I had a great time with my teammates. My friends. We shut that shit down and ended up back at someone's apartment, where I got even more shitfaced and turned down every single girl who approached me.

Literally every one of them.

The guys asked me if I was sick. Derek put his hand to my forehead and everything, the asshole. I'm not sick. Unless what I'm feeling for Ruby is some sort of disease.

Then I'm ill as fuck.

Same thing, different day, the following week. I'm busy with school and practice and strength training and keeping my elbow on ice because it's been hurting like a bitch lately.

Play the game on Saturday—gain another win—celebrate at Logan's again. Turn down girls again.

It's been over two weeks since I messed around with Ruby and I haven't touched another girl. Thought about another girl. All I can think about is her. Her softly panting breaths in my ear. The sounds she makes when she's coming. The flush that coats her skin when she's aroused. The scent of her pussy. How wet she gets. How delicious she tastes.

Everywhere.

I'm a man obsessed and I see her almost every single day.

Every. Single. Day.

It's wearing on me. I've jacked off so much I'm pretty sure I have calluses on my palm. Yet it doesn't ease the incessant need building within me. The need for more Ruby.

Any way I can get her.

She's avoiding me too. I can tell. She keeps her distance but isn't cold or unfriendly. Nah, that's what makes it worse. She flashes these pretty little smiles my way every time our gazes connect, which twists my gut into knots. The need to talk to her is strong. The urge to touch her is even stronger.

But I keep my distance because I am a man of my word and I'm not about to get her into trouble. Or get myself into trouble. Just having her nearby while I practice is good enough. Catching her gaze track my every move during practice?

Even better.

It's a Thursday night and I'm at a bar that's not Logan's because I'm looking for a change of scenery. I came with Javier and Evan because we've grown closer and I like the way they're not constantly looking for a woman to fuck. Javier is happily taken and completely in love with his girlfriend. Evan isn't a complete manwhore, looking to get laid all the time, so I appreciate that about him. And then there's me.

Holding out for a woman I technically can't have until the end of the season.

I'm laying off the drinking too. Trying to keep a clear head and healthy body and my coaches, trainer and nutritionist are all praising me for staying on track. They have no clue I've been working out so much lately because I'm trying to work off all of the sexual frustration I've been dealing with.

It's a lot.

We're at a newer place downtown called Dirty Habit and it's really cool. Lots of exposed brick and mood lighting. Plenty of seating and a giant bar counter with a variety of beers on tap. I'm only sipping on one beer because I'm the designated driver tonight and not in the mood to get drunk.

The place isn't busy like Logan's, but there's a steady stream of people and it fills up quickly. To the point that I'm glad we got here when we did and nabbed a table before they all filled up.

Women drift over to our table and we chat them up. Always polite, though Javier rarely looks up from his phone when they're talking to us. Almost like he's afraid of them. I'm not interested in any of them, but I know I have to at least be polite. Gotta perform for the fans—and the fangirls.

"What's your deal?" I ask Javier after yet another group of women stop by our table and he barely looks at them.

He sets his phone on the table, sending us a look that's hard to read. "Just wait until you're in a serious relationship. You won't want to look at a single female who comes near you."

"And why not? Shouldn't your girlfriend feel confident and trust you completely?"

"My girl is the jealous type." He shrugs. "I can't even be friends with a woman. She gets all freaked out, especially since we're in a long-distance relationship."

"I guess I can see that," I say, thinking of Ruby. As usual.

Is she the jealous type? Would she be pissed if I talked to women all the time? I'm doing it right now and not a single one of them piques my interest. There was a blonde who came to our table earlier. She was cute and friendly and she had a great body. I notice these things, can appreciate these things, but am I interested in her?

No. I'm not. I'm not even with Ruby, yet she's all I can think about.

Grabbing my beer, I drain the last of the alcohol, setting it down extra hard, frustration rippling through me. Javier and Evan are involved in their own conversation and I scowl at the crowd filling the bar, hating how grumpy I feel.

I think I need to get laid. At the very least, kiss a pretty woman.

But there's only one woman I want to kiss.

"Maybe I should order another beer," I announce, knowing without a doubt that it's a terrible idea.

"I thought you were our DD," Evan says.

"Oh, I am." I push my empty beer away from me, tipping it over and causing it to roll across the table. Javier hops up from his chair and grabs it before it falls to the floor, where it most likely would've shattered. "Thanks, man."

"You're moody lately," Evan says, nudging me in the ribs. "What's your problem?"

Women. A woman. A beautiful blonde woman with green eyes and the best smile you've ever seen. Who gasps and moans whenever I touch her. Who's got the prettiest, tastiest pussy out of any of the women at this place. A pussy I haven't even fully fucked yet, and here I am, thinking about it.

Fantasizing about it.

Wanting it.

Fuck, I want her.

As if I conjured her up in my own mind, she magically appears in this bar. What are the odds? I shake my head and close my eyes for a moment, telling myself I'm just seeing things, but when I open my eyes again, there she still is, standing in front of the entrance, her roommate Natalie right by her side and a few other unfamiliar women standing behind them.

Huh.

I grab the empty beer bottle that Javier deposited in front of me once more and tip it to my lips, disappointed it's empty. "I definitely need another beer. Think I'll go get one."

Before either of them can get a full sentence out, I'm out of my chair and headed toward the crowded bar, my gaze scanning the room since I lost sight of Ruby's blonde hair. I edge my way through the crowd and lean against the counter, waiting for the bartender to acknowledge me, still on the lookout for my newfound favorite thing.

Favorite person, not thing.

Ruby.

"Yo, Ace Townsend," the bartender greets me. "How are you, man? Welcome to Dirty Habits."

"Thank you." I hold out my hand to the guy who's about my age, maybe a little older, and he gives me a fist bump. "This place is pretty cool."

"Yeah? Thanks. My dad owns it." He props his forearm on the bar, smiling at me. "Played a great game last weekend."

"Thank you."

"Worried about this Saturday?" The bartender's eyebrows shoot up.

We're playing against one of our biggest rivals, and it's going to be a tough one. "Can't get too worked up over it."

"You've got this in the bag." He pushes away from the counter, pointing his fingers at me. "What can I get you?"

I order another beer, which he insists is on the house, so I take it, gripping the bottle in my hand as I turn to glance around the room, searching for Ruby.

Still can't find her.

I keep walking, my stride slow as I smile and nod at people I pass by. A group of women stop me, all of them surrounding me with flirtatious smiles and exaggerated giggles, some of them bold enough to touch me.

"You look so good out on the field, Ace!" one of them squeals, her hand landing on my forearm and giving it a squeeze.

"Hey thanks." I smile at her and take a sip from my beer.

She flutters her lashes at me. They're long and thick and definitely fake, and I wonder how she can keep her eyelids open. "I'm coming to this Saturday's game too."

"Can't wait to see you there." I lift my beer toward her, hating that I just said that. I don't mean a word of it and I probably got her hopes up.

Her eyes flash. They're dark brown and currently gobbling me up. "I'll make a sign for you."

"Okay." I don't know how to respond to that.

She scoots closer, the overwhelming scent of her perfume washing over me, making me want to sneeze. "I think you're the hottest guy out on that field."

My chuckle is nervous, when normally this sort of thing doesn't bother me. "Oh yeah?"

"Definitely." She nods, her hand back on my arm. "Want to go somewhere more private?"

"Right now?"

Her smile is knowing. "Yes, of course, right now."

"Let's ease up a little bit there, sweetheart. Get to know each other better first."

The disappointment on her face is obvious. "Are you turning me down?"

"Are you trying to hit on me?" I take another sip of my beer. "Let me at least finish my drink."

Her smile is back, bigger this time. "And then you'll leave with me?"

I don't plan on going anywhere with this chick. I need to be honest with her.

"You know what?" When she nods eagerly, I continue, "Probably not."

Her face falls. "Oh."

"Yeah." I take another swig. A bigger one this time. "Oh."

She screws her face up, her lips puckered into an unattractive pout. "You're kind of a dick."

"And you're kind of pushy." I tip my bottle toward her. "Better luck next time."

"Men," she practically huffs out before she turns on her heel and stalks away.

I watch her leave, faintly amused, contemplating if I should drain my beer and grab another one when I catch a familiar scent. Hear a familiar voice.

"Pissed off another one, huh, Townsend?"

The relief at hearing Ruby's teasing makes my knees fucking wobble, which never happens. I glance to my right to find her standing there, looking hot as fuck because it doesn't matter what she's wearing or how much makeup she has on her face or whether her hair is curled or not.

In my eyes, Ruby is hot as fuck no matter what.

"She was—a lot," I tell Ruby, staring into her green eyes a little too long.

Amusement dances in her gaze. "Came on to you too strong?"

"Yeah." I can't stop staring at her. She's so fucking pretty. The shirt she's wearing is tight and cropped, showing off that toned stomach of hers, and she's got on a pair of jeans that are kind of baggy, but I know how slender those legs are. The gentle flare of her hips. The dip of her waist. The curve of her perfect ass.

Damn it, I've got it so bad for this woman. Does she even know? Understand the hold she has on me?

"You like to chase?" she asks, her sweet voice pulling me from my thoughts.

Again, I decide to be honest.

"I like blondes—specifically one." I shift closer to her, dipping my head so my mouth is at her ear. "With a sweet pussy and my cum dripping all over her tits."

Her eyes go wide when I pull away and I wonder if I took it too far. She blinks at me, quiet for way too long, and I study her, my gut starting to churn.

Then she reaches out and rests her hand on my arm, just like the pushy girl did only a few minutes before. The moment her fingers touch my skin, it's like an electric current is running through my veins and straight to my dick, making it stand at attention.

"Meet me in the women's bathroom in five minutes," she murmurs, before she turns.

And walks away.

25

RUBY

My heart is racing as I leave Ace behind and I don't look back. It's like I can't. But I can definitely feel his eyes on me, hot and heavy, watching my every move. My legs are shaking as I push my way through the crowded room and when I finally spot the bathroom, I practically run inside.

The room is massive and dark. The stalls are large, with a single light pendant hanging above each one. The bulbs cast a warm, golden glow, but it's still dim in here.

Perfect.

I go to one of the sinks and wash my trembling hands, sudsing them up with lots of soap before I rinse them. Trying to kill time before Ace joins me.

God, he better join me.

A toilet flushes and a woman comes out of the stall and smiles at me, washing her hands quickly before she dashes out, the door slamming behind her. I wait by the sink, noting how silent the room is, and I glance around.

I peek under the stalls.

I'm the only one in here.

Thank God.

I didn't even consider what would happen if there were other women in here and Ace just strutted in. His presence would cause a commotion. Some women might freak out. Some might demand he leave.

Fear squeezes my stomach at the thought. Why did I believe this was a good idea again? We probably won't be able to make this work. And I don't even know what I was expecting, asking him to meet me in the bathroom.

I do know what he whispered into my ear practically turned me inside out, it was so hot. Referencing what happened the last time we were alone together. Like he still thinks about it.

Like he still thinks about *me*.

This man is going to destroy me, I just know it. And I'm going to enjoy every single second of his destruction too.

The door suddenly swings open, Ace standing there, his gaze finding mine immediately. We stare at each other from across the cavernous bathroom, neither of us speaking a word. He has no right to look as gorgeous as he does in the simplest outfit. A pair of jeans and a white T-shirt that clings to his chest and arms, emphasizing his muscles. It's been what...two weeks since our last moment together? And I swear he's bulkier than he was before.

My hands tingle at the opportunity to touch him.

"Are we the only ones in here?" he asks, his deep voice settling right between my legs, making me throb.

I nod, my voice gone.

He starts heading toward me, his steps hurried, his hands reaching. Landing on my waist, steering me backward, until my butt hits a stall door and it slaps open. We're crowded into the stall in mere seconds, the lock sliding into place, Ace turning me so my back is pressed against the wall and he's directly in front of me. So close, his warmth seeps into my body, making me hot.

For him.

"I missed you," he murmurs, just before he dips his head and nuzzles my neck with his nose.

I close my eyes, my mouth falling open at that first contact of his skin on mine. The fact he admitted that he missed me. I would've never said that out loud. I still haven't. But he confessed his feelings without hesitation and I...

I love that.

"We've seen each other almost every day," I remind him, setting my hands on his very broad, very hard shoulders.

"It's not the same as touching you." His lips move against my neck, a shuddery breath escaping me. "Having you close to me."

His hands slide upwards, along my rib cage, pausing right under my breasts, his thumbs pressing into my skin. As usual, I'm not wearing a bra. I hate them and he knows it and he doesn't even hesitate.

Within seconds, he's fully cupping them, kneading my flesh, his thumbs rubbing back and forth across my nipples, making me want to cry out. Instead, I bite my lower lip, a soft moan sounding from behind my teeth when he drags his hot, wet mouth down my neck.

"You feel so good, Red. It's been way too long," he mutters against my cheek, kissing me there. It's a sweet gesture, yet there's nothing sweet about the way he's touching me. His hot body pressed against mine, his knee nudging between my legs. I spread my thighs, allowing him access, and the next thing I know, his mouth is hovering above mine, his knee pushed firmly against that needy spot between my thighs, making me see stars.

Already. That's all it takes. A few rushed minutes in a bathroom stall and I'm on the edge of coming.

"We need to make this quick," he whispers against my lips. "Someone might catch us."

I would die if someone caught us. I would also die if he decides to put a stop to the hottest encounter of my life.

"Let's make it quick then," I encourage, my voice soft. I run my hands down his chest slowly, savoring the hard muscles beneath his smooth, hot skin. His body is absolute perfection and if I could, I'd yank his shirt up and stare at him for a little bit.

But I don't think we have enough time.

He slips his hands down to my ass, lifting me up and I go with him, my legs wrapping around him as I tilt my hips forward, brushing against the bulge in his jeans. He's hard and huge and I wrap my arms around his neck, my mouth finding his.

The kiss is instantly hot. A tangle of tongues and clash of teeth. Wet, greedy lips and warm puffs of air. He groans. I whimper. He slides his fingers in my hair, curling it around his fist. I shove my hands in his hair and tug, making him growl.

The sound leaves me weak and I'm grateful he's got me pinned against the door or else I'd probably be on the floor.

We kiss and kiss, until my jaw aches and my lips feel raw. He's thrusting against me, nice and slow, driving me out of my mind and when the bathroom door suddenly slams open, a bunch of giggly women entering the room, Ace goes still.

I crack my eyes open to find him watching me. He shifts away from me, our gazes still connected, his hand settling over my mouth, fingers clamping tightly to silence me.

A whimper sounds beneath his hand and his expression

becomes stern. I can practically read in his gaze that he's telling me to be quiet. I must be really fucked up because I can't stop thinking how sexy this is. How he's got his hand over my mouth and his knee pressed against the seam of my jeans. He applies more pressure, making my clit pulsate, and I close my eyes, lost to the sensations this gorgeous, dominating man is giving me.

I feel him lean in close, his cheek pressed to mine as he whispers in my ear, "You're being too noisy."

I say nothing in response as he pulls away from me slightly. His hand still covers my mouth, his knee still firmly against my crotch, his other hand resting on my side, his fingers slipping beneath the hem of my cropped shirt. He surrounds me, leaving me breathless and dizzy and filled with the need to consume him just like he consumes me.

God this man. He's overwhelming in the absolute best way.

The women are chatting so loudly, it sounds like there are at least twenty of them in the room, though it's probably not even ten. A few of them enter the stalls. Others remain at the sinks, checking themselves in the mirror, I'm sure. Applying lipstick and gossiping about the night.

"Saw Ace here," one of them says.

Ace's gaze turns amused. A little curious.

"He's so hot," another one adds.

"He rejected me," says yet another one.

Ace's eyebrows shoot up at that statement.

"Girl, he doesn't know what he's missing."

"That's what I thought. He'll regret turning me down."

He shakes his head, chuckling. Removes his hand from my mouth so he can kiss me.

And he doesn't stop. He keeps kissing me, his hand dropping to the front of my jeans, fingers fumbling over the button and the zipper. He drops his knee too, disappointment crashing inside me, replaced by total euphoria when he slips his hand into the front of my damp panties, rubbing my clit.

I don't even know how we're making this work, but we are. He's getting me off with his talented fingers, his wicked mouth and sweeping tongue. The women being on the other side of the stall only makes it hotter. That we're doing this in secret. That anyone could discover us.

He rubs me harder. Faster. I can't catch my breath. Can't focus, can't even think. All I can do is feel, the sensations radiating through my veins, sparking my blood. I thump the back of my head against the stall door and close my eyes, that familiar feeling building within me.

I'm close. Like he knows it, he slows his pace, his fingers sliding up and down my pussy, just as he pushes one inside me, his thumb resting against my clit.

It's sweet torture, what he's doing to me. How delicious it feels. How he's driving me out of my mind. One by one the women eventually leave the bathroom, and it's surprising to me, how the place empties out so quickly that we're the only ones left. This would never happen at Logan's. The bathroom is always busy.

"Finally," he mutters against my lips, just as his hand becomes busier. Bringing me to the brink. Leaving me hanging there until I fall over the edge, my body shaking.

His mouth lands on mine the moment the orgasm hits me, his lips swallowing my cries, my moans. I cling to him, riding out the orgasm, riding his freaking hand, and when the trembling finally subsides, I've got my face buried against his neck, my arms around his shoulders, my hands buried in his hair yet again.

"Fuck, you're so hot, Red," he murmurs against my

forehead before he kisses it. He removes his hand from my still throbbing pussy, tugging the zipper up, though he's not quite able to close it. "I should go."

He carefully sets me on my feet, smoothing a hand over my hair, pushing it away from my face while I gape at him, still dazed from my climax. Confused as to why he'd just...leave.

Like this is it.

"Ace—" I clamp my lips shut, unsure what to say next.

His smile is small. Even a little sad. "I know, baby."

That's it. That's all he says before he reaches behind him, undoes the lock and then slips out of the stall. I can hear his hurried footsteps slap across the floor, the door opening and closing, leaving me in silence.

Leaving me alone.

I take a fortifying breath and release it slowly, my heart still racing. My head still spinning. I don't know how to explain exactly what just happened, but I feel changed.

I feel like I want to toss aside all responsible thought and chase after Ace. Beg him to take me home so we can continue where we left off. Is he purposely trying to drive me out of my mind?

Because it's totally working.

26

ACE

It's Saturday. Game day. Another one played at home and against our biggest rival, so the crowds are thick in the stands. Pretty sure the stadium sold out and even though we're in the locker room, I can hear the roar of their voices, cheering along with the band, who came out early to put on a special performance.

My stomach is in absolute knots. I'm freaked the fuck out and think I might puke.

"You look green," someone notes as they pass by me.

"Gee thanks," I mutter after he's gone, annoyed. All eyes are on me. My teammates. My coaches. Every fucker out there ready to watch me either win this game or...

Lose it.

I refuse to lose it.

"You okay?"

I turn to see Evan standing in front of me, a look of concern on his face. This guy is different from the majority of my teammates. He's not such a macho asshole all the time. In fact, Evan doesn't ever really act like that at all. Not that the rest of the guys on my team are complete dicks, but Evan is a decent human.

And I appreciate that more than he could ever know.

"I'm nervous," I admit truthfully. Something I never do because I prefer to keep up the pretense that I've got my shit handled. If anyone ever saw a lick of doubt in my face or actions, forget it.

They'd lose all faith in me.

I'm supposed to be the team leader. I can't show weakness. I need to be strong and prove to everyone—my team, our coaches, our fans—that I've got this.

But damn, sometimes the pressure just gets to me.

At least practices are going better for me. Just having Ruby on the sidelines almost every day is enough to keep me going. To the point that even when she's not there, I feel okay. Because I know she's going to be there again.

Eventually.

"Bro. You've totally got this." Evan offers his hand and I take it, giving him a high five. He clasps hold of my hand, giving it a shake, his gaze locked on mine. "You're going to kill it out there."

"I hope so."

"Nah, man. Don't put that uncertainty out into the universe." This comes from Javier, who's just approached us. "You gotta say without any doubt that we're going to destroy them. We're on our home turf. We've got this. You're going to be great, QB."

"Put it out into the universe?" I ask, scratching the back of my neck.

Javier rolls his eyes. "Listen, that's my girl talking. She's always saying stuff like that. She talks about manifesting and shit. It sounds like a load of crap, but I'm starting to think she's onto something. Like, that kind of thinking works, you know?"

"Sure." I nod, having no idea what he's talking about. Manifesting?

All I do know is that I'm jealous of his relationship. Jealous he can have one and I can't. And I'm the guy who didn't want a relationship. Who avoided that sort of thing because I couldn't commit.

Now I actually want to commit and she can't do it. It fucking sucks.

I wonder sometimes if it's the fact that we can't be together, and that's why I want Ruby so much. We always want what we can't have, right?

Shit, I don't know. What I do know is I'm going out of my mind and if I'm not thinking about football, I'm thinking about her. She haunts me day and night and I don't know how to get over her.

The problem? I don't want to get over her. I enjoy wallowing in my obsession with the one and only Ruby Maguire. Having her out on the field during practice when the social media team joins us, I'm always relieved when I see her smiling face. Hell, I play along with her schemes and let her film some of us as we mouth the words along to trending songs and make goofy ass posts for them. I look like a damn fool, but she reassures me that the fans are eating this shit up. Especially the women.

It's wild, how much our social media followers have grown since Ruby and Gwyneth implemented their ideas. I've been keeping track and they're killing it. Ruby even encouraged me to post some of their content as well and she sent a few videos to me, which I put on my social media and now mine is growing too.

That girl is smart. Savvy. Kind and funny and why all the

guys on the team don't flock to her leaves me confused. And grateful.

I might have to kick someone's ass if they make a move on her. It might be unspoken, but that girl is mine.

She belongs to me.

Maybe they sense my feelings toward her. I don't know. I'll make any excuse to talk to her, but it never feels like enough. I want more. More time with Ruby. Listening to her. Watching her smile. Hearing her laugh. I'm completely entranced with her and it's fucking killing me that we avoid each other.

Well. For the most part.

Still think about that moment in the bathroom, though. It's taken permanent residence in my brain—might've helped me through a few lonely nights when I only had my hand to keep me company.

There is nothing I enjoy more than getting Ruby off. Seriously. It's my favorite thing to do. Maybe even more than football.

It's pretty damn close.

Just knowing that we're in this together, that we seem to feel the same way about each other—it's reassuring and eases some of my game playing anxiety. And while I'm a fucking nervous wreck on game day, I remind myself I just have to push through it. I can do this.

I can.

Coach eventually calls us over so he can give us a rousing speech. This one is more encouraging than usual, because we're out for blood. We haven't lost to this team since before Cam was our quarterback and now that I'm here, I need to maintain the record.

"You just know they've poured over our game film," Coach Mattson says near the end of his speech. "Just like we've poured over theirs. They're looking for any way they can take down Ace, but we're not going to let them. Y'all need to guard that boy with your life. No sacks today. I refuse to let it happen."

My linemen all nod, grumbling their agreement.

"And there will be no interceptions either." Mattson points right at me. "We can't afford any mistakes out on that field. If they outplay us, that's one thing. But if we keep making stupid mistakes that give them the advantage? Then we handed the game to them. We can't do that."

"Right," I say with a nod, breathing deep. "We've got this."

I have to believe it. Believe in myself. If I don't, I'll just fuck up and do as Coach says.

Hand them the win.

Well, fuck that.

27

RUBY

I'm literally sitting on the edge of my seat.

This game has been such a nail-biter, I think I'm going to pass out from anxiety. The back and forth, the teams outplaying each other every single quarter. Ace has played a magnificent game, but the problem is, the other team has played a really great game too.

They're both struggling to score. It's a battle on the field, and thank God it's almost over.

"God, there's still seven minutes left in the quarter," Gwyneth mutters, checking the scoreboard for like the millionth time. "I don't know how much more of this I can take."

"It's a lot," I agree, my gaze never straying from the field. We currently have the ball and Ace is in a huddle with the rest of his offense, all of them screaming 'let's go' just as they break up and get into position.

I scoot forward, my ass nearly falling off the bench, my breath lodged in my throat as I listen to Ace's deep voice call out the play. The ball is hiked to him and he jogs back a few steps, his head swiveling left and right, searching for the open player he can throw the ball to. He finally throws it, the ball spiraling through the air, my gaze tracking its every movement.

The ball falls into the hands of the safety, who clutches it to his chest and runs it in.

Touchdown.

We leap to our feet, hopping up and down, Gwen and I clutching each other. The relief currently sweeping over me is enough to leave me weak, but I can't get too confident yet. I check the time on the board.

We still have more than six minutes to go.

It's like this for the rest of the quarter and I realize that whoever has the ball at the very end of this game will determine the winner. It's not necessarily about skill. It's more about who's lucky enough to have that ball.

God, I think I might throw up.

As the clock winds down, I realize the other team is trying to play it to their advantage. Trying to keep that ball as long as possible to not give our team any chance to make another score. I know Ace and his team would do the same thing and I hate this for him.

My gaze drops to where he sits on the bench on the sidelines, staring at the back of his head. His hair is a riotous mess and his white uniform jersey is dirty. Smudged with grass stains and God I swear that might be blood.

Maybe not. I don't think he's really taken any hits today.

I tear my gaze away from Ace to watch our defense and the other team's offense on the field, a gasp escaping me when one of our defensive linemen intercepts the ball. The stadium erupts in cheers, everyone around us leaping to their feet and screaming at the top of their lungs and Gwen and I do the same thing, continuing to jump up and down. Yelling our encouragement as the lineman sprints across the field as fast as he can, heading straight for the end zone, two guys from the opposing team following him. Reaching for him...

Until he ends up in the end zone, the referees holding their arms up in the universal signal that he just scored a touchdown.

We completely lose it, Gwen and I clutching each other, screaming our heads off. My gaze tracks Ace's every move as he runs out onto the field, grabbing the guy who scored the touchdown and slapping the back of his helmet.

My heart is ready to burst with happiness, it feels so full.

Everyone seems to calm down once the extra point is kicked in. So little time remains on the clock that the rest of the quarter is just a formality. Once it's deemed impossible for the other team to manage another chance at scoring, the game is over.

The Golden Eagles win.

"Oh my God! We won!" I squeal, reaching for Gwen and giving her a hug.

She returns the gesture before pulling away, keeping her hands on my shoulders. "We need to get down there and film some content."

"Totally agree."

Since the social media team is allotted one person on the sidelines at every game, it was Eric's turn to be down there. He gets the best field footage out of the three of us, so it makes sense for him to film all the plays. Gwen, though, was down there during the first game.

I'll be down there the next home game, which is in three weeks. Our team has a bye next week, and an away game after that.

Even if we're not on the field itself during a game, we still have pretty great seats since we get to be in the media section. One of the many perks of being on the football team's social media crew.

"Who do you want me to talk to?" I ask Gwen as we leave the stands and head toward the gate, where the guard will eventually let us out onto the field.

"I want to talk to the guy who scored the last touchdown," Gwen answers, which isn't a surprise. "Think he'll film with me?"

"Of course, he will," I say without hesitation. "Guess I'll go talk to Ace."

Ooh, such a hardship. Don't know how I'll manage it.

We're eventually let on the field and Gwen and I go our separate ways; she in search of the beefy lineman who ran in that final touchdown and me in search of our golden boy QB. The very man who had me pinned against a bathroom stall door, his hand in my panties, his fingers making me come only a few days ago.

Yikes.

I wander around the field, stopping to talk to some of the players and film them real quick, while asking them silly questions on camera. There are all sorts of people out here and it feels more crowded than usual. I try my best to ignore the panicky feeling growing inside my chest, but it's no use. I'm freaking out.

I can't find Ace.

My disappointment grows with every step and I glance over my shoulder toward the exit gate. I should probably go. Text Gwen and see if she wants to meet up and go over anything. The last home game we just went our separate ways after we were finished but maybe...

Ugh, maybe I'm just feeling lonely and wishing I had someone to talk to. Like Ace.

Turning, I head toward the exit gates, my head held

high, smiling at anyone who passes me when I swear I hear someone calling my name.

No. I'm imagining it.

But then I hear it again. Though it's not my name that's being called. It's my nickname. And there's only one person who calls me Red.

Coming to a stop, I turn, my smile growing when I see Ace striding toward me, still clad in his uniform and safety pads, looking broad and dangerous and a gorgeous mess. My heart starts racing when I see that gleam in his eyes and he's heading straight for me, his steps determined.

He only stops when he's directly in front of me, and I drink him in. He does the same to me, our gazes eating each other up almost greedily. His helmet is gone, his hair is sticking up all over the place and he's a little sweaty around the temples. There's this glow in his eyes and this look on his handsome face that has me feeling all melty and gooey inside, and not in a bad way.

No, in the very best way.

"Red." His voice is warm and deep and reaches right inside me, grabbing hold of my heart and giving it a giant squeeze. "You came to my game."

"Wouldn't miss it," I say way too brightly. I wince, mentally telling myself to calm down.

His smile grows. "Wasn't Derek's interception amazing?"

"Wait a minute. That was our Derek?" How did I not put it together? Am I in such a haze that I can't even think clearly while watching a football game, my focus solely on the man in front of me?

"It was our Derek," he says with a nod, his expression amused. I think he might've liked that I used the word 'our.' "He's so proud of himself. He's going to be insufferable tonight."

"He helped win the game," I point out.

"Yeah, he did." Ace tilts his head to the side, his hot gaze raking over me slowly. "You look good."

"So do you," I say without hesitation because oh my God, it's true. I don't care how dirty he might be or if he smells. He's glorious.

He chuckles. "I'm a mess."

A sexy, want to rub myself all over you, mess, is what I want to say, but I keep my thoughts to myself. "Nothing a shower can't fix."

His gaze darkens. Talk of showers means nakedness and I'm sure his mind went there. Because mine certainly did. "What are you doing tonight?"

Resist him! Tell him you've got plans! Spending time with him leads to nothing but trouble!

"Nothing," is how I answer, my voice weak. Like my resolve.

"We're all going to Logan's here in a bit, but afterward, we're having a little get-together at our apartment. Just a few people coming over, nothing big," he explains.

I hold my breath, waiting for him to ask me what I'm afraid he's going to ask.

"That sounds fun," I whisper, hating that I'm going to have to reject him. I can't just show up at a party by myself and act like I'm there for funsies. It'll look weird. People will suspect there's more between Ace and me then we let on.

I can't do that. I can't risk losing my job.

"Think you could maybe stop by?" His brows shoot up in question, and it kills me to say no. Especially because he never hesitates when he asks me.

I slowly shake my head, my stomach sinking. God, this is awful.

He exhales roughly. "I figured you'd answer like that."

"It's just—"

"You don't have to explain yourself," he says, cutting me off. "I understand."

Oh God. I've ruined everything. He looks uncomfortable as he stares off in the distance, his jaw working, his lips in a straight line. And maybe even a little upset. Like he'd rather be anywhere than here and I don't want to ruin his night. The team should be celebrating. He shouldn't be worrying about me.

"Congratulations," I tell him, hoping he knows how sincere I am. "It was a great game. You played magnificently."

Ace turns to me, his gaze locking with mine. "Thank you."

I smile, feeling sad, and God, Ace looks sad too. Like we're two sad sacks and this is just so heartbreaking to me. I can't even bother him by asking if he wants to film anything because it just doesn't feel right. I know Gwen will question what happened later, but I don't know how to tell her what's really going on. And if I did tell her, she's such a rule follower that she'd most likely report me and I'd lose my job.

Can't risk that.

"What if..." My voice drifts and Ace takes a step closer, his interest clearly engaged. "What if you came over to my place later?"

"And not show up at the party at my house?"

I nod, knowing how risky this is, but suddenly not giving a damn about it. I miss him. I want to see him.

"Will you go to Logan's?" he asks.

I shake my head, still not saying anything.

"Why not?" He frowns, his disappointment clear.

"Natalie's working tonight. She's the only one I'd end up going with anyway." I shrug.

"Will she be home later?"

"Probably."

"Are you wanting me to...what? Sneak into your room?"

"No."

Ace frowns.

"You can come to the door like a gentleman," I finish.

His smile returns. "You really do want me to come over, huh, Red?"

My entire body is on high alert, eager to have his hands on me again so yes. Yes, indeed, I definitely want him to come over.

"Sure," I say nonchalantly, shrugging. "If you want to."

"Oh, I want to," he says without hesitation.

"Then what are you waiting for?"

"I don't know." He shrugs. "For a proper invite?"

I take a step closer to him, noting that he appears as tall and as broad as the mountains that surround our little college town. Ugh this man. He is seriously going to be the death of me and I'm going to die a happy woman as long as he's involved with it because lordy, all he has to do is look at me and I want to die.

Looks like I need to give him what he wants. That invitation.

"Would you like to come over to my place later?" Resting my hand on his chest, I rise up on tiptoe and he bends down at the same time, meeting me in the middle so I can whisper in his ear. "If you're lucky, I might be waiting for you in my bed. Naked."

He pulls away slightly so he can look into my eyes, the heat in his gaze scorching me. "I hope like hell that I'm lucky tonight."

"Maybe you will be." I smile, crossing my arms in front of my chest. "But then again...maybe you won't."

He rubs a big hand across his jaw. "Don't tease me like that, Red."

"I think that's your favorite part about me," I say. "The teasing."

"I don't know." His gaze skims over me again, settling on all the spots of my body that tingle for him. "I pretty much like all your parts."

I giggle.

Ace chuckles.

I'm clearly putting everything at risk, but in this very moment?

I don't care.

28

ACE

Everyone is celebrating us tonight at Logan's. Every round of alcohol is purchased for us. Beer. Shots. Expensive liquor that should be sipped that we're shooting instead because we're idiots and the majority of us are looking to get fucked up—it doesn't matter what, people are sending it to us. I feel like we won a damn championship game, though I guess this is close enough.

I can't lie, it feels good, basking in everyone's adoration. We're loved tonight and I want to savor the moment. I really do.

But I can't stop thinking about Ruby and her invitation. Mentioning that she'll wait for me in her bed.

Naked.

Jesus, this woman. Seeing her wear our school colors ignited something inside me that keeps growing. I want to see her in my jersey. My number on her chest, my last name on her back. Fuck, that would feel like a claiming. I don't care about anyone else who wears my jersey—well, I do love it when they wear the T-shirts and root me on because they're fans, you know? But Ruby isn't just a fan.

She's...oh shit, who am I right now, thinking like this?

Fuck it.

Ruby is my girl. That's how I see her at least. And even if we can't be together yet, I'm hoping—fingers crossed tightly —that we can be together someday. After the season? Which means not until December or even January, if we make it to a championship bowl.

Back to the waiting for me naked part. That'll be the best part of my whole day. At the very least, it's on par with winning the game. Though I'm not quite sure how she's going to do it.

How she'll manage the naked in bed part since she needs to come to the door and let me in. But I guess I shouldn't worry about the logistics. I should focus on the idea of beautiful, luscious Ruby bare beneath the sheets. Wet between the legs.

Waiting for me.

I check my phone for what feels like the twentieth time since I arrived at Logan's, wishing for a text from Ruby, but so far there's nothing. I don't know the proper length of time for me to stay and celebrate, but I'm hoping it's an hour, tops. I already told Javier I won't be returning to our house for the after-party. He seemed disappointed, but he was also cool with it. I didn't mention any names when I said I was going somewhere else and he didn't ask either. I appreciate that he respects my privacy and always do the same for him.

"Stop checking your phone." Derek gives my arm a shake. He's extra obnoxious tonight and with every reason. Scoring that touchdown after the interception was a glory moment for him and he deserves to celebrate. "There are so many people here tonight ready to celebrate you. So many *women*. Live a little, QB."

"Yeah. Sorry." I offer him a smile, pocket my phone and reach for the beer someone bought for me, polishing off the rest of it. "Still a little keyed up, I guess. Stuck in my head."

Derek contemplates me for a moment. "You know what you need?"

"What?" I ask warily.

A sly smile appears on Derek's face. "To get laid."

Yeah, I do. Kind of hoping that happens tonight, if I'm lucky, but I need to play this off with Derek. He can't know that's my plan. He might start asking questions I don't want to answer.

I'm about to say something when Derek talks right over me.

"I know you've been on the straight and narrow here lately and not going out with any women, and while I don't get it, we all have our thing that we stick to during the season and maybe you go anti-pussy. I'm not sure. I don't remember you doing that last year."

"I didn't," I interject, but he keeps talking.

"If this is helping you play better, then more power to you. But you gotta blow off some steam eventually, my man." Derek claps me on the back, grasping hold of my shoulder and giving it a not-so-gentle shake. "You're going to get all that—you know—built up inside you."

I frown. "What are you talking about?"

Derek shrugs. "You know."

"I don't know."

He rolls his eyes and leans in close. "Cum. Semen. Jizz. Whatever you want to call it. It's gonna build up inside you and eventually you're gonna blow a gasket."

Derek is talking pure nonsense, but it's fun to play along with him.

"You're probably right," I say, my voice and my expression dead serious. "If I don't watch it, my dick might explode."

He shoves me away from him, making a dismissive noise. "You know what I mean, ass wipe. Just—go find a pretty lady tonight and let her suck your dick or something. You're too damn edgy."

"Uh huh. Maybe."

Derek shakes his head and we both turn our backs to each other in an obvious show of avoidance. I shake my head, reaching for the fresh beer that was just placed on the table in front of me and take a big gulp. Damn, I really don't want to be here. I don't want to find some pretty random girl and let her suck my dick either. That sounds...fucking awful.

I'd rather celebrate tonight with one woman in particular. Not some stranger. I don't want to use a girl for release. Yeah, yeah, I know that's exactly what I used to do like a complete asshole, but I'm not about that life anymore. I've somehow become a one-woman man, and the one woman I want, can't want me back. Not fully.

That's really messed up. How did I end up in this situation again?

It's when I'm sipping on my fourth beer that I feel it. A tingling awareness that slips over my skin, making me sit up straighter and take notice. I can feel her. She's here. At Logan's.

Ruby.

The crowd parts and she appears, still clad in the red CU T-shirt she was wearing at the game and those black denim shorts that show off her long, golden legs. Her blonde hair is pulled into a high ponytail tied with a red ribbon that's the same color as her T-shirt and damn, she's fucking adorable.

I want to sling her over my shoulder, slap her perfect ass and cart her right out of here so I can get her alone and fuck her properly. On a bed and everything. I'd take my time and savor her. Touch her everywhere. Kiss her everywhere...

"Hey, your little buddy is here." Derek nudges me in the ribs, waving a hand in Ruby's direction. "She sure is hot."

"Don't even look at her," I mutter and Derek's eyes go wide, his mouth dropping open for approximately two seconds before he bursts out laughing.

"Look at you, getting all territorial over a girl." He shoves me and I topple over a little, even though I braced myself. The fucker is strong, I'll give him that. "She know you're hot for her?"

I say nothing.

"She hot for you?" He tips his head toward me, a giant shit-eating grin on his face.

I still remain silent.

"Whatever. Keep your little secret. I imagine that makes everything ten times hotter." Sometimes Derek is too smart for his own good. "Just watch it. Everyone will find out eventually and that's going to be a big deal."

"What's going to be a big deal?" I ask, guzzling all the beer down that I can swallow. I'm suddenly nervous. My palms are sweating and everything.

"You and Ruby Maguire, my friend. She's a hottie. And a Maguire." Derek frowns. "Wait a minute, you can't be with her. There's some sort of clause the social media team has to sign after that one chick lost her marbles and posted dick pics online."

"What the hell are you talking about?"

"That's why that clause was put into place. There was this one girl who had a baseball playing boyfriend and she was on their social media team. It was no problem until they split up and she put all of his naked pics on the university's Facebook page or whatever. It was bad. Shit hit the fan and that's why they added that pesky little amendment to the contract. No fucking around with athletes. The university doesn't want to risk another fiasco," Derek explains.

My gaze stays on Ruby as she stops to chat with a group of women that she seems to know. She's animated, laughing and gesturing with her hands, stopping to listen to whatever the other women have to say. It's only when I finally let my gaze stray to the other women that I realize she came with Gwyneth of all people.

Interesting.

"Sounds like a stupid clause," I say, still staring at Ruby.

"Only because you're looking at her like a starving man and she's a giant slab of meat you want to gnaw on for the rest of your life."

I send him a measured look. "I really don't need your commentary."

He's grinning again. "And I'm really loving this. Don't fuck things up for yourself, QB. Keep a steady head. What if she turns into a vengeful witch out to get you if you don't give her what she wants?"

I'd give Ruby whatever she wants. Orgasms. Flowers. Chocolate. Plenty of hugs. She wants to make out all night? I'm down. Cuddle in bed naked? Yes, please.

"She's not like that," I say in defense of her. "And do you really think all women are like that?"

"Some are."

"She's not," I say firmly.

"Hey, guys."

We both swivel our heads to find Ruby standing at our table, Gwyneth just behind her with an unsure expression on her face.

"Maguire," Derek greets. "See me out on the field today?"

I roll my eyes and Ruby laughs.

"I definitely saw you," she says. "You were amazing."

"I know, right?" Derek is literally preening under Ruby's attention and it's a sight to see.

Scratch that. The true sight to see is Ruby smiling at Derek, her gaze sliding to mine like she can't resist. Damn it, she's gorgeous. That T-shirt clings to her perfect tits in the best way and I curl my hands into fists, keeping them in my lap. I'd much rather lunge for her, grab her and never let go, but I don't.

I can't.

"You all played pretty great," Ruby says, her gaze only for me.

"It was a tough game," Gwen adds, stepping closer to the table. "You struggled but by the end, you all came out on top."

"You're damn straight," Derek tells Gwen, his gaze narrowing. "And thanks for the critique, Gwennie."

She rolls her eyes. "Don't call me that."

"Don't like nicknames?"

"I don't like you."

"Not sure why. All the women love me." Derek leans back in the booth, spreading his arms across the back of the seat. "Right, Acey baby?"

I turn to him. "Acey baby?"

He shrugs one shoulder. "You need a nickname."

"What's yours?"

"Big D." He grins.

"You wish." I send a look to Ruby and she's still smiling. "Care to join us, ladies?"

Ruby's smile fades. "You sure that's a good idea?"

"We're just friends hanging out and celebrating the big win, right?" I'm daring her to deny it. Daring her to walk away. Can she?

I know I couldn't.

29

RUBY

I keep my gaze glued on Ace, contemplating what I should do. How I should answer. The smart move would be to keep walking. I didn't plan on coming here tonight. It was Gwen who suggested we show up at Logan's, which surprised me. She never wants to do this sort of thing. She told me so herself.

Yet here we are. Out at the most popular bar, celebrating the football team's big win. And here's Ace, already trying to get me to sit next to him, which I will gladly do. But in front of Gwen?

Risky.

"Come on, let's sit with them." Gwen nudges me in the ribs and I'm helpless to do anything else but slide into the booth, ending up pressed right next to Ace's side since there's not much room left once Gwen slides in after me. We're all crammed into this booth, cozy as can be, and oh my God, the man is as hot as a furnace.

"Hey, Red," Ace murmurs low enough that only I can hear him and I smile, sucking in a breath when I feel his hand settle on my thigh, giving it a gentle squeeze. His voice, his touch sends a zap straight to my core.

"Hi," I squeak out, feeling foolish. He just smiles that secret smile, turning away from me when the guy who's sitting on the other side of Derek says something to him.

Never removing his hand from my leg either.

"God, there's so much testosterone in this room. I can practically see it floating in the air," Gwen mumbles to me.

"You're not used to hanging out with guys?"

"I have two sisters." When I turn to her, I see this vulnerable light glowing in her eyes. "And I've never really had a —boyfriend."

"Never?" I'm really not surprised by this revelation.

"Ever," she whispers, swallowing hard. Her gaze turns panicked and she glances around the table. "I need a drink."

"We'll get you one," Ace says, lifting his arm up in the air.

A server just so happens to be passing by and she stops when she sees Ace waving at her, a seductive smile curling her lips. "Whatcha need, Ace?"

He leans forward so he can see Gwen around me. "What do you want to drink, Gwyneth?"

Her eyes go wide and I can tell she feels uncomfortably singled out, when Ace is just trying to help her. "I don't know."

"What sort of drinks do you like?" he asks.

"Something fruity?"

Ace turns to the server. "Get her something fruity and delicious. And full of lots of alcohol. Please."

"I don't want to taste it," Gwen adds.

"You heard her." Both his smile and demeanor are absolutely charming and he turns it on me. "What do you want to drink, Red?"

"Something strong and sweet," I tell him, glancing up at the server. "Whatever you make her, I'll have the same."

"Got it. Two Frosés coming right up." She points her pen at Ace. "You want something, babe?"

Babe? Did she really just call him that?

An unfamiliar emotion rises within me, leaving me flustered. Even dare I say a little...angry? Say what?

God, I think I may be jealous.

"I should probably slow down," Ace says to the server, that smile still firmly in place. He doesn't have to do a damn thing, just exist, and women fall at his feet, believing he's flirting with them. And I get it. He's handsome. Magnetic. He enters a room and instantly commands it. There are people—mostly women—lingering on the peripheral, all of them trying to play it cool but sneaking glances in the table's direction, dying for the opportunity to talk to the team.

Really? They're dying for the chance to speak to Ace.

"Have another beer," Derek says. "And get us a round of shots."

"Shots of what?" the server asks.

"Whatever you've got that's the strongest." Derek grins, turning to look at us. "We're gonna get fucked up tonight."

The server leaves and I relax a little, glad she's gone. She was pretty and seemed interested in Ace but maybe she acted like that because she's a good server who just wants tips.

Or maybe she wants my man.

I blink, going still. Wait a minute. *My man?* Am I serious right now? We're not even close to being in a relationship, and I'm already thinking like this? We've hooked up a few times, had plenty of conversations, but that doesn't mean he's my man. Plus, he's told me before that he doesn't do relationships, though lately he hasn't acted like that.

No, lately Ace Townsend acts like he's completely obsessed with me.

Well, the feeling's mutual.

"You good?" Ace asks me, giving my thigh another squeeze. His hand hasn't left me yet and no one can tell since we're hidden by the table.

"I'm great." I turn to him, surprised to find him so close. Kissing close. I study his face for a moment, getting lost in his handsome features. He definitely showered after the game, of course, and he smells like heaven. He's freshly shaven, his jaw and cheeks clean and smooth and my gaze lingers on his mouth for a little too long. His lips are the perfect shape, and they're freaking magical when they kiss me...anywhere he chooses.

I remember him going down on me and just like that, my panties are wet.

"You look a little flustered." He leans in, his mouth at my ear for the briefest second. "Thinking about anything in particular?"

His hand slides up, his fingers brushing against the spot between my thighs and a shiver steals through me.

"No. Not at all," I practically choke out, sending him a look that I hope he interprets as, *freaking stop it*.

He just smiles, the jerk, his thumb pressed firmly against me. "Hey, Gwen, did you guys get some good footage at the game?"

She brightens, nodding enthusiastically. "We definitely did. I saw some of Eric's footage too since he was on the sidelines. He got the interception Derek made."

"Of course, he did," Derek says, sounding smug. "That was epic."

"It really was," Gwen agrees and I'm surprised she'd say

that but...it's deserved so maybe I shouldn't feel that way. "Such a great play."

"Right? I was stoked." Derek rubs his hands together, leaning into Ace and practically crushing him as he speaks to Gwen. "I've never run so fast in my life. And I'm a big guy. Speed is not on my side."

"It was in that moment," Gwen says, and I can tell Derek is eating this up.

They talk about his play, while Ace and I sit there silently, sharing secret smiles, his hand still on my leg, his thumb still gently pressing against the throbbing spot between my thighs. A reminder that he wants me. That he's into me, and all I can do is sit there and silently marvel over that little fact.

Am I a fool for wanting to pursue this with Ace? Maybe. I definitely am if we get careless and I put my job at risk.

The server returns with huge drinks full of red slushy liquid that she sets down in front of me and Gwen. I stare at the drink for a second before I look up at the server. "What is this?"

"It's a Frosé. It's a rosé slushy with extra alcohol. Limit two because it'll get you drunk quick," the server explains.

Gwen's eyes go wide and she turns to me. "I drove here."

We came to Logan's in separate cars because I figured we might want to leave at separate times. Subconsciously, I wanted to leave with Ace because when it comes to that man, I'm a total ho for him.

"That's what Ubers are for," Derek says to Gwen. "You can leave your car downtown. It'll be no big deal."

"I don't know..."

"Just drink it, Gwennie," Derek encourages once the server has left us. "Come on."

I pull my drink toward me and take a sip from the straw, wincing a little. Damn, that's strong.

"How is it?" Gwen asks warily.

"Delicious," I immediately say.

"Uh huh." She studies the drink like it might strike out and bite her. "I don't know."

"Drink, Gwen," Derek commands, just before he starts chanting.

Gwen-nie! Gwen-nie! Gwen-nie!

The other guys join in and start chanting. Even Ace and I join in and soon the entire back half of the bar is screaming her name and she's turning about a thousand shades of red. I can tell she's an equal mixture of mortified and a little bit thrilled, and finally, she pulls the drink toward her and takes a long sip from her straw.

And immediately starts coughing.

I rub her back. Ace pushes a glass of water across the table toward her and she grabs it, taking a long drink before she finally says, "I don't really drink alcohol much."

"What a way to kick off the night then," I tease her. "Take it easy on that straw. Sip it slowly."

"Will do." She nods, glancing about the room before she turns to me, leaning in close to murmur, "Do you think Eric will show up?"

I back away from her, my face showing my surprise, even though, deep down, I'm not surprised by her question whatsoever. "I don't know. Did you tell him to come by?"

"I did." She nods, misery flickering in her eyes for the briefest moment before it's gone. "I hope he does."

"Are you into him, Gwyneth?" I keep my voice light and teasing because I don't want to pressure her or freak her out.

"He's an idiot," she spits out.

"Most men are."

"Oblivious."

"They're that too," I agree.

"And he always thinks he's right. Like he knows better than I do." She shakes her head, reaching for her Frosé and taking a steady sip from the straw. "Just because he's a man doesn't mean he's a total authority of football."

"Agreed. You've come up with some pretty great ideas," I tell her.

"Thank you." She peers at me, her expression turning serious. Which is her usual look, but I swear this is even more serious. "Can I tell you something?"

"Absolutely," I say with a nod.

"I thought you were going to be awful. That you got the job only because of your last name and who you're related to," she admits.

I'm not shocked by this confession either. "I figured as much."

"I know I can be a bit...judgmental sometimes." She takes another sip of her drink, wincing. "It's my worst trait. I'm just...I have a hard time trusting people."

"I'm glad you gave me a chance," I tell her, wanting her to know that I mean it. "I think we work well together."

She smiles faintly. "I do too. It helps that you care about the team. Making content. The girl last season...she just wanted to hook up with as many players as she could."

Uneasiness slips down my spine and I mentally tell it to take a hike. "I definitely enjoy creating content, especially the type where the guys can make fun of themselves. And I like brainstorming ideas with you and putting it all together."

"I totally agree! I'm just so glad to find someone who's into it and not doing the job just to get close to football play- ers. I mean, I get why anyone would want to get close to them. They're fun, they're attractive. They're a good time," Gwen says.

I'm finally shocked by something Gwen said. "You actually *like* them?"

"Oh yeah. I find them intimidating, I can't lie, but there's something about hanging out with a giant group of guys who are a team. Who support each other. You get caught up in it, and it's...exciting. Doesn't hurt that they all have gorgeous bodies and faces." Gwen takes another, longer sip from her drink and I realize I need to catch up to her.

I sip from my Frosé, digesting what she just said. I had Gwen all wrong. I thought she hated the team and did the job because she...I don't know, had to? But that makes no sense. If you're going to work in social media and with athletes, shouldn't you have respect for the sport? At least a little bit?

"But they're not my speed," she continues. "Football players. I like my guys a little more on the quiet, nerdy side."

"Like Eric?" I ask, my voice low.

She nods, suddenly appearing miserable. "Just like Eric."

"Did you just mention my bro?" Derek asks us out of nowhere. God, I really hope he wasn't listening in on our conversation. "Eric?"

"Derek and Eric," Gwen murmurs. "You guys' names rhyme."

"Right? Any time one of you screams his name, I get excited for a second, thinking you're calling me," Derek says, his smile sly as he studies both of us.

I groan. "Please don't start flirting with us. We're not interested."

"Oh, come on, Maguire. You know you want me." The cheesy grin that now appears makes me roll my eyes. "And

Gwennie, I just got half the bar cheering for you. I deserve a reward."

"You don't deserve shit," Gwen tells him, slurping down her drink. Her cheeks are flushed and her eyes are sparkling and I realize why there's a two-drink limit on this concoction. She's already buzzed. "I'm not interested in you, Big D."

He chortles. "Whoa, you know my nickname?"

"*Everybody* knows your nickname," Ace says, reentering our conversation after talking to the guy on the other side of Derek. "You proudly tell everyone and their mother all about it."

I laugh. Ace squeezes my leg yet again, making my stomach—and other, lower parts of my body—flutter. We share a look and I think of what Gwen said. How she's so glad I'm not interested in getting with anyone on the football team.

I'm definitely not interested in the entire team. Not even a few of the players.

Only one.

30

ACE

I'm drunk.

I've tried my best all season to watch my alcohol intake and stay on the healthy track. I've managed it pretty well too, but tonight was a cause for celebration and I let go.

Apparently, so did everyone else. The entire bar is full of stumbling, loud and obnoxious drunk people, the majority of them being my teammates.

We deserve to cut loose. It's been an intense week and what makes it even better? Next week is a bye. No game scheduled means our practices aren't going to be as intense. Hell, we even get an extra day off from practice, plus game day off. It's gonna feel like a freaking vacation.

But it'll go by fast and the week after that, we'll be back in action. Hitting it hard.

I'm ready for the lax schedule. My class load is picking up and I'll be working on my assignments this upcoming week. Not interested in thinking about any of that though. I've got other things to concentrate on currently.

Like the pretty, warm blonde snuggled up to my side.

I've had my hand on her leg all night and she hasn't protested once. Let's face it.

Ruby Maguire is as into me as I'm into her.

Damn if that isn't reassuring.

Eric eventually swings by our table, looking like a nervous chump afraid to speak, and after a few minutes of idle chatter, he takes off with Gwen of all people, which has Ruby wiggling in her seat, a mysterious smile on her pretty face.

"What's your deal?" I ask after they're gone.

"I shouldn't say anything but..." Her eyes are wide as she stares at me. "Can you keep a secret?"

"I think you should know by now that I'm a pretty good secret keeper," I drawl.

Her cheeks flush pinker, if that's possible. The alcohol already has her nice and rosy. "Gwen likes him."

"Who? Eric?"

"Shush." She rests her fingers against my lips and I'm tempted to nip at them but I don't. I'm just glad she's touching me in front of everyone. "You're so loud. Can you be quiet? Just for a minute?"

I nod and her hand drops away. "And yes. She likes Eric. I think he likes her too."

"That's cute."

"Aren't they lucky? There's no clause about anyone on the social media team dating each other." Her wistful sigh makes my heart ache.

Yeah, she's totally into me. And I'm totally into her. But we can't do anything about it. Not publicly.

I hate that stupid clause.

"They're pretty lucky," I agree, sliding my hand back up so it's firmly lodged between her slender thighs. Swear to God I can feel the heat emanating from her pussy, which has got me thinking all sorts of dirty thoughts. "I'm glad you came here tonight, Red."

"Me too." She leans in briefly, her hair brushing my cheek and I breathe deep, catching a whiff of her delicious scent. "It's been fun."

"How's that drink working out for you?" I nod toward the giant glass of slushy alcohol. She's on her second one so she's got to be feeling it.

"It's delicious." She smiles, leaning into me again, her face practically in mine. "Pretty sure I'm a little drunk."

"Oh yeah?" I bop her nose with my index finger and she rears back a little. "I don't take advantage of drunk girls."

"That's too bad." She mock pouts. "I'd totally let you take advantage of me."

I reach for her, resting my fingers against her lips, just like she did to me only moments ago. "Better be quiet there, baby. Don't want anyone hearing you."

When I remove my hand from her mouth, she continues staring at me, murmuring, "I love it when you call me baby."

Just like that, my dick is hard. Well, I've been sporting a semi all damn night having her close and my hands on her, but the way she looks at me right now, that sweet little confession...

"Yeah? Better than Red?"

"I like that too," she whispers, reaching for her drink and taking a long sip.

My gaze fixes on her mouth wrapped around that thick straw and I'm sweating. Thinking of the time she gave me a blow job and I blew all over her tits. Why haven't we done that again? Why haven't we kept up a steady stream of secret hookups? What the fuck is wrong with me?

"We should go," I tell her, the need to get her alone suddenly overwhelming.

"Aw, can't we stay a little while longer?" The sexy little pout is back and I want to kiss it off her lips.

"Okay." I lean back and she does the same, mimicking me. "We can stay as long as you want."

I decide to torture her. While I'm talking with my team-mates, I've got my hand still firmly planted between her legs, my thumb slowly drifting up and down the seam of her denim shorts, teasing her pussy. Even though I act like I'm paying attention to my friends' conversation, I'm wholly concentrating on Ruby's reaction.

The way her breathing shifts. Becoming faster. Shallower. Her thighs clamp together, trapping my hand, but I don't let up. I don't want to.

It's like I can't.

Out of the corner of my eye, I watch her reach for her drink and choke it down, her tongue sneaking out to lick at her lips when she finishes and fuck, I want to groan. I want to shove my fingers down the front of her shorts and see how wet she is.

I'd bet big money she's soaked.

All for me.

Eventually I feel her side press more firmly into mine and next thing I know, she's resting her head on my shoulder. I ease up on the pussy teasing, glancing toward her at the same time she shifts her head to look up at me from her spot on my shoulder and I lose myself in her pretty green eyes for a moment.

"I'm drunk," she whispers. "And horny."

That's our cue to leave. "We need to get the fuck out of here."

She lifts away from me, her brows drawn together like she's confused how she got there in the first place. "We can't leave together."

"I'm not letting you leave this place alone," I say fiercely. There's just no fuckin' way.

"Um." She glances around, but no one is paying attention to us. Not a single person in the bar cares what we're doing right now. "I'll leave first and you wait a few minutes then come outside and meet me."

"No." I shake my head, ignoring the sad expression on her face. "I'll leave first. I'm not going to let you stand out there all by yourself, waiting for me."

Her eyes go soft. "Aw, you're so protective."

"You don't even know the half of it." She has no clue. I can't stand the idea of her being hurt or alone out in the dark, shivering while standing in front of the bar. Dudes walking by, leering at her. No way. Fuck that.

I want to take care of her.

"I'll text you in a few." Removing my hand from between her thighs, I give her ass a nudge. "Scoot out, baby. I've gotta go."

Her eyes light up at me calling her baby—did it on purpose, I'm not an idiot—and she slides out of the booth, standing to the side and giving me room. I touch her waist briefly, murmuring, "Sit back down. I'll text you in a few and you can come out and meet me. I'll get a car for us."

She nods, her expression solemn, her green eyes extra big. "Okay."

I watch her practically fall back into the seat, smothering the laugh that wants to escape. She's so damn cute.

Beautiful.

Sexy.

Fun.

Easy to talk to.

Sexy.

Wait, did I already think she was sexy? Yeah, she deserves to be called that twice.

Sending her a meaningful look, I head deeper into the bar, finding Javier and pulling him aside so I can talk to him. "Hey, I'm out of here."

Javier glances around the space before returning his gaze to mine. "You meeting someone somewhere?"

"Yeah." I rub my jaw, not about to reveal who I'm meeting. "You still having people over?"

"Maybe. I don't know. We're having a pretty good time here and besides..." He shrugs, his grin faintly embarrassed. "My girl promised me a naked FaceTime sesh if I go home soon."

"Bro, you better jump on that." I grab hold of his shoulders and give him a slight shake. "I'll see you later."

I get the hell out of there before any of my teammates notice, but that doesn't stop other people from talking to me. It takes me an extra fifteen minutes to leave Logan's. It's mostly guys congratulating me on the win, but there are also a few women who tell me I did a great job, flirting it up.

Not interested. I'm too eager to get Ruby alone. In bed. Naked.

Finally, I'm standing in the alley to the left of Logan's ordering a car. It'll be here in seven minutes and I check the time before I send a quit text to Ruby.

A group of loudly laughing women exit the bar, all of them squealing when they see me standing in the alley.

"Ace Townsend!" one of them screams.

"See ya around, ladies." I offer a wave and turn my back to them, making like I'm going to leave. They sound disappointed but keep moving and I nearly sag with relief when they're gone.

I need to get the hell out of here.

Within minutes, Ruby is in the alley with me and we head to the back of the building, where the tiny parking lot is. I instructed the driver in the notes to pick us up there and when his car appears, I usher Ruby inside the back seat, following after her and slamming the car door.

"Ace!" The driver catches my eye in the rearview mirror and I want to groan out loud. I can't get any peace. "I thought that was you."

"Hey," I say weakly, pleased when Ruby snuggles close to me, her face pressed against my chest. I slip my arm around her shoulders.

I chat with the driver the entire ride back to her place while Ruby remains quiet. Cuddly. Her arm is curled around mine and her hair is practically in my face and I don't mind at all. This moment is nice, being able to sit with her freely without judgment. Who's this guy gonna tell? He's a former student at CU and still lives in the area, and this is his weekend job to earn extra cash that he's saving so he can buy a house.

Yeah, I know a lot about this dude because he's giving me his entire life story.

By the time we pull up in front of Ruby's apartment building, I have to nudge her to get her moving. "We're here, Red."

We spill out of the car, me taking Ruby's arm to stabilize her. The moment the car drives away, I take her hand, momentarily disoriented. I know I've been here before but... "Where's your apartment?"

"This way." She gestures with her free hand and starts walking, leading me to her front door.

"You think Nat is home?"

"She works pretty late on Saturday nights. She usually works the tables in the bar. That's where the best tips are,"

Ruby explains as she turns left and steers us up a set of stairs to her apartment.

I loom behind her as she unlocks the door, impatience making me eager, and when we're inside the apartment, I'm on her like I have no control. Pinning her to the door, reaching for her and cradling her cheeks in my hands, tilting her head up so I can study her pretty face for a moment before I swoop in and kiss her.

A soft sigh leaves her the moment our lips touch and I keep it gentle, restraining myself. Brushing my mouth against hers again and again, her lips parting with every pass. Until I tease her with my tongue, her tongue immediately meeting mine. Flicking. Circling. Until I can't take it anymore and deepen the kiss.

She moans, her body going limp, her hands sliding down my chest, fisting the fabric of my shirt. I press more firmly against her, holding her against the door, letting her feel what she's doing to me, and when she finally breaks the kiss first, I can tell she's giggling.

"What's so funny?" I dip my head and rain kisses down the length of her neck.

"You're always kissing me against a door." A shiver moves through her when I gently bite the spot where her neck and shoulder meet. "We should go to my room."

"Is that an invitation?" I lift my head away from hers, the lust coursing through my veins as I take her in.

God, she's beautiful. And so damn sweet. All that silky blonde hair and those big green eyes. Or are they hazel? Right now, they're glowing green, eating me up, and my skin fucking tingles as her gaze sweeps over me.

Ruby nods, letting go of my shirt and reaching for my hand. "Come on."

I let her drag me down the hall and into her tiny

bedroom. She hits the light switch and the lamp on the bedside table turns on, casting the room in a gentle glow. She turns to face me, walking backward toward the bed, her expression full of promise. "I can't believe *the* Ace Townsend is in my bedroom. Again."

"Oh, don't start giving me a hard time, Red. I'm not that big of a deal." My gaze slides over her, lingering on all of my favorite parts. There are too many to name so basically I'm ogling her like some sort of freakish pervert, but from the glimmer currently lighting her eyes, I can tell she doesn't mind.

"You're a huge deal, Ace. You were great out on that field. So commanding. In control. The entire bar was there for you tonight, and you deserve all the accolades." She sounds in awe of me and I can't lie.

Pride floods my veins. It means something, that she thinks I'm a big deal. I don't care what anyone else thinks about me.

Just her.

"They were there for the team, not just me," I correct because I can't take all the credit for the win.

That game was brutal. I was sweating big time and secretly terrified of fucking everything up. But I didn't.

We won. And I'm hoping I can claim Ruby Maguire as my prize.

31

RUBY

I have Ace in my bedroom and I'm suddenly nervous. My palms are damp and my heart is racing and I'm experiencing a serious case of self-doubt. I don't know why. He's made it more than clear that he likes me. That he wants me. And we've hooked up before. What we've already shared was pretty amazing, so I know it'll be good between us.

Scratch that. It's going to be *great* between us.

So why am I panicking now?

"You're so modest," I finally murmur as I take a step away from him, letting my gaze sweep over him freely. Everything lately with Ace feels so...covert. Like we're spies having to sneak around to see each other. Communicate with each other. I don't like it. Not really. I'd rather let the world know what we're doing.

At least the campus.

"I'm just giving credit where it's due. I can't play like that without them. I need that team just as much as they need me. Maybe even more." He rubs his chin, his narrowed gaze lingering on me. "So. What are we waiting for, Red?"

My stomach jumps. "What do you mean?"

"Shouldn't we be getting naked by now?" He cocks a brow.

My body grows warm at him using the word *naked*.

All sorts of images pop into my brain, all of them involving Ace with no clothes on.

"You start first." I wave a hand at him.

"If you say so." He reaches for the back of his shirt and pulls it off in one smooth move, revealing his magnificent chest.

I clamp my lips together so I don't do anything embarrassing while I stare at him, like drool.

"Your turn," he drawls when I still haven't said anything.

Slowly I tug my CU shirt off, revealing the white lacy bra I wore special for the occasion. As if I knew this moment would happen.

I was definitely hopeful.

His gaze turns heated as he takes me in. "You have the best tits I've ever seen."

Laughing, I roll my eyes. "Best *tits?* Your language is rather coarse, Acey Baby."

A growl leaves him and I giggle even more. "Did you really just call me that?"

I nod. "You don't like it?"

Without warning, he lunges for me, making me gasp, taking me down so I land on the bed behind us, with him on top of me. His hands are everywhere at once, tickling me, making me laugh harder, but then he cups one breast, his big hand completely covering it and the laughter dies in my throat.

Swiftly replaced by a soft moan.

"Guess I only like it when you call me that," he

murmurs, his face in mine, so close I can feel his breath feather across my lips. "No one else."

He lifts away from me before I can say anything, tracing the lacy trim of my bra with his index finger, gooseflesh rising on my skin. He does the same to the other breast, his barely-there caress making me squirm, wanting more. When he reaches for the clasp between my breasts and slowly undoes it, I breathe a sigh of relief.

This is what I've been craving since our last encounter. His hands on me. The delicious way his touch makes me feel.

Ace sweeps the cups away from my breasts with the back of his hand, dragging his knuckles across my hard nipples and I sink my teeth into my lower lip, my eyes falling closed when he does it again. He shifts his hand back and forth over my nipples so lightly, they start to ache with need.

"They really are pretty," he murmurs, and I crack my eyes open to find him staring at my chest with longing. His gaze lifts to mine and his expression turns somewhat guilty. "I'm a tit man."

"No kidding," I tease.

He pinches my left nipple, making me hiss in a breath. "I'm also an ass man." He slips his other hand beneath me and palms my ass, giving one cheek a squeeze. "And a leg man."

"So you like all the parts." My breath stalls in my lungs when he sweeps his hand down the outside of my thigh, making me quiver.

"Only your parts." His smile is soft. Intimate. "I guess I'm a Ruby man."

Oh my God. He shouldn't say things like that. My heart is soaring out of my chest and my head is filled with all sorts of ridiculous thoughts.

Like what we share could turn into something real, which is impossible. I need to keep this moment light. Sexy.

"More like a Ruby fan?" I counter.

"Whatever you want to call it." He leans down and brushes his mouth against mine, pulling away before I can really kiss him back. Such a tease. "I'm going to savor you tonight."

His deep voice seems to vibrate right through me, leaving me breathless.

"Oh." That sounds absolutely wonderful.

It also sounds like pure torture.

"I want to touch you everywhere." He kisses my cheek, his hand sliding down to rest on my stomach. "Kiss you everywhere."

I nod, needing to hear more.

"And after I make you come at least once, maybe twice, I'm going to fuck you." He removes his hand from my stomach to rest it on my throat, his fingers curling around it lightly. "You want that?"

I nod, loving how he calls it fucking. No guy has said that to me before, and I know it's a small thing, but it's also a really hot thing. As in, it's making me hot.

But I'm already so far gone for this man, he could call it boning and I'd probably find that sexy, when really? That word is most decidedly not.

His mouth finds mine once more and I lose myself in his deep, drugging kiss. Getting swept away by his searching tongue and persuasive lips. His hand is still clamped around my neck, his fingers exerting the slightest pressure and I close my eyes, savoring the sensation. His thumb rubs along my jawline. His other fingers streak across my throat. It's sensory overload and I love it and I never want him to stop.

What makes it even better?

He's doing this because he knows I like it and God, I do. I actually love it. It feels like he owns me and for some weird reason, that's what I want. For Ace Townsend to claim me. Own me.

Completely.

We kiss for long, wondrous minutes, his hand eventually moving away from my neck to drift down the length of me. I'm trembling when he touches my breasts, his fingers playing with my nipples. Shivering when he touches my stomach, sliding his fingers beneath the waistband of my denim shorts. He undoes the button and slips the zipper down with ease, a whimper escaping me when I feel him touch the thin waistband of my skimpy panties and then he slides those magical fingers beneath the sheer fabric, sinking into me.

"Always so wet," he murmurs against my lips. "Fucking love that about you."

He shouldn't use the word love so freely around me. A girl could start to get the wrong idea.

I spread my thighs open, allowing him more room and he takes advantage, his fingers searching me. Rubbing my clit in slow, tight circles. Ratcheting up those sensations growing within me with every stroke. I lift my hips, seeking more of his touch, my mouth hungry, my hands reaching for him, holding him to me. Until I finally have to break away from his kiss so I can catch my breath, overwhelmed with sensation.

"Baby, we need to get these clothes off of you," he says, and I can't take it when he calls me that. Baby. It's the sweetest thing. The sexiest thing.

What's sexier is this big man taking care of me. Shifting down the mattress so he can tug at my shorts, pulling them down my legs, his mouth following after his hands. He kisses each hip bone. My stomach. The tops of my thighs. The inside of my thighs, his lips so soft, so damp, I almost shoot off the bed.

Eagerly I kick off my shorts and spread my legs wider, wanting him to hone in on my pussy and he does.

Oh God, he does.

I reach behind me, grabbing at the pillow and clutching it to the back of my head as he tugs my panties aside, revealing my glistening wet pussy. Pausing, he glances up at me to find I'm already watching, a slow, sexy smile curling his lips and I want to throw a pillow at his beautiful head.

I also want to beg him to never stop what he's doing.

"Want me to lick it?" he asks, his voice so deep it sounds like he's growling.

I nod furiously, desperate for him to lick it.

"Beg."

"Wha?" I frown, finding it difficult to speak full words.

"Beg for it, Red. I wanna hear you beg for my mouth and my fingers on your pretty pink pussy. Can you do that? Tell me what you want, baby. Let me hear it."

This man. What in the world? No one has made me beg for anything before. And certainly never like this.

He dips his head, his tongue swiping across my clit, making me cry out before he pulls away again. "Beg for my tongue. You know I can make you come with it. You're already close."

I'm so close. He'd probably only have to breathe on my clit and I'd fall apart.

He teases it again, just with the tip of his tongue, and I suck in a harsh breath, nearly choking on it.

"Come on. I wanna hear you use your manners."

We stare at each other for a moment and I realize...he's giving me what I want. What I crave. Hot sex for one night.

And he's going to make me beg for it.

"P-please, please," I stutter, spreading my thighs as wide as I can. This big, broad man is currently lying between them, his face right at pussy level, and I am dying to feel his mouth on me again. "I need you to..."

My voice drifts and I close my eyes.

He traces my folds with a single fingertip, driving me out of my mind with lust. "You need me to what?"

"Lick my pussy," I whisper, closing my eyes for a moment. It's not a word I say out loud. Pussy. Not really.

He does exactly that, flattening his tongue and covering as much territory as possible with that wicked tongue of his and lord save me, it feels amazing. "What else do you want? Get creative. Tell me exactly what you need, and make it as dirty as possible."

I hesitate and he must see something flicker in my eyes because his expression gentles.

"You're safe with me, Ruby." His voice rings with sincerity. "You can say whatever you want. Ask for whatever you want. No judgment."

His words are like a dam breaking inside me.

"I want you to fuck me with your fingers and your tongue," I whisper. "I want you to suck my clit. I want you to put your whole mouth on my pussy and suck and lick me. I want to ride your face, and after you make me come, I want you to kiss me so I can taste myself on your lips."

His gaze darkens and he gives me exactly what I want, sliding two fingers inside me at once and steadily pushing them in and out of my body, curling them. Touching something deep with every thrust that has me slowly unraveling. I lift my hips, arching into his hand and when he replaces his fingers with his mouth, I grip the back of his head, holding him to me, much like I did the last time we did this.

He doesn't seem to mind as I basically smother him with my pussy. God, he eats and eats at me, giving me what I asked for. His lips and tongue toying with my clit, drawing me closer and closer to the edge. I feel like I'm going to fall straight over it at any moment. As if I'm freefalling in the air, and there's no net to catch me. It's exhilarating.

It's terrifying.

He grabs hold of me, his hands slipping beneath my ass, lifting me up, his mouth still attached to my pussy and my hands fall away from his hair. I grind against his face, whimpering. Moaning. Ohhh...

Oh.

"Ace." His name falls from my lips on a pant and he zeroes in on my clit, his tongue and lips working the bit of sensitive flesh. Circling. His fingers teasing the crack of my ass, sliding closer to a spot no guy has ever touched before. He spreads my ass cheeks with those big hands, fingers dipping deeper, tongue flicking at my clit and shit.

That's it.

I'm coming.

Coming.

"Oh God," I choke out as the orgasm hits me hard, my head spinning, my entire body shaking. He never lets up, his mouth working me into a frenzy, my clit becoming so sensitive that when it's over, I'm pushing him away from me because I can't take it anymore.

It's too much. He's too much.

Truly, he's not enough.

"Roll over," he demands and I automatically do as he says, turning over onto my stomach. He yanks me into position so I'm on my knees, my upper body still pressed into the mattress and I wiggle my ass back and forth like the shameless woman I've become thanks to him, shivering as the cool air hits my heated flesh.

I can feel him looming behind me. Hear him kick off his shoes—oh my God, he just did all of that to me with his shoes on, and I don't know why, but the idea makes me giggle.

Ace pauses. "Are you laughing at me?"

A shiver pulses through me at the sound of his deep voice. God, he sounds like sin and sex. "No."

"Better not be." He smacks my ass, his palm connecting with my flesh, making me jolt forward, a moan falling from my lips.

Heaven help me, that felt *good.* I never thought I was into spanking. Seriously, the idea of it always sounded kind of silly to me, but what he just did?

I swear I'm dripping down the inside of my thighs, it was so hot.

"Look at you." His tone is admiring as he contemplates me and I can hear him get rid of his jeans. Most likely his underwear too. I'm tempted to turn around and check to see if he's naked, but there's something so delicious about lying here with my face basically buried in the pillow I find myself clutching and my ass sticking up in the air. I spread my knees a little, wanting him to see all of me and he smacks my butt again. A little lighter this time but still hard enough to sting.

To burn.

I feel that burn all the way to my clit.

"You are a dirty girl, Red." He massages the spot where he just slapped me, his touch gentle, making me tremble. "I plan on fucking you like this someday."

Oh, the promise in his voice. I can barely take it.

"From behind?" I ask hopefully.

"Mmm, hmm." The mattress sags when he climbs onto the bed, his hands on my hips as he pulls me into him. I feel the brush of his cock against my exposed pussy and good God, all I want to do is back up even more and feel him slide into me. Just like this.

"Why can't we do it now?" I ask, my voice muffled by the pillow I'm clutching.

He goes still, his large hands spanning my hips, his cock right there, poking at me. He's long and hard and I'm dying to feel him slowly enter me. Dying to experience the delicious friction.

Oh god. I could come again just *thinking* about it.

"You really want me to fuck you like this?" He sounds surprised.

"Yes, please," I practically scream into the pillow.

"I do love a woman who's polite," he says jokingly, pulling me into him, his cock sliding along my folds, teasing them. Between my lower lips. Back and forth, nice and slow, driving us both out of our minds. "Fuck, you feel good like this, Red."

"So do you," I whisper, rocking against him.

We keep this up like we're unable to stop, the mattress creaking with our movements, both of us panting. He increases his pace, his cock slipping inside me, just the tip, and we both pause, the guttural groan coming from deep inside Ace's chest sparking something primal inside me.

I want to hear him make that sound again. Now.

"Fuck me, you are so tight." He inches inside, just a little bit more, and I whimper. "I need a condom."

I go completely still, his cock barely inside me, my chest aching with the need to just push back and engulf him completely but...

"I don't have any condoms," I admit.

He's quiet for a moment, like he's struggling to find words. "I don't either."

My stomach sinks.

"Oh my God," I whisper. "Are you serious?"

"I mean...yeah." He pulls out a little.

Pushes back in a little.

I moan, enjoying the torture.

"You're Ace fucking Townsend. Biggest player on campus," I remind him.

"Don't remind me," he mutters. "I haven't fucked anyone in ages."

"Define ages."

"Since you came back into my life."

"Wait...what?" I'm shocked.

Is he for real?

"I'm serious." He runs his hands up and down my sides, making me shiver. I can't get enough of him touching me. "I've never fucked anyone without a condom before."

Is he just saying that?

No. I get the sense that Ace respects me. Actually likes me. We get along. Conversation is always flowing and I want to know more about him. I think he wants to know more about me too. I like this man. He wouldn't lie just to have sex with me. If that was the case, he would've tried something a long time ago, I probably would've fallen for it and we'd already be done-zo.

"Really?" I ask.

"Really," he says firmly.

I went on birth control my senior year in high school and I've never stopped taking it. Should I tell him that? It's not foolproof and I don't know his sexual history so I'm the type who likes to double up on safety. I don't like putting my health at risk and babies?

Yeah, no. Not for at least ten years.

"Me neither," I admit softly. "And...I'm on birth control."

He rocks his hips, sliding in deeper, the bastard. Trying to remind me of how good it feels like this. "I'll pull out of you before I come if you want."

"Come all over my tits again?" I ask teasingly.

His hips buck against me. "Damn, woman, don't say those words. Conjures up all sorts of images in my brain."

Aw, he's so cute. And sexy. And easy to rile up.

But I forget about all of those thoughts when he slides deeper, entering me until we're both completely still, getting used to each other. I feel so full of him, stretched out completely because he's long and thick. Like a dream dick, if I'm being real with myself, and of course Ace has a dream dick.

He's a dream guy. It makes sense that he'd come properly equipped.

"Lift up, baby. Brace yourself on your hands," he demands, and I do what he says, sending him deeper, making us both moan.

Gripping my hips, he steadily fucks me, sliding in and out, slow and easy. Driving me out of my mind with pleasure. I knew the friction would be good. That slow drag of his cock inside of me pulling almost all the way out before he plunges back in. Over and over. I can feel his fingers trace along my folds that surround his cock, his gaze hot on my skin, and I don't even have to see him to know this is happening. To feel it.

"This is sexy." He drifts his fingers back and forth over my pussy, along his dick. "Watching you take me."

I duck my head and moan at his words, my tits swaying with his every thrust as he increases his pace. We fuck like this for so long, I marvel at his stamina, at the fact that he's driving me closer to orgasm yet never quite getting me there. Like he's drawing it out on purpose.

He most likely is.

"Jesus, I can't take this." Ace pulls out of my body completely, grabbing my waist and giving me a tug. "Roll over."

I glance over my shoulder at him. "Why?"

He flips me onto my back with ease, his body hovering over mine as he grabs hold of his cock and guides himself into me. I'm so wet, he slides home easily and I lift my hips, meeting him halfway. "Because I want to look at your beautiful face when I make you come."

Oh God. He says things like that and I want to melt. I want to fling myself at him and never let him go.

Ever.

32

ACE

I'm torturing myself. Torturing Ruby. But I want to draw this moment out. The first time I have actual sex with her, and I want it to be a memorable experience.

For both of us.

The shock on her face from my admission was worth me telling the truth. I don't normally care about watching a girl's face when she comes. I'm a selfish bastard—before I was always in it for myself.

This night with Ruby though?

I want to watch the orgasm consume her. I want to stare into her beautiful eyes and kiss her luscious lips and fuck her into oblivion. I want to hear her whisper my name, feel her pussy pulsate around my dick as she wrings my own orgasm out of me.

Fuck, I'm about to come just from the thought of it.

Bracing my hands on the mattress on either side of her head, I ram into her over and over, until she's got her head thrown back and her throat on display. Bending over her, I race my mouth over her skin, kissing the spot where her pulse throbs. It matches the same beat as her cunt, and fuck, she's squeezing me. Tightening around me, strangling me—

"Oh God. *Ace.*" She draws my name out, the rhythmic pulsing of her pussy sending me closer and closer...

Until I'm desperate to pull out of her, groaning as semen spills from my cock all over her lower belly, dripping across her mostly bare pussy. Coming all over her as if I have no control over myself.

Which I don't. Not when it comes to this girl.

"Holy shit," she murmurs, her eyes cracking open to stare up at me. "Wow."

I smile, dipping my head to kiss her. "Yeah. Wow."

She reaches down, her fingers drifting across her stomach, smearing my cum all over her skin. "Want to rub it in?"

Jesus. This woman. My cock is already standing at half attention thanks to her saying that.

"Do you want me to rub it in?" I don't give her a chance to answer, batting her hand away so I can streak my fingers through the liquid. I hold them in front of her mouth, and she parts her lips, her eyes going wide. "Lick it off."

I sink them into her mouth and she does as I tell her, her tongue lapping at my fingers and yeah, I just shot cum all over her and my cock is hard like it's ready to go again. There is nothing sexier than an eager to please woman licking your semen off your fingers like it's her favorite dessert.

And right now, Ruby is sucking my fingers like they're my dick. Meaning she's doing a damn good and most thorough job.

When she's finished, I collapse on the mattress beside her and yank her into my arms, holding her close. We're quiet for a moment, trying to calm our breathing. Our racing hearts.

"I have a question," I say after a few minutes.

"What is it?"

I rest my cheek against hers, whispering close to her ear, "What's your opinion on ass play?"

She bursts out laughing. "I've never really thought about it before."

"Well, think about it. With me." I rub the side of her hip, savoring her smooth, soft skin. "Because I want to play with yours."

"Using what?"

"My fingers." My arms tighten around her waist, pulling her closer. "My mouth. My tongue. Eventually my cock."

She's silent for a few seconds. "Are you into that sort of thing?"

"Not really. Until you," I say with all honesty.

Only because I want to claim every single part of her and make her mine.

If I said that out loud, would it freak her out?

Hell, would it freak *me* out?

"Then, I'm interested," she says firmly.

I kiss her because fuck yes, that's the answer I was looking for. Is Ruby Maguire turning into my dream girl?

Apparently, the answer is yes.

MONDAY MORNING and I'm striding across campus, whistling a showtune like I'm in a Disney movie and sunshine is shooting out my ass. I feel so fucking good, so on top of the world, absolutely nothing is going to keep me down.

Not a damn thing.

Ruby and I fucked around all Saturday night and well into Sunday morning. The girl can give as well as she takes and damn, it was a life-changing experience. By the time I snuck out of her apartment in the early morning sunlight, I was exhausted. Went home and slept pretty much all day.

And now I'm wandering around campus bright-eyed and bushy-tailed like my mom used to say, on high alert as I scan the area in search of Ruby. Desperate to see her pretty blonde head.

She's nowhere to be found.

I texted her earlier, but she didn't answer. I didn't let that deter me though. We texted last night for a little bit and it got dirty with her describing exactly what she wanted to do to me next time we were alone, and damn, I had to jerk off to thoughts of Ruby on her knees while I fucked her mouth with my cock.

Because that's what she wanted to do—she described it in vivid detail.

See? Dream girl material. I'm a lucky fucker and I know it.

I go to all of my classes and try to concentrate. Eat lunch with some teammates and idly listen to their conversations, my thoughts consumed with Ruby. By the time I'm in the locker room getting ready for practice, I'm practically vibrating with excitement at the thought of seeing her with the rest of the social media team out on the field.

I'm barely changed into my practice gear when Coach Mattson calls for a quick meeting that's met with a lot of groaning and moaning, which just pisses him off.

Uh oh. Hope someone didn't fuck up.

"I don't want to crap all over our big win this weekend, but we've had some complaints," Mattson announces.

"Complaints about what?" I ask, resting my hands on my hips, vaguely annoyed.

Who the hell could complain about us? What have we done? Not a goddamn thing if you ask me.

"An anonymous report came in that some members of the football team were fraternizing with members of our social media team Saturday night at Logan's." Coach's gaze scans all of us surrounding him. "Is that true?"

Dread coats my insides, turning my annoyance into worry just like that. "What exactly are you talking about?"

"There were female members of the social media team sitting with some of you guys at the bar," Mattson says slowly, his gaze fixed on me. "You were named, Ace. And so were you, Derek."

"Oh, gimme a break. We were chilling with Maguire and Gwyneth. It was no big deal," Derek grumbles.

"Ruby Maguire?" Coach asks. "Knox's little sister?"

I hate that he put it like that. Most of the time I forget she's Knox's sister. She's just Ruby to me.

"You know she's on our social media team," Derek reminds Mattson.

"Right." Mattson scrubs his hand across his jaw. "Well, it's a big deal to the athletic director. We have an image to uphold and he wants no trouble with the department, especially the football team, while you're in season. You partying with those girls could look bad, especially after what happened a few years ago."

"That chick was psycho," someone else adds, earning a stern glare from Mattson.

"We reserve no judgment here. We don't know the actual circumstances between them. And you never know what could happen. Alcohol and partying and women—that's a dangerous combination. Things can get out of hand quickly and next thing you know, you've got a woman hellbent on ruining you. None of you can take that risk."

I can't imagine Ruby hellbent on ruining me, like Coach says. I think she likes me too damn much to want to fuck with me.

"We're barely into the season, boys. I need all of you healthy and keeping your dicks out of trouble," Mattson continues. "From what I understand, the women on the social media team are getting a talking to as well."

My stomach drops at the idea of Ruby getting in trouble for hanging out with us at the bar on Saturday night. "It was pretty harmless, all of us together at Logan's."

"We were just celebrating," Derek adds.

"I understand, but there's a clause included on the agreement everyone on the athletic social media teams has to sign. They can't date an athlete. Meaning our social media gang can't date any of you assholes." Mattson jabs a finger in the air.

"Too bad," Derek drawls. "I was really checking Eric out Saturday night."

Everyone groans and laughs, with the exception of Mattson. His expression is stone-cold serious. "This isn't a laughing matter. The university isn't going to risk any trouble again. We all know and understand that hormones can come into play at any time. But you're all adults. You can have a professional relationship with the social media team —and that's as far as you take it. Understood?"

We all nod and grumble yeah, and by the time we're out on the football field, I'm sick to my stomach.

It's too late. Ruby and I took it pretty damn far. We've had sex—multiple times in one night. All I can think about is her. How am I supposed to keep our relationship strictly professional?

Give me a break. We're too far gone for that.

I put in a halfhearted performance during practice and

thank God we don't have a game Saturday because I'm worthless.

"Still hungover?" Javier asks me at one point after I throw another bomb.

"Nah. Just...tired." I shrug, unsure of how to answer.

More like I'm preoccupied. Worried. And still horny. A confusing swarm of emotions and feelings I don't quite know how to process. It doesn't help that no one from the social media team shows up during practice. Where the hell are they?

Where the hell is Ruby?

33

RUBY

Our department advisor Marilee is waiting for us in our office when we show up at our normally scheduled meeting time, a sour look on her normally sunny face. The three of us exchange glances before Gwyneth steps forward and bravely asks, "Is everything okay?"

"I need to speak to the three of you. Well, only you two." Marilee indicates me and Gwen. "It's about what happened Saturday night."

My stomach literally bottoms out and I'm afraid I might puke up the salad I ate at lunch. Does she know I had sex with Ace Saturday night? How? Who told her?

"What about Saturday?" Gwen asks, sounding genuinely curious.

"There was a report that the two of you were spending time with the football team at a bar downtown." Marilee sniffs, pushing her glasses up her nose.

Relief floods me at her not mentioning the sex part, but still.

This isn't good.

"We were at Logan's, yes." Gwen nods, her gaze quickly going to mine before she returns her attention to Marilee. "And we spent some time with the football team."

"That's not allowed."

"They asked us to join them," Gwen explains. "As friends. We're kind of a part of the team, you know? And we were there celebrating their big win."

"I was there too," Eric adds.

"You were?" Marilee looks over at him, surprised.

"Yeah. I hung out with them as well."

"That doesn't seem to be a problem," she says firmly.

"Why? Because I'm a guy?" Eric's tone is almost hostile.

"Well...yes," Marilee says.

"What if I was gay?"

Marilee frowns. "Oh...are you?"

"That's not the point. You're making Gwen and Ruby feel bad for hanging with the football team—guys we spend a lot of time with already—like what they're doing is wrong. Yet when I hang out with them, it's no big deal."

"The sexual component always comes into play—" Marilee starts, but Eric cuts her off.

"It shouldn't. Men and women can be friends. It's no big deal."

"It's true," Gwen adds. "Nothing happened that night. We were there to celebrate our team. That's it."

"Yeah. That's it," I echo.

God, I'm a giant liar. Later that night, I had Ace's dick in my face. In my mouth. In my body. We were wrapped up in each other all night long and it was awesome and I'm dying to do it again.

Marilee studies all of us, her gaze touching on each of our faces, her frown deepening when she lands on Eric.

"I feel like you're trying to turn this into a bigger problem," she tells him.

"And I feel like you're being unfair just because they're women. They know how to conduct themselves with the football team. We all know what our responsibilities are and we're not going to jeopardize anything," Eric says. "Shouldn't you be sticking up for them, considering you're a woman too?"

"Eric," Gwen says, her tone faintly chastising. There's a pleading look in her eyes, like she's dying to tell him to shut up.

Marilee visibly bristles. She doesn't like being challenged, that's clear. "I merely wanted to let you know about the matter, and if you want my advice, I would suggest not spending any personal time with a football player. Especially at a bar where everyone can see you."

One more sweeping look and then she marches out of the office, slamming the door behind her.

Gwen slumps forward, pressing her head against the desk for a moment. "Did you have to argue with her, Eric?"

"She was being so sexist! It's not like you were flirting with the football team." Eric scoffs.

I keep my lips pressed together so I don't say something stupid like, oh I was!

Because I was flirting with Ace all night.

"Right, because I was too busy flirting with you." Gwen lifts her head, her gaze going to mine. "You never heard me say that."

"She did," Eric says.

"I did," I agree, my gaze bouncing between the two of them. "Are you guys—"

"We don't know what we are," Gwen says, cutting me off.

Eric remains quiet, but he's smiling, ducking his head.

My earlier worry is forgotten. I'm grinning at them like a fool. "Ooh, you two! What happened Saturday night?"

"None of your business," Gwen says at the same time Eric answers, "We kissed."

"Oh my God!" I'm hopping up and down like a child, clapping my hands. "That's so cute. You two make a good couple."

"Don't rush things," Gwen says.

"I agree," Eric tells me.

This man is clearly into her and she's freaking out. We need to have a talk, but I can tell Gwen doesn't want to have it now.

"We're not going to practice today." Gwen rises from her chair and starts pacing around the office like she's nervous. "I wanted to work on editing the footage we got over the weekend and putting together some posts, and now after what Marilee said, I think it's a good idea if we steer clear from the team for the week."

"The entire week?" I ask, sounding sad.

"Gwen, that's being a little extreme," Eric tells her.

"Do you have a better idea?" Gwen crosses her arms in front of her, defensive.

"Yeah, I think I do. I agree we should stay here this afternoon and work on all the footage we got during the game, but later this week? Those guys are going to be a lot more relaxed since they don't have a game Saturday, including the coaching staff. You should put together some of those lip-syncing videos you like so much." Eric makes the slightest face. He still thinks those videos are ridiculous, but he doesn't give us too much grief over it. "What do you think, Ruby?"

"I think that sounds perfect," I say with a firm nod.

Gwen sighs. "Fine. Let's get to work then."

I'll miss seeing Ace out at practice, but it might be best to stay away this afternoon. I'm guessing they got a talking to as well, and I wonder how he took it. Will he freak out and not want to see me anymore?

I doubt he would give up on me that easily.

Would he?

He better not.

❧

ACEY BABY: **What are you doing?**

Me: **Avoiding football players at all costs.**

Acey Baby: **Including me?**

Me: **Especially you.**

Acey Baby: **Ouch. That's harsh.**

Me: **Did you hear that someone snitched on us?**

Acey Baby: **Yeah. We got a big speech over it, though I have to admit, it didn't feel like that big of deal. So we hung out at the bar. It's not like anything happened.**

Me: **We were talked to as well and I quietly freaked out because something definitely happened.**

Acey Baby: **No one knows about us.**

Me: **Right and we need to keep it that way.**

He doesn't respond for a few minutes, and of course, my stomach twists into knots and I worry about what he's thinking. How he might be reacting.

Acey Baby: **I can't stop thinking about it.**

Acey Baby: **Can't stop thinking about you.**

Butterflies flutter in my stomach and I glance up at the ceiling, searching for strength, but there's none to be found. I know what I should do: turn him away. Tell him we need to play it cool and not hang out because this is dangerous. This kind of talk? Him saying he can't stop thinking about me?

It's not good. It's not good at all.

Acey Baby: **Let's hang out.**

Me: **Tonight????**

Acey Baby: **Yeah. I want to see you again.**

Acey Baby: **Get you naked again.**

Acey Baby: **Fuck you all night. What do you say?**

It's a terrible idea. Despite the way my pussy tingles and my entire body turns to mush at him saying he wants to get me naked again and fuck me all night—sheesh, way to get a girl excited—I know I should say no. At the very least I should lie and say I'm busy.

My phone rings and I answer it automatically, Ace's deliciously deep voice filling my ear and making me shiver.

"You took way too long to respond."

"I don't know. Is it a good idea, us seeing each other?"

"It's a great idea."

"They're cracking down on us. What if someone finds out?" He'll get a talking to and I'll get fired.

I definitely have more at stake than he does.

"Trust me, no one will find out." He sounds so sure of himself that if he were standing in front of me, I would smack him for being so confident. But then he goes and lowers his voice, becoming intense. "I need to see you."

More tingling and I clamp my thighs together to try to stop it. "Why?"

"Don't ask me questions, Red. Just tell me I can come over." He sounds vaguely irritated. A little impatient.

"But—"

He cuts me off. "Like I mentioned earlier, I'm dying to fuck you again. Eat that sweet pussy of yours. Maybe even fuck your mouth if we have time? What do you think, Red? Sound good?"

His tone is rough, his breathing ragged and I sigh into the phone, feeling weak. "Okay. Come over."

"See you in ten."

34

ACE

I meant what I said. I'm at Ruby's doorstep ten minutes later, my fist raised and ready to knock when the door swings open and Ruby's head pops out. She looks left, then right. Then left again before she grabs my hand and drags me inside, slamming the door behind me.

"What the—"

"We have to be careful," she says, interrupting me. "Come on."

Without waiting, she heads toward the short hall that leads to her bedroom and I trail after her like a dutiful dog because I'm not a stupid man. Where that sexy woman goes, I will follow, especially when it involves privacy and a bed.

She shuts the door and locks it, turning to face me, and that's when I can really take her in. And sweet Jesus, she's worth staring at for a moment because damn.

Her hair is in a sloppy bun on top of her head and she has no makeup on save her lips, which are coated in the faintest sheen. She's got on some thin black shorts that are cut so high I bet her ass cheeks hang out of them when she bends over and one of her infamous T-shirts.

This one is pale blue and cropped, showing off her toned stomach, and it has a saying across the front of it in dark blue lettering.

YOU WISH.

"Ah, Red. Your shirt." My gaze lingers on the words, how they track across her tits perfectly, just like the last one. "I don't have to wish."

She frowns. "What do you mean?"

"All of my wishes have already come true." I grab her hand and yank her to me, her body colliding with mine, sparks igniting between us. "Now that I'm here."

She rolls her eyes. "Give me a break, Acey Baby."

"You really going to keep that up?" I raise my brows.

Ruby is grinning, she's so pleased with herself. "Hmm, definitely. That's your name in my phone now."

"No fucking way."

"I'm serious."

"You're fucking with me."

She shakes her head. "I'm not. Hold on." She swipes her phone off her nightstand and opens it, tapping at the screen until she turns it and shows it to me.

There's my phone number listed in her contacts, accompanied by the name *Acey Baby*.

"That sucks, Red," I groan, shaking my head.

"I think it's cute." She deposits her phone on her nightstand before she turns to me, her hands on her hips and looking sassy as hell while she contemplates me. "This is a terrible idea, by the way."

"What is?"

"The two of us. Together." She shakes her head. "Right now. I could lose my job, Ace."

The seriousness of her tone, the way she's looking at me...shit.

I feel bad.

Standing up straighter, I glance over at the door, knowing I should walk out. Leave her alone for the next couple of months. Anything worth having is worth waiting for, isn't that how the saying goes? Ruby's worth it.

I know she is.

But I've had her already and I want her again. I know what it's like to kiss her. Touch her. Take off her clothes. Eat her out. Sink my dick into her welcoming pussy and fuck her until she comes. I know what she looks like when she comes and she's beautiful. Sexy.

And I want to see that look on her face again. I want to be with her. Damn it, I'm weak. Weak for her.

"You want me to leave?" I ask, my voice so low I can barely hear it.

She stares and I get this sense she hates that I put the ball in her court, so to speak. She probably wanted me to walk out and leave her alone, but it's not that easy. I can't just walk away from her.

I don't want to. I don't think I'm capable of it. She wields some sort of power, spell, whatever you want to call it, over me and I'm not ready to give up on her, or on us.

But if that's what she wants, then I'll give it to her. I'm not going to be the reason she loses her job. She could end up resenting me, hating me and I don't want that to happen.

I need to be the bigger man and walk.

"I'll go," I say when she still hasn't spoken. I head for the door, my hand reaching out, fingers brushing the handle when I hear her voice.

"Don't leave," she whispers.

I turn and she's right there, practically tackling me against the door as per our usual deal and then she's kissing me, swallowing my groan when our lips connect. Her hands are already slipping under the hem of my long-sleeved T-shirt, fingers brushing against my abdomen, making me hiss in a breath. My dick is already standing at attention and she's barely touched me. Hell, I've barely touched her.

"Just one more time with you," she murmurs between kisses. "That's all I want."

Hate to break it to her, but one more time between us won't be near enough.

But I don't say that. With our mouths still fused, I turn her around and steer her toward the bed, guiding her there until she settles on the edge of the mattress and we break apart.

She's reaching for the waistband of my black joggers, already tugging, and I settle my hands over hers, stopping her. "What's the hurry?"

"I want you." She slips her hand from beneath mine and drifts it down the length of my dick, making it leap beneath her touch. "And clearly you want me."

"We don't need to rush it." I repress the groan that wants to escape when she curls her fingers around my shaft. Jesus. "We've got all night."

Pausing, she gazes up at me, her eyes wide and unblinking. "I want to do as much as possible with you tonight."

"We will, baby." I release her other hand and cup her face, tilting it up so I can stare into her pretty eyes. "I'll let you use me and abuse me all you want."

Her smile is faint. "Promise?"

"For you? Anything."

"I want to give you a blow job," she admits without hesitation.

"Who am I to stop you?" I release my hold on her face and let her get to work. She yanks my joggers down and I help her, stepping out of my slides before I kick off my sweats. Bend over and whip off my socks real quick because there's nothing less sexy than me standing around in just my socks and nothing else.

I bet Ruby would be cute completely naked with only a pair of socks on her feet. But she's an exception.

She's sexy no matter what.

"Have I told you how unbelievable your body is?" she asks, her greedy gaze eating me up.

Look, I know I'm in top condition. I work out so damn much I have to be. I'm in the best shape of my life and that's because it feels like every single game is high stakes. I have to win. I have to prove to everyone watching—NFL scouts I'm talking to you—that I've got what it takes. I'm on top of my game, literally.

It feels good though, that the beautiful woman who's currently looking at me like I'm a tasty snack and she's about to consume me is offering me compliments. I'm going to revel in them.

"You haven't," I say truthfully, scratching my fingers across my stomach.

Her eyes turn molten the longer she stares. "Well, your body is amazing. So many muscles." She hesitates. "Have you ever..."

She doesn't say anything else and my curiosity is aroused, along with everything else. "Have I ever what?"

"Touched yourself," she whispers. "In front of someone else?"

I'm shocked she'd ask.

"Not that I want all the details because I don't. No way do I want to know who you stood in front of and jerked off because that's none of my business but—"

"No one."

She frowns. "Really?"

I nod, dropping my hand from my stomach. "Why? You want me to do it in front of you?"

"Yes," she says without hesitation, her gaze stuck on the front of my boxer briefs. My dick is currently making a tent out of them, dying to escape. "I want to sit right here and have a front row seat."

"Red, you are so fucking pervy," I murmur, loving every perverted part of her.

She rolls her eyes. "It's not that big of a deal."

"Right, I just jerk off in front of girls on a daily basis." I shake my head. "For the record? I don't. But for you? I'll make the sacrifice. I just need one thing from you."

"What's that?"

"Keep your eyes on me the entire time," I say, my voice so deep, it sounds like it's rumbling from my chest. "Got it?"

She nods, leaning back on the mattress, bracing her hands on top of it. "Got it."

"And whatever I ask you to do, do it," I add.

"Okay." Her eyes darken, as if she senses I'm going to ask her to do something equally pervy.

She's a smart girl, my Ruby.

Slowly I take off my boxer briefs, my cock springing free and pointing straight at her. Her gaze zeroes in, her eyes practically crossing as she stares at it and I almost laugh. I mean, this is a little crazy, right?

But not really. I'm sure people do this sort of thing all the time. What's the problem with me showing her what I like?

"Lick my hand, baby." I extend it toward her, palm up. "Get it nice and wet for me."

She grabs my wrist and drags her tongue across my palm, the excessive saliva coating my hand and then my perverted girl adds a little extra to it by spitting on it.

Holy. Shit.

I grab the base of my dick, curling my fingers around it and slowly slide my wet hand up, then down the shaft. She watches carefully, her gaze tracking my every move and I bend my knees a little, thrusting my hips. Trying to get my dick in her face.

When I increase my speed, she frowns, a little line forming between her brows. "Doesn't that hurt?"

"No," I bite out, hissing in a breath when I squeeze just below the head, precum filling the slit. "Feels fucking good."

"You're so rough with it."

"I know what I like." I squeeze harder. "And I'm not scared that it's going to hurt."

"Wow," she whispers when my hand begins to move faster. "You're so big and thick."

"Goddamn, you are perfect for my ego," I say between clenched teeth, taking a step closer to her. "Lick the tip, baby. Clean me up."

She leans forward, her tongue sneaking out to lick at the precum, lapping it up with a few quick, teasing strokes. The lash of her hot tongue on my erect dick makes my skin tingle and I'm tempted to ask her to do it again.

But I don't have to ask because she actually does it again, her gaze lifting to mine as she circles the flared head with her tongue. "I told you I wanted to do this."

"You did."

"Let me join you."

"Okay," I say weakly, unable to stop her when she takes over, my hand falling away from my dick and suddenly I'm filling her hot mouth with my cock. She inhales, her cheeks caving in as she sucks extra hard and I flex my hips, desperate to thrust. Ready to take over and fuck her mouth in earnest.

But I let her do her thing, breathing heavily as I watch her enjoy torturing my ass.

Well, torturing my dick more like.

She teases and plays with it. Sucks just the head like it's her favorite candy. Traces the veins with her tongue, gripping the base of my shaft and squeezing, giving her all, but fuck. It's not enough. My sweet little Red, trying so hard.

"Let me take over," I demand and when I pull my dick from her mouth, I see the disappointment flash in her gaze. "Spread your legs."

Ruby does as she's told, parting her legs and bracing her feet on the floor. Swear to fucking God she looks a little damp between the thighs. Has she soaked through her shorts already? Damn. "Take off your shirt."

The shirt is up and over her head and gone in seconds, revealing she's not wearing a bra. Her nipples are hard and flushed a deep rose color and my palms literally ache to cradle them, but not yet.

Not yet.

"Take your hair down," I murmur, reaching for her, cupping her cheek. My thumb drifts over her skin, marveling at how soft she is. How beautiful. Eager to please and willing to do anything.

She reaches up with both hands, mine still on her cheek, and yanks the tie out of her hair so that it falls around her shoulders in haphazard waves. I remove my hand from her cheek and gather her hair at the nape of her neck, holding her in place. "Open your mouth."

The moment her lips part, I'm feeding her my cock. Inch after inch, I slide it in, crooning at her to relax. To open up more. To let me take it deep.

Until her mouth is stuffed full of me and her eyes are watering. She looks so pretty. So fucking sexy.

I start to fuck her mouth, pulling all the way out, the head resting on her lips before I slip back in. I do this over and over again, the visual getting to me quick. How easy she's making this, the silky softness of her hair knotted around my fingers, the faint gagging noises she makes when I go extra deep, my cock bumping the back of her throat.

She doesn't complain. Just takes it like a champ and fuck this girl.

This girl.

I pull out of her mouth, grabbing the base and tapping the head against her still parted lips. "I'm gonna come," I warn her.

Ruby sits up straighter, her tits bouncing and I'm tempted to come on them again but nah.

"I want—to come on your face."

Her eyes go wide for only a second and then she's smiling, her tongue sneaking out for a lick. "Okay."

"Or would I rather come down your throat and make you drink it down?" I ask myself. And her.

Her skin flushes with pleasure at my words.

"Suck it, baby." She does as I tell her, her lips suctioning just the tip, her tongue teasing. My balls draw up and that familiar tingling sensation starts at the base of my spine, radiating throughout my body, settling in my dick.

Yeah. I'm fucking close.

I give myself firm, quick strokes, tapping the head against her lips and she tilts her head back like an offering.

Like a sacrifice.

That's what finally does it. Her tits thrust out and those hard little nipples. My fingers tangled in her hair. Her pink tongue lapping at my dick. I'm coming, the semen dripping from my cock and all over her lips and chin, and fuck.

What a sight.

35

RUBY

Something is wrong with me. I have to be like...a sexual deviant or whatever to love what Ace just did to me. He fucked my mouth and wasn't kind about it. Not like he did things to me that I didn't want but...

It was dirty, what we just did. His fingers in my hair hurt and I liked it. Gagging me with his thick cock and I wanted more. Like who am I? Who have I become?

The girl who's into weird shit, that's who.

But is it really that weird? We're just having fun, right? I don't know.

What I do know is that being with Ace is pushing me out of my comfort zone and I'm enjoying every second of it.

After he came all over my mouth and chin, he helped clean me up—by gathering up all that cum with his fingers and making me lick them off—and now I'm lying on the bed with him on top of me, naked and huge and hot and even a little sweaty.

I don't care. I like him sweaty. Love his damp, smooth, hard skin. I want to rub myself all over him so I can smell like him. I want to touch him everywhere I can, even the forbidden spots. I remember seeing on social media a whole talk about how men shoot off like rockets when you touch them just behind their balls. Or from a finger in their ass.

Would he let me finger his ass?

Probably.

I can feel his balls right now through my thin shorts. He's all snug and nestled close to my pussy and I spread my legs a little. As much as I can, considering his heavy weight on me, and his shaft is suddenly right there, pressed up against me. Half erect already.

The man is insatiable.

"You have too many clothes on," he mutters against my neck, making me shiver.

"Only my shorts," I remind him.

"Too much." He reaches for the waistband of my athletic shorts, tugging them down and I shove at his shoulders so he rolls away from me.

I immediately miss his weight, sucking in a breath when he pulls my shorts down, revealing that I...

"No panties?" He glances up at me, surprise etched in his handsome features.

Slowly I shake my head, nibbling on my index finger.

"I love a woman who's full of surprises." He removes my shorts in seconds, tossing them on the floor, his big hands resting on the inside of my thighs. He spreads them wide, staring at me as I grow wetter by the second, but it's not because of the way he's looking at me. Oh no.

It was his dangerous choice of words.

He *loves* a woman who's full of surprises.

Such as me.

No way does Ace Townsend love me. Everything has happened so fast. I'm not sure if I love him quite yet. That's just...

That's way too quick.

Do I like him?

Oh yes.

Care about him?

Definitely.

Love him?

I'm...falling for him. That's for sure.

He goes down on me and I just take it, moaning with every thrust of his fingers. Whimpering at every swipe of his tongue. He flips me over onto my stomach, spreading me wide from behind and licks me everywhere...back there and *oh God*.

His tongue teases the most forbidden hole I've got and never would I think I'd like that but...

Holy shit, I love it.

He licks it. Strokes it. Inserts just the tip of his finger inside it, encouraging me to basically hump the mattress while he does and I do it. Like a woman with zero self-control, I grind my pussy against the bed, while Ace has his face buried between my ass cheeks and I'm falling apart in minutes, coming so hard, I swear to God I pass out.

Nothing but black. No sound. No thought. Just pleasure radiating throughout my body. Pulsating in my core.

When I come to, Ace is already climbing off the bed and is in my connected bathroom. The faucet turns on and he's washing what I can only assume is his face and hands. I tug the sheet up, covering my still trembling body and when the water shuts off, he's standing in the open bathroom doorway seconds later, studying me.

"I, uh..." His voice drifts and he shrugs, his erect cock bobbing with the movement. "Had to clean myself up first. Before we—"

Excitement bubbles in my veins at the *before we* part.

"Right." No cross contamination going on here. I appreciate his cleanliness.

He climbs into bed with me, his big body taking up almost all of the space. I have a puny double bed because my room is so small. My parents wanted to buy me a queen but it would've taken up most of the space and...

Oh my God, when was the last time I talked to my parents? I've been so busy and I miss them.

A thick with muscle arm wraps around me, pulling me into an equally muscular chest and I go willingly, my back to his front, his cock poking my ass. I lie there, all thoughts of my parents gone, my body on high alert, ready to continue the night's activities.

Orgasms so far? One each. Hoping for more.

"Really only one more time, huh?" He nuzzles the side of my neck, his rumbly voice making my stomach dip and twist.

"One more time, what?" I ask, my body relaxing as he continues rubbing my neck and shoulder with his nose, his wide hand spanning my stomach.

A woman could get used to this. A big, manly man in her bed, about to fuck her until she can't walk, but being sweet about it first.

"You said one more time. Then that would be it." He kisses my shoulder, his lips soft. "For us."

Can I take that back? I didn't mean it. There's no way I want this to be over. I like him too much.

I mentally curse clauses and agreements and women who get their revenge by posting dick pics all over official university social media. She ruined it for the rest of us, and God, life is really unfair.

"Do you want this to be it for us?" I ask, my voice wary. A

little shaky even. I swear I quit breathing and my heart even stops beating while waiting for his answer.

"What do you think?" He thrusts his hips against my butt, nice and slow, his cock reminding me that yes, he's invested and always ready to go. "I just ate your ass, Red. Pretty sure I'm in it to win it."

What...what does that even mean? "In it to win it? Win what?"

He chuckles and the sound is so warm and sexy, it makes my pussy ache. "I figured you'd zero in on the eating ass part."

I'm only mildly embarrassed about him mentioning that, but I'm more curious about the other part. "What are you trying to win?"

"You." He kisses my shoulder again. My neck. His lips are soft and sweet and I remember that this is the man who just said he ate my ass and suddenly I'm giggling.

And I can't stop.

"Why are you laughing?" he asks, sounding mildly offended.

"I don't know. You say crazy stuff." His hand slips from my stomach to my pussy, his fingers teasing my slit and a soft huff of air escapes me. "You're a contradiction."

"How so?" He slips his fingers deeper, pinching my clit between them, the slick sound of his fingers in my pussy horny music to my ears.

From the way his cock is twitching against my ass, I'm guessing it's the same for him.

"You say you're trying to win me, which is just...it's a little romantic."

"I like romance." His mouth is at my ear, teeth nipping the lobe.

"But then you talk about eating ass and instantly turn it dirty," I whisper.

"You liked it when I said that. Don't deny it."

"I did."

"And you liked it when I did that too."

A shiver moves through me at the reminder. "Uh huh."

He's grinning against my shoulder. "You humped your bed."

"Shut up."

"You're fucking filthy, Red."

"You love it."

"I do."

We're quiet for a moment, me marinating in my feelings. In his words. Feeling so utterly content, I don't know how it could get much better.

"Enough with the dirty romance talk," he finally says, his fingers still in my pussy and his mouth still at my ear. "Wanna fuck?"

"Be still my heart," I tease.

He laughs, tugging on me. "Wanna ride me, cowgirl?"

"Yes, yes, I do." Don't need to ask me twice.

I climb on top of him, straddling his hips and bracing my hands on his chest. He watches me with a grin on his handsome face, his blue eyes sparkling, his hair a mess, his skin coated with that delicious sheen of sweat. I bend over him and lick the spot between his pecs, earning a grunt for my efforts, my ass brushing against his dick.

He's salty and delicious and oh, I am such a sucker for this man.

Lifting up, I kiss him and he devours me, the kiss a mess of teeth and tongue and eager lips and hot moans. We're sloppy and we don't care, our hands wandering. He's palming my ass, teasing me from behind. My hands are mapping his skin, marveling at all the strength I feel beneath my palms.

This man could easily break me. Damage me beyond repair. Instead, he's so incredibly gentle. His hands are currently roaming over me, landing on my breasts, giving them a squeeze. I arch into his hands, sucking in a breath when he pinches my nipples, rubbing them with his thumbs.

"Need inside you," he says at one point, as if he's lost his ability to speak in full sentences and I lean back, his cock brushing my entrance. Teasing him. "Now."

I rise up, grabbing the base of his erection and lowering myself upon him, sinking down until he's completely embedded inside me.

Oh my God. He's so deep. So thick and throbbing and connected to me completely. He should probably have a condom on. Sex this good is bound to cause us nothing but trouble in the future.

Not that I'm tempting fate or anything like that, but my God.

Ace lifts his hips as if he's trying to get me to move and that's my sign. I roll my hips, circling to the left, to the right. Back to the left again. He's got his hands on my waist, holding me in place and I straighten my spine. Gather my hair in my hands and lift it to the top of my head, putting on a show.

"Holy fuck," he mutters, his eyes glazed over as he watches me. As I continue to move. I've been on top before—exactly once, with another guy not worth mentioning—and I was an utter failure. This time I want to do it right.

For Ace. For me.

I rock back and forth, grinding down, my clit brushing

against the base of his dick and my entire body trembles. "*Oh.*"

"Like that?" His hands tighten on my waist, fingers pressing into my skin as he guides me up and down, lifting his hips at the same time I bear down. Pleasure shoots through me and I drop my arms, my hair falling all around my face until I tilt my head back and pant at the ceiling.

Who am I in this moment? I don't feel like myself. I'm a woman transformed by a magical cock and magical hands and magical sex. He keeps talking, almost murmuring to himself, and I zero in on his deep voice, trying to decipher the words.

"...so fucking beautiful. You take my cock so good, Red. Yeah, baby."

He presses his fingers right at my clit and I cry out. I am basically bouncing on this man's dick and at one point, I fear I might break it in half, but he's encouraging me at first. Until his hands slide down to my hips, his grip tightening as he murmurs, "Keep still."

"Wha..."

Ace thrusts up into me again and again. Hard. Harder. His entire body flushes red, the cords in his neck standing out, the muscles in his arms strained. He fucks me, grunting with every thrust, making me moan. Making me lose all sense of myself and my body until I'm nothing but lust and hormones and tingling sensations that make my toes curl.

That first spurt of semen floods my body and I squeeze my inner walls, gripping around his shaft, making him groan. He's pressing against my clit, tight little circles that ratchet up the intensity until I'm coming too. My pussy throbs, squeezing him over and over until I collapse on top of him in a sweaty heap, my face in his neck.

My lips on his skin.

His big hands land gently on my butt, massaging me there, his cock still embedded in me. We lie like that for I don't know how long. The room silent save for our pounding hearts and rapid breaths. I close my eyes and swallow hard, wondering if I'll be able to climb off him or if I'll just slide off and land on the floor in a puddle when he murmurs...

"Want to do that again?"

A contented sigh leaves me and I brush a kiss to his chest. "Yes, please."

36

RUBY

I t's like this for a month. Four glorious weeks of illicit meetings with Ace behind closed doors. Always at my place because for some reason, Natalie is never around much anymore. When I see her on those rare occasions and ask her about it, she always gives me some off-hand excuse about classes and work and how she doesn't have a lot of time with her intense schedule, and I eventually stopped asking because I felt bad.

I'm over here having the absolute time of my life, while she's working her ass off and I have major guilt.

But I don't feel guilty enough to stop because why would I? Ace Townsend is, frankly put, a sex god.

And he's *my* sex god.

His unwavering interest in me is giving me the self-confidence boost I never knew I needed. That this gorgeous, athletic, smart, everyone-wants-him man is interested in me and no one else?

It's heady stuff. His attention toward me makes me feel like I could possibly conquer the world.

When I came back to my home state to attend college at

CU, I wasn't feeling that confident. More like I believed I was a complete failure. I left Colorado in the hopes to find a different life and I couldn't cut it.

I was low. Even feeling a little alone. My parents are in California. My sister took off and is living her best life as a devoted NFL girlfriend, and my brother is actually in the NFL. They're living our parents' life while I felt like a giant fuck-up.

Well, not anymore. Now I'm on top of the world. I have a handsome, sexy, successful man who's totally into me and I'm doing well in my classes. And at my job.

Ugh, my job. I need to stop reminding myself.

That's the only difficult part. The sneaking around and keeping our relationship under wraps. It hasn't been easy for Ace. He's offering up all sorts of excuses to his team-mates and his roommates as to why he can't hang out or why he's always leaving and I think it's wearing on him.

I know it would wear on me.

It's almost a relief when he has an away game because then we're forced not to see each other for a little while. Despite it being absolute torture and I can't stand being away from him for too long, it's also a lesson in learning how to be adults and deal with separation in a mature manner.

Okay, that sounds like a load of crap, but I'm trying to convince myself that I'm growing up.

My biggest issue currently is lying to Gwen. We've become even closer these last few weeks and she's been telling me everything about her and Eric. I've become her relationship guru, which is hilarious because I don't know shit about having a real relationship, but Gwen has put all her trust and faith in me. Any bit of advice I dole out, she takes it. She believes in it. She believes in me.

And that hurts. It cuts to the bone. I watch her and Eric

fall for each other harder as every single day passes, and I'm jealous. They don't have to hide their feelings. Everyone can know, though I doubt very much Marilee is aware of it—or anyone else who's part of the athletic department administration.

There aren't any rules or clauses in the agreement that we signed that say they can't be in a relationship, so they're safe. Unlike me.

I want to tell Gwen the truth about me and Ace, but I'm so scared that she's such a little rule follower, she might end up confessing our sins.

And I know I would get fired.

It's late at night and I'm trying to concentrate on writing a paper that's due next week, but I can't focus for shit, so I give up and leave my room to grab a snack. I know there's ranch dip in the fridge and a new bag of potato chips on the kitchen counter, and while it's almost eleven at night and the last thing I need is to consume a bunch of sodium before I go to bed, I'm still creeping down the hall. Heading for the kitchen, I pause, an unfamiliar sound making me go completely still.

What...what is that?

I crane my head toward the living room, my heart pounding in my throat. The lights are off. I didn't think Natalie was home yet but is that...is that her?

And is that noise I'm hearing the sound of lips connecting. Parting. Reconnecting?

The rustle of clothing, a soft moan flits through the air and I realize someone is making out.

In our living room.

Feeling brazen, I march into the living room and reach for the nearest lamp, flicking it on. Sucking in a shocked gasp of horror when I see who's wrapped up around each other on our couch, their mouths fused, hands in each other's hair.

My roommate and...

Big D?

Derek?

They break away from each other at the same time, Natalie ducking her head against Derek's barrel chest, while he grins at me, his cheeks ruddy. Like he's...what?

Embarrassed?

"Yo, Maguire."

"What the hell are you doing here?" I practically scream.

He lets go of Natalie and rubs at the corner of his mouth, contemplating me. "Um, what's it look like to you?"

Is he seriously the one asking me questions? Please.

"Are you two hooking up? On my couch?" I am screeching. And I sort of don't care because I'm absolutely floored by this turn of events.

Natalie lifts her head, and I take in her flushed face and bright eyes. "We're not hooking up."

"Then what would you call it?"

"Kissing on the couch?" Derek offers. I glare at him and he goes quiet.

"I thought you hated this guy," I say to Natalie, lowering my voice like we're sharing secrets with him sitting right there.

"Hey," Derek protests, sounding offended.

"Shush," I tell him before I turn to Nat. "Seriously, what's going on?"

Natalie's expression turns sheepish and she leans her head against Derek's chest, a faint smile curling her lips. "We're...dating."

My mouth drops open. "You're kidding."

"Afraid not."

"You don't got faith in me, Rubes?"

"Oh my God, do not call me that," I tell Derek. It sounds too close to pubes. "And no, I have zero faith in you. You're a player. You've said that from the moment I met you."

"Well, I'm a changed man thanks to Natalie." He slings his thick arm around Natalie's shoulders, nearly engulfing her as he tugs her close and drops a sweet kiss on her forehead. "We've been seeing each other for a month."

A month?

"I think a little longer," Natalie corrects him. "Six weeks?"

So basically as long as Ace and I have been seeing each other. This is...

This is wild.

"Why didn't you tell me?" I ask Nat, kind of hurt, though I have no right to be.

After all, I haven't told her much about me and Ace beyond that one initial hookup. I declared I was on a man ban and never brought him up again.

"I don't know. I was a little embarrassed. Not of you, babe." She pats Derek's meaty bicep. "Just of our situation. We both have reputations we're not exactly proud of. Plus, we tried the fuck buddies thing last year and it sort of fell apart."

"Okayyyyyy."

"We wanted to take this slow and make sure it would actually work before we made any big announcements," Natalie explains. "I just—I didn't expect to tell you like this. When you catch us kissing in the living room."

"I didn't know what was happening," I admit. "I was just coming out here to get a snack."

Her smile is rueful. "Sorry."

"Hope it wasn't the bag of potato chips you wanted to snack on," Derek says.

I groan. "You ate them?"

He nods, looking guilty. "Sorry. Nat brought me over here to feed me. There's no food in our house."

"That's not true." Natalie nudges him in the ribs. "Well, he's right about the lack of food at his place but we came over here because I forgot my laptop and I have a paper due in the morning."

"And you got distracted enough to start making out on our couch?"

"After I caught him eating our chips." She indicates the crumpled bag I didn't notice before that's discarded on our coffee table.

"Derek, you owe me a bag of Lay's Potato Chips," I demand.

"Yes, ma'am." He salutes me, jumping to his feet and offering his hand to Natalie. "Ready to go, babe?"

She takes his hand and he pulls her up, hauling her into his arms, kissing her right in front of me. All lovey dovey and sweet and my goodness, my brain is confused by all of this.

It's Big D we're talking about here. And Natalie. The two people I never believed could be serious are...

Serious.

Who knew?

I watch them leave, trying to shove aside the weird emotions swirling inside me while they blatantly touch and flirt with each other right in front of me. What they have is what I want. What I wish I had.

With Ace.

The moment they're gone, I'm grabbing my phone and sending Ace a text.

Me: **You awake?**

He answers almost immediately.

Acey Baby: **Yep. You okay?**

I smile, touched by his concern. I love that's the first thing he asks. He really is sweet.

And a complete savage in bed.

Lucky me.

Me: **I'm bored, hungry and horny.**

Acey Baby: **Is this a cry for help?**

Me: **Yes.**

Should I ask him to come over?

Yes. Yes, I should.

Me: **Come over.**

Acey Baby: **What are you hungry for?**

Me: **Surprise me.**

Acey Baby: **You really want me to come over?**

Me: **I'm alone and a little hungry. I need protection. And food.**

Acey Baby: **I'll be right over.**

37

ACE

I throw on an old pair of threadbare gray sweats and a CU red hoodie with bleach stains and make my way to Ruby's apartment in record time, only stopping at Taco Bell because it has a twenty-four-hour drive-thru. I buy a variety of items—tacos, burritos and chalupas and haul ass the rest of the way, eager to see her.

Eager to take care of her.

I never thought I'd want to be with a girl for such an extended period of time, but I'm proud to say I'm not sick of her yet. In all actuality, I'm more entranced with Ruby now than I've ever been. She's just so...fascinating. I like hearing her talk about her day. Her past. Her present. What she hopes for her future. I like hearing her stories about her family. How close they are, and how someday she wants a bunch of kids too.

Though she made that confession and immediately tried to play it off, like she wasn't thinking about having kids with me.

Honestly? When she said it, I couldn't help but think of having kids with her.

She'd be a good mom. She comes from a good family. She's smart and thoughtful and sexy and funny and friendly and caring and...

I've got it bad for her. So fucking bad.

And I don't know what to do about it.

This no-dating clause thing is a real drag. I'm tired of hiding what we're doing, but I have to be respectful of Ruby's job. I don't want to be the reason she loses it.

But this is truly some straight-up bullshit.

By the time I'm at her front door, she's already got it open and letting me inside, reaching for the Taco Bell bag before the door is halfway closed.

"Oh my God, that smells amazing," she murmurs, dropping the bag onto the tiny kitchen table and digging her hand inside. When she pulls out a chalupa, she groans. "My favorite."

"I got a bunch of stuff," I say, watching as she unwraps the chalupa and takes a big bite. "I wasn't sure what you wanted."

"I want all of it." She waves her hand at the bag, her mouth still full. "Unless you, uh, want something."

I grab a basic taco and unwrap it, taking a bite though I know I shouldn't. This definitely doesn't qualify as part of my nutritional meal plan to keep in shape.

Once she polishes off the chalupa, she grabs her water bottle that's sitting on the table and takes a big sip before she plucks a taco from the bag and starts tearing into that too. I watch her, wondering if she's hormonal or about to start her period or whatever. She seems preoccupied and unusually hungry.

"Are you all right?" I finally ask after she still hasn't said anything.

A sigh leaves her and she drops her half-eaten taco onto

the wrapper that's spread out on the table with a plop. "I'm eating my feelings."

"Say what?"

"I'm eating my feelings," she says slowly, like I'm an idiot.

"Oh, I heard you, I just don't know exactly what you mean."

She throws her hands in the air. "Derek and Natalie are dating."

I blink at her, startled by her rapid change of subject. Shocked more by what she said. "They are?"

Ruby nods, seemingly miserable. "Isn't it great? They've been together for like six weeks. I think they're in love."

I take a step closer, reaching out to tuck a strand of hair behind her ear. "Why do you sound so sad about it?"

"Because I'm jealous." She backs away from me, grabbing her taco so she can nibble on it. "They're not the relationship type."

"Okay," I say slowly.

"They both admitted that to me."

"Did they tell you they were together?"

"I caught them kissing on our couch. Like full-blown making out, their hands everywhere. It was...oh God, I was so shocked. Like this is the last thing I expected. Natalie's told me before that she hates him."

"Doesn't sound like she hates him anymore."

"She doesn't," Ruby wails. "I think she might love him. God, I hate this."

She polishes off the taco, wipes her hands and mouth with a napkin and then stalks off, headed down the hallway.

"Where are you going?" I call after her.

"Running away from my problems!" she yells.

This woman. She makes absolutely no sense.

I follow after her, grabbing her arm before she can sneak

off into the bathroom and turn her to face me. "Ruby. Baby. Tell me what's bothering you."

"I'm tired of keeping this secret."

"Keeping what secret?" I'm fairly certain I know what she's talking about but I'm just making sure.

"Us. You and me." She sounds miserable. "I like you."

"I like you too." I try to ignore the way my heart swells, but there's something about the way she just said that.

"I want everyone to know we're together." She pauses, her eyes going wide and she nibbles on her bottom lip. "Wait a minute. I'm probably getting way ahead of myself."

"Are you?"

"You tell me."

I'm starting to sweat. Do we have to have this discussion now? Right now? In the doorway of her bathroom after she just ate her feelings?

"I am," she says, not giving me near enough time to speak. She yanks her arm out of my hold. "Thanks for the snacks, Ace. You can go now."

"I thought you said you were horny," I remind her.

"Only for men who are totally into me," she retorts.

"Ruby." I pull her away from the open doorway and pin her against the wall, staring into her distressed green eyes. I brace my hands on the wall on either side of her head, pressing my pelvis against hers. Proving to her that I'm totally into her. "Baby. You're killing me here."

"Don't call me baby." She closes her eyes. Releases a shuddering breath. "I hate it when you do that."

"You do not." I press my lips to her temple, kissing her there. "You're a jumble of emotions right now."

"I know." She ducks her head, her hands reaching out to pluck at the front of my hoodie. "Your sweatshirt is bleach-stained."

"Thanks for letting me know," I tease her, drifting my fingers through the ends of her silky hair. "Talk to me, Red."

She glances up, those eyes still full of so much emotion. She's never acted like this before toward me, and I'm more than a little confused. "I just—I know you don't want to talk about this. Not right now."

"Maybe I do," I tell her, my voice soft.

"It's dumb."

I cup my fingers around her chin, tilting her face up. "Nothing you say is ever dumb."

"Really?" She sounds so unsure and I hate that I could be the reason she feels that way.

"Really." I kiss her forehead, letting my lips linger for a moment before I pull away. "Tell me what's on your mind."

She's quiet, closing her eyes for the briefest moment before she speaks.

"Do you ever want...more?" Her lower lip trembles and it breaks my heart to see it. "With me?"

She whispers those last two words, so unsure, my girl. And yeah, I can't lie.

Sometimes I'm a little unsure too. What are we doing? Where is this going?

But I know the truth. The answer is right here. Standing directly in front of me.

"I think the fact that we're still in this is answer enough. Right?"

She nods, but I can feel the doubt radiating from her.

I remember what I told her a few weeks ago. The night I joked about eating her ass—which I continue to do on the semi-regular and she freaking loves it. "I'm in it to win it."

Her face brightens the slightest bit. "Really?"

"I told you that before."

"After we had a particularly dirty sexual experience," she says primly.

I chuckle. "You don't need to play little miss innocent for me, baby. We're in this. I'm into you."

A sigh leaves her and the sound is so soft, so fucking sweet, it lands in the base of my balls, making them tighten. "Sometimes a woman just needs to be—reassured."

"I don't reassure you enough?" I frown.

"Our situation isn't very reassuring." She rests her hand on my chest, her gaze imploring. "I hate having to keep everything a secret. I just want everyone to know we're together."

It doesn't even faze me that she said we're together. We are. It's not like we've had a serious talk and declared ourselves exclusive with each other, but I don't see anyone else.

She doesn't see anyone else either.

We have sex without condoms most of the time, and if that isn't a big commitment, I don't know what is.

"I want everyone to know too, but your job—"

"I know, I know." She cuts me off, sounding miserable. We've gone over this before. We know what's at stake.

"Hey." I touch her face, my fingers drifting across her cheek, thumb pressing against the corner of her mouth. "I hate seeing you down."

"I don't know why I'm so emotional," she practically whines.

"What'll make you feel better, baby?" I dip my head, brush my lips against hers. A spark ignites between us, encouraging me to kiss her again. One more time.

And again.

"Can you answer one more question for me?" she murmurs against my lips.

"What is it?"

"What are you hoping to win?" she asks, her tone cautious.

I go with my gut and answer her.

"I've already told you this before, Ruby. I'm in it to win *you*." Which is the truth. I'm fucking obsessed with this woman. She's all I think about. All I want.

"You really want to be with me?" Her voice is so soft, I almost don't hear her.

"Are you serious?" I pull away, so I can stare into her eyes. "It's only been you since school started. You're all I think about. You're the only one I want."

Her eyes shine. Fuck, is she crying? She wasn't lying when she said she's extra emotional. "You're the only one I want too."

I crush her lips with mine, cupping her face, communicating without words that she's it for me.

I don't know when this happened. When I realized that I'm halfway in love with this woman, but here I am. A complete goner for Ruby Maguire.

Wait, there's no halfway in love with her. I am in love with her. How do I tell her? How do we make this work without her having to give something up?

Life is really fucking unfair sometimes, I swear.

38

RUBY

"Oh, your apartment is so cute." Mom enters my place ahead of Dad, stopping in the living room and slowly looking around, her hands resting on her hips. Her gaze lands on me and she smiles. "I love it."

I return the smile. "Thanks, Mom. We like it too."

"Where is Natalie?"

"She had to work but she'll be at the game and she's going to sit with you guys," I answer, my gaze tracking my father's every move.

He's currently examining the window that overlooks the parking lot, a faint frown on his face. "This window doesn't look that secure."

Always watching out for my safety. I love that about him.

I go to where he's standing and pull on the cord that lifts the blinds, showing him the stick that sits in the sill, preventing the window from opening beyond a tiny crack. "We're safe, Dad. Every window in the apartment has these."

Ace made sure of it after his climbing through my

bedroom window incident. He installed a new screen on my window the very next day and had these rods made for all of our windows, even Natalie's because he's just that great.

Ugh, sometimes I can't stand how great he is. Especially when I can't publicly share his greatness.

Pretending not to care about him is becoming harder and harder.

"Good," Dad says, nodding his approval.

I wish I could tell him Ace is the reason we're safe. Ace is the reason for a lot of things in my life, all of them positive and wonderful. But I have to keep my relationship with him quiet for only a few more months.

Months. That sounds impossible, but we can do it. I know we can.

My parents came to visit me for the weekend and they're going to a football game because as Dad says, he wants to see me in action. It's my turn to be on the sidelines to get footage.

Really? I think my dad just wants to watch the team play. I know he's excited for me and is proud of me, but I also know where his true love lies.

With my mom and football.

"Are you excited for today?" Mom asks. They arrived last night and I picked them up from the airport. We went to one of their favorite restaurants for dinner and then we hung out at their hotel for a little bit before I headed home. Now they're picking me up before we go to the game.

"I'm a little nervous," I admit. "I've never been alone on the sidelines before, filming content."

The last time it was my turn, they allowed two people from the social media team to be down there and I went with Eric. Now I'm on my own.

"You're going to do great," Mom says firmly as she

wanders into the kitchen and opens the refrigerator. I want to roll my eyes because I know she's checking on what we've got inside, which isn't much. "Are you eating okay, honey?"

See? "Nothing but junk food and Taco Bell runs," I tell her.

She shuts the fridge and turns to look at me. "Please tell me you're at least drinking plenty of water."

I point at my water bottle sitting on the kitchen table. "I pee day and night."

"TMI," Dad teases. He likes using acronyms. Says it keeps him feeling young.

"I just worry about you," Mom says, her voice full of concern. "Just because you don't live with us anymore doesn't mean I don't want to take care of you."

"Aw, Mom." I go to her and wrap her up in a big hug. "You have Dad to take care of, and he needs as much help as he can get."

"I resent that," he mutters, making us laugh.

"He doesn't let me fuss over him much," she admits, squeezing me. "Though neither do any of my children."

I pull out of her embrace and smile at her. "I'm eating okay. I promise it's not always Taco Bell."

"At least have a taco from there," she says. "They have lettuce."

Rolling my eyes, I show them the rest of the apartment before we end up back in the living room.

"What time do you have to be at the stadium again?" Dad asks once he's settled on the couch.

"Soon." I pluck my phone from the back pocket of my jeans and check the time, surprised to see I have a text notification from Ace.

Acey Baby: **Miss you. Good luck today.**

I'm smiling, just staring at my screen when Dad says, "Who's the text from?"

I jerk my head up, my smile fading. My brain scrambling. "A friend."

His phone rings and he checks it, holding it up to show my brother's name flashing on the screen. "I'm going to take this."

Before we can respond, he's already on his feet and out the door, standing on my front balcony and talking to Knox.

I send a quick text to Ace.

Me: **Shouldn't I be the one wishing you luck today?**

I accompany it with a bunch of heart emojis and pocket my phone.

"What friend has you smiling like that?" Mom asks, her tone curious.

My face flushes. I can feel the heat sweep over my skin and God, I hate myself right now. "It's no one."

She just looks at me.

"Seriously."

"Uh huh." She leans forward, resting her arms on her thighs. "Is it a boy?"

The look on my mother's face has my resolve weakening into dust. Just like that, I open my mouth and the story pours out.

I tell her everything. Well—I leave out the sexual stuff because yikes, I'm not going to admit all that to her—but I let her know that I'm involved with Ace and we're totally into each other, but we can't be because of that stupid agreement I signed.

"You really like him," Mom concludes when I finish speaking. I can't believe my dad is still outside talking on the phone.

"I do," I say, vaguely miserable.

"You always said you wouldn't date a football player," she reminds me.

"I guess I lied." I shrug. "He's just so—*ugh*. There's something about him. He's confident and sweet and kind. He's the reason we have all of those sticks or whatever in the windows. He's protective and he's nice and we have fun together. He makes me laugh. He's a good kisser." Mom laughs and I think my face is now on fire. "I think he cares about me."

That's a lie. I *know* he cares about me.

"Are you in love with him?" Mom asks.

The door slams open before I can answer, Dad striding inside with Knox still on the phone. Dad switches it to speaker and says, "Go ahead and tell them what you did last night, Knox."

"I asked Joanna to marry me," my brother announces.

"Oh my God!" Mom squeals, leaping to her feet and rushing toward Dad so they can both crowd around the phone. "I need every single detail, Knox. Where's Joanna? Can you FaceTime us? I want to see the ring!"

Within minutes we're watching Knox and Joanna on my father's phone screen, Joanna holding up her hand and showing us the giant diamond on her finger. Mom is practically crying, she's so excited. Knox and Jo can't stop smiling at each other and Dad is proud.

"Congratulations, you guys," I say, thrilled for them. Envious that they can bask in each other's love and don't need to hide it.

"Thank you, Ruby. Where's Natalie?" Joanna asks me. "I keep trying to call her and she won't pick up."

"She's at work, but she should be off soon," I tell her. "Text her and tell her to call you later. She'll want to hear this."

"I will." Joanna pauses, her gaze sticking on me. "Ruby, would you be one of my bridesmaids? I know I should do some elaborate thing where I send you all gifts with my request and I'll do that eventually, I swear—"

I interrupt her, unable to help myself.

"Are you serious?" I rest my hand against my chest, honored. "I would love to be."

There's more excited-talking about a wedding and what time of year is best. The call ends pretty much after that, Joanna eager to try to get a hold of her best friend. I sneak a glance at my phone while Mom and Dad are still chattering away about the upcoming nuptials and I read Ace's response.

Acey Baby: **We've got this game in the bag, just like you do. You're going to do great.**

Me: **So are you.**

Acey Baby: **It'll be nice to have you on the field with me.**

Me: **You have to ignore me. Pretend I don't exist.**

Acey Baby: **Impossible. You're all I see.**

My heart swells. He says the best things, and they never feel cheesy either.

"Should we go soon?" Dad asks, and I can tell he's eager to leave.

"Let me grab my stuff and then I'll be ready."

I send Ace one last text.

Me: **See you soon.**

Acey Baby: **Can't wait Red.**

∾

IT'S JUST about the end of halftime and I tilt my head back, marveling at the gorgeous weather. The air is crisp and cool and the sky is blue, dotted by the occasional white fluffy cloud. There's a cool breeze that sweeps through the stadium that makes me shiver and I'm grateful I wore my CU hoodie. By the time this game is over, it's going to be cold.

We're winning with four touchdowns to their one and I get the feeling Ace was right. It's going to be an easy win. So far, I've recorded some great footage and I can't wait to share it with Eric and Gwen, who are currently sitting in the stands, not too far from where my parents and Natalie are sitting.

Our team jogs out onto the field accompanied by the roaring crowd and my gaze finds Ace. And his finds me too, like we're two magnets drawn to each other and the slow, easy smile that spreads across his face has butterflies dancing in my stomach.

He's so freaking handsome. And strong and capable and confident. Women scream for him throughout the game. Make signs with some pretty inappropriate stuff written on them. I know this sort of thing goes on all the time and I should be completely immune to it, but when it comes to the guy I'm dating in secret?

It's annoying. I want to tell them all to back off. That Ace Townsend is mine.

But I can't do any of that.

My phone buzzes and I check it to find a text from Gwen.

You're doing great! Can't wait to see what you filmed!

I smile at my screen, happiness bubbling up inside of me. Who knew grumpy Gwyneth could be so encouraging? She's definitely not so moody thanks to her and Eric being together all the time.

The game continues on and it's such a relief that it's

going to be a big win. The tension has completely evaporated from the sidelines and the team is joking and laughing with each other, easy grins on their faces. I check the scoreboard for the time when our defensive line runs out onto the field, grateful to see we only have a few minutes left when I sense someone approach me.

"Hey, Red."

I turn at the familiar drawl to see Ace standing there, a little distance between him and his teammates, his focus one hundred percent on me.

"Hi." I'm breathless, my heart hammering in my chest. Just having his attention on me, even for a little bit, can almost feel like too much.

"Looking good out here." His gaze slowly scans me from head to toe. "I like having you close."

"You might've mentioned that already," I tease him, feeling flirtatious since no one is paying any attention to us.

You know, just an entire stadium full of people could be watching us, but no biggie.

"I meant it." His gaze locks with mine. "Whatcha doing later tonight?"

I shrug. "Hanging out with my parents. They want to go to dinner."

He nods slowly. "That sounds nice."

The expectant look on his face tells me he wants to go with us, and I—I want him to come too.

"Do you have plans after the game?"

"Not sure. The usual? Logan's and whatever." He shrugs those broad shoulders, the breeze ruffling his hair. It's grown out a little and it flops over his forehead in the most appealing way. He wears a headband a lot of the time to keep it out of his eyes and when he does, I always think he looks adorable.

Clearly, I have a total thing for him and believe he's adorable no matter what.

"You want to come with us?" Oh, this is dangerous, but we could write it off to my dad wanting to meet him. Dad always enjoyed meeting Knox's teammates so that tracks.

Ace's eyes light up. "You wouldn't mind? People wouldn't...say anything? About us together?"

I slowly shake my head. "We'll go somewhere far away from campus. Not like anyone is going to catch us."

"You don't mind if I go?"

"Why would I mind? I want you to meet my parents."

"I want to meet them. And not because your dad is who he is. I want to get to know them because well...you know." He smiles.

I smile too.

I know. Because we're basically together and this is the next step. An important step. Introducing Ace to the family.

Oh my God. This feels serious.

Glancing around, I take a few steps closer to him, my voice low so no one can hear us. "I'll text you after the game and tell you where to meet us, okay?"

"Perfect." He's grinning. He looks very pleased with himself. Extra confident. It's a good look for him. "I'll see ya later, Red."

A whistle blows, and without warning, Ace slaps my ass before he jogs out onto the field, leaving me standing there in shock. What was that?

God, hope no one noticed.

39

ACE

I was nervous as fuck thinking about meeting Owen Maguire the entire drive to the restaurant, where I was meeting Ruby and her parents, but he's proven to be a pretty cool dude. We spent the entirety of dinner talking about football and stats and Knox and Cam. How they're doing in the NFL. He asked if I have professional aspirations and I said of course.

He praised my game play and I basked in his words. Did my best to impress his wife by minding my manners and doing my best to be polite. All while Ruby watched me with amusement lighting her gaze. Like she thought me trying to be good was hilarious.

I've never really met parents before, beyond talking to them before I picked up a prom date or whatever, and that was a long time ago. I've never stayed with a woman long enough to get the parental introduction and I was just fine with it.

When Ruby mentioned going to dinner with her parents, I was desperate to go. Ready to ask if I could if she didn't invite me herself.

We're mostly done with our dinner and making idle conversation when Mr. Maguire's gaze narrows, sliding from me to Ruby and back to me again.

"You two are friends then?"

Ruby and her mom go silent, exchanging secret looks.

This is my cue to step it up and say what Ruby really is to me.

"I like your daughter a lot, sir."

"As friends?" Owen asks again, his brows shooting up.

"Well, yeah. I like her as a friend, but it's—more than that."

"We're together, Daddy." Ruby scoots closer to me, curling her arm through mine. "It's just—complicated."

"How so?"

"No one can know we're together until the season is over," Ruby says.

"And why the hell is it like that?" His gaze slides to me, his green eyes that are so like Ruby's turbulent with emotion. "Is this some kind of weird superstitious thing you've got going on? Because if that's the case, you need to know I'm about to call you out on your bullshit."

"Owen." Ruby's mom reaches over and settles her hand on her husband's leg. "Calm down."

"It's kind of my fault," Ruby says, catching her dad off guard. She goes on to explain the agreement she signed to work with the social media team, and how she can't date an athlete. "Once the season is over, we'll be able to go public."

He contemplates me again, his expression not as hostile as it was a minute ago. "How do you feel about this?"

"I hate it," I say truthfully. "All the sneaking around. Not being able to tell everyone Ruby is mi—my, uh, girlfriend."

She literally squirms in her chair at my use of the word that feels so damn foreign on my tongue.

Girlfriend.

We've never officially discussed it. Never come right out and labeled ourselves in that way but how else am I going to describe it—her—to her parents? That we like spending all of our free time together and most of that free time is spent...having sex?

Yeah, that wouldn't go over real well.

Though it's more than that with Ruby and me. It goes beyond sex. I like her. I enjoy her company. I want to know about her.

I want to know everything about her.

"You two are serious," her mother says, a secret smile on her face.

"Mom. Stop," Ruby moans, sounding like an annoyed teenager. "We're just...seeing where this takes us."

"Did you tell him about your brother?" her father asks.

"What about him?" I glance over at Ruby, who's smiling helplessly.

"He asked Joanna to marry him last night," she says.

"No shit?" My brows shoot up and I realize too late I cursed. I turn to Chelsea Maguire with an apologetic smile. "I'm sorry, Mrs. M."

"I told you not to call me that," she chastises, her voice soft. "Please. Call me Chelsea. And I've heard worse. After all, I'm married to a man who uses the f-word like it's a sport."

"I stand by my assertion that it's the most versatile word ever created." Owen sits up straighter, his eyes dancing with mischief, while his wife just shakes her head.

They're cute together. Act like they're still into each other too, which is nice to see. I glance over at Ruby to find she's already watching me, a glow in her eyes I've never noticed before.

"They're going to get married, huh?" I turn to the Maguires to find them watching us very closely. I push past wanting to squirm much like Ruby did only moments ago and smile at them. "Congratulations."

"We're not the ones getting married," Owen points out.

"I know but it's your son who just got engaged to the woman he loves, and that feels like a pretty big deal." I lean back in my chair, reaching out to settle my hand on the back of Ruby's chair. "I like Joanna. She seems nice."

"We adore her," Chelsea says. "She also asked Ruby to be in the wedding."

"Oh yeah?" I can imagine her in a pretty dress, standing at the altar near Joanna. Or even better, her wearing a wedding gown, walking down the aisle on her father's arm.

Headed straight for me.

Sitting up straighter, I swallow hard, shaking the image from my brain. What the fuck? Marriage? Now that's pretty fucking serious. We're only twenty-one. I'm not ready for marriage yet.

But the idea of spending forever with Ruby? That sounds...

Perfect.

"It'll be fun," Ruby says, smiling at me.

It's like this for the rest of the evening. Talk of family stuff. Ruby sending me flirtatious glances. Her parents watching me carefully, almost like they're waiting for devil horns to sprout from my head or for me to say something wrong.

But I realize they're just curious. I'm dating their youngest daughter and they want to know more about me. It's natural. I want to know more about them too.

We're leaving the restaurant when Ruby grabs my hand

and gives it a tug, whispering in my ear, "Meet me at my place?"

I pull away slightly to look into her eyes. "You sure?"

She nods, her lips curled into this inviting, almost sexy smile. I glance around, making sure her parents aren't paying attention before I lean in and drop a quick kiss on her pretty lips.

"You got it."

That smile on her face is a sight to see. "I might be a while. You want my key?"

"Nah, it's cool—"

She's already unhooked the key from her keychain and hands it to me. "Just let yourself in. Natalie won't be there. She's out with Derek. Wait for me."

We say our goodbyes in the parking lot. Her dad shakes my hand extra hard. Her mom wraps me up in a smothering hug, telling me she's so *glad* we got to meet. I hug Ruby and kiss her cheek, my hand lightly patting her ass and I swear her mom caught me doing it, a mischievous look on her face when our gazes catch.

Busted.

I crank up the music on my drive over to Ruby's apartment, feeling on top of the world. I'm having a terrific season. I just met Ruby's parents and they seem to like me. Pretty sure me and my girl are going to take things to the next step—as soon as we can reveal our relationship, that is.

Life is good.

I've got no complaints.

I enter my darkened apartment and make my way to my bedroom, slowly opening the door to find there are candles flickering on every available space inside. My dresser, the bedside table, my tiny desk. Little votives scattered everywhere.

And there's a bare-chested Ace sitting in the middle of my bed, leaning against my mountain of pillows, his phone lying discarded by his side on the mattress.

"Hey," I murmur, drinking him in, surprised by the romantic mood he's set up while waiting for me to return.

"Hey," he returns, his lips curled in a barely-there smile.

"Sorry that took so long," I say, shutting the door behind me and locking it. I admire him for a few more seconds, a smile curling my lips. "My parents love you, by the way."

"Really?"

He sounds pleased and even a little unsure and that's so cute.

"Really. Dad likes that you're a football player, though he's never going to let me live down the fact that I said I would never date one." I roll my eyes.

"I'm just that convincing." He rubs his hands together and I laugh, pushing away from the door and heading toward the bed. Considering my room isn't that big, it only takes me a couple of steps and I'm standing at the foot of the mattress.

"You've got way too many clothes on," he observes as I get rid of the coat I had on. "Maybe you should take some of that off."

"Maybe you should help me," I counter, but he slowly shakes his head.

"I like watching you strip."

He likes watching me do a lot of things, I muse, kicking off my shoes before I tug the hoodie over my head and dump it on my desk chair. I make quick work of my clothing, until I'm just in my bra and panties, the cool air nipping at my exposed skin.

"It's freezing," I say as I yank back the covers and slip into bed beside Ace. He scoots down and turns so we're facing each other, the candlelight casting his handsome face in a warm glow and I just stare at him for a moment, going over everything that happened today.

Us down on the field together. His big win. Him slapping me on the ass on the sidelines. In front of my mother. Meeting my parents. I'm so relieved they like him, but I knew they would, so it's not that big of a surprise.

How he called me his girlfriend. How good it felt, to hear that word come from his lips. How right. We might not have the most normal relationship in the world, but that will change by the beginning of the new year at the latest. I can wait that long.

I'm a patient person.

Sometimes.

"What are you thinking about?" he asks.

"Not much." I shrug one shoulder.

"You're a liar. I always know when you're thinking. You get a line right..." He touches the tense spot between my eyebrows. "There."

"I'm thinking about what a good day it's been," I admit, my voice soft. "And it's all thanks to you."

"Oh yeah?" He looks pleased with my confession and I scoot closer, seeking his warmth. He reaches toward me and scoops me up, pulling me into his body. I throw out a hand, my fingers brushing against his naked upper thigh and I realize he doesn't have any clothing on.

And he's already hard.

"Yes," I confirm, snuggling as close as I can as I slip my arm around him. "You're naked."

"No shit?" He raises his brows, teasing me.

That's my favorite part. How he makes me smile. Makes me laugh. He knows when to be serious, but he's a lot of fun. It's like the more time we spend together, the more compatible we realize we are and it's a mutual thing. I don't have to chase him.

And he doesn't have to chase after me.

We just...fit.

And I love it.

I love him.

The realization makes everything expand inside of me—specifically my heart. I always wondered when it would happen. When I would find a guy that was just as into me as I was into him and now that it's here, that the moment is actually happening, it feels...

Good.

No, more than good. It feels...

Right.

So right.

"A girl could get used to this kind of treatment." I slowly run my hand up the smooth, muscled expanse of his back. "Coming home to find her boyfriend surrounded by candles and waiting for her naked in bed."

"I was feeling romantic."

"Here's the thing—lately you're always feeling romantic, Ace." I tip my head back and smile up at him. "That's my favorite quality about you."

He dips his head, his mouth brushing mine. "It's been a good day, I agree. And that's all thanks to you."

He repeats my words back to me and I let my hand drift down, skimming the muscular curve of his ass. He has the best body ever. I could spend days mapping it with my hands.

My mouth.

I have before. He lets me do whatever I want to him and it's never a hardship because he always benefits from my exploration.

"Did you really mean it when you called me your girlfriend?" I ask, suddenly filled with the need to know.

He pushes my hair away from my face, his expression gentle as he studies me. "What do you think?"

"I need to hear you say it," I whisper, feeling the tiniest bit insecure.

I know this man is into me. That he cares about me. But sometimes, a woman wants to hear her man say it out loud.

"Ruby Maguire, I want you to be my girlfriend," he murmurs, leaning in to kiss me again. His lips are so soft and warm. They hold the power to revive me. Make me feel lighter. Make me feel whole.

Make me feel loved.

"I want to be your girlfriend," I whisper against his lips, kissing him again, my tongue sneaking out to lick. His tongue meets mine and we get lost in each other for a few seconds. Until he pulls away and cups the side of my face with his big hand.

"I hate hiding what we're doing." His tone is fierce and his blue eyes blaze with frustration.

"I hate it too." I settle my hand over his, trying to reassure him. "But we don't have to hide it for much longer."

"I want everyone to know that you belong to me."

My heart feels like it might explode, it's so full of emotion. "So territorial."

"I am," he says without hesitation. "I didn't know I had it in me, but when it comes to you, I am. You're mine."

"I'm yours," I whisper, unable to deny it.

His hand slips down, landing on my throat and curling around the front. I love it when he does this and he knows it. My eyes fall closed and my lips part, his fingers exerting the slightest pressure when he says, "I'm in love with you."

I open my eyes to find him studying me with a mixture of pain and love swirling in his eyes. It's written all over his face. Like it took everything out of him to admit that.

"I will do anything for you. Do you realize that? You want us to keep this quiet to save your job, my lips are sewn shut. You want me to squeeze your throat because it gets you off? I love that. I will do it for you every single time. You like it when I pick you up Taco Bell when you don't even ask, and you love it...you absolutely love it when I eat your ass." He chuckles when I shove at him. "You do, Ruby. You love everything I do for you. And I love doing those things for you because I'm in love with you."

Leave it to Ace to make the sweetest love confession ever and also mention eating my ass. This man...

"I love you too. I love everything about you. How protective you are, how smart. You're kind and funny and sexy and you never hesitate when I ask you for something. You go above and beyond to make sure I'm happy. Satisfied." I climb on top of him, causing him to fall onto his back so I'm now straddling him. "It's like you were made for me."

"You were definitely made for me." His hands land on my ass, slipping beneath the thin fabric of my panties to knead my flesh. "I love everything about you too, Red. Thank you for letting me go to dinner with your parents tonight."

I make a face, resting my index finger over the center of his mouth. "Don't mention them when I'm lying on you and we're practically naked."

"I'm naked. You're not." He tugs at my panties, pulling them down so my ass is half hanging out of them. "We need to rectify that."

We do. My bra and panties are discarded in seconds and we're kissing. Touching. Hands roaming. My fingers curling around his shaft. His slipping between my thighs, his other hand clamped around my breast, holding me like he's never going to let me go. His magical fingers bring me to the brink of orgasm and then he stops, rolling me over onto my back so he can climb on top of me, his thick cock probing at my entrance.

When he slides in, it feels like he's coming home—which is corny, I know it. I sound like a romance novel or some silly movie but it's so true. We cling to each other as he pushes inside of me again and again. Doing it missionary style, which isn't our preferred position.

I prefer it on top. He prefers fucking me from behind. Says he gets balls deep—direct quote—and I can't deny that the orgasms are always pretty life-altering when we do it that way.

But tonight is different. There's a connection between us

that can't be denied. This man admitted that he loves me. And I admitted that I love him. What we're doing doesn't feel like just fucking anymore.

It feels...transcendent.

He presses his mouth to my neck as he works his hips and I lift up to meet him thrust for thrust, my arms winding around his neck. My fingers burying in his soft hair. I bend my legs at the knee and brace my feet on the mattress, which only sends him deeper and we groan into each other's mouths. Desperation sifts through my veins, making me cling to him tighter, our mouths locked. Tongues tangling.

I can't get enough of him. He acts like he can't get enough of me.

When he slips his hand between us and toys with my clit, I start chanting.

"*Don'tstopdon'tstopdon'tstop.*"

"I'm not," he whispers into my ear. "I've got you, Red. I'm never going to let you go."

My orgasm slams into me and I can't respond. I can't think, I can't even breathe. All I can do is cling to him as he continues to move inside my body, my inner walls strangling his cock, squeezing his own orgasm right out of him. He's panting against my neck, groaning as the shudders rock his big body and when it's over, we lie like that, wound together.

"Goddamn," is the first thing he finally says, which makes me giggle. He kisses my shoulder, his lips lingering. "That was..."

"Amazing?" I supply for him.

He pulls away slightly so he can stare down into my eyes. I greedily stare back, marveling that this man is mine. That he loves me. I remember when I met him almost a year ago, and how cocky he was. How I didn't like him that much.

Oh, that's such a lie. I was wildly attracted to him from the start and pissed at myself for being just like my mother. My sister. Falling for a football player.

Now I can't imagine my life without him.

"Amazing," he murmurs, dipping his head to kiss me. "I love you, Ruby."

"I love you too, Ace."

"Want to do it again?"

"You know it," I readily agree, grateful the man works out all the time and is in his physical prime.

His stamina in bed is one of my favorite things about him.

Oh, that and his heart.

41

RUBY

I enter the social media headquarters Monday afternoon to find Marilee waiting inside, Gwen and Eric nowhere to be found.

"Hello, Ruby." She rises to her feet, her expression serious.

I stop in the open doorway, my fingers clutched tight around my backpack strap. "Uh, hi."

"Do you have a moment so we can talk?"

"Sure." My stomach churns and I try to swallow but my mouth is too dry. "Is everything okay?"

Marilee doesn't respond to my question. "Let's go chat in Jim Williamson's office, all right?"

My advisor. I haven't seen that guy in weeks. Months even.

This is...this is serious. Shit.

Did someone find out about me and Ace?

God, I think I might...cry.

Or puke.

Take your pick.

I follow Marilee to Williamson's office where he's waiting, his expression grim as I settle into a chair across from his desk, Marilee to my right. I remember how jovial he was when I first met him. How enthusiastic he was to have me be a part of the athletic department.

Now he looks like he's just arrived at my funeral.

"We'll just cut to the chase," Jim says, leaning forward and resting his forearms on top of his desk. "It's been brought to our attention that you're seeing Ace Townsend."

I blink at him, the denial on the tip of my tongue. Instead, my shoulders sag and I lean back in my chair. "It's true."

Jim frowns. Glances over at Marilee before returning his gaze to me. "It is?"

Oh God, was this a test? If I'd denied it, would it all be swept under the rug and forgotten?

I wouldn't forget. This has been torture, pretending we're not involved. Sneaking around. Meeting each other at night, always alone, rarely hanging out with anyone else. We can't even be friends because the athletic department gets suspicious and people are always watching.

It's ridiculous. I'm tired of it.

"Yes." I blow out a breath. Throw up my hands. "It's all true. Ace and I are together. We're boyfriend and girlfriend."

"We have a strict policy that anyone on the social media team cannot date an athlete," Marilee starts, her voice stern. "You signed the agreement."

"I know."

"Your position will have to be terminated."

I close my eyes for the briefest moment, hating the idea of losing my job. Of not being able to work with Eric and Gwen anymore. I'm going to miss them. I'm going to miss making silly content and laughing with Gwen. She's become one of my closest friends and I adore her. I care about Eric too. They make a great couple and witnessing their relationship grow has been fun.

I'm tempted to ask why they can be together and Ace and I can't, but I don't want to get them in trouble either so I remain quiet.

"Do you understand why we have to do this? Becoming involved with an athlete while you're working for the athletic department has the potential to make things— sticky if the relationship doesn't work out. We can't put the department's reputation at risk. Or the players'," Jim explains.

"Right but who cares what happens to the person on the social media team though. They're just collateral damage," I say bitterly, jumping to my feet. "Can I go now?"

"Do you have any belongings in the office here?" Marilee asks me.

Probably, but I don't want to go back there and get it. Not with Marilee hovering over me and making sure I'm not stealing anything or whatever.

Not that she would actually do that, but maybe? I feel like a criminal enough.

Just because I fell in love with the guy. This is seriously so unfair.

"We care about you too, Ruby. We're just watching out for you," Marilee says, and when I spot Jim's sympathetic nod of agreement, I'm tempted to lash out. Tell them both they can shove their opinions up their asses and march out of this stupid office with all of his trophies and photos. Holding on to the glory days like a pathetic loser.

But I do none of that. I don't want to look like an asshole.

And I don't think Jim Williamson is a pathetic loser. That's just my anger and frustration talking.

"Can I ask a question?"

They both share a look before they nod in tandem.

"How did you find out? About me and Ace?"

"There's—speculation online," Marilee admits.

I gape at her. "What?"

"One of the broadcast channels caught Ace slapping you on the as—backside on the sidelines during the game."

Oh God. I remember that slap. I even remember worrying someone might have noticed it.

I didn't expect it to get *filmed*.

"And considering you're the daughter of Owen Maguire and the sister of Knox, the public knows who you are. So there's been speculation," Marilee continues.

"And anonymous reports that the two of you are together," Jim adds. "We've received a few emails about the two of you over the last month or so."

People out there still ratting us out. Guess they have nothing better to do.

God, I hate this.

"Is there anything else you need to tell me?"

"We will have your final check ready for you by the end of the day," Marilee says, her tone efficient. "I'm sorry it didn't work out for you."

"Me too," I say sadly, turning on my heel and fleeing Jim's office. Hightailing it out of the athletic department building before I possibly bump into someone I might know.

I think about what Marilee said the entire time I walk across campus, headed for the parking lot so I can jump in my car and go home. How she said she's sorry it didn't work out for me. A year ago, this would've sent me into a spiral. I would've been devastated. Losing a job that's in my major all over a guy? I would've beat myself up endlessly.

But Ace isn't just a guy. He's the man I'm in love with, and he's in love with me. Marilee is wrong.

It did work out for me.

42

ACE

We're almost done with practice for the day when our social media team finally appears on the sidelines of the field.

Minus my girl.

I frown in Eric and Gwen's direction, noting how pissed off they both look. And not at each other either. Their heads are bent close together and they're talking—a lot. With animated gestures and matching scowls on their faces.

A scowl is Gwyneth's natural expression, but lately, she's been smiling more and that's because she's with Eric. They make a good couple. Ruby encourages their relationship, even though I know she finds it extremely unfair that they can be together, but we can't.

I have to agree.

Eric and Gwen don't even bother filming us. By the time practice is over, they're waving at me to come over and talk to them and since curiosity gets the better of me, I'm on them in seconds.

"Where's Ruby?"

The look on Gwen's face is pure misery mixed with anger. "They fired her."

My heart drops into my balls. "Say what?"

"She got f-fired. I-I can't believe it." Gwen bursts into tears and Eric wraps his arm around her shoulders, pulling her into him, his expression grim when he looks at me.

"They let her go this afternoon. They found out you two are together."

"Do you know how?"

"Ruby called it speculation online about the two of you. Do you know about it?"

I get tagged in a lot of shit. It's constant, especially after a game. I haven't had a chance to scroll through it all yet, and sometimes...I don't even look at it all. It's too much and I get overwhelmed.

Besides, I spent most of Sunday with Ruby at her apartment and then I went home and worked on homework for the rest of the night. I've been busy with school today. Practice.

"What kind of speculation?" I ask.

"Something about you slapping her butt on the sidelines," Eric says.

Gwen lifts her head, her face covered in tears and her eyes blazing red. "I saw it. You smacked her ass in front of thousands of people and of course, someone caught it. Many someones."

Her tone is accusatory and I guess I can't blame her. I did slap Ruby's ass because I'm always touching it. I sort of forgot myself, which is typical when I'm around her.

Shit.

"I cost her the job." My voice is hollow and a ragged exhale leaves me. "This is my fault."

"No way—" Eric starts but Gwen cuts him off.

"Yep. It's all your fault, Townsend. And now we've lost her. God, it's so unfair." Gwen curls her hands into fists, pulling out of Eric's embrace, and I swear for a second I think she's going to lunge for me. "You have to make this right."

"How?" I ask incredulously, wishing I had my phone so I could call Ruby. But it's in my backpack back in the locker room.

"I don't know. Go talk to Marilee," Gwen retorts.

"Gwen, calm down. There's nothing he can do. The policy was already in place and Ruby broke it," Eric says, sounding completely logical.

"This is such bullshit." Gwen glares at me, jabbing her index finger in my direction. "I hope it was worth it. You better not dump her after this. I don't know if she'll be able to survive it."

"We need to go," Eric says to Gwen firmly, sending me a sympathetic glance. "We'll talk to you later, Ace."

He steers his girlfriend in the opposite direction and I watch them walk away, my entire chest aching.

Gwen's right. This is my fault. I shouldn't have slapped Ruby's ass on the sidelines during a game. What the hell was I thinking? How could I be so careless? I don't even want to check all the stuff I'm tagged in now. It's probably that ass slap on an endless loop accompanied by all sorts of rumors and lies. No one knows what Ruby and I have beyond us.

Launching into action, I run toward the locker room, eager to get the fuck out of here and head to Ruby's. She needs me right now.

And I need to be there for her.

～

I SHOW up twenty minutes later on Ruby's doorstep, furiously knocking on her door. I sent her a quick text asking if I could come over and she said sure, like it was no big deal. Like her life hadn't just been completely altered by losing the job she loves so damn much, and I expect her to answer the door a tear-stained, red-eyed mess.

But when the door swings open, I swear she's the prettiest I've ever seen her, clad in a pair of black joggers and a cropped fitted black T-shirt with gold lettering that says:

I was born fucking cool.

"Oh my God, you brought Taco Bell." She reaches for the bag and snatches it from my hands, turning and heading for the kitchen table. "How did you know I was craving it?"

Blinking, I enter the apartment and close the door behind me, watching as she starts going through the bag. Looking for a chalupa, I'm sure. "You always crave the Bell when you're upset."

"Funny thing is, I'm not actually that upset." She drops the still wrapped chalupa on the table, studying me. "Gwen told me you guys talked."

"She's mad at me."

"She's mad at the situation," she stresses. "I don't think she's actually mad at you."

I don't bother arguing with Ruby. She didn't see Gwen and how pissed she was.

"I'm sorry," I tell her, hoping she realizes how sincere I am. "I fucked up."

"How?" Ruby is peeling the wrapper back from her food, lifting it to her lips and taking a big bite. "Oh my God, this is good."

"I'm the one who slapped your ass. I did this to you."

"You're always slapping my ass." She shrugs.

"Not in public. Not in front of thousands of people and

with cameras everywhere." I shake my head, wondering how she can eat like it's no big deal while I'm standing here sick to my stomach. "I cost you your job."

"I think Marilee enjoyed firing me," Ruby says conversationally. "I never did like her much."

"Ruby." My voice is so stern, she jerks her head up to meet my gaze, her green eyes wide. "Tell me what happened."

She launches into the story, giving me every excruciating detail. Making me feel worse and worse, to the point that I have to pull out a chair and sink into it, propping my elbows on the table so I can bury my face in my hands.

The guilt I'm experiencing is goddamned overwhelming. This is the last thing I ever wanted to do. I cost the woman I love her job. All with a careless smack.

I'm such an asshole.

"And then I got mad," she continues. I don't have to look at her to know she's taking another big bite of her chalupa. Damn, she loves those things. "I was so pissed. I had all sorts of hostile thoughts about Jim and Marilee. How could I take them down, you know? Make their lives a living hell?"

I lift my head to study her, shocked by her revelations. "Are you serious?"

"Oh yeah, it was a vengeful phase that lasted maybe ten minutes?" She shrugs, polishing off her chalupa. "Then I got over it and realized they were only doing their job. This is on me. I signed that agreement that said no dating and I went and fell in love with you anyway."

She smiles, her hand rustling in the bag once more as she plucks out another wrapped chalupa. "I shouldn't eat this." She drops it on the table and starts unwrapping it. "But I'm gonna."

I stare at her for a moment, in shock at her nonreaction. "Are you mad at me?"

"Why would I be mad at you?" She sends me a look. "I'm in love with you."

"I love you too," I say automatically. "But this is a big deal. You found a really great job in your major and you were killing it. All the football teams' social media pages have grown like crazy and that's because of you."

"And Gwen," she points out. "Eric too."

"And you," I stress. "You're an integral part of that team."

"I'm going to miss them so much." Her voice is wistful.

"You're going to resent me for getting you fired."

"I am not." She rolls her eyes. "Don't you see? I might've lost my job but I got you, Ace. And now we don't have to hide anymore. Everyone will know we're together and won't that be such a relief?"

I stare at her hard, making sure this isn't some kind of trick. That she's being nice just to suck me in and then unleash on me...

But then I remember this is Ruby I'm looking at and she's always upfront with her feelings. There are no games with this woman. I love that about her.

I love her.

She loves me too.

"You're not mad," I finally say.

A sigh leaves her. "I can't deny that I'm sad about losing my job, but I talked to my parents already and Dad said that whenever there's a setback in life, something better always comes. I believe him."

"What did your mom say?" I brace myself for the answer.

"Oh, she said she's not surprised an ass slap took us down. You did the same thing to me in front of them after dinner." Ruby laughs, the sound easing the churning in my gut some, but not quite enough.

I can't manage to laugh. I'm just too fucking relieved that this girl isn't pissed at me. That her parents don't hate me.

"I still feel bad," I admit. "And responsible."

"It's going to be okay." Ruby reaches across the table and rests her hand on my forearm. "Now I can wear your number at games. I can tell everyone who will listen to me that you're my boyfriend. I need to buy your jersey."

"I will give you my jersey," I say vehemently, enjoying the idea of seeing Ruby with my number plastered all over her in the stands. "We can tell the whole fucking world we're together."

"See? It's not so bad, me losing my job." She's smiling, her second chalupa lying discarded on the table as she focuses on me instead. "I told my parents I could become a content creator on my own and they said I should."

"You totally should." My stomach suddenly growls and I reach for the bag, grabbing a burrito and unwrapping it. "You can do whatever you set your mind to, Red."

Her smile is soft as she watches me eat the burrito and I pause, wondering why she's looking at me so weird. "You okay?"

"I just...I love you," she says with a sigh. "A year ago, if this had happened to me, I would've had a panic attack and thought the world was over."

I'm frowning. "And now?"

"Now I feel confident about myself and where I'm going. This isn't that big of a deal. I can find another job." She smiles. "A lot of my confidence is thanks to you."

"Baby, I am not the sole reason for your confidence. You did that on your own," I tell her truthfully. "I'm proud of you."

"Thank you. You know what? I'm proud of me too." She glances down at her partially eaten chalupa and curls her lip. "Want to go make out?"

I have a mouthful of burrito in my mouth. With onions. "Uh..."

"You can brush your teeth first," she suggests brightly. "I need to."

"You want to make out?" I set my burrito down.

She nods. "In the shower."

"You want to take a shower?"

"And make out, yes."

"Wash all your troubles away?"

"No, I want to make out with you naked in the shower and possibly give you a blow job. What do you say?" She's laughing, pleased with herself, and I'm hopping out of my chair, grabbing her hand and dragging her toward her bathroom.

"I say that sounds like a great idea." I pull her into my arms and kiss her, burrito with onion breath and all. "I love you."

"I love you too." She kisses me back.

"I'm proud of you."

"Thank you," she murmurs. "Everything is going to be okay."

"Yeah, it is." I pull her into my arms. As long as we're together...

Everything is going to be just fine.

43

RUBY

"It's really nice being able to sit next to you at a game," Natalie says, her attention completely focused on the field below us.

I nudge her shoulder with mine, my gaze on the sidelines where Ace currently stands among his teammates, watching our defense work it out on the field. "I totally agree."

"You went all out too."

"I had to." I am completely decked out in number ten gear. I'm wearing a Townsend jersey with a long-sleeved thermal shirt underneath because it's freezing cold outside, but I refuse to wear my coat over it because I want everyone to see his name across my back. I've got a knit hat on my head with the number ten stitched on the front and a puffball that wobbles on my head every time I move, plus I drew the number ten on each of my cheeks in red glitter paint.

I'm Ace Townsend's number one fangirl. None of the girls in his fan club—last I heard, they disbanded once it came out that we're together—can match my enthusiasm for this man.

Not a single one of them.

The game is intense and I'm a yelling, shrieking maniac for most of it. Barely able to control myself. Natalie keeps telling me to stop screaming in her ear but I can't help it. The game is exciting. They're all playing so great but then...

During the last quarter, the other team scores a touchdown during the last seconds and wins the game. Our team *lost*.

It's devastating.

"I'm a bad luck charm in the stands," I tell Natalie as the stadium clears out quickly. It's so cold and the skies are dark gray. A storm is looming and the wind is making everything worse. "I feel terrible."

"It's not your fault they lost," Natalie reassures me, though from the look on her face, she's got me feeling full of doubt.

Maybe it was my fault.

Ugh, I hate this.

By the time the team is out of the locker room and ready to head out, we're already gone. Waiting for them back at our apartment because who wants to go to Logan's to celebrate? We lost.

This is new territory for Ace and I'm nervous. He's been on such a winning streak and I don't know how he's going to feel. Will he be sad? Mad? Frustrated? All of the above.

Probably.

We order a couple of pizzas because we both agree the guys should eat their feelings and by the time they show up, Natalie and I are both anxious, worried over their reactions.

But they enter the apartment like they both live here, laughing and talking.

"I'm starving," Derek announces, his gaze zeroing in on Natalie who stands helplessly in the kitchen. He goes to her and hauls her into his arms, giving her a long, vaguely inappropriate kiss that I have to turn away from so I don't just blatantly gawk at them.

The moment I turn, Ace is right there, his arms held out like he wants me to walk into them so I do. He holds me close and I cling to him, breathing in his delicious clean smell, trying to communicate with him without words that I've got him. It's okay to lose a game. He's still amazing.

"Those fuckers were sneaky," he murmurs into my hair.

I pull away from him slightly so I can look into his eyes. "I hate that they won."

He shrugs those impossibly broad shoulders of his. "You win some, you lose some."

Hmm. He's being so cavalier about it, which isn't at all what I expected. "I thought you would be upset."

"I'm pissed that we lost, can't lie about that, but what can I do? We still played a great game. In the end, they got the better of us," he explains.

I touch his cheek, his stubble prickling my palm. "I'm proud of you."

"Oh yeah?" His brows shoot up.

"Yes." I drop my hand from his face. "Your reaction is very...mature."

"I learned from the best." He ducks down and kisses me and it turns passionate in an instant. I circle my hand around the back of his neck, keeping him in place as I part my lips for his seeking tongue—

The doorbell rings and we jerk away from each other, me smiling helplessly. "We ordered pizza."

"Oh, thank fuck," Derek groans, tearing away from Natalie and stalking toward the front door. "I'll pay for it. That way you guys can't be pissed if I eat most of it."

Natalie and I share a secret look. We ordered three pizzas just in case because we're not dumb.

Ace and I end up locked away in my room after we devour our late dinner, the two of us automatically shedding our clothes before we dive beneath the covers. Drawn close together so we can warm each other up.

And do...other things.

Eventually.

"It was fun, watching you play like a normal spectator," I tell him.

"I like the photo you sent me, decked out in your Townsend gear," he says, nuzzling my cheek.

I'm currently wrapped up in his arms and he's behind me, our bare legs tangling, his erection poking at my butt. "I wish we could've met out on the field after the game and taken photos together."

"No way were we hanging out on that field for long," he mutters. "We had nothing to celebrate."

I squeeze his arms that are wrapped around my middle and wiggle my butt, bumping against his cock. "You still played amazing."

He's quiet for a moment and I savor the stillness in my room. The way his big body is curved around mine, protecting me. Savoring me.

"I appreciate you saying that," he finally says, his voice soft, and when he lifts up, I turn my head, pressing my cheek against his chest.

"I love you," I murmur.

"Baby, you can't even begin to comprehend how much I love you," he says, his voice ringing with the emotion.

"I think I have an idea." I turn in his arms to face him, tilting my head back so I can look into his eyes.

"Thank you for loving me," he says, his voice serious.

"For supporting me no matter what. For always having my back."

"You do the exact same for me." I swallow past the sudden lump in my throat, overcome with emotion for this man.

He grabs my hand, resting it on the center of his chest. "Feel this? That's my heart beating for you. It's yours."

I curl my fingers slightly, scratching his warm skin, the steady thud of his heartbeat pounding against my palm. "I'll cherish it forever."

"You better. It wants no one else." He's smiling, his head descending, those magical lips landing on mine and I lose myself in his kiss.

Lose myself in his arms.

There is nothing better in life than being loved by this man.

Nothing.

EPILOGUE

Ruby

D*ecember*

"I CAN'T TAKE THIS!" I'm screeching as I leap to my feet, the air stalled in my lungs as I watch our offensive line get into position, my boyfriend right in the back center, his deep voice booming across the field, calling out the plays.

The football players shift into motion, the ball is hiked to Ace and he backs up a few steps, his feet constantly moving, his head swiveling. I can't take my eyes off him, my heart beating so fast I swear it's going to bust out of my chest and when he throws the ball, I watch it arc through the air, spiraling, soaring into the hands of a waiting tight end.

The player turns, tucking the ball against his chest and

running with all his might straight into the end zone, scoring yet another touchdown.

Natalie and I are hopping up and down, cheering and screaming. I won't have a voice by the end of this game. I've become that girlfriend. The one who screams at the refs when they make what I deem a bad call. The one who antagonizes the opposing team and shit-talks them when they're out on the field.

Not too badly, but I always say a few rotten things to make myself feel better.

Ace gives me grief over it, saying I should maintain a certain level of good sportsmanship or whatever, but I can't help it. He's my man and I'm going to defend him.

So there.

The season is almost over and our team is playing in a championship bowl. This game is huge. The fact that Ace and the rest of the team got here during his first year as the first-string quarterback? It's a big deal. My man feels on top of the world and he should.

That's where he belongs.

We're midway through the fourth quarter and the latest touchdown just cemented their win for the most part. After that one loss, I don't like thinking we've won until the time on the clock officially runs out, so I'm still wary but feeling good.

Natalie, on the other hand?

"We've got this." She raises her hand and I give her a high five, both of us grinning at each other. I let her revel in her confidence because she's enjoying this. Cheering on Derek. Being in a relationship. For two people who claimed they weren't interested in anything long-term, they sure do seem to work well together as a couple.

My gaze snags on my other favorite couple who are both

on the sidelines, their heads bent close together as they examine whatever footage Eric just got. Yep, Gwyneth and Eric are still going strong and we've even had them over a couple of times when Natalie and Derek are home too. Eric eats those moments up, being able to talk football with Ace and Derek, while us girls hang out. We've all become closer and I love my friend group.

I especially love Ace.

Ugh, how did I get so lucky?

The opposing team calls a timeout and Natalie glances over at me.

"Did you ever hear back from the baseball team?"

I'm grinning and nodding like a fool. "We're still in negotiations about pay, but pretty sure I'm going to take the job."

"Oh my God, that's so great!" Natalie grins, reaching out to squeeze my hand.

Here's the crazy thing. After word got around that I was let go by the athletic department? Teams from other colleges started reaching out, asking me to come work for them. Considering I want to get my degree first, I had to turn them all down, but when our very own baseball team reached out and asked if they could hire me as a content creator outside of the social media team provided by the athletic department?

That's when things got interesting.

Nowhere does it state that an individual team can't hire someone to promote them. They want me to work in tandem with their assigned social media team, and they don't want me to sign the regular agreement either. I would be freelance. The athletic department put up a stink at first, but eventually had to back down and let it happen.

The best part about this? They're also hiring Gwen. They want us to put together fun content like we did for the football team because their social media audience is seriously lacking.

I can't wait to get to work. I know Gwen is excited too. Our boyfriends aren't too thrilled that we're going to be hanging out with the baseball team all of the time, but they have nothing to worry about.

We're not interested in those guys anyway.

When the opposing team gets the ball, Natalie is screaming just like I was, encouraging Derek, who's out on the field, ultimately sacking their QB. You can feel the satisfaction pouring off of him as he struts across the field, and I can't help but laugh.

The team doesn't manage to score. Our boys roll back out there and while another touchdown doesn't happen, they do get a field goal, pushing our score high enough that with the time left on the clock, they'll never meet it, let alone rise above it.

We won.

Natalie and I are giddy for the rest of the game. When it's finally over, we're on the field as soon as they let us on it, the two of us separating so we can go in search of our favorite players. I find Ace almost immediately, being interviewed by some pretty redhead holding an ESPN microphone in her hand, and I wait, watching him speak to her, my chest swelling with pride.

He looks tired, but happy. His hair is an absolute sweaty disaster and his uniform is a mess. He got sacked during the first quarter, but he didn't let it get him down. Didn't let it get into his head.

Ace played a strong game, proving that he's a strong leader who doesn't fold under pressure. I'm so proud of him, I feel like I could burst.

He catches sight of me when he's still talking to the

reporter, a slow smile appearing on his face and my heart trips at the sight of it.

Ugh, I love him so much. And he loves me too. We're a little ridiculous sometimes.

I wouldn't change a thing.

The reporter wraps up filming but keeps talking to him and he finally pulls away with the best words ever. "Hey, my girlfriend is waiting for me. I gotta go."

My smile grows as he heads for me, gasping when he picks me up and spins me around. He's laughing and he sounds so happy, my heart soars. As light and carefree as his mood.

He sets me back on my feet but doesn't let go of me, his hands on my waist, fingers splayed wide. "We won."

"You won." I brace my hands on his chest and rise up on tiptoe, meeting him halfway for a far too quick kiss. "You were so good out on the field tonight."

His expression turns serious. "We all were."

My smile grows. He always gives his team as much credit as himself and I love that about him.

"You were," I agree.

"Ace!"

We both turn to see his parents approaching us, walking together hand in hand. I met them for the first time a few days ago, when they arrived in town for the game and I already adore them so much. His mom Wendy clearly dotes on her son and is pleased that Ace has found a girlfriend who dotes on him too. And his dad Scott is obviously so proud of his only child. They're great people.

No surprise, considering I think their son is pretty great too.

"You were amazing," his dad says, just before they hug. Wendy and I watch them, and I laugh when Ace grabs his mother and swings her around much like he did to me only a moment ago.

"There you guys are," says a deep familiar voice and I turn to find my uncle Drew and my dad standing together, matching smiles on their faces. "Ace. Great game."

"Drew Callahan," my boyfriend says, his voice ringing with awe as he steps away from his parents and walks toward my uncle, his hand thrust forward. "Wow, you came to my game."

"I convinced him it would be worth it," my dad says, winking at me. I already knew Uncle Drew and Aunt Fable were coming, but I kept it a secret from Ace.

Looks like it was worth it. I'm afraid he might cry, he's so overwhelmed that one of his childhood idols is standing in front of him.

"Where's Mom?" I ask Dad.

"She went to the car with your aunt. They both complained it was a little too cold, and besides, we're all going to see each other at dinner, right? Though my wife did want me to tell you congratulations," Dad says to Ace, who nods slowly in acknowledgement, as if he's in a daze. He probably is, still staring at my uncle like he can't believe he's there.

It's cute.

An announcement is made and Ace has to go to the fifty-yard line to receive the championship trophy with the rest of the team, and we all watch, me standing between my dad and uncle, feeling so proud to be here. To enjoy this moment and celebrate the man I love and his team. Ace's mom wipes tears from her eyes and rests her head against her husband's shoulder, clutching him. I feel tears fill my own eyes and I blink them away, refusing to let them fall.

Even though they're happy tears.

There is no one I'm happier for than this man who loves me. Who stands by me and supports me no matter what. I do the same for him. His wins are mine and I can't wait to celebrate him with everyone else tonight.

Can't wait even more to celebrate with just the two of us alone, either.

THE MOMENT we come home from the restaurant and we're in my bedroom, Ace is on me. His mouth on mine and his hands busy, trying to remove my clothing. I do much the same, unbuttoning the flannel he's got on and moaning in frustration when I see the pristine white T-shirt he's got on underneath it.

"Too many layers," I grumble, shoving his shirt up so I can see the tattoo he recently got.

It's simple. Small. Just a single word over the center of his chest, right where his heart is. It says...

Yours.

I trace each individual letter, while his hands undo the button on my jeans then pull down the zipper. "I love this tattoo," I murmur.

"I know you do," he says. "Want to get one like it for me?"

"Where?"

He bends down in front of me, tugging my jeans down my legs. I toe off my shoes and kick off the jeans. "I was thinking right here."

He palms my ass with both of his hands and I burst out laughing.

"You would want a tattoo on my butt that says 'yours'."

"It is mine." He cups my ass cheeks, giving me a squeeze. "I can't get enough of this ass."

"It still gets us in trouble," I remind him.

"Ah, but what a way to go, am I right?"

He's kneeling in front of me, a wide smile stretched across his face, and I reach for him, drifting my fingers down his cheek. "You're kind of weird."

"You love it." He turns his head, kissing my palm.

"You're right. I love you."

"Love you too, Red."

"Forever?" I ask him, needing the confirmation.

His eyes glow as he stares up at me, nothing but love shining in his eyes.

"Forever."

ACKNOWLEDGEMENTS

Well, I didn't think this would happen, but Ace Townsend turned into one of my all time favorite characters I've ever written. There is something that's just so easy and sexy about him. And then there's Ruby - while she's suffered through some self-doubt in her life, once she comes back home and starts college at good ol' fictional CU, she comes into her own. Ace and Ruby are just so so good together and I had the time of my life writing this book. I was eager to write every day while working on it, and that doesn't always happen, let me tell you. And I don't like to play favorites but...this is definitely my favorite of the series. Boy obsessed for the win!

I'm sad it's over. This is the end of an era, so to speak. If you've been reading me for a long time, then you know what I'm talking about. The Callahan/Maguire family has been in our lives for over ten years! I've had some requests for next gen books, and here's where I admit I have some ideas brewing. A crossover between series perhaps? That's all I'm saying for now...

This book is for the readers. Sports romance is my fave. I

know those dang Lancaster kids have taken over, but there is nothing better than writing about a sexy football player and the woman he falls for. This type of story brings me joy and I hope it brings you joy too.

Everyone at Valentine PR, thank you for taking care of me - Nina, Kim, Valentine, Daisy, Sarah, Amy (my child), Kelley, Meags - you ladies are the best! Nina, as usual you helped make this story shine and I appreciate you for it!

Thank you to my editor Rebecca for all that you do. Thank you to Sarah for the proofread and keeping the details straight.

Emily Wittig designed the gorgeous covers for this series and I'm still in love with them. The purple goes so well with the other two and I wanted to be in a Lavender Haze so....yes. Perfection.

If you enjoyed **PLAYING TO WIN**, it would mean the world to me if you left a review on the retailer site you bought it from, or on Goodreads. Thank you so much!

He just wanted a decent book to read ...

Not too much to ask, is it? It was in 1935 when Allen Lane, Managing Director of Bodley Head Publishers, stood on a platform at Exeter railway station looking for something good to read on his journey back to London. His choice was limited to popular magazines and poor-quality paperbacks – the same choice faced every day by the vast majority of readers, few of whom could afford hardbacks. Lane's disappointment and subsequent anger at the range of books generally available led him to found a company – and change the world.

'We believed in the existence in this country of a vast reading public for intelligent books at a low price, and staked everything on it'
Sir Allen Lane, 1902–1970, founder of Penguin Books

The quality paperback had arrived – and not just in bookshops. Lane was adamant that his Penguins should appear in chain stores and tobacconists, and should cost no more than a packet of cigarettes.

Reading habits (and cigarette prices) have changed since 1935, but Penguin still believes in publishing the best books for everybody to enjoy. We still believe that good design costs no more than bad design, and we still believe that quality books published passionately and responsibly make the world a better place.

So wherever you see the little bird – whether it's on a piece of prize-winning literary fiction or a celebrity autobiography, political tour de force or historical masterpiece, a serial-killer thriller, reference book, world classic or a piece of pure escapism – you can bet that it represents the very best that the genre has to offer.

Whatever you like to read – trust Penguin.